Moo

Jane Smiley

MOO

ALFRED A. KNOPF

NEW YORK

1995

This Is a Borzoi Book
Published by Alfred A. Knopf, Inc.

Copyright © 1995 by Jane Smiley

Library of Congress Cataloging-in-Publication Data

Smiley, Jane.
    Moo : a novel / by Jane Smiley.—1st ed.
      p.   cm.
    ISBN 0-679-42023-1
    I. Title.
PS3569.M39M66   1995
813'.54—dc20   94-12840
                                         CIP

Manufactured in the United States of America
Published April 7, 1995
Reprinted Five Times
Seventh Printing, April 1995

For Phoebe, Lucy, and Axel James, with love

Part One

1

Old Meats

FROM THE OUTSIDE it was clear that the building known generally as "Old Meats" had eased under the hegemony of the horticulture department. Its southern approach, once a featureless slope of green lawn, was now an undulating perennial border whose two arms embraced a small formal garden defined by a carefully clipped and fragrant boxwood hedge. In front of that, an expanse of annuals flowed down the hillside and spilled across flat ground in a tide of August reds, golds, and yellows. Here and there, discreetly placed experimentals tested the climate. Right up against the long windowless southern wall of Old Meats, someone, sometime, without benefit of application, grant, permission from administration or grounds crew, without even the passing back and forth of a memo, someone had planted, then espaliered, a row of apricot and peach trees. In midsummer, just at the end of summer session, they were seen to bear fruit—heavy burnished apricots and big peaches swollen with juice that later disappeared and never seemed to reappear on the salad bars or the dessert bars in any of the dorms or fraternity houses. Nor were they sold at any hort department fund-raising sale, the way apples, Christmas trees, and bedding plants were. They just appeared and disappeared, unnoticed by most though legendary to the few who had stolen fruit, who kept an eye on the seed catalogues, wondering when these cultivars, the Moo U. cultivars, might be introduced to the open market.

In fact, though it stood much in the way of foot traffic from the Bovine Confinement Complex, the Business College, the Chemistry building, the foreign travel office, and graduate student housing, and though, as generations of freshman geographers had found, it stood on the exact geographical center of the campus (unless you included the recently constructed Vet School two miles to the south, which threw everything off), and though it was large and blocky, Old Meats had disappeared from the perceptions of the university population at large. This was fine with the horticulture department, for certain unnamed members and their student cadres had just this summer laid out an extension of the perennial border to the east, curving in wanton floral revelry toward Old Meats' unused loading dock and Ames Road. So much, said the Chairman in private meetings with the rest of his faculty, for their *assigned* garden site, out by the physical plant and the bus barn, on a dead-end road that no one travelled unless lost. Guerrilla action, as he often remarked to the woman everyone including their children thought was his wife and whom he had met in SDS at the Chicago convention in 1969, was as protean and changeable as the needs of the people.

It was also true, however, that Bob Carlson, sophomore work-study student, was as invisible to the horticulturists, though he passed them every day, as Old Meats was to the rest of the campus. No busy digger or mulcher ever noticed him unlock the door beside the loading dock and enter, though he did it openly and in full view, often carrying bulky sacks. To them, Old Meats was a hillock in the center of the campus, a field for covering with vines and flowers; to Bob, it was a convenient job, an extension of his life on the farm, but instead of helping his dad feed and care for a thousand sows and their offspring, Bob tended to only one hog, a Landrace boar named Earl Butz. Right on Earl's pen, Bob had taped up a sign that read, "Get big or get out." Every time Bob saw that sign it gave him a chuckle. It was just the sort of joke his dad would appreciate, even though, of course, he had agreed to tell no one, not even his dad, about Earl, Earl's venue, a sparkling new, clean, air-conditioned, and profoundly well-ventilated Ritz-Carlton of a room, or Earl's business, which was eating, only eating, and forever eating.

Just now, as Bob entered, Earl Butz was at the trough, but he noted Bob's arrival, acknowledging the young man with a flick of his ears and a switch of his little tail. Earl Butz was a good worker, who applied himself to his assigned task with both will and enjoyment. Already today he had cleaned the back end of his trough, and now he was working industriously toward the front, offering the low-pitched hog noises that expressed his suitability to his lot in life. Earl Butz had been eating for eighteen months, which was just exactly how old he was. He was white, white as cream cheese or sugar, and fastidious. Bob had noticed that every day, during his breaks from eating, he liked to nose and kick clean straw into a nice nest near the trough and far from the toileting area. Earl Butz also liked a bath, and had no objection to the lifting and cleaning of his trotters. He was an agreeable hog, and Bob liked him. At Christmas, Bob had purchased some large, sturdy red toys (a big ball, a hoop that hung from a ceiling beam, and a blanket) from a kennel catalogue. They had been Earl Butz' first toys, and he played with them when he could fit the time into his work schedule.

Bob filled his trough, emptied and refilled his water reservoir, and scratched his back with a stick. He had been tending Earl Butz since November. He visited him five times every day, and Dr. Bo Jones, Earl's owner, said that he was the best caretaker they'd found. Bob took the compliment for what it was, a testament to the fact that he felt more comfortable with Earl than he did with anyone else he had met since coming to the university. He had his own reasons for not telling his dad about Earl Butz, and they all revolved around the worry his family would experience when they found out that although he was doing fine in his classes, and eating and sleeping well, he had made no friends among the twenty-four thousand other students on the campus, and spent the time he should have spent at parties and bars in his room writing letters to kids from his high school, five letters to girls for every one to a guy, since girls liked to get them and always wrote back, and guys, well, it was hard to tell about guys. They all, at their jobs and colleges, seemed to be partying hearty and getting lucky on a regular schedule.

It was this very knowledge, that all his old friends were having the time of their lives, wherever they were, that had finally kept Bob on the campus all summer. His dad, though he missed the help with the farmwork, couldn't sneer at the money—more than Bob would make at the A & W at home, and a real bite in the tuition bill. And, of course, it had never occurred to Dr. Bo Jones that Bob would even think of abandoning Earl Butz. The rapidity with which the two had become associated, even twinned, in Dr. Bo Jones' mind would have astounded him, had he thought about it. But he was not in the habit of introspection.

"Hog," he said, "is a mysterious creature, not much studied in the wild, owing to viciousness and elusiveness. Can't get the papers, you know, to take yourself to Uzbekistan, even if you had the funding. Never been a hog that lived a natural lifespan. Never been an old hog. Hog too useful. Hog too useful to be known on his own terms, you know. What can I do with this hog, when can I eat it, what can I make of this hog, how does this hog profiteth me, always intervenes between man and hog. When I die, they're going to say that Dr. Bo Jones found out something about hog."

What the doctor was busy finding out about Earl Butz was how big he might grow if allowed to eat at will for all of his natural lifespan. To that end, he was fed corn, alfalfa, middlings, wheat, peanuts, soybeans, barley, a taste of molasses, and skim milk powder on a schedule devised by Dr. Bo Jones and contained in a secret file labelled "16TONS.Doc" on his home computer. Its companion file, into which he entered, late at night, the results of Earl Butz' weigh-ins and other tests, was labelled "WHTYUGT.Doc." Bob had never seen a printout of either file. He just received weekly instructions and turned in weekly test scores. It was a job. Dr. Bo Jones wasn't unlike some of the eccentric farmers you might meet back home. Bob considered that reassuring.

He spent about half an hour with Earl Butz. This time of day, Earl was pretty busy. Mornings he was more playful. By ten, when Bob always returned for a last check, Earl would have turned in, sleeping soundly, his mounded bulk rolled up against the orange metal slats of his pen as if for comfort.

Outside of Earl's pen, Old Meats was dim and empty. The classes in slaughtering and meat cutting that had once been held there were long removed to the purview of the junior college forty miles away, along with hotel cooking, barbering, auto mechanics, cosmetology, and everything else that Bob's dad and uncles would have considered respectable work. These days, no parade of animals marched to the holding pen and then, one by one, to the slaughtering floor. The meat locker was just a room now, its heavy door removed. The white enamel demonstration tables, still bolted to the cement in the stage area of the teaching amphitheater, canted dustily toward the center drain. No water ran from either spigot at the back of the area, nor from the faucets into the long, enamelled washing basin, nor had any use been found around the university for this equipment. Possibly it was not inventoried on any computer in any office, and had, therefore, ceased to exist.

Out in the twilight, Bob saw that the horticulturists had retreated for the day. Shadows lengthened across the lawns toward a warm August dusk. Where a woman was walking alone from the Ames Road parking lot, within days thousands of students and hundreds of faculty would be traversing the paths and sidewalks. Bob was looking forward to getting to know the new apartment-mates he had found in May, but maybe he preferred this sight. The woman's dark, thick hair was piled in a loose bun. She wore a vibrant orange and yellow skirt, long and fluid, a crisp white sleeveless blouse with a sharply pointed collar, and orange shoes tied around slender ankles. Her summer tan stood out against the white of her blouse, and she didn't look like any T-shirted undergraduate or crisply permed sorority girl Bob had ever seen on the campus. He wondered if she knew how she looked, if she had planned to look that way, or if, as often happened to him, she might come upon a mirror or a plate glass window and surprise herself with the way her dressing effort for the day had turned out. At least she would be pleasantly surprised. Bob's usual experience ran quite the other way. She opened the door to Stillwater Hall, and disappeared inside.

2

More Than Seven Thousand New Customers Every August

UNDERGRADUATE CATALOGUE, 1970–71: The experimental dormitory, Dubuque House, offers freshman students new and enlightening responsibilities for living, studying, and socializing in an unusually well-integrated and modern living situation. At Dubuque House, white students and Afro-American students plan meals together, share housekeeping duties, and largely govern themselves, free of the more customary houseparents. Most importantly, these students learn to respect each other, and to find common ground for lasting friendships. Because students prepare their own meals and maintain their own grounds and living quarters, the college is able to offer a 5 percent rebate on tuition and room and board expenses.

UNDERGRADUATE CATALOGUE, 1989–90: Unique to universities of this size and type, Dubuque House offers undergraduate women the opportunity to experience multicultural diversity on a daily basis. Activities and house governance promote debate and self-determination—no rules are imposed by the university administration except basic rules of conformity to campus-wide standards of upkeep. Originally a beautifully maintained and elegant mansion that predates the university itself, Dubuque House is a uniquely homey and noninstitutional place for undergraduate women to live, but more importantly, it is a place for women of all ethnicities and backgrounds to come together in cooperation and respect. Physically challenged students will find that Dubuque House is well suited to their special needs. Because students prepare their own meals and maintain their own grounds and living quarters, and because the university is deeply committed to the ideals of multicultural diversity that Dubuque House represents, a 20 percent rebate on tuition and room and board is offered to Dubuque House students. Assignment is on a first come, first served basis.

IN SPITE OF the detailed *Let's Get to Know Each Other* booklet that the university had sent to each student on the fifteenth of July, the only thing Mary Jackson really knew about her roommates and the other Dubuque House students was that they probably couldn't have afforded the university if they didn't live in Dubuque House. Certainly, she could not have. Living in Dubuque House lowered her expenses below even what they would have been at the University of Illinois, where she would have had in-state tuition, and so she was here, sitting on her bunk with her suitcases, watching her roommates arrive and smiling every time one of them or one of their parents looked her way. Her bus from Chicago had gotten in at seven a.m. but she tried hard not to show the effects of her long night—four hours in the bus station because her sister had to drop her off before going to work, then ten hours on the bus next to a very small white man in dark blue Keds who stared at the ceiling with his eyes open and kept his hands folded in his lap the whole time, even when they stopped for a snack and a rest-room break. His likeness to a corpse had been contradicted only by his occasional giggles, unaccompanied by movement or change of any kind, and toward the middle of the night, Mary had begun to wonder if he were some sort of a robot or mechanical man being sent secretly from one lab to another, more cheaply on the bus than by UPS Next Day Air.

Without seeming to, disguised by apparent perusal of the catalogue, Mary was glancing at Keri, Sherri, and Diane, who bustled back and forth as if they owned the place already, and knew each other already. In fact, Sherri's mother unconsciously claimed all three of them as her daughters, because she called each of them "honey." To Mary, she had said, "Oh, you're Mary. From Chicago. Hello, dear."

They had CD players and little TVs—well, Sherri had a little TV—and lighted makeup mirrors. Their parents had brought them, though Sherri's mother and father were the only ones still around, and they were dressed better than their parents, as if merely enrolling in college had raised their socioeconomic status. Mary had nice clothes, too, ones she had worked hard for over the summer, clerking in a drugstore, and chosen carefully, but it was clear in an instant's acquaintance with Sherri, Keri, and Diane that her clothes were nothing like theirs—too urban and eastern, as if she had consulted New York editions of *Mademoiselle* and *Glamour* and they had consulted special midwestern editions. Her sister had told her to wait and buy when she got to school, but the windows at Marshall Field's had been too seductive, the experience of riding the El north and walking into that mythic emporium with money in her pocket too irresistible. Now her clothing budget was used up and she would just have to wear what she'd brought, no matter what.

She looked around. Their room was nice, though, with moldings and deep closets and big windows. Big enough for four—not like rooms in the new dorms. The university meant to have students in Dubuque House, and that was for sure.

As for Sherri, whose desperate wish was that her father would leave and take her mother with him, she had memorized word for word Mary's self-portrait in the *Let's Get to Know Each Other* booklet, as well as the self-portraits of Keri and Diane and of every other girl who looked nice or fun. Mary had written, "I am the first girl in my family to go to college, and the only girl in my high school class to go out of state. I have never been out in the country! I have never seen a cow or a pig! My hobbies are reading, shopping, and planning to travel. I would like to go to Africa, India, Japan, and Hawaii. I plan to major in statistics and to become an actuary. I am really looking forward to meeting all the girls in Dubuque House."

Sherri's own self-portrait read, "I grew up in a small rural community. One-fourth of my high school class will be going to the same university as me, so I chose Dubuque House because I figure I won't see any of them over here. I have lost sixty-two pounds in the last year. I have a photographic memory, and I was a straight-A student in my high school. I hope to major in early childhood development. I have twelve younger brothers and sisters, so four in a room will seem kind of lonely to me. I do not plan to have any children of my own after I get married." Glancing up from time to time to where Mary was stretched out, going over her course catalogue, Sherri wondered what her secrets were. Sherri herself had three. One of them was that she had let her boyfriend Darryl go all the way with her just last night, and then broken up with him anyway. The second was that she had stolen her sister Patty's new rose-colored sweater, which might not be discovered until mid-October, if she was lucky. The third was that Mary frightened her, even though she didn't want that to be true, and actually blamed it on Darryl, whose attitudes about most things were far from enlightened and he wasn't the sort of boyfriend that the new thin her intended to have any truck with in the future. Somebody foreign was what she was thinking lately.

It was true that Mary had a secret. Her secret was that she felt blue and not especially hopeful. The confidence and anticipation that had brought her here now looked like a series of misjudgments, and the obstacles she had seen to going elsewhere, even to staying in Chicago and going to junior college, which she had disdained, now seemed flimsy and self-created. She lifted up her catalogue so the others couldn't see her.

Diane's secret, hidden behind a manner of energetic, practically electric friendliness, was that she would be out of here and into a sorority as soon as she could. Her very unpacking and arranging, which she accomplished with her customary organized alacrity, was a cover for how soon she would be out of this room, this dorm, this world of girlish uncertainty and unformed style. A sorority, particularly Phi Delta Pi, say, or Delta Delta Delta, was where you perfected your manners, where you learned how to talk to strangers, men and women, but especially men, with just the right mixture of enthusiasm, courtesy, and flirtatiousness, where you learned how to pass a tray without servility and to give orders without giving offense. In a sorority, techniques for pleasing men without giving in to them were part of a traditional wisdom that your very skin drank up like Oil of Olay. The right sorority, in short, was the first step to a successful executive career. Of course there would be classes and the acquisition of actual knowledge, but plenty of women had that and were still stuck in middle management. Diane didn't intend to tolerate such a fate. Diane's mother, who had gone to some experimental college in upstate New York in the sixties, had made living in Dubuque House a condition of Diane's matriculation, and maybe it wouldn't be so soon that she could find the money to live at a sorority house. But Diane knew very well that her mother, who majored in Techniques of Social Activism and Political Disruption, was remarkably susceptible to those charms of persuasion and intimidation that would be so useful in the future, that sorority girls knew all about. In the meantime, and while thinking all of this, she kept up a pleasant stream of conversation with the other girls and with Mrs. Johnson, who saw that this girl Diane was organized and outgoing but not pushy and self-centered the way so many girls were these days, and she thought what a nice friend Diane would be for Sherri.

Sherri thought Diane was going to drive her crazy inside of a week, she was just like her sister Patty, who was always sucking up to Mom so that you wanted to blow biscuits and Mom ate it right up until you wondered if the woman was of normal human intelligence, but she had to admit that Diane had a terrific haircut, very short around the sides, but long and springy on top. Her hair was something Sherri worked on every day, and intended to color tonight or tomorrow, as soon as she could, because there was an ad on the radio that said in the nineties color was an important part of a good haircut and maybe her mother had never covered her gray hair and did look exactly like she had borne thirteen children, but an eighteen-year-old college girl had to establish high standards from the outset, and if that weren't true, then why had she lost sixty-two pounds to begin with?

As for Keri, Mrs. Johnson pegged her as one of those very pretty but vapid girls who went to college because they didn't have anything else to do with their time. She was sweet enough, the way she took the last bunk, though she had gotten there second, and she tried, rather ineffectually, to engage the black girl in conversation. She was the kind of girl with her future written all over her, just like so many women Mrs. Johnson knew, with well-to-do husbands and children who ran wild, women who never raised their voices, but always threw up their hands. They hid out at the country club and voted Democratic and seemed to think that keeping their figures was a sufficient lifetime accomplishment. Certainly it wasn't their fault that they were like that—society LET them be like that instead of shaking them up once in a while—but it was a useless sort of girl, in the view of Mrs. Johnson, and at least Sherri, with all her sullenness and complaining and fighting with her sisters, had some gumption, and if she could keep her weight down, which Mrs. Johnson would NOT mention before leaving, because Sherri was right that it was her own business, but if she could keep her weight down and make the right friends, she would do well enough in college, though an intellectual she most assuredly was not, and maybe find herself, which discovery Mrs. Johnson hoped to God would happen soon, like before Thanksgiving, because another summer like this one would do her in.

Now Sherri's dad had finished hanging her bulletin board, and she tacked up pictures of the enormous sibship one by one, Patty, sixteen, down to Lizzie, eighteen months, and silence fell over the six people in the room as she did this.

They were a pleasant-looking family, thought Keri.

To Mary, they looked like twelve pictures taken at different ages of the same white person with blue eyes and light brown hair.

Diane wondered if Mrs. Johnson had understood what was making her pregnant.

Mrs. Johnson had no general thought, except that it was time to get home, and Mr. Johnson was trying not to cry in front of all these women, but really, leaving your oldest girl at college, a college as big as a small city, just leaving her there—he went out into the corridor.

"Don't rush off, Hal. Sherri, go give your dad a kiss good-bye, he's taking this kind of hard. Then come back here and find that sweater of Patty's because I know you took it."

Keri thought her secret was safe. No one from her high school had come to this university—they'd all stayed in Iowa. So, for one thing, she could tell everyone she was from West Des Moines, and for another, she would never have to refer once to her year's reign, now just ended, as Warren County Pork Queen.

3

The Midwest

TIMOTHY MONAHAN, associate professor of English and teacher of fiction writing, had never returned to the campus more than twelve hours before the beginning of his first class, and often cut it closer than that, to two hours, or even ten minutes. His profession as a novelist, he thought, gave him that kind of leeway for eccentricity, and although he was not in fact as eccentric as he might have wished and as certain writers he knew actually were, what did not come naturally could be cultivated, as he often told his students to their everlasting benefit.

This year, it happened that the beginning of the semester overlapped Bread Loaf by three days, so that he had to cut it very close, both to give as much of himself to his Bread Loaf students as he could and to begin his university students on the right foot, which he didn't trust any of his colleagues to do for him. He had spent the entire summer on the East Coast, and had left Vermont about four the previous afternoon. His foot heavy on the accelerator, he had stopped for only two hours just before dawn and taken a short nap.

That nap had, in fact, been rather eerie. He had pulled into some parking lot just off the interstate when it was still the "dark night of the soul," as Fitzgerald had called it, and stretched out as well as he could across the bucket seats of his perfectly maintained '79 Saab. He had awakened suddenly, uncomfortably, and with a sense of urgency. The first thing he had seen upon lifting his head was two cars across the lot, pulled up side by side, the driver's windows adjacent. A package was passed. Tim lowered his head. The cars sped away in opposite directions. A drug deal, fair enough, that wasn't the eerie part. The eerie part was the way something pinkish gray, some blanket-like, bowl-like thing arched above him, and met the ground very low down on every side. He could not for the life of him figure out what this was, and his heart began to pound, until he realized it was the sky meeting the flat of the land. He sat up. He was back in the Midwest. He rubbed the sleep out of his eyes and noted this sensation for later inclusion in a book. He reached between the seats and started the car, but his heart was still pounding.

Even so, the summer had gone well, carrying him from writers' conference to writers' conference, the best known being Bread Loaf, Wesleyan, and Warren Wilson, but it was not for him to disdain the others, as they had supported him since the tenth of June with only a one-week break at his mother's house on the Cape. Wesleyan was the exposition, followed by Maine, Nantucket, Virginia Beach, Sea Island, Asheville, Camden, and Vassar as the rising action. Then Bread Loaf was the climax, his first time there, and he dared to think he'd made a pretty good impression on both students and administrators, drinking enough, but not too much, flirting enough, but not too much, getting discreetly laid but sticking to one person, and one who was nearly his own age and nearly his own rank in the Bread Loaf hierarchy. Discretion was, perhaps, the lesser part of eccentricity, but then at Bread Loaf, discretion was eccentricity. He'd found the atmosphere markedly invigorating.

And distinctly different from the atmosphere of the revered agricultural and technical institution of higher learning that had turned out to be his employment fate. Not Yale (where Hersey had been), not Princeton (where Oates still was), not the University of Michigan (Delbanco), or of Wisconsin (where Lorrie Moore got to enjoy the fabled pleasures of Madison), not Duke (Reynolds Price), or Iowa (Frank Conroy). Even so, a good job, an enviable job, two courses a semester, little committee work. The advertisement that had attracted his application eight years before had attracted 213 other, unsuccessful applications. Seventy-two from writers who had one book, as he had had, twelve from writers with two books. These were figures he was always cognizant of, never mentioned, but also never forgot. Reciting them to himself was his charm against his besetting sin of envy.

He stopped off at the house he had rented for the eight years, a two-bedroom bungalow of some charm across from the campus, carried in a suitcase, showered, changed, and emerged. An hour till class, time enough to walk. He cut through the student union, where the dishes offered for lunch were bar-b-qued beef w/ sauce on bun, scalloped potatoes w/ ham, pork loin sand., and vegetarian steamed vegetables w/ rice. No clams, bluefish, duckling, or crabcakes in sight. As he neared Stillwater Hall, the numbers of people he knew and greeted thickened, until he had, in fact, spoken to ten or twelve friends, two women he had dated, and one woman he had lived with for two years. Such as it was, this was home. He accepted that.

He picked up his class lists and sorted the summer's first-class mail from flyers, memos, and brochures.

He spoke in a friendly but not fawning way to the chairman.

He flirted with the secretaries, all of which, he knew, were on to him.

He made a lunch date with the woman he had lived with for two years, who had followed him into the office, and with whom he was on very good terms, especially since she was married now, to a guy in Soils Science, and, by the look of her, about three months pregnant (he could always tell, but he would let her tell him).

At last he strolled down the stairs toward his classroom in the basement and the sixteen strangers he would know far too intimately by the end of the semester.

Here it was that he gazed upon a sight he had never seen in Stillwater Hall, the sight of a beautiful dark-haired girl with the natural exotic grace that midwestern women never had. She was replacing a pin in her hair, then she was picking up her briefcase, which students never carried, so he deduced that she was some kind of faculty member, then she was putting her hand on the knob of the classroom door right next to his classroom door, and then he was saying, "Can I help you?" and she was saying, "No," and he was saying, "I'd certainly like to," and she was throwing him an amused glance, and he was thinking that forty-five classes in the semester were forty-five chances to make a favorable impression, and he had better take his time, and if she heard his class through the wall laughing that would be a good start, so he went in and told a joke and they did laugh, and it did reach the ears of Cecelia Sanchez and she did smile.

Cecelia Sanchez, assistant professor of foreign languages and teacher of Spanish, too found the Midwest eerie, but it was not only the flatness that threw her. Each day of the past two weeks she would have picked a different source of dislocation. Right now it seemed eerie to look out on twenty-one blond heads, in rows of five, unrelieved by a single brunette. Last night she'd thought the humidity was going to suffocate her. A few nights before, her rented duplex had seemed uncannily muffled by trees. Sometimes it seemed that everyone she saw, everyone in every room, was determined to be very very quiet. In the almost empty streets there was no shouting, no music. When she went into stores, the customers seemed to be gliding around on tires. Salespeople appeared beside her, smiling significantly, murmuring, apparently ready to flee. No one wanted to negotiate or even talk about a purchase. You were supposed to make up your mind in some kind of mysterious vacuum. The smiling itself made Cecelia uneasy, because it didn't seem to lead to anything, and whatever the distinctions were between types of smiles, they were so fine that she couldn't make them out. On all sides, her neighbors were dead quiet, the hum of air conditioners substituting for conversation and argument. She saw men in gas stations exchanging sentences a single word long and understanding what they were getting at.

This was her second class today. In the first class, a second-year group that met at eight a.m., the students sat silent and attentive, their faces straight, their posture excellent. They raised their hands and waited to be called upon. The girls wore so little makeup that the one set of plum-colored lips, and perfectly outlined and filled in they were, belonging to a heavyset girl in the front row, throbbed like a beacon. Cecelia had not been able to take her eyes off them, and that, too, made her feel weird.

Though only twenty-six, Cecelia had never thought herself provincial—her parents were from Costa Rica and Mexico. She had lived in L.A. and San Francisco. She had been married to an Anglo and spent time with his family in Oregon, and that white family had talked and argued plenty. She had even known transplanted midwesterners— now that she thought about it, it was they who had rolled their eyes in amazement when she'd revealed the location of her new job. But she'd been so relieved to get a good job, a job like there used to be in the old days, before the era of a course here and a course there, all for little money and no benefits, that she hadn't paid any attention. A job away from Scott, the Former, and her parents, who'd had less sympathy with her divorce than with her marriage, and little enough with that. Anyway, what could be bad about a town with low rents and no crime? And it wasn't exactly bad, it was just quiet and dreamlike; except for the humidity (which did give her hair a wonderful bounce), it was a cool, Anglo, keep-your-distance-and-we'll-all-get-along kind of heavenly vision, where, as she had overheard in the departmental office, someone's wallet had been found on the street and turned in to the police, who called and said they'd send it over in a squad car, the officers didn't have anything better to do at the moment. It was true that no one had asked her more than the most perfunctory questions about herself and that even good friends at parties she'd gone to talked to each other about the weather, their gardens, and the athletic teams with a detailed interest that dumfounded her, but the blankness of this was maybe a fair exchange for the anxieties and conflicts of home.

She read the roll. The students, like those in the earlier class, expressed their presence with a slight change of posture or the lifting of a finger or chin. She counted them all present, baffled at how she was supposed to read the roll-sheet and detect their gestures at the same time. Then she had an idea. She said, "For the first two weeks, I would like you to sit alphabetically, starting here." She tensed for the inevitable wise-guy remark—"Hey, Professor, what's an alphabet?"—the sort of smirking, half-charming, getting-to-know-you-getting-to-know-all-about-you remark at least one of her students of the last three years would have shouted out, but it didn't come. She pointed to the front desk to her left, then read out the roll again. All but one of the blonds noiselessly took their places. She said, "Yes?"

"I'm a late add?" said the leftover girl. "The registrar sent me over here for permission? Because the class was full?"

"Name?"

"Lydia Henderson." Lydia's voice surged out, musical and vibrant.

"That's fine." She assigned the girl a seat.

"Hola," she said. The semester had begun.

4

The Common Wisdom

IT WAS well known among the citizens of the state that the university had pots of money and that there were highly paid faculty members in every department who had once taught Marxism and now taught something called deconstructionism which was only Marxism gone underground in preparation for emergence at a time of national weakness.

It was well known among the legislators that the faculty as a whole was determined to undermine the moral and commercial well-being of the state, and that supporting a large and nationally famous university with state monies was exactly analogous to raising a nest of vipers in your own bed.

It was well known among the faculty that the governor and the state legislature had lost interest in education some twenty years before and that it was only a matter of time before all classes would be taught as lectures, all exams given as computer-graded multiple choice, all subscriptions to professional journals at the library stopped, and all research time given up to committee work and administrative red tape. All the best faculty were known to be looking for other jobs, and this was known to be a matter of indifference to the state board of governors.

It was well known among the secretaries in every office and every department that the faculty and administrators could, in fact, run the Xerox and even the ditto machines. They were just too lazy to do so.

It was well known among the janitorial staff that if you wanted to maintain your belief in human nature, it was better never, ever to look, even by chance, into any wastebasket, but to adopt a technique of lifting and twisting the garbage bag in one motion and tossing it without even remarking to yourself that it was unusual in weight or bulk or odor.

It was well known among the students that the dormitories, like airlines, were always overbooked, and that temporary quarters in corridors and common rooms happened by design rather than accident. It was also well known to the students that there had been three axe murders on the campus the year before, that the victims' names had started with "A" or "M," and that the murderer had never been found, and that the university would do anything to hush these crimes up. It was well known to the students that the chili served in the dorms every Thursday noon contained all the various kinds of leftover meat from the preceding week, even meat left on plates. Some students found it tasty anyway. It was a further tenet of popular student belief that the bars stopped checking IDs at midnight Fridays and Saturdays. This happened, in fact, to be true.

It was well known to all members of the campus population that other, unnamed groups reaped unimagined monetary advantages in comparison to the monetary disadvantages of one's own group, and that if funds were distributed fairly, according to real merit, for once, some people would have another think coming.

IVAR HARSTAD, the provost, knew all these things and plenty more. Only his secretary, Mrs. Walker, whom he called "Mrs. Walker," while she addressed him as "Ivar," had been around the campus longer and knew more. One of the things that Ivar knew about Mrs. Walker was that she would only tell him what she knew if he asked the right question, so he spent a portion of his time meditating over what he might ask Mrs. Walker and how he might phrase the question. He understood that this was much like being married, but he had no firsthand knowledge of that. He lived with his twin brother, Nils, the dean of ag extension, in a large brick house with two sunporches in the best neighborhood in town. One thing he knew was that he and Nils bore the disrespectful appellation of "the Albino Nordic Twins," but Mrs. Walker had assured him that this moniker was no longer in widespread usage, since Jacob Grunwald, who had put this name about as a disgruntled seeker after the job Ivar had now held for fourteen years, was long gone elsewhere, and had in fact died of the heart attack he deserved.

Foremost in the provost's internal data bank just now were the results of his morning meeting with the President of the university and His inner circle of administrative advisors. They were not positive results, did not redound to the university's professed goal of excellence in every area, or even the provost's own secret goal of adequacy in most areas. Cutbacks, on top of cutbacks already made, were in the air, though no one had yet used the word, which was a technical term and a magical charm to be used only at the time when items in the budget were actually being crossed off. It was a technical term in that you could refer to "shifting resources" and "reallocating funds" right up to the moment you told some guy that his research assistant was being fired and his new lab equipment was not being ordered, and it was a magical charm because it instantly transformed the past into a special, golden epoch, the grand place that all things had been cut back from.

One thing that Ivar had noticed at the meeting was the way that the president and his right-hand and left-hand men, Jack Parker, federal grant specialist, and Bob Brown, human cipher, pushed back from the table as the word "cutback" entered the discussion. It was clear from their manner that the actual cutting back would be beneath the three of them—they were adopting a regrettable-but-necessary-I'm-leaving-for-the-airport-right-after-the-meeting sort of detachment. It was perhaps for this reason that the actual amount to be cut from the budget had not seemed to faze them—the three of them dealt only in numbers. What the numbers would buy, whether copying machines or assistant professors, they did not precisely know. Or at least, the president and Jack Parker, a hawk-nosed man with close-set eyes who Mrs. Walker told Ivar had once been a private investigator, did not know. Bob Brown, balding, round-faced, ever-smiling, seemed to know either everything or nothing. In his two years on the campus (at a salary higher than Ivar's own) he had not yet divulged what he did know. His only distinct characteristic was his habit of referring to the students as "our customers."

Though his computer screen was shining with color and information, Ivar was biting the eraser of his pencil and marking in little tiny writing on a little tiny piece of paper, etching the little tiny names of enormous corporations, potential investors of great big sums of money. Like everyone else at the meeting, he was preparing a list for Elaine Dobbs-Jellinek, associate vice-president for development, whose whole job was made up of the sort of approaching, stroking, grooming, and teasing that these corporate contracts, or "grants," demanded. Until the advent of Jack Parker, she had approached, stroked, groomed, and teased the federal government, too, but now Jack did that, spending most of his time in Washington, D.C., where, Ivar couldn't help imagining, the first thing he did when he got to his hotel room, before he even cast his glittering gaze around the room for evidence of hostile intrusion, was to pull out his .357 Magnum and set it on the table beside his bed. Elaine's beat was corporate headquarters in places like Wichita and Fargo, where university-trained engineers and agronomists had built empires based on flow valves and grain sorghum.

Associations of mutual interest between the university and the corporations were natural, inevitable, and widely accepted. According to the state legislature, they were to be actively pursued. The legislature, in fact, was already counting the "resources" that could be "allocated" elsewhere in state government when corporations began picking up more of the tab for higher education, so success in finding this money would certainly convince them that further experiments in driving the university into the arms of the private sector would be warranted, that actually paying for the university out of state funds was irresponsible, or even immoral, or even criminal (robbing widows and children, etc., to fatten sleek professors who couldn't find real employment, etc.).

Ivar stared at the tiny scrap and counted the names, ticking each with the tip of his pencil. Fifteen names that only he could read. Then he pressed the button on his phone. Mrs. Walker's voice came through like the voice of God. He said, "Mrs. Walker, tell me again the amount of the possible reallocation."

"Seven million." That made it true.

"This early in the fiscal year."

"This early in the fiscal year."

"Thank you."

"You're welcome."

No single donor had ever come up with seven million, except for a named building with a bust of said donor bigger than life in the lobby. But though perhaps somewhere some billionaire on his deathbed was longing for a respectable home for his wealth, Ivar hadn't heard of any.

Good-bye to Nuclear Engineering.

Good-bye to Women's Studies.

Good-bye to Clothing Design and Fiber Science.

Good-bye to Broadcast Journalism and the university radio station.

Good-bye to Oceanography.

Good-bye to the Geological Station in Colorado.

Good-bye to the university chamber orchestra.

Good-bye to every secretary hired in the last six months.

Good-bye to Xeroxing, hello to dittoing.

Ivar turned his paper over and wrote down another name, then another. He sighed.

It was all true, what everybody knew, all true about the Marxists and the vipers and the indifference of the legislature. Only the axe murders weren't true. Those, he had heard, took place on some campus in northern California.

5

Secular Humanism

MARLY HELLMICH did have a semester of college. What she remembered most clearly was how her freshman English teacher wrote the words "critical thinking" on the board, and then, after some discussion, during which all of the students, including Marly, expressed discomfort with the idea of "critical thinking," the teacher had written the phrase "Critical thinking is to a liberal education as faith is to religion." After the semester, Marly understood that the converse was true also—faith is to a liberal education as critical thinking is to religion, irrelevant and even damaging. The wiser course, she had decided, was to cast her lot with faith and forget liberal education, and that was what she had done, and she had felt much better for it, while at the same time noting the irony that her unskilled labor was worth more to the university than it was to any of the other employers in town. And so she had spent all of her adulthood in the arms of the university after all, serving the cause of critical thinking, or at least the critical thinkers, with what, some days, seemed like all her strength.

Father saw the university as a set of one-way streets in the middle of town that sometimes were confusing, and always snarled traffic. When he used to drive more, he would come home perennially surprised—"I don't know what they're doing down there, but it took me twenty minutes to get through." Marly's brother, who worked in a feed mill in a nearby town, saw the conspiracy of secular humanism moving forward at the university every day on every front by measurable degrees. Computers, he told her, had been designed specifically to forward the progress of secular humanism—"Christians had to count one thing at a time, so they went slow. The secular humanists weren't going to stand for that, nosiree. The computer is the atom bomb of secular humanism. You ever seen a computer that acknowledges the Lord? The computer is the greatest false prophet there ever was. I wouldn't touch a computer with a fork."

Marly's view was more complex. What she saw was a stream of people who often didn't acknowledge her, and so felt free to look and act with complete unself-consciousness as they were passing down the food line. Almost the only thing she was ever called upon to say was "Lift your tray, please, the plates are hot." Almost the only thing anyone ever said to her was "I'll take some of the pork," or whatever. Almost everyone was slow, as if contemplating the food put them into a dream, and a lot of people had to be prompted to choose. A few had the irritating habit of throwing their trays onto the top of the steam table and saying, "I don't care, just put something on it," thereby leaving the choice to her. People started eating while they were waiting in line.

But of course food behavior wasn't the end of it. Boys walked through the line pushing trays with one hand and feeling their girl–friends' rear ends with the other. Couples kissed passionately every time the line paused Fingers went to noses, hands to rears. Once in a while someone absentmindedly stuck a fork handle or a pencil in his ear and twirled it. Tears streamed, and not only down the faces of women and girls. There were bursts of laughter at nothing. People sang and muttered. People pushed trays, their own and those around them, off the tray rails. Food was spilled, plates were broken, tempers were lost, apologies were made (or sometimes not). People fell down, even though the busboys were careful to clean up and to set out the "Slippery Floor" sign. People read books and had arguments in line. On more than one occasion, food had been thrown as soon as she served it.

Once, fifteen years ago or so, a man had stuck his fork right into the back of the man ahead of him, as far as it would go. Everyone in line had started saying, "Oh my God oh my God oh my God." Blood might have spurted out, except that it was winter, and the victim's tweed sport jacket had soaked up most of it. The commons supervisor had come out and taken charge, calling an ambulance and the police. She had walked the victim over to a table, and he had sat there, very straight, wincing but not talking. The supervisor wouldn't let anyone pull out the fork. Marly never understood why. Another time, late on the dinner line when there weren't many people in the food area, three fraternity pledges had exposed themselves to her. She had just lifted the plates onto their trays when they stepped back and there were their penises, dangling like little purses in front of their jeans. "Thelma!" she had called out, and when the supervisor appeared and the boys were hurriedly zipping up, she had said, "These boys have something to show you." Then she had looked them, especially the biggest, who was first in line, right in the eye, and said, "Do it again, NOW!" and they had done it, and Thelma had turned them in to campus police and they had been expelled from school.

There were all physical types, from the blackest Africans to the palest northern Europeans (probably Nils Harstad, the dean of extension, who was a member of her church, defined this end of the spectrum), from the tallest—maybe seven feet—to the shortest, maybe three. They rolled through in wheelchairs, hobbled through on crutches, lifted their trays with hooks (farm accidents, most of those), carried white canes, followed guide dogs, watched her lips, wore hearing aids. They twitched and hunched and limped, or they seemed to dance. Breathtaking beauties of both sexes passed through the line. People who were quite the opposite of that did, too. There were girls who had shaved their heads and boys who had hair to their waists, and vice versa. A few had tattoos on their faces, more had them on their arms. People in thousand-dollar suits stood next to people in torn sweats and T-shirts, but everyone had on shoes and shirts. That was a health rule and the only sort of uniformity. Most of them spoke English, but probably she had heard, or even been addressed in, every major language in the world. She just kept smiling, because here exactly was her task, the task set by Jesus, to love the sinner even though you might hate the sin. Or, as she interpreted it, even though people were crabby and snappish and impolite and angry with each other and weird and hard to look at, being either enviable or grotesque, even though they were lusty and argumentative, and even though she had seen people eat some of the food that was supposed to be weighed at the checkout, stealing routinely, and right in front of her as if she weren't there, she DID, mostly, love them as she knew she ought to.

What she really liked to think about was how far they had come to walk through her line—not only from all corners of the campus, but also from all corners of the world. She liked to think about them setting out, all on their own, one by one, from thousands of different spots, tracing meandering courses on their feet, in cars, on buses and trains, on airplanes of course. She liked to think how predictable it was, that at seven a.m. and eleven-thirty a.m. and five p.m., so many would be taken by the same urge, and then streams of them would converge on the commons, and in spite of all their differences, they would all be after the same appeasement of the same appetite, and then they would leave, no longer like converging liquids but like the dissipating atoms of a gas.

She worked hard and she didn't like her job. She was tired of her coworkers and beginning to fear the sight of Jane and Amanda, two older women who'd been ladling food since the Second World War. She was so hungry to quit her job that she could taste it, but she didn't see the people she had served over the years as participants in a secular humanist conspiracy. There were too many of them and they were too wrapped up in their appetites to be as focused as her brother thought they were. If secular humanism arose out of their activities—and surely it did, that was the evidence according to every preacher—it arose from a natural mixing of desires and appetites, the way an odor arises from a natural mixing of flavors. The secular humanists and the critical thinkers didn't really offend her, maybe not as much as they should have. It was easier, once you were among them, to accept and even enjoy their flow.

6

Creative Writing

Assignment: Dialogue—dialogue is one of those elements of fiction writing that is at least as much of a skill as a talent, but you need to train yourselves to listen carefully when people are speaking, and to hear how they choose to phrase things as well as what they want to say. Eavesdropping is a habit fiction writers get into. Fiction writing will lead you into a number of socially unacceptable practices.

Your assignment is to eavesdrop upon and to write down about two pages of dialogue. Do not use a tape recorder. I want this dialogue to be filtered through your ear and your hand. Try the commons, your dorm dining room, the TV room at your fraternity. You'll find a place. To protect the innocent AND the guilty, do not use names or describe the speakers. "Girl 1" and "Boy 1," etc., are good enough. No copies necessary, we will read these aloud.

GARY OLSON positioned his desk a little closer than usual to the door of his room and turned off the CD player. Then he switched on his computer and opened a file labelled "CWASS.Doc." Bob, he knew, was quietly working on statistics problems—he'd checked that with a trip to the bathroom. Lyle and Lydia, his quarry, were lounging on Lyle's bed just the other side of the door. He could see their feet, hers bare, his sporting thin dark green socks that Gary thought typical of Lyle, whose idea of style was anything his mom sent from home. Gary himself wore only white athletic socks and Air Jordans. He turned the screen a little so that even if Lyle or Lydia looked in the doorway, they wouldn't be able to see what he was writing.

GIRL: I'm hungry. Are you hungry?

BOY: You had that ice cream cone.

GIRL: That was just dessert.

(Silence)

GIRL: Are we going to that party tomorrow night?

Boy: What party?

Girl: You never listen.

Boy: I was listening. I know what party. I was just joking.

Girl: What party?

Boy: That friend of yours in, uh—

Girl: On Auburn Terrace. Melissa, on Auburn Terrace. I'm, like, talking to you all the time, and you're, like, thinking about something else. It never fails.

Boy: You know where it is, why should I? You'll remind me no matter what.

Girl: What's that supposed to mean?

Boy: Nothing. Did you put on some weight?

Girl: No. (*Pause*) Yes. Just, like, two pounds, though. You can't tell. Can you tell?

Boy: A little.

Girl: You can't tell. You're guessing. Does it look bad? Where do you see it?

Boy: Around here.

Girl: Here? or here? Exactly where?

(*The bedsprings creaked*)

Girl: I don't see it. Well, maybe a little here.

Boy: The back looks worse.

Girl: What back? What do you mean?

(*Pause*)

Boy: Your ass.

Girl: My ass looks bad from the back?

Boy: It doesn't look *bad*.

Girl: You said it looked bad.

Boy: I said it looked *worse*, not bad yet.

Girl: Almost bad?

Boy: No, no. Not even almost bad.

Girl: How long till bad? On a scale of one to ten, where ten is bad.

Boy: Shit.

GIRL: Tell me.

BOY: Just lose the two pounds.

GIRL: It's water weight. It'll go away by itself.

BOY: *(unintelligible)*

GIRL: What?

BOY: Nothing.

GIRL: Tell me.

BOY: You'll get mad.

GIRL: No, I won't.

[Gary thought, Yes, Lydia, you will.]

BOY: It better.

GIRL: It better what?

BOY: It better go away.

[Gary thought, What a dope.]

(Silence)

(Silence)

GIRL: You asshole.

BOY: Me asshole! You asked!

GIRL: I didn't push. Really you wanted to tell me. You think I'm
fat.

BOY: No, I don't. You're fine.

GIRL: Fine but not good, right?

[Gary thought, Two pages, that's enough.]

He saved his file and printed it out, secreted it in his binder, turned
off the computer. He didn't feel too bad, not as bad as he usually felt,
trying NOT to hear Lyle and Lydia talk. Maybe Mr. Monahan was
right about how if you faced up to some horror and wrote about it,
you felt better about it, you made it yours, and smaller than you.
Horror was exactly the word for Lyle and Lydia. Bob said not to pay
any attention, but Bob spent most of his time with a hog somewhere.

Lydia appeared in the doorway and smiled at him. She had a great
rolling voice and beautiful smile, she was petite and her hair was thick
and honey-colored. Given a choice, Gary would have put her in a
much different story.

7

Homo Economicus

DR. LIONEL GIFT, distinguished professor of economics, was, as everyone including Dr. Gift himself agreed, a deeply principled man. His first principle was that all men, not excluding himself, had an insatiable desire for consumer goods, and that it was no coincidence that what all men had an insatiable desire for was known as "goods," for goods were good, which was why all men had an insatiable desire for them. In this desire, all men copied the example of their Maker, Who was so Prodigious and Prodigal in His production of goods that His inner purpose could only be the limitless desire to own the billions and billions of light-years, galaxies, solar systems, worlds, life-forms, molecules, atoms, and subatomic particles that He had produced. Perfect in the balance He incarnated of production and consumption, He represented a model that the human race not only COULD strive for, but MUST strive for. In this, his private theology, Dr. Gift felt that he had reconciled faith and relativity, self and the vastness of time and space. In fact, every time astronomers demonstrated that there was more out there, and that it was farther away than anyone had thought, every time a physicist successfully quantified vastness, or even minuteness, for that matter, Dr. Gift felt a genuine thrill, the thrill of toiling toward the holy.

At the same time, men were not perfect in their insatiability. While in the large, it never failed them, in the small, they tended to jump from one item to the other, wanting today a steak and tomorrow a tomato and the next day chicken Kiev. As far as insatiability was concerned, the spirit may be willing, but the flesh was weak, time was limited, the purity of desire was fettered by circumstances. You could say, though, and Dr. Gift often did say, that this was our very humanness, this was what made us interesting, from the point of view of economics, and even poignant, in a sense. And it certainly provided the avenue for getting ahead. Our differing desires put us into different markets, and that allowed for creativity, entrepreneurship, original thinking, progress. It was an inspiring cosmology that drew

Dr. Gift out of himself, spirit-wise. His clear and potent explanation of these and other principles of economics to beginning students (or "customers"—Dr. Gift felt that Bob Brown's habitual appellation for the matriculators at the university was both subtle and inspired) had won Dr. Gift two university teaching awards, and he was always ready to remark that these meant more to him than all the other prizes and citations of his long career, more than the photographs of himself with presidents and prime ministers that were scattered around his office, more than everything except the money and consumer goods that the money had bought him over the years. To value those goods above all was, of course, in line with his deepest principles. Other universities were always after Dr. Gift, but he made the principled stand that as long as this university paid him the most money (enabling the consumption of the most goods), here was where he would stay.

Like God's, Dr. Gift's condition as a male was uncontaminated by any infusion of the female. He was unmarried, had never desired children, and devoted himself to teaching, research, and consulting. He was a busy man, and the highest-paid faculty member, by far, on the campus.

There were whole countries that Dr. Gift had made what they were today. So far they were small countries—Costa Rica was the only one most people had heard of, so he stopped mentioning the others because he always had to say what they used to be called or where they were near, which, he thought, diminished their importance and therefore his accomplishment, but Costa Rica everyone knew about. Costa Rica was a paradise, and in gratitude for what he had done for them, the Costa Rican government had given Dr. Gift a house overlooking a very nice beach on the western coast. This boon illustrated another of Dr. Gift's principles, that gifts were consumption of another kind, but still consumption, still a manifestation of insatiable desire—payment for services already rendered, or down payment for services to be rendered later. The longer he lived, the better deal the house would turn out to be for the Costa Rican government, because the cost of maintenance of the property had been transferred to him, while the sense of obligation (or repayment) that he now felt and that they could assert both privately and publicly could be drawn upon for many years to come. It was true, as the Chinese said, that the acceptance of a gift should never be undertaken lightly. But Dr. Gift

felt that strong principles and a clear understanding of costs and benefits forearmed a recipient against economic surprises.

In addition to his other work, Dr. Gift had been chair of the university promotion and tenure committee for the last two years. It was
the most sensitive committee on the campus, the one most fraught
with politics. The benefits of every positive decision were modest,
the costs of every negative one potentially disastrous. It was a small
committee, but it needed a strong and principled leader. What repaid
Dr. Gift for his time and hard work were the connections he made
and strengthened with other important members of the university
community, whose specialized knowledge could be had at lower cost
if they felt a personal tie with him. Another thing he told his customers
was that one of the great accounting unknowns of the modern age
was how to value knowledge. It was an exciting field.

One profitable practice, in Dr. Gift's view, was meeting with the
committee once or twice before any departmental materials were referred to it, and so he sent out a memo calling a meeting in the second
week of classes, and so he reserved the economics seminar room, and
so he sat at the head of the walnut seminar table and watched the
other members file in.

Dr. Helen Levy, professor of foreign languages (French and Italian),
set down her thermos of black coffee and nudged her briefcase under
the table with her foot. She considered this meeting the real beginning
of the school year because this committee, which she had sat on the
previous year, had a way of burdening your life. She glanced around,
smiling at each member as he or she came in. The group, for the first
time ever, was a miracle of political correctness, an unstable compound
that on this overwhelmingly white, male campus would mutate after
this year to the more usual, and more comfortable, ratio of all white
men except for one "designated minority." This year, though! Helen
smiled right at old Gift, the complacent fool. His habit of oily pontifi-
cation, with which he had greased every conflict last year, greased it
and greased it until out of misplaced deference or simple fatigue the
committee had given in, that habit wouldn't do him a bit of good
this year. Helen had sat on other committees with all of these people,
deplored all the time spent in meaningless argument, but this time,
however fatuous in substance, the effects she foresaw in balking old
Gift would be splendid indeed. She said, "Well, Lionel, have a pleasant
vacation?"

"Vacation?"

"Summer recess."

"Oh, yes. Well, the weather was pleasant, but of course my work proceeds seamlessly, year-around."

"Getting and spending?" Helen smiled.

"More or less, yes. On many levels, yes. A cogent way of putting it."

Dr. William Garcia, professor of psychology, could see them taking up their roles as soon as they walked into the meeting room. Father Lionel, humorless, even, you might say, witless, big with gravity though actually a rather small man. Mother Levy, full of a feminine power that was profound but essentially reactive, bringing sustenance in the form of coffee to the meeting, which she would certainly offer around at some point. Sister Bell, the youngest, perhaps the most brilliant, probably (and she hadn't even opened her mouth, and Garcia had never actually met her before) the most recalcitrant (though she would experience her recalcitrance as authentic rebellion). Brother John Vernon Cates, a black man who had fled to science and would fruitlessly strive to bring "facts" to bear on every conflict between Mom and Dad. And finally himself, of course, a lifelong mediator— he could already feel the tension and it already hurt him. He was better in groups of boys, as he had been great, in his youth, on the playground, big enough, quick enough, good-looking enough, well-meaning enough, good at sports. Most men, in fact, were competent in groups that mimicked the playground, incompetent in groups that mimicked the family; that was why all-male committees ran the most smoothly. He had published a paper about it in the *Journal of Social Psychology* that had been cited in fourteen other papers. He was not sanguine about this year's committee work, foresaw a tangle of controversies involving every member's whole personality structure, with appeals to professionalism (which often worked in groups of men) ineffectual and resented. He said, "Professor Levy. Weren't we on the parking committee together some years ago? I seem to remember that."

"Oh! The parking committee! I thought the perk for that would be a special permit or something. Do you know I got ten tickets that year? Would you like a cup of coffee? There are some cups over there. This is a nice French roast."

Garcia shook his head. "This late in the day, it disagrees with me."

There, they had done it. She had made him her son, and he had made her his mom, and made himself sickly, to boot. He could say almost anything for the rest of the semester, and she would probably agree with it. He looked at old Gift, who was grinning, as usual. Did they call economics the dismal science? They should have saved the term for psychology.

Dr. Margaret Bell, a brand-new full professor of English at thirty-four years old, who had been the most heavily recruited faculty member in the history of the English department eight years before, thought that serving on committees with Cates the Chemist was the bane of her existence. Student Judicial Committee, Minority Student Affairs Steering Committee, Black Studies Hiring Committee, Dean Search Committee, Black Awareness Month Committee, Library Committee, Faculty Senate Salary Committee. She had served on eight university-wide or college-wide committees that took up an average of four hours per week. When she had called her dissertation advisor at Harvard and complained about this, she had been told, "You have two courses of action and you have to pursue them both. Draw the line at one committee per year, and work to hire more black faculty members so that you can spread the wealth around." Well, she had gotten used to the committee work, and often used the time to think through knotty logical points in papers she was writing, but she hadn't gotten used to Cates the Chemist, who had the least amount of personality she had ever encountered in a man, much less a black man. After years with him, listening to him talk, following the train of his thoughts, she had diagnosed his problem as some sort of brain damage that had left him without instincts. His entire response to every stimulus was cerebral and had to be thought through. Dr. Bell, who urged her students to call her "Margaret," thought it one of the weirdest disabilities she had ever seen, and she might have regarded it with dispassionate interest except that he also considered it his responsibility to discount the instincts of others and draw the regard of the committee back to "facts." He always did this in measured tones, usually after she had spoken, as if in reaction to some wild irrationality that she represented. In social situations, he was overly formal, as if all he had to offer was exceptional manners. His wife was from Ghana, a pleasant woman but hard to get to know, and amused at Margaret's single status. Her usual greeting when they met was "And how old are you now, Miss Bell?" as if she had some sort of right, earned through marriage, to take an interest in Margaret's personal life. Margaret knew she was from a village, one of the twenty-seven children of a man with five wives, so she had decided this interest was kindly, but even Margaret's mother had given up asking her about men, so where did Cates the Chemist's Wife get off? Margaret pursed her lips and said to Helen Levy, "I heard you spent the summer in the French Alps?"

"A month, just a month, but delicious. How about you?"

"I did an NEH seminar at Princeton with Carol Gilligan."

"I'm impressed. How was it?"

"I'm still suspicious, reluctant, full of doubts, but the seminar was great."

"Ready?" orated Dr. Lionel Gift.

John Vernon Cates looked at him and wondered by what strange and tortured intellectual process economics had come to be known as a science.

Meanwhile, Dr. Gift had sized them up. Of the four, Garcia and Cates were the most likely to bring in a corporate grant large enough to dent the budgetary shortfall the provost had told him about. Cates' lifetime figure was pretty impressive. More corporations were interested in atomic clusters than you might suspect. Garcia wasn't far behind Cates, because he sometimes studied corporate life, and corporations loved to be found interesting and worthy of study. He glanced at Bell. An unknown quantity, and he was a little afraid of black women, anyway. So he said, "Helen? How about taking notes today."

Professor Levy lifted toward him her coldest smile, and said, "Lionel, forget it."

They stared at each other until Dr. Garcia, with a sigh of resignation, took out a pen and a yellow pad.

8

The First Memo

FOR MANY YEARS, the chairman of the horticulture department, known to himself as "Chairman X," had lobbied to change the start date of the fall semester to September 10, the average first frost date for the university's climatic region. Chairman X was an observant man, and he had noticed that one day every year, right around the first frost date, everyone on the campus woke up refreshed, the local news media referred to "good sleeping weather," and the work of the semester moved into high gear. For the horticulture department, of course, this sense of new beginnings was mixed with the end of the growing season. The plant succession that had begun in March with snowdrops and early crocuses would soon flicker out in a blaze of orange chrysanthemums and show its last pinpoints of color in bittersweet and ash berries hanging like embers in the general misty brown of the world. *That* was the time to be sitting indoors and reading books, the time to be glancing out windows and reflecting, and even if the university population at large didn't know that, their bodies felt it. Nevertheless, Chairman X had let his efforts in this direction slide. The task of putting thirty-two thousand people in touch with their senses was finally beyond him.

It was, in fact, September 10, always an important date to him, as was May 20, at the other end of the season, when he noticed that something was going on in Old Meats. There were, of course, no lighted windows, no vehicular activity. There was only the sight of a student entering the door beside the loading dock, using a key. When Chairman X tried the lock a few minutes later, the door did not budge. Chairman X resumed his inspection of the perennial border, which was still blooming vigorously because the first frost was later than average this year, but he did not move on to the experimental beds, instead returning to the beginning of the perennial border. His inspection had now become a pretense, and he self-consciously fingered leaves and stems and blossoms, looking for signs of parasites or disease. He had already decided, for example, that planting delphiniums annually was becoming too much trouble, and that perhaps delphiniums referred too cravenly to eastern and English gardens. Perhaps it was time to break away more decisively from that model. Taking up the delphiniums once and for all would constitute a statement about where this garden was, what that meant. He straightened up. A boy in a blue shirt, certainly the same student who had gone into Old Meats, was walking away from the building, already a good fifty paces off. Chairman X called, "Hey!" but the boy didn't hear him, or at least didn't stop, and Chairman X decided not to run after him, only to note him, and to resolve that he would get to the bottom of this mystery. Actually, Chairman X was surprised to discover in himself this sense of jealous proprietorship over Old Meats, but that's the way it was, wasn't it? Even the ugliest and most worthless pieces of property had the power to set your feet upon the capitalist road.

When most people thought of the campus, they thought of the buildings and their distinctive features—the bell tower of Lafayette Hall across the quad from the complementary dome of Columbus Hall, one housing higher administration, the other housing the school of agriculture. Other buildings ranged from these in two casual arms— Auburn Hall, Pullman Hall, Corvallis Hall, the Frankfort College of Engineering, Ithaca Hall, the Clemson School of Art and Design. Some of these buildings were notable for their architecture, others notable because they needed to be rebuilt and modernized, but as a group they made a harmonious backdrop, to Chairman X, for the many grand trees that had been planted among them, maples, oaks, Russian olives, redbuds, dogwoods, dark glades of Douglas fir. For a week in spring, pink and white crab apples planted everywhere made a fragrant heaven of the campus. The early tree man who had planned and planted all these trees had been an unsung genius. It had, in fact, taken Chairman X a whole semester, off and on, to find out his name, which was Michael Hailey. Shortly thereafter, the horticulture department had raised the funds for a granite bench to be placed in the fir glade, inscribed "to the shade of Michael Hailey, who gave us this shade."

But not only did Chairman X rarely consider the buildings as an important factor on the campus, he never considered the campus as anything but an arbitrary thought, a passing microclimate. What he felt and saw were the larger, gently rolling sweep of the deep geosyncline far below (still, in fact, rising, though infinitesimally), the layers of rock and aquifer (Bozeman shales, Burlington limestones, with upthrusting Laramie sandstones) above that, the skin of subsoil and topsoil above that, then the whispering interface between earth and atmosphere, and the humid, thick air that was prey to every weather system sweeping from the west. And above that the jet stream, above that the sidereal realm of the astronomy department.

The mutable, almost fluid landscape where the campus sat like a stone in a stream rolled gently downward from the northwest to the southeast, a hospitable slope that ended in low bluffs overlooking the Orono River. All the ponds and creeks on the campus emptied into a tributary of the Orono, the Red Stick, which ended in a small man-made lake, Red Stick Lake. Most of the time, the Army Corps of Engineers allowed moderate flow from there into the Orono. To the west, low morainal hills rose in a semicircle, and Chairman X had found many rare plants in the thin hardwood forests that clad those slopes. The earliest white settlers in the region had known clearly enough that the hills were better for hunting than plowing, and for that Chairman X gave thanks.

The campus tempted most of its denizens to nest—to crawl into their books and projects and committee work and pull their self-absorption over their heads like bedcovers, but Chairman X never lost the sense of that slope, and the sweep of forces across it. Whatever was produced on the campus, from toxic waste to ideas, flowed uncontrollably into the world, and, frankly, it made him nervous. Even those whose lives consisted of giving advice to everyone from home orchardists to national governments around the world displayed this odd sleepiness, in the view of Chairman X, but of course his view, often expressed, was not a popular one. The Lady X, the woman he would have been married to by now if they had remembered to get married and found a convenient time (in a few years, when the children would be at summer camp?), told him that he was misinterpreting the midwestern demeanor from the perspective of his own East Coast impatience, but as usual, he felt, she was too forgiving. She didn't know Nils Harstad, after all, the dean of extension and everything Chairman X deplored.

Every day, Chairman X had to endure the pleasant, reasonable voice of Dean Harstad calming him down. "Say," he would remark, "you've been spreading those radical ideas again. The books are there. The hort answer-line people just have to re-e-e-ad from the book. Don't have to make it harder than it is. These folks who call in, they don't like to go off on a tangent, you know. No time for that."

Dean Harstad had unbounded patience, the very patience that drove Chairman X bananas, patience as a weapon. At meetings, when Dean Harstad was delving deeply into his patience, he would close his eyes. It was a remarkably infuriating gesture, especially to Chairman X, who had probably never closed his eyes voluntarily in his whole life.

Chairman X had a private fantasy of killing Dean Harstad. While normally a believer in the larger forces of history, and ready at any time to discount a theory of history that privileged "great men," Chairman X did feel that there were key individuals, uniquely destructive, who could not be replaced, after whose demise life on the planet would actually be better, and Dean Harstad was one of these. Hitler, Stalin, Nils Harstad. The urge to violence was what Chairman X, a flower-man, a believer in perennials, struggled against. Neither vegetarianism nor Buddhism, neither long study of Japanese gardening theory nor the example of the Lady X, a mild and generous woman, had quenched his desire to kill Dean Harstad, preferably with his bare hands, staring right into the eyes, forcing him, at the last moment, to recant, to regret, to know his life as worse than bankrupt.

Chairman X consciously released his grip on the shovel he was throttling, and hung it gently on its hook in the tool building, then washed his hands, and went up to his office to write a memo. It read,

From: Chairman of Horticulture Department
To: Provost's Office
Subject: Morgantown Hall ("Old Meats")

I have noticed activity around the loading dock entrance to Old Meats. It was my understanding that the building is abandoned and part of the structure is condemned until renovations have been approved. You might look into what's going on over there, in case some students have gotten keys and are using the building for nonacademic activities.

Of course, this memo would never reach the provost, nor was it intended to. The Chairman stuck it into a campus envelope and addressed it to Mrs. Walker, provost's office. That was how you got anything done on this campus.

9

A Party

DUBUQUE HOUSE HAD always been known, with a thrill among the customers and a shudder in the administration, for parties. For a few years in the mid-eighties, the resident assistants had, of their own accord, gone through the dorm and removed mirrors from the bathrooms. Even without shards of glass and sharp metal frames, even with bags checked at the door and paper cups for beer, it had been surprising what the drunken customers could transform into weapons, and every party had ended in a fight, and every fight had ended in one or two hospitalizations. In 1986, the administration had quietly decided to end coeducation in Dubuque House. With no male customers living there, plenty of security, and strict instructions to the female customers to lock their doors and keep them locked until they went to bed, THEN to lock themselves in, the rate of unfortunate incidents had dropped almost to zero, and the administration had turned its attention back to fraternity row. It was too bad, some thought, that you couldn't bar male customers from the fraternities, too, or, even, from assembling in groups larger than three anywhere on the campus, but given the impossibility of that utopia, the best you could hope for was keeping them confined to their own area. That was what fraternity row was for.

Dubuque House parties were still the best on campus. Actual bands, good ones, came from Chicago and Kansas City, and actual dancing took place far into the night. Without boys and boys' rooms, there was less danger of rape, and the dorm was far enough from fraternity row, all the way across the campus, that a girl would have sobered up from the walk before she was halfway there. Those who passed out and were left by their dates under bushes and trees were picked up by campus security and efficiently taken home. There had never been a case of injury through exposure to the weather, though that was something Ivar Harstad and the student affairs office worried about every year.

Mary, Sherri, Keri, and Diane, all of whom were shocked by how poorly they were doing in their classes, but none of whom had confided this to the others, assuming that the others were doing well, were dressing with careful exhilaration for their first college bash.

It could not be said that they were getting along well as a general rule. The most they felt for each other was relief at the familiarity of someone and some place in the wilderness of people and ideas they had entered upon three weeks before. Even so, getting ready was fun. The possessiveness each had been feeling about her clothes and makeup, the fear each had had that something might be used or borrowed without permission, had fallen away the moment Sherri said to Diane, "I have the perfect belt for that dress!" and then pulled out the perfect belt—black patent leather with a silver buckle shaped like a morning glory—and handed it over. Soon after that, Keri was wearing Mary's purple miniskirt instead of the tasteful flowered print dress she had planned on, and Mary was trying on one of Diane's hats. She hardly ever wore hats, but she had to admit that if she crushed one side a little bit, and cocked it over her eye, it gave her a very interesting look. And she liked the parrots marching around the band. They matched the orange and yellow blouse she had been planning to wear for a week. Then Diane said to Keri, "Oh! You've got Red Door! I love that!" and they all had to put some on, and discuss how best to put it on—spray it onto a cotton ball, then touch your hot points, or, as Keri insisted, spray a little cloud, then walk through it, *once*. Sherri walked through it twice, now that she was a redhead.

Mary said to Keri, forgetting herself just a little, "Girl, you look sexy in that purple skirt!" and Keri's face turned beet red, because looking sexy in that very purple skirt had been a fantasy of hers since the first day, when she watched carefully as Mary unpacked her clothes, and took note of every item. Her own clothes hung in a wan pastel lump in her side of the closet. When she got dressed in the morning, she didn't even look at what she was putting on, knowing that it would look okay and much the same as yesterday. Instead, she looked at what Mary was putting on, which was an education. The thing about Mary, Keri thought, was that she was so effortlessly herself. She snatched things out of the closet and threw them on, making fashion decisions faster than a speeding bullet. Everything about Mary, Keri thought, was a positive contrast to herself, and while she was afraid to actively model herself on Mary, she thought by studying her, she might soak up something that would give her more energy, make being herself less of a labor.

Sherri said, "I heard at these parties you get two guys, or more, to every girl, and lots of different types of guys, not just fraternity guys. I heard even some foreign students come."

"You mean, like, from New York City?" said Diane. "That would be foreign enough for me. Exactly."

Sherri puckered her lips speculatively into the mirror, then said, "What I dread is if kids from my high school show up. I wish there was a big banner, 'Fishburn High, this is not for you, stick with your own kind.' "

Keri said, "What kind is that?"

"The gawky kind. Besides, one of them is sure to tell my old boyfriend if they see me dancing with someone else, God forbid I should flirt or kiss or, as my mother would say, throw my body around in a suggestive manner."

Mary said, "Didn't you break up with him?"

"I did, but it takes two to break up."

"That's the truth."

"Well, girls," said Sherri, "how do we look?"

They stood up and gave each other the eyeball. Sherri tucked the label into the back of Diane's blouse. "Fabulous," said Diane. "Super fabulous," said Sherri. Keri smiled and smoothed her purple miniskirt, Mary opened the door, then locked it behind them. They could hear the band rumbling from the dining room two floors below.

Across from the campus, in a bar near the physics and astronomy building called "the Black Hole," Gary was working on his roommate Bob. "Shit. It doesn't matter what the guys are wearing as long as you've got jeans and sneakers on. The thing is to check out what the girls are wearing. I'm not going to hike all the way back over to the apartment so you can put on a different shirt, and I'm not going to let you go by yourself, because you'll find some excuse to stay there, so let's just go."

The clientele of the Black Hole consisted largely of students who, if asked a question about what single nutrient they might choose to have with them on a desert island (or in a black hole), would answer unhesitatingly, "Bud." All earnestly believed that beer *was* the perfect food, and that this knowledge had been kept from them by a conspiracy of adults. While Bob knew this wasn't true, he frequented the

Black Hole because it gave him someplace to go that was decidedly different from his apartment but not unlike Earl Butz' confinement room with the lights off. He said, "I hate parties. I like anti-parties, like the Black Hole here."

"Shit. If you don't watch out, you're going to go right back to your dad's farm and think that a night out means going down to the Country Tap."

Bob didn't say anything because that's exactly what his dad and uncles did think.

Gary stood up suddenly and said in a fed-up tone of voice, "Well, I'm going."

Bob brought his glass close enough to his face to see it in the dim light. It was empty. Since sometimes in the Black Hole you had trouble catching a waiter's eye and getting a refill, he stood up, too. "Okay, okay," he said. He had known Gary about a month now. While he didn't think they were quite friends, having no history together, for now the sense of Gary's companionship was comforting.

The evening air was so perfectly cool as to seem like a cloud of pleasure suspended about them, specifically FOR them. Bob's spirits lifted. Gary knew lots of the girls who went by in perfumy groups. "Hey," they would say, and come up to him, "Hey, Gare. Done those chem problems yet? Suzy Allison was looking for you, I saw her in the Union. Cool shirt. Hey. Hey." Bob admired the way Gary fended them off and strung them along at the same time. Instead of stiffening at their approach, the way Bob felt himself do, Gary loosened, let them in close. But he always kept walking. "Hey, Cheryl, wow, you look terrific. Hey, Carla, hey, Barb, call me." With just his fingertips, he touched them on the elbow or the shoulder. It was a technique of such delicate instinctive intimacy that it made Gary seem like a visitor from outer space, like no male that Bob had ever known.

The lights of Dubuque House seemed to surge on the heavy beat of bass and drums that could be heard from inside. Doors and windows opened to the cool air, and customers were standing everywhere, as many girls as boys. Bob handed over his six dollars, had his hand stamped, received tickets for two beers, and pressed himself after Gary into the crush.

It was then that Diane, who had been standing with her mostly full cup of Diet Coke, watching the dancers, was pushed suddenly backward, and Bob received her in his lap, followed by another girl, who stumbled over them. "Holy Moly" was what Bob heard Diane exclaim into the shoulder of the other girl, and then a guy in a Garth Brooks T-shirt came down and Bob felt his ankle twist and give underneath the pile. Even so, as soon as they all landed they seemed to bounce, as others turned and pulled them up, and then everyone, including Diane, was looking at Bob and saying, "You all right, man? You're okay, aren't you?"

"More or less." He tried to stand up, but that was impossible, so he hopped and hobbled toward one of the tables pushed against the wall. Diane followed him. That was the consolation.

She looked great, with her hands on her hips and her short haircut like an exclamation point and all her girlish elements, too, the cologne and the smooth skin, and the fine blond hair on her forearms and the exasperated look on her face, which was the look above all others that drew him. She said, "You were standing practically on top of me. You didn't give me an inch to move!"

He said, "I was just trying to get through. I wasn't standing there."

"I bet that hurts."

"Well, yeah. Yeah, it does."

"It's swelling right up. I can see that from here."

"Maybe it's broken." He thought first about Earl Butz, about how he was going to get across campus without a car.

"It's not broken."

"How do you know?"

"Nothing cracked. I would have heard something crack."

It was true that she had been that close, and closer. Closer than any other girl since he'd come to college. He smiled. She said, "Shit. Now I suppose I've got to find you a way back to your dorm. What's your major?"

"Agronomy."

"Are you kidding? Where are you from?"

"About a hundred miles from here."

"I can't believe it!"

Clearly, she was really angry. He said, "You don't have to do anything, except maybe take these tickets and go get us a couple of beers."

"I don't like beer."

"Well, get yourself a Coke."

"Diet Coke."

"Get that, then."

"All right, all right." She stomped away. Now this was a girl, Bob thought, who was not like any girl he knew, and this was the girl he wanted.

Across the room, Mary was standing half-hidden by a post and watching Keri. She was sure that Keri hadn't seen her, which was just fine, because if she were to see her, she would certainly come over in a friendly way and start asking questions. Of all the room-mates, Mary had found Keri the least compelling. She aroused in her neither incipient antipathy nor incipient affection. Keri's beauty, which the other girls often commented on, looked right out of a magazine to Mary, and white girls in magazines reminded her of the Barbie dolls she had had as a child. They were around, and sometimes she played with them, but her mother always called them "those things," as in "Put those things away," or "Those things are the silliest-looking things I've ever seen." Thus Mary had held Keri in low regard, until now. Now Mary watched her and marvelled.

Her face was flushed, her blond hair disordered from dancing. The skin of her neck and shoulders shone with perspiration. Two beers had put her in a laughing mood, and four guys were standing near her, staring at her and laughing with her. Others, farther away, were attuned to her, too, and kept glancing in her direction as if they couldn't help it. She sat half on a table with her foot on a chair—the purple skirt showed lots of leg, and it was good leg, long, well defined, and smooth, but the most interesting thing about her to Mary was not that she gave off light and heat for the first time that Mary had seen, but that she also gave off safety. There wasn't a single man looking at her. Looking at her had turned them all into boys. This was an aspect of Barbie-hood that Mary had never given any thought to, that Barbie created Ken, anatomically incorrect to the very core of his brain, where he understood as well as he understood his own name that Barbie was inviolable.

Inviolable was exactly what Mary herself wanted to be, safe here at the university, safe back in Chicago, safe in her future, safe without thinking about it or looking around her or waking up in the night wondering whether the doors and windows were locked. Though her Chicago neighborhood was not the frequent scene of gunfire, she would have liked to walk safely there without wondering about which passersby were carrying what weapons. Not being safe was very time-consuming, more so in that she felt less safe than she was, which meant she gave it more attention than she needed to, which meant that her sense of danger was accompanied by a nagging sense of wasting time that could be used for better things. Friction, a drag on her energy, something she had to work herself up to, whether she felt like it or not.

Conditions at the university were not precisely the same, but anytime you went among whites all day long, you couldn't help feeling exposed to looks, attitudes, even sometimes gestures, and if you went around with the other black students, there were longer, more speculative, more aggressive looks from the white students, often met by the equally aggressive looks of your companions. Keri was never taxed in this way. Probably, given statistics that Mary was well aware of, Keri was not as safe as she felt, but it was hard not to envy the natural joy of the safety that she did feel, the freedom it allowed her to throw back her head and laugh, kick up her leg, look square into the eyes of the nearest guy, to abandon herself to the good time that came to her as a beautiful white blond woman, a good time that she didn't have to seek, like Sherri, or probe, like Diane, or resist, like Mary herself. There was reason to envy her, and standing off by herself, more unexposed than usual, Mary could admit that she did envy her.

10

Same Night, Different Party

HELEN LEVY GAVE a dinner party every weekend. She had big copper pots with silver lids hanging above the six-burner range, and large brightly colored bowls and stacks of big platters and two soup kettles, four-gallon and eight-gallon, and a table with three leaves that could seat up to twenty, and she had windows all along the length of the tiled kitchen counters that looked out upon her herb garden and her vegetable garden and her edible-flower garden. Instead of her former husband, who had cost her a lot of money, she had a man who helped in the garden who cost much less. She had a desk in the kitchen. She had cookbooks in French and Italian, including Vietnamese and Moroccan cookbooks in French and Ethiopian cookbooks in Italian. She had written one book in the old days, when one book was enough for a full professorship and since then she had confined herself to gustatorial research into recipes, kitchen techniques, and cooking equipment. She would never publish again, but most assuredly, given her root cellar, freezer, and food dryer, neither would she perish.

Guest lists came to her in dreams, and this week she had dreamed up seven possibilities—Cecelia Sanchez, who needed to be introduced around; Timothy Monahan, who seemingly did not need to be introduced to Cecelia; Ivar Harstad, whose relationship with Helen was as discreet as it was long-standing; Dean Jellinek, who lived next door and worked in Animal Science; his girlfriend, Joy, who was about five feet tall and as big around as a baseball bat (Equine Management); Margaret Bell, whom Helen was growing more and more fond of the longer they sat on that horrible tenure committee; and Dr. Bo Jones, whose relationship with Helen had ended fourteen years earlier, but who loved the bouillabaisse Helen was serving, and whose wife, Carla, Helen's good friend, was away visiting their daughter and her new baby. Only Dean and Joy formed an actual pair, so only they were having trouble getting along. One of Helen's principles was never to invite more than one couple for every six singles, ever since the birthday party she had given for her former husband where each of the four couples invited had squabbled on the road and turned back, leaving Helen and Howard to eat all of the osso buco and the chocolate fondue by themselves, an extended interaction that had led them into a fight, as well.

Helen didn't mind if a dinner party wasn't successful. There were so many of them, after all, and the food was always good, but this party had gone well, all the way through the frozen raspberry mousse and chocolate-dipped orange wafers she was now clearing from the table. Dr. Bo had been discoursing about hogs, which allowed the other guests to ruminate peacefully and think their own thoughts, when Margaret broke in suddenly and exclaimed, "You know, this reminds me of something I hadn't thought of in years. Before I ever went to school, we used to go to my great-grandparents' place in the country, and it seems like everybody there lived in terror of the hogs. I remember there was a mule and also a horse, and if we rode them into the woods, we had to be careful to never fall off, because then the hogs would get us. It seems to me that we were told they would eat us. Are hogs carnivorous?"

Dr. Bo pressed himself back in his chair until it creaked, and said, "Hungry hog'll eat almost anything. Used to be common practice to let 'em forage in the woods, and the veneer of civilization lies very lightly on the hog, very lightly indeed. You say to that hog, 'Adapt,' and that hog will adapt, whether to a life of ease or a life of brutish warfare. All over the world, hog and human take each other's measure. It is a delicate alliance, as your folks would have attested."

Swept up in her newly discovered train of memory, Margaret said, "And back home, we never had pork. My father couldn't stand pork!"

"Where are you from?" said Joy.

"I grew up in Kansas City, but all of my father's family lived in Arkansas. That's where those hogs were. I think I was only five the last time we visited there."

Dean said, "I'm surprised you remember it. My family moved when I was five, and I can go right to the house we lived in before and not recall a thing."

Dr. Bo, not to be turned from his favorite subject, said, "That hog, that southern hog, would have been lean and very fast. Rich in the hams, dark in the shoulder."

Margaret said, "My grandmother did bring the ham to the table as if—you know, she always said, 'Jesus himself ate ham at the Last

Supper,' and my uncle always said, 'Jews don't eat ham, Mama,' and then my grandmother would look at him and say, 'Well, how do you think they knew he was a Christian and not a Jew, then?' "

Everybody laughed.

Dr. Bo tried for one last fact. "Spanish brought the hog, set 'em free all over the Caribbean so they could come back the next year to a ready food supply. Ecological disaster, of course." Helen set a cup of coffee in front of him, and he drank deeply of it.

There was a long pause in the conversation, not unusual when Dr. Bo was a member of the party. Helen knew that most of the guests were trying to develop some interest in, and feeling for, the information they had just been given about hogs. She said, "Shall we take our coffee into the living room?" Twenty minutes left, a half an hour at the most, even though it was only ten-thirty. This group was predominately youthful, and that meant sobriety. She looked across at Ivar. In her first year at the university, they had met at a party given by a couple in the psychology department where the whiskey drinking, as at all parties then, started at six, dinner was brought to the table toward ten, and heads were sometimes laid upon the table between courses. The last drop of brandy was licked from the rim of the last bottle long after midnight. At that particular party, in fact, the hostess's elderly mother, bourbon in hand, was discovered, along about nine, to have passed away in her chair. She was left to herself, just her legs covered with an afghan and the drink removed from her grasp, until the roast beef and coffee could sober everyone up. Helen had been impressed by the aplomb with which the hostess had gazed down at her mother, thoughtfully sipped her own drink, then returned to the kitchen and taken the rolls from the oven.

Timothy Monahan accepted brandy, turned the glass in his palm, and looked at Cecelia, who had seated herself beside Joy Pfisterer. The problem, he was tempted to think (but thinking this way was always a temptation), was that his fame didn't penetrate here, and so couldn't work in his favor, for example with Cecelia, the way it did out East. The stories in *Granta* and *The Paris Review*, the pieces in *7 Days*, even the reviews he'd done for the *Times* meant nothing here. They didn't speak nearly as much for him as the bad review he'd gotten (with picture) in *People* magazine spoke against him. After that appearance, eleven of his students had mentioned that their mothers had wondered if that Timothy Monahan were him? With such a review, you were tempted to say no, the short answer, or to explain the difference in America between high culture and low culture, the long answer. At any rate, just to use the scientific method, this summer, his triumphal progress from writers' conference to writers' conference had proved sexual as well as professional, and there they knew his name beforehand and here he had to explain to every new acquaintance that he was in the English department and what he did there, often to be greeted by polite "Hmms" as if even an explanation weren't enough to establish his identity. Apparently Cecelia had been so immersed in her courses and dissertation that her ignorance of his work was as total as anyone's. In this flirtation he was conducting, he had had to rely entirely on his personality, never a good idea.

Margaret sat down beside him and took a sip of his brandy. He said, "Hey, kiddo."

She said, "I haven't had much of a chance to talk to you tonight. Did you put together your review materials?"

"I turned them in Thursday. But you aren't going to see them for months, right?"

"I'm not going to see them. As a member of your department, I have no input at all."

"Well, that's probably for the best, eh, Dr. Bell?"

"Oh, I don't know." She smiled, possibly with some affection—Tim couldn't tell. His affair with Margaret, three years in the past now, had been firmly grounded in his understanding that she had never read any of his work. Then, one Sunday over breakfast and the *Times*, she had made a little noise, one little noise, at a review of the third novel by a writer he knew and detested, a total fraud whose whole approach to the novel was unserious in the extreme, whose style was second-rate and had been since Tim had known him at Columbia. It was an appreciative noise, so Tim had looked up, said, "What?" and Margaret had pointed out the review, and Tim had snorted, and then Margaret had said she was including a paper about this joker in her book, and Tim had said, "Well, in that case, you really OUGHT to read my work," and she had said, "I have, you know that," and they had looked at one another and he had never felt an iota of desire for her afterward; try as he might, all the unspoken opinions that had changed hands in those few minutes still shrivelled him right up, it wasn't even vengeful. He smiled and said, "Well, there is a conflict of interest."

She nodded, and said, "Did you sell your new book yet?"

"It's at Little, Brown, now."

"A sale would make a big difference. With three, you'd be in there absolutely. No amount of ignorance or perplexity on their part would matter at all."

Tim shrugged. "A sale would make a big difference" was his life's watchword right now.

"I'll be back." Margaret stood up and headed toward the bathroom.

Cecelia stretched and yawned, touched her hair to see if the pins were falling out. The gesture lifted her breasts, which were large, and marvelously concentrated his attention on the loose white cotton of her blouse. He heard her say, "Actually, I walked. My duplex is only a few blocks."

Before Joy could say a word, he was in there. "Say, I walked, too. I'd be glad to walk you home." Fleeting amusement crossed her features, but she said, "All right, Tim."

He said to Joy, "We teach in adjacent rooms."

Cecelia said, "Yes, and his class is always laughing and my class is always droning."

"Well, they read their work aloud to each other, and they find themselves very funny."

Joy looked at him in a serious way. He said to her, "What do you do?"

"Right now, we're on parasites. Next week, inoculations."

"Of what?"

"Oh. Of horses. And I manage the university's horse herd and run the riding club." She fell silent, still looking at him. Clearly she was a person for whom conversation was not an end in itself. He returned her gaze for a while, then said, "Well, Cecelia, let me know when you're ready to go."

He picked up his coffee cup and looked into it, then drank a sip. The party was winding down, and there wasn't much left to do. He had schmoozed with the provost twice already, complimented Helen on the food, listened to the Jellinek guy go on and on about bovine cloning and the vet guy do hogs. He had contemplated how he might fit Margaret's early childhood recollections, which were certainly picturesque, into something he might write, and he had noted, on his visit to the bathroom, which was upstairs, the drugs Helen was taking or had taken, the names of the cosmetics she bought in France, the price of a new sweater she'd left lying on her bed. He had opened her bathroom closet and noted boxes of tampons, which meant she hadn't gone through menopause yet, and a couple of diaphragm cases, ditto, with the additional implication that she was still sexually active. The rumors were that her sexual activity had once been various and unstinting. Tim was glad to see that cooking hadn't replaced that. Tim was glad, in fact, to see any evidence of sexual activity at all around the university. Every so often he wondered, with a touch of self-consciousness, if he were not a solitary toiler in that particular cabbage patch. There were other, much more interesting rumors about Helen, too, ones that gave you to contemplate age-old philosophical questions. Tim sat, staring at his brandy, contemplating these questions, until he had finished it.

After that, he smiled at the provost, who smiled back in that knowing but secretive way of his, and then Cecelia said, for him to hear, "Well, I guess—" and Helen said, "Must you—" and that was that.

Dr. Dean Jellinek, Animal Science, and his great and good friend, Joy Pfisterer, walked silently to his house next door, as befitted a couple who had been arguing for three days, and had only set aside their differences for the evening in the interests of appearance. He let them in and turned off the porch light, glancing toward the upstairs, which was dark. Joy said, "Chris must have gone to bed after all. I don't hear the TV." They stood in silence, listening.

"I'll check the computer room in a minute. Are you going home or staying?"

"I have to get up at five."

"People get up at five around here. Other people sleep right through it."

"It's easier—"

"Fine, call me as soon as you get in the house."

"Dean—"

"Joy. Stoshie isn't around anymore. I don't like you going into an empty apartment." The apartment wasn't yet empty, Joy thought. There were still almost two weeks before she would be moving into Dean's large and pleasant house.

"There's so much to do before the new renters move in over there, I just—"

None of these topics were the source of their disagreement, but clearly, thought Joy, anything could be sucked right in, even Stoshie, her elderly Dalmatian, whom she had put to sleep a month before (kidney failure). Joy put her hand on the doorknob. "Give Chris a good-night kiss for me."

"The provost thinks funding is likely. A lot of funding. A couple million for exploratory research."

"Great." Now they were right in it.

"He named four or five sources right off, a couple that I hadn't thought of. There could be real speed."

"Good. Speed is good."

"Joy—"

"What?"

"I need your support on this. This is going to make up for the other."

"You've got to get over the other anyway, without anything making up for it."

"I can't. You know perfectly well that now, forever, they'll call it the Dichter Technique. It could have been called the Jellinek Technique."

"But he doesn't own that technique! You don't have to pay him to use it—"

"People who have put their lifeblood into developing something just work their lives away in obscurity while someone else rises to the top."

Cloning. Cloning. Dean was obsessed with cloning, and wore his obsession for all to see. It was true that he had put his life's blood, or, at least, ten years of work and money from lots of grants, into working out a technique for the transfer of nuclear material from one calf embryo to another by placing the two eight-cell calf embryos between two electrodes, turning on the juice, and thereby causing the embryos to become one, though Joy was not quite clear on exactly how this happened. And it was also true that Dean had been writing up his article on these successful nuclear transfers, fussing a bit over his style, thinking he had an edge, some publication leeway, when, lo and behold, Dichter et al. from UC Davis had blindsided him with an article in *Nature*. That was in the spring. Since then, Dean had sat around the house, bemoaning all the conferences he hadn't managed to attend, all the minute ways in which it must be that he wasn't quite in the loop—he hadn't heard a word, no one had told him a thing—though he was sure everyone knew, his grad students, his colleagues, his connections at the FDA, the editors at all the journals he published in. But now he had come up with a new idea and Joy had made the mistake of showing skepticism and he had been mad at her for three days.

It was a great idea, simple in the way of all great ideas, as cloning was a simple idea. Cloning, Dean had often told her, came to everyone slightly differently. It had come to him years before, the story went, when Chris was just a baby watching Saturday morning cartoons. They'd been sitting together on the couch, eating father-son bowls of Rice Krispies, and it had come on TV, one image of a puppy that suddenly reproduced itself into a drill team. They barked, they wagged their tails, they turned their heads, all together, and just then he, Dean Jellinek, had seen cows, beautiful black and white Holsteins in a green pasture, all marked the same, all turning their heads, all mooing, all switching their tails, all in unison, a clone herd, the perfect herd of perfect cows. Why would you do it, he thought just then, and the answer was simple, too, always the sign of a good answer: you would do it because it was beautiful and because you COULD do it.

He had staggered to his feet with the beauty and simplicity of it, and set down his cereal bowl on the couch, where Elaine's elderly schnauzer had taken care of the cleanup. He had staggered out of the house and gotten into his car to go to the lab, leaving Chris by himself without even realizing it. Elaine had returned from the supermarket to find the two-year-old hard at work adjusting the reception dials on the TV so that every channel received only static.

But the picture in his mind! Green meadow, blue sky, identical black and white cows all turning their heads toward him at the same time with the same gesture! Divorce, custody, solitude, new love, all had intervened between that time and this, but desire propelled him insistently, relentlessly, toward this picture. Then Dichter et al. came along, and it was very much like watching the only woman you ever loved marry another man and take his name, except that, in Dean's personal opinion, there were many potential wives, but only one or two simple great ideas.

Joy reached up and pulled his head down for a good-night kiss. He was stiff, and wouldn't bend. She smiled in a teasing way, and said, "Come on. We'll see. Don't be mad anymore. I hate not getting along. Anyway, it's not me you have to convince, it's the people with the money. You're a great grant proposal writer."

"Am I?" He knew she would say yes.

"You are. I have faith in YOU. It's just an unusual idea to me. I'll get used to it."

He was mollified. He bent down and gave her a long, warm kiss. He whispered, "It could work."

MEANWHILE, Tim's flirtation with Cecelia was progressing better than he suspected, and better than Cecelia considered wise. The fact was that he was very good-looking in THAT WAY (as Cecelia described it to herself), and when she got up on the mornings of their adjacent class meetings, she dressed more carefully and with more pleasure, she felt less of the tedium of routine, and the day before her seemed shorter in prospect. Her sense of the quiet around her had not diminished, had induced in her an answering sleepiness. When she mentioned this to her father on the phone, he had reminded her of her first day in first grade—the room had been so quiet in contrast to kindergarten that she had fallen asleep at her desk and then fallen out of her chair and been sent home. After that, her academic career had more or less prospered, until now. The students drilled industriously, but in a kind of murmur. One time she had instructed them to shout their answers, but after three or four they had subsided, embarrassed, into the drone they were comfortable with. Other days, she made them walk around and address one another conversationally; she made them pretend to argue or to haggle; she saw at once that they would back down in any conflict, be suckered in any market transaction, and that they considered their reticence a form of becoming modesty. Little did they know that they were putting her to sleep, that she could not remember any of their names, that she had less interest in them than in any group she had ever taught.

Nor were her colleagues much better. They invited her for dinner or lunch, but there seemed to be a general taboo against introducing any remotely unpleasant subject in the presence of food. And everything at all real was deemed unpleasant: the fact that her father, a doctor in Mexico, was a gardener in Los Angeles, and her mother, an accountant in Mexico, was a bookkeeper; interethnic conflict in L.A. in general; her divorce; the association of one of her cousins with an L.A. street gang—the kind response of any interlocutor when she stumbled upon one of these subjects was to assume that she must be ashamed to talk about such things and to relieve her of the necessity.

Departmental conflicts, which were many, it turned out, were spoken of only by allusion and only in low voices. Whenever Cecelia felt she was showing a flattering interest in the personal lives of her new acquaintances, they said, "Oh, you can't want to hear about that, it's so ordinary." When, in the departmental office, she happened to eavesdrop upon others' conversations, they were invariably talking about gardening, remodelling, or problems in the schools, three subjects she could not have been less curious about. One signal conversation, which she had lingered near for ten minutes, between two woman German professors, had concerned a support group they both belonged to for people with an overwhelming compulsion to tear up their clothes and braid them into rag rugs.

In this dreamy sea of quietude, Timothy Monahan stood out, would have stood out even if he had not looked THAT WAY (black hair, blue eyes, thin face, large hands). He was not direct and volatile like the men she had grown up with, but everything he said, and he said a lot, was inviting. It invited laughter or disagreement or outrage, even, or sex, or thought, but it always invited some response, and promised that all responses were interesting, worth his attention. Cecelia knew (thus her caution) that this habit of his was not any more a moral virtue than the face was, or the natural physical grace. She had mistaken qualities of style for elements of character before, and clearly she was disoriented and vulnerable, and he sensed that and that was another reason to be cautious. Look at him. Right now, walking down the street, he was inviting disbelief. "You know," he said, "she has two vaginas."

"You can't know that."

"I swear."

"She's told you that?"

"Two complete sets of female reproductive organs."

"I'm offended that you should tell me this."

"Don't you think it's enhancing? I do." He smiled wickedly at her.

"I think it's her business, not mine or yours."

"It's interesting."

"I'm going to put this out of my mind as soon as we stop talking about it."

"Why? It's just an anatomical fact."

"How naive of you to say so."

"You were in her kitchen. You saw all those giant bowls and pots and pasta servers and flower planters and colanders and orchids and that big red amaryllis and the Georgia O'Keeffe reproduction on the wall. It's the theme of her life, but it's still just an anatomical fact. I think of it as a kind of test. I'm sure some people are quite uncomfortable at her parties. I happen to be extraordinarily comfortable. It just depends on how you feel about women. But everybody knows."

"Everybody *believes*. Belief is never knowledge, no matter how strongly held."

"Some know, then. And some of them have told."

"I don't know." Cecelia knew she sounded snappish. She glanced at Tim. He couldn't suppress a smile. "You're teasing me!"

He shrugged. "Interesting idea, though, isn't it?"

"You'll say anything."

"Maybe."

Her porch loomed. She stopped in the street. "Thank you for walking me home."

"Hey." He grasped her wrist and drew her toward him.

She removed his hand. "I don't like being teased."

"It's true, then."

"Then I don't like that sort of gossip."

"It's a game, then. Like writing a novel. A game of meditating over objects of the imagination."

"You can't come onto my porch, and don't try to kiss me. I'm annoyed with you, and I hate it if men find that arousing."

"Okay. But I will watch you in the door."

"Okay."

"Then I'll walk back to Helen's and get my car." As always, he spoke with playful equanimity. She turned on her heel, mounted the porch steps with dignity, and jammed her key into the lock. He shouted, "Night, Cecelia. I'll call you tomorrow!" as if he didn't care whether he woke up the whole neighborhood. Cecelia winced at the noise bursting in the silence, maybe for the first time ever.

11

Born Again

NILS HARSTAD, dean of extension, heard it all—the click of the door lock, the footsteps downstairs, the give of the steps muffled by carpeting as his brother, Ivar, mounted toward his bedroom. Nils looked at the clock, 3:43, but he neither turned on the light nor sat up in bed. Normally he wouldn't have been awake anyway, but tonight, at fifty-five years old, he was on the verge of a new life.

He was not exactly repudiating the old life—there was nothing to repudiate, of course. If anything, he had poured himself freely out, giving of his knowledge and his strength with little prospect of reward. The early days in the field had been the best, the days of super-seeds and crop production that seemed miraculous to the village farmers who came to stare at his demonstration plots. The sixties! The era of splendid acronyms like SEATO, UNESCO, CARE. Virile young agronomists, their hatless thatches of hair bleached by the sun, blown by the wind, their muscular strong hands begrimed with earth, had spread out all over the world, carrying with them the knowledge of hybrids and fertilizers and mineral supplements and machinery and drip irrigation and drainage (not to mention grants and gifts and low-interest loans and investments) that their agronomical elders had carefully incubated through the war and into the prosperous fifties. It had fallen to Nils and his colleagues to bear the good news—an end to hunger! granaries filled to bursting! orderly ranks of children, all races, creeds, and colors, marching off to school with their bellies full!

Nils shivered and drew the quilt up to his shoulders, shaking off the old, claiming the new. The plan had come to him just at bedtime, first as the recognition that Marly Hellmich, a young woman at his church, was clearly attracted to him. He was thinking how flattering that was, that she must be thirty, or even younger, and that her manner of expressing this attraction was nicely done—circumspect, almost bashful—and then he had turned on his electric toothbrush and given what he thought was his full attention to cleaning his teeth and stimulating his gums—and by the time he'd switched off that little motor and stood in silence again, the plan was formed—a marriage, many children, the life of Christian fatherhood that he had missed and thought lost to him.

The key, of course, was one or two artificially induced multiple births that would make up for lost time and, as a side benefit, bring science into the service of the greater glory of God and the enlargement of Nils' church. You could not overestimate Nils Harstad's gratitude to his church, for through its doctrines and the support of both the minister and the other members, he had, after almost a lifetime, found an end to doubt of all kinds—doubt of the Lord, doubt of himself, doubt of the goodness and rightness of Providence, doubt of the way he had made in the world. Every year on the anniversary of his entrance into the church, he woke up and marvelled at, and then gave thanks for, this ongoing reassurance. He felt, in his very being, the daily approval of the Lord.

The effects of this end to doubt were nothing less than miraculous— an end to anger (now he dealt with every university problem with the sort of patience he had only longed for in the past), an end to resentment, especially of his late wife, whom he always felt had entered into his world and his work only with reservations, an end to the lifelong loneliness of missing his distant parents and sensing a basic disjunction between himself and Ivar, for even though they looked alike, talked alike, and had some of the same interests, only Nils knew how different they were at the core—so different that their being identical twins had always struck him as a simple impossibility or, perhaps, an illusion of appearance foisted on them by others. Since joining his church, he had been far easier with Ivar—far more able to tolerate their disagreements with good grace, far less inclined to give in just to end conflict. Of course, his differences with Ivar had widened with his growing commitment to Creation Science, a theory Ivar, as a physicist, wouldn't even discuss, but which Nils found far more doubt-soothing in every way than the theories of relativity, evolution, and the big bang. For the last five years, Nils Harstad had been a man with a smile. But the future, populated by a pleasant wife and five or six obedient children, would make him a laughing man! The gift of faith gave him no doubts about this, either.

4:02. What if he did stay up all night? He hadn't stayed awake in exhilaration for decades—it was something to offer up, a new vision to set against all the disappointments over the years, all the fallings-short, all the almosts-but-not-quites of his marriage and his career and his life, since conception, with Ivar. Because of course those heady days of the sixties had proved hollow and illusory. World hunger had gotten away from all of them—mostly, Nils thought, due to unfortunate weather—as his enigmatic wife had gotten away from him. It was all very well to tell yourself, as he had been doing for years, that all you could do was give it your best shot. He did not feel blameworthy—that was the point—he felt disappointed. But maybe Heaven, of which he also had no doubt, at least as far as he was concerned, was where this delightful sense of rightness and goodness and perfection that you always had with a good idea lasted forever, as it of course could not with others working against you, and your own failures of judgment and energy and will letting you down as well.

Ah, thought Nils, and he reached into his pajamas and took hold of his member. It was firm and hand-filling. He brought to bear upon it the image of Marly Hellmich's plain, trustful face, her likely virginity, what he imagined as her quiet history of faith, frugality, devotion to others (he saw her in a long dress and a bonnet), and it expressed to him no doubts.

12

A Rule Broken

MRS. LORAINE WALKER KNEW where all the bodies were buried, including the ones in the university graveyard between the baseball practice field and the Clemson School of Art and Design. She knew that a ball hit into the graveyard was known as "the ultimate home-run," and left to lie, in accordance with traditional campus superstition, until the following Halloween, when new recruits to the baseball team were deployed to find them, with flashlights, in the dark. As she thought this was a harmless and rather charming tradition, she allowed it to continue, and instructed the grounds crew who mowed the graveyard to leave the balls there.

On the other hand, the determination of some art and design students to erect *objets* among the stones she met with absolute resistance, largely because she found the taste of the students offensive and unbeautiful. No matter who called her from the college, if it was the dean or even the dean's secretary herself, Mrs. Walker told her that the university had rules. It was true that the university did have rules, but the university's rules were a subset of Mrs. Walker's rules. Her set included rules that the university would have had if the university had known that it needed them, so she felt justified in terming those "university rules," too.

Mrs. Walker had been secretary in the provost's office for twenty-two years, through the terms of three provosts. She found Ivar, with whom she had worked since his ascension to the post, compliant and industrious. He generally fulfilled the tasks assigned to him on his own initiative, with minimal help from her. He sought advice readily, always a good quality in an administrator, and did his own Xeroxing. He dressed appropriately for the office in dark suits and white, long-sleeved shirts. Nothing mint green, which highly offensive fashion choice seemed to be a favorite of the president of the university, whose secretary had always been overindulgent and, in Mrs. Walker's opinion, always would be. Ivar was respectful without fawning and only occasionally needed personal encouragement. He was, she often reflected, markedly better than Jacob Grunwald would have been, and she was glad to have chosen him. He had worked out well.

Mrs. Walker espied the messenger from the mail room in the hall. She looked at her watch. 9:32. Four minutes early. This improved her mood. He brought the mail in on a dolly, and set it where he knew he was supposed to—campus mail on her right hand, U.S. mail on her left. She spoke pleasantly to him, and he replied in kind. One of her rules was always to be pleasant, no matter how trying the circumstances. He was gone by 9:38. She reached for the U.S. mail. There were fifteen first-class pieces addressed to Ivar. After reading them all, she put fourteen in her reply basket and one in his. It was from the president of the TransNationalAmerica Corporation ("TNA—We're in all you do"; the corporate symbol was a tasteless circle of stars, thirteen, she counted them, on a dark blue field). In fact, the president's name rang a bell, but the TNA Corporation did not.

It took her longer to process the campus mail, because the envelopes had to be saved for reuse (an idea and policy of hers long before the days of recycling). Gray university memo forms she stacked together and read through. It was then that she saw Associate Vice-President Robert William Brown, or, as he called himself with a smile, "Just Plain Brown," outside the door to her office. He was standing close enough to be looking at her, but she saw very clearly that it was not until she and he made eye contact that his hand went to the doorknob. He entered on a snail's trail of congeniality. "Mrs. Walker," he said, with a practiced nod.

"Associate Vice-President Brown."

"Marvelous day for this time of year, don't you think?"

"The end of September frequently offers superior weather in this climate. Sir."

"Oh, goodness, no need for that. You know, minimizing the expressions of hierarchy within the organization seems actually to mitigate its negative effects and to draw all the employees at every level into a more profound dialogue with one another. Some of the best ideas come from staff and even blue-collar employees."

"May I help you, Associate Vice-President Brown?"

He pulled out a handkerchief and wiped it over his forehead. He said, "I'll just wait over here," and he went to a chair beside the door into the Xeroxing room and sat down. He occupied himself by gazing out at the brilliant morning and humming tunelessly under his breath.

Later on, she did piece together exactly what happened. After reading a number of the memos, ten or fewer, she noticed that it was time for her break, 10:00, and she set the rest of the memos on the right side of her desk. She stood up, picked up her handbag, and went into the bathroom. As she did so, Eileen, a secretarial assistant, remarked that the office seemed warm, and Mrs. Walker gave her permission to open a window. While Mrs. Walker was in the bathroom, Eileen opened the second window, the window across from Mrs. Walker's desk, rather than the more customary first window. A breeze from that window must have lifted the top memo off the stack and floated it across the small space between Mrs. Walker's desk and the radiator, where it slid up and under, beyond the view of the janitor, who otherwise would have found it that night. When Mrs. Walker returned to her desk, of course, she had Eileen correct her mistake, but the lost memo, about unauthorized use of Old Meats from that funny little man who ran the horticulture department and wouldn't allow anyone to call him by his name, had evaded her.

Just Plain Brown had left.

Had his presence disconcerted Mrs. Walker just a bit? A grain more than she suspected? Whatever the cause, she noticed the TNA letter in Ivar's basket again and picked it up. Arlen Martin. Ah, yes. She remembered him clearly now, and not fondly. Mrs. Walker tapped the corner of the letter lightly on her desk while she made up her mind, and then, with her usual dispatch, she threw the letter away.

That was what started it all.

13

The Keynote

Dr. Lionel Gift's lecture, entitled "Costa Rica: The Lessons of Development," was packed to the walls. Dr. Gift estimated an audience of 740 or 50, and he was practiced at estimating audiences. It did not matter to him that nearly the entire audience was composed of students ("customers," he reminded himself) required to attend and looking forward to quizzes (to prove attendance, if not comprehension), nor that most of the economics department was conspicuous for their absence (while he made it a principle to go to every lecture presented by an econ faculty member and to ask at least one searching question). An audience was an audience, and, as he often quoted himself, "Ears cannot be closed." Something would get through, and something was a beginning.

As Ivar had persuaded him to give this lecture without an honorarium, Dr. Gift was using a paper he had given twice before, once for ten thousand dollars, to a group of corporate executives interested in investing in Latin America, and once, for twenty-five hundred dollars, to an Ivy League university that had been courting him. That university had been somewhat surprised at the fee he charged them for what was, essentially, the presentation of his credentials for their consideration, but he had pointed out the unwisdom of services and knowledge given gratis (which devalued them in the marketplace and persuaded buyers that they were of little worth). Afterward, they had made a nice offer, but not nice enough.

Nevertheless, Dr. Gift now felt that the price of the lecture had depreciated into the "pro bono" category, and furthermore, it was good business to keep Ivar Harstad happy, so he agreed to having his name plastered all over the campus ("World-renowned economist, advisor to presidents" was the phrase he had suggested when the publicity office had called him), and to put on a blue suit, and to display himself to and for the university—to the customers and for the benefit of the eight potential corporate donors he had greeted when he entered. The provost sat to their left, the president sat to their right, Bob Brown behind them, beaming his perennial, and to Dr. Lionel Gift, ever-approving smile. The corporate executives all sat in a row, leaning back, each one's ankle resting arrogantly on each one's opposite knee, each one fancying himself a Hollywood producer about to make or break a star. Dr. Gift gave this row the sort of knowing, collusive, and self-confident twinkle they always fell for, and began.

As he began, Cecelia, who had required the lecture of her classes just to give them some sense of the lives of some of the people who spoke the language they were learning (though these people rarely said, as her students often did, "I have the ball and Juan has the stick," or "Please tell me whether the toilet is in the next street"), felt the man sitting next to her jump in his seat. She shifted away from him. Then he said, in a low voice, "What shit!" and then he actually spit on the floor between his shoes. Cecelia looked around for another seat, or even a place to stand, but the room was amazingly crowded. She should have given the campus more credit for interest in the outside world, that was clear. Perhaps the insulated blankness she thought she perceived was simply a manner that hid untold depths of curiosity.

The man next to her exclaimed, "Oh my God!" and four or five people turned and looked at him. Cecelia said, "Please be quiet! You're acting very rude!"

He said, "Are you listening to this bullshit?"

She said, "Yes, I am!" and the four or five starers chorused, "Shhhhh!"

It was only then, when he had to be quiet, but also to do something that would distract him from the torrent of drivel that was pouring off the podium, that Chairman X noticed Cecelia. He noticed that she was wearing dazzling silver earrings made of the beaten bowls of old spoons, and these made him notice the definition of her neck as it dovetailed into her throat, and this made him notice her remarkable full, wide, and sharply cut lips, and after that, he turned away because he was afraid to notice anything more.

Giving his lecture for the third time freed Dr. Lionel Gift from paying much attention to it. He had a naturally expressive style of delivery, honed over the years in elementary-econ lecture halls. He knew, without even thinking, to address the middle rows of the hall, but to occasionally "shoot" the listeners in the back corners. He knew how to make eye contact and solicit the attention of those who were thinking of other things. He knew that that little shit from horticulture was making his usual fuss and would later ask his usual pugnacious question. He listened with appreciation to the wise words of his lecture rolling out of him, as he depicted, for these customers, the beauty that Costa Rica had become in the last ten years—how nicely tied into the world market it was now, how its GDP had risen and risen, how, while some economic sectors had shown surprising declines, such as fisheries, others had flowed into the gap, such as export of tropical hardwoods and beef. New roads, new schools, new public works, a successful restructuring of debt, stable cash cropping on newly opened agricultural land. Dr. Gift smiled and smiled, showing charts of GDP (which, he explained, was enough like GNP for his audience to think of it as the same thing) where the line rose and rose without faltering; no lurches, no dips, no hesitations.

Upon Chairman X certain words and phrases had a noticeable electrifying effect: "world market"—he writhed; "surprising decline"—his mouth gaped in a silent scream; "export of tropical hardwoods"—his feet began a tattoo on the hardwood floor. At "cash crop" he leaned over so far toward Cecelia that he nearly fell out of his chair. Cecelia heaved him upright. He muttered, "Sorry," and subsided until the chart came out, when Cecelia began to feel his chair rock against hers. By this time, however, she had decided that he must be the unfortunate victim of some sort of illness, possibly Tourette's syndrome. One cousin of her former husband had been thus afflicted, and Cecelia had come to like him very much, and hardly notice the outbursts. And so it was that the more explosive Chairman X became, the more sympathetic Cecelia became, thinking of that cousin, and how she had lost touch with him since her divorce.

In spite of this distraction, Cecelia was enjoying the lecture. Although she hadn't actually been to Costa Rica since before she could remember, a trip there, an extended visit, was one of her happiest plans, a delicious present for herself and her mother, as certain as if it had already been bought and put away. It would be no hasty sojourn or ill-thought-out vacation, but a progress of delight and enlightenment, the fabled tropical sights alternating with invigorating visits to relatives. Cecelia was confident both that she would come up with the money before too long and that her mother would let go of her strange reluctance to make the trip ("Of course I want to see them," she always said, "but it's so far away. There's so much to do here. Your father—"). Dr. Gift's words were very dry, not at all evocative of the deep green cloud forest Cecelia could not remember, or the fragrances of the hillsides she knew she would recognize when she made her return. Dr. Gift didn't make it sound like what it was, which was a place much more splendid than anywhere else. It was hard to believe what the program said, that he visited there regularly.

Irritated, Cecelia looked around. Most of the students sat upright but removed, like horses asleep on their feet in a field. Their pencils had fallen out of their hands, and their notes drifted to an end about a quarter of the way down the first page. It was always true, Cecelia thought, that ignorance was the prime element of boredom. She sighed. The lecture also made her think of her mother in Los Angeles, the way, over the years, the extra effort of living there seemed to have taxed every part of her—her spirits, her temper, her warmth, her looks. Dora Sanchez did not thrive in L.A. Cecelia thought her habitual thought about the calming and rejuvenating effect of the trip. She would bring it up at Christmas. This time she would really—

AND WHAT WERE the lessons of development in Costa Rica? Dr. Gift swelled his oratory to a preacherly roundness. First and foremost, RATIONAL coordination of a nation's local market mechanisms with world market mechanisms worked to the mutual satisfaction of everyone's demands—which in theoretical terms were, of course, insatiable—and the local officials were capable of acting RATIONALLY once principles were explained to them. Second, the control of the international monetary community reenforced the RATIONALIZA-TION of an individual nation's choices, working to bring it into the fold. Third (and here he looked to the eight-man gallery seated between the provost and the president), the greatest single component in the growth of any small nation was the RATIONAL investment of well-run corporations. As one man, the gallery nodded with measured agreement. Fourth (and here he looked at the assembled customers), there was a world of opportunity out there for an enterprising young American man (he looked at the customers again and made a quick recount) or young American woman. He quoted one of their songs: "The future's so bright, I've got to wear shades," thus startling the students into embarrassed laughter. Thank you.

Chairman X shot like a rocket out of his seat, not just to ask a question, but also to relieve the buildup of frustration. He had not actually formulated his question beyond "What kind of ignorant asshole are you?" but Gift's gaze turned his way, and he knew he would be called upon as soon as the applause died down. The room was warm. He tugged at the collar of his shirt. He knew he was going to sound shrill and IRRATIONAL, that he was going to fail in speaking for his cause and in fact speak against his cause, because even if his words came out ordered and reasonable, his face would be red, the emotion in his voice would be readily apparent, and anyway, he was so well known around the campus as a crackpot that his opinions would be discounted as soon as he opened his mouth. Gift said, "There. In the middle," and Chairman X knew that was him. He opened his mouth, curious to see what would come out. He heard himself say, mildly, "What have been the effects of this development on Costa Rica's natural biological systems?"

"Very much within the bounds of acceptable exploitation, even positive, as sectors which have no value become valuable through use."

"But how much has been lost?"

"Nothing has been lost, but a great deal has been gained. Let's allow some of the others to speak, shall we. Back in the back there."

Allowing the others to speak was fine with Chairman X, who was choking with rage and seeing a reddish fog enclose him from both sides. He sat down and attempted to slow his breathing. This would, possibly, be the occasion of his first stroke. The Lady X had begged him not to come, to avoid, as she said, the occasion of sin, but he had to hear what they were saying, how they were presenting themselves. The red fog cleared. The lovely woman next to him said, "I thought that was a good question. Thank you for asking it," and her voice soothed him. "My mother's family is from Costa Rica." He looked at her and she smiled ruefully. "I don't think they've participated much in the general rise."

Across the room, Ivar Harstad tried to pick the back of Chairman X's head out of the crowd. He seemed to be sitting beside that new woman in Foreign Languages. Ivar, too, had appreciated the question, and considered Gift's reply evasive, probably owing to ignorance. Was there a grant in there somewhere? Ivar took out his notebook and wrote a tiny little note to himself to call the horticulture department in the morning.

14

The Provost Is Tempted

ARLEN MARTIN WAS a little Texan with jug ears who was worth a billion dollars and it both surprised the provost that he had turned up and didn't surprise him at all. It certainly did not surprise him that he had turned up in the company of Elaine Dobbs-Jellinek, who probably didn't know about the ten-year-old scandal, and might not have cared if she had known. Arlen Martin's name was one the provost had not written down, nor even spoken aloud in his ruminations over corporate grantors, but it had been in his mind, and clearly that was enough.

Elaine had a theatrical way about her. In her three years as associate vice-president for development, her wardrobe had grown progressively more flamboyant in color and cut, so that now she looked just like a TV anchorwoman. Each year she was thinner, too, magnifying the similarity. And each year she travelled farther afield, looking for funding. She knew exactly what she was doing, what those executives in Fayetteville and Tulsa would be impressed with.

Arlen Martin, though, was a horse of a different color. He had risen through so many social classes, and travelled through so many latitudes and longitudes that he was comfortable with everyone. And he was so rich, anyway, that the duty of accommodation fell to others, not him. Ivar stood up and came around his desk, hand extended. Elaine Dobbs-Jellinek exclaimed, "Ivar, Arlen says no introductions needed!" Clearly, she viewed this as a compliment.

"No," said Ivar, "I remember Mr. Martin very well. How are you, sir?"

"Now don't 'sir' me, Dr. Harstad. I know perfectly well who here has a high school diploma and who here has a pee aitch dee!" Elaine laughed hysterically at this joke. Mrs. Walker's face, where she stood beside the doorway, was impassive, her "Indian" face. Not many people knew that Mrs. Walker was half Menominee, but Ivar did. It was the half of her that he was most intimidated by. Mrs. Walker knew all about the scandal, probably more about it than Ivar did. Ivar said, nervously, "Well, sit down for a few minutes, Arlen. Elaine?"

"Wait till you hear, Ivar. Something very exciting is about to happen."

Hmmph, said Mrs. Walker, or rather, without speaking, she launched this hmmph into the air of the room and allowed it to float there. Elaine's womanly response was an even brighter smile. Like everyone else on the campus, Elaine didn't dare underestimate Mrs. Walker. Arlen, however, did. He said, "Well, I could use a cup of coffee, Ivar. I'm dry as a bleached bone. How about having your girl bring some in."

Elaine coughed, then said, "Let me get it, Mrs. Walker."

"Nah," said Arlen, "I need you here for support. Dr. Ivar Harstad, well—"

"I'll get it," said Mrs. Walker in her most deadly voice.

"Good, good, good," carolled Arlen, with just the cheery insouciance of a character in a horror movie who must die a horrible death within ten minutes. Mrs. Walker retreated and closed the door behind her.

Ivar was resolved not to get involved with Arlen Martin under any circumstances. It was clear he was no longer in chickens, but he had been ten years before, and he had given a grant to the university for the purpose of investigating the health effects on chickens of a diet made up partially of dead chicken offal—ground-up bone meal, ground-up dried blood and innards, and feathers, etc. In his many chicken factories at the time, the chicken cutters sent the wings, breasts, thighs, and legs to the supermarket and everything else to the rendering facility, where it was ground, cooked, and mixed with grains and prophylactic drugs. It was a practice widespread in England, where Arlen also had chicken factories, but frowned upon by the USDA. A study showing wholesomeness was just the ticket, and a professor in Animal Science had signed on. When the study showed that both the eggs and the killed carcasses of the chickens on the Martin diet showed higher levels of salmonella contamination that could not be satisfactorily controlled by antibiotics also added to the feed, the first thing Ivar had done was to give up eating chicken.

Arlen had assumed that the study would remain unpublished, and asserted himself to realize his assumption. Jolly to the end, he had attempted to destroy the reputation not only of the scientist who had received the grant, but also of the graduate student who had helped him and the journal who had published the results. An addition to the library he had planned to fund had disappeared from the drawing board. Had it been built, Ivar thought, it would have disappeared from the campus. The faculty at large had taken the moral high ground, one of their normal perks as a faculty, and strongly disapproved of Ivar's every attempt to find a compromise. There had been a vote in the faculty senate, condemning him and calling for his ouster, which had not passed, but had hurt more than his reputation.

The study had been published.

Other studies discrediting that study had been published very quickly thereafter.

The USDA had, albeit reluctantly, approved the Martin system of chicken feeding.

A salmonella scandal had hit the British egg industry.

Ivar had stopped eating eggs as well as chicken.

Arlen Martin had risen above chickens, spent two years as the American ambassador to Switzerland, and returned to buy up some companies and double his net worth.

You could not call them friends, but as Arlen himself had once said to Ivar, "You and I are closer than you think. Someday you're going to look at me, and I will look just as familiar to you as your oldest pal, and you'll kind of like me, after all. Just you wait and see."

And it was true. For all his resolve, Ivar felt no personal aversion to Arlen Martin.

Martin said, "I hear you got a budget shortfall of seven million."

"We are laboring under some budgetary constraints, but there are no actual"—he cleared his throat—"cutbacks as yet."

"Mmmm hmm."

"I don't think we have to take the unrealistically optimistic view with Mr. Martin, here, Ivar. He knows what there is to know."

"Well, Elaine," said Ivar, "that doesn't surprise me."

"Waters' son dates my daughter, you know," said Arlen. "Met at college, out there. Princeton."

Waters was the vice-chairman of the state board of governors. Ivar nodded.

"Now, the thing is, I know you guys skim a percentage right off the top, and I don't mind that. I recognize that you can't do good research if you don't keep up the physical plant, and I know a lump sum over here bumps some general funds over to here, and so on.

Accounting is accounting, and I define accounting as an art rather than a science.''

Elaine laughed again.

"You know, we've brought six companies under the TransNational wing in the last six years, some big, some not so big. That gives us control of eleven diverse companies in all, and, of course, a goodly debt. Not much left over for research and development, for, let's say, the physical plant aspects, and the personnel. So I look around me, and I say, who's got the physical plant and the personnel, and I don't have to look far, do I?''

Ivar, whose nodding agreement had become unpleasantly rhythmic, said, ''No, probably not,'' and consciously stilled his head.

"Our interests continue to coincide, Dr. Harstad. I got hybrid seeds, you got plant genetics. I got steel roller mills, you got materials science and industrial engineering. I got airplane engine parts, you got aero-space engineering. I got chickens, beef, and llamas, you got animal science. I got a chemical company that specializes in pesticides, you got entomology. I got a big accounting and PR firm, you got a business school. Are you catching my meaning, Dr. Harstad? Why should I hire R and D people just to read what your R and D people already know?''

"Of course," said Ivar.

"Your own governor says that alliances between education and business are the wave of the future, Dr. Harstad."

"Technology transfer," murmured Elaine.

"You don't have to convince me of general principles, Mr. Martin."

The door opened, and Mrs. Walker brought in a tray of coffee and cookies. She set it in front of Elaine. There was silence until she left the room.

"Call me Arlen."

"Arlen."

"Well, there you go."

"Arlen, let me speak frankly. The principles you speak of are generally agreed upon, but your particular history with this university is a more significant factor in the equation. I don't know that the faculty would allow such an association even now, given the heat of opinion ten years ago."

"It's up to you to explain reality to them, then. Jobs. Cutbacks, that sort of thing. Besides, I can understand my own mistakes. I've made plenty of them. I'm not so hotheaded as I used to be. Trans-

National casts a wider and more diversified net than Martin's Flavor-best did. I say, invest everything in chickens and pretty soon you're thinking like a chicken. You know how chickens think? I do, because I raised chickens as a boy. Chickens are always looking for little bits of things in the dirt. They don't conceptualize on a higher plane. You step back from chickens and you start conceptualizing on a higher plane. That's my philosophy."

"Even so."

"We got a lot to offer one another."

Elaine nodded vigorously, then said, "Ivar, I don't think you should overestimate the sort of punctilious view that the faculty is going to take. My own personal sense of things is that bygones CAN be bygones if your office and my office handle things properly. But Mr. Martin has too much to offer this university, ANY university. I'm sure he knows that any research funded by his group of companies must be done according to academic standards of disinterestedness. I'm sure we can rely on that." She beamed. Her shining eyes caught the electric blue of her suit and promised the end to all difficulties. The President, a newcomer of some two years' standing, she knew was on her side, even though at his last dinner party, he'd talked to Jack Parker for seventeen minutes and thirty-seven seconds, and to herself for only twelve minutes and three seconds.

Ivar said, "Well, specific proposals carry the most weight."

Arlen said, "The whole faculty doesn't know, as a rule, about any individual project or grant?"

"No, they don't," said Elaine.

"There you go," said Arlen.

Ivar's heart sank. For a few minutes, the three of them sat thoughtfully, sipping coffee. Finally, Arlen stood up. Elaine immediately popped out of her chair. Arlen said, "We'll talk again."

"Yes," said Ivar. "Elaine, I need to speak to you for just a moment about another matter."

"I don't think—" said Elaine.

"Only a second."

"Go ahead," said Arlen. "Don't stand on ceremony with me." He went out. In the office, Mrs. Walker was just beginning her mail routine for the morning. She was the last to glance up when he entered. She pointed to the hard wooden chair beside her desk, the chair where students with appeals, complaints, and problems always sat. She said, "You may sit there."

"That's all right, ma'am, I'll stand."

She said, "Sit."

He sat. He put his ankle up on his knee and jiggled his leg. She said, "Don't do that."

He stopped.

She read through her mail deliberately. Of course, she clearly remembered the TransNationalAmerica letter she had thrown away without opening, but she did not intend to waste her time in fruitless regret.

He thought of offering her an extremely well-paid job, just on the basis of her authoritative manner.

Elaine emerged, and said, "Oh! I'm sorry there isn't a more comfortable chair for you, sir."

Mrs. Walker glanced at her.

They left rather hurriedly.

Mrs. Walker picked up her phone and buzzed Ivar, who was waiting to hear from her. She said, "I have three words for you, Ivar."

"And they are?"

"Bovine Spungiform Encephalopathy."

"I'm sorry?"

"Let's say that my sheep has a brain disease called scrapie, and that I send my sheep to a rendering plant where his or her remains are rendered into cattle feed, and then my cow begins to stagger around and fall down, and when I autopsy my cow I discover holes in her brain like the holes in a sponge—"

"Spungiform?"

"Exactly. I have not been careful in my feeding practices. I have encouraged a strange and terrifying disease to cross species boundaries. I am continuing to sell my beef and milk, though."

"Where am I doing this?"

"England, my old stamping ground."

He said, "The source of your information, Mrs. Walker?"

"My friend Mrs. Lake subscribes to the Sunday *Times* of London. Just by chance."

"No. You're right. Thank you."

"You're welcome."

She hung up her phone and picked up her campus mail.

15

A Proposal Made

ONE OF THE Christian acts Marly Hellmich had set herself was to behave in a kindly fashion toward all members of the church, and so, for five years, she had behaved in a kindly fashion toward Nils Harstad, and he had received her kindness more or less as she expected—he was polite in return and he got along well with her and the others. This strategy of low voices and turning aside from anger had worked well for ten years to prevent the sort of acrimonious split that had divided the congregation at the end of the seventies, resulting in the establishment of a splinter church on the north side of town that still harbored fifty or sixty misguided souls, including Marly's own brother and sister, though her father, uncle, two aunts, and all the cousins had stayed on this side of town. The rift ran so deep that there were plenty on both sides of town that were still not speaking to one another. She had heard that the north-siders continued to cherish contentiousness in their hearts, which proved that they always had done so, but the south-siders were as smooth and easy among themselves as passionate believers could be; their strategy had served them well. All you had to do whenever it became too strenuous was offer the effort up to the Lord, and that seemed to work well enough.

It ran through her mind that something had changed with Nils Harstad, but what with preparing for the service, then serving the church supper afterward (a Wednesday night tradition), and cleaning up from that, and listening to Marge Overbeck's story of her kidney stone, she didn't think much else about it until she was leaving and Nils Harstad asked if he could walk her home.

"Well, Nils, I have my car, but if you need a ride, I can easily give you one."

"No. I have my car."

"Oh, well, then—" She was confused, unsuspecting.

"How about a stroll around the block?"

The most she thought, the absolute most, was that he might ask her out to a movie, but actually, he was too old for her. He would be in his fifties, and she was only thirty-five. She preferred men, when she got the chance (which wasn't often with her job and Father to take care of), younger, darker, and from out of town. Certainly from beyond the surveillance of the church. She said, "I'm a little late tonight—"

And he said, no kidding, "How about getting married?"

Marly had to admit that this made her mad. She had not pegged Nils Harstad as a ridiculer of women, but she had been wrong before. Looking at him, she felt a powerful annoyance overcome her, but she spoke softly and turned away from anger. "Don't you think this is sudden, Nils? Our friendship in the church isn't accompanied by any special friendship just between us, do you think?" She had found with her father that asking questions was much more productive than making statements.

Nils cleared his throat. "Many cultures find that a preexisting friendship between the parties to an engagement isn't necessary to marital concord."

"Pardon me?"

"I've seen you. I've watched you. I think the Lord has made his wishes known to me."

Well, if he put it that way. That way of putting it gave Marly pause. She said, "I need to pray over this and think about it. I need to listen to what the Lord says to me."

"I certainly honor that."

"Fine, then."

He took the casserole dish that she was carrying out of her hands and accompanied her to her car. By this time, his car was the only other vehicle in the parking lot. It was a Lincoln, about a year old. She got into her own eight-year-old Dodge Omni with a new self-consciousness, especially when he opened the door for her and said, "I don't do things lightly, Marly. I know my own wishes."

The only thing to do was to pray about it, even if it took all night to get some kind of sign, so after carefully brushing her teeth, she knelt beside her bed and fixed her attention. When she got up an hour later, she knew what the Lord wanted her to do, and in the morning she still knew it, so she called in sick and set about following His orders.

First, she went to the university library and checked the budget book out at the reserve desk. She noted that Nils Harstad, dean of extension and professor of agronomy, earned $121,000 a year.

Second, she looked Nils up in the phone book and drove past his house. It was large, probably four or five bedrooms, brick, and surrounded by expensive plantings.

Third, she called a realtor and told him she was new in town, come from California, and looking for a big traditional brick house in the best neighborhood. What should she expect to pay? "Weeeeelllll," he said, "IF one should come on the market, which doesn't happen very often, you'd be looking at a quarter million, depending on the shape it's in. Can I take your name?" She hung up.

Fourth, she meditated over the entry in the phone book. Apart from Ivar, who lived at the same address, there were no other Harstads in the phone book and no teen-line, which meant either young children (unlikely) or married children or none.

Fifth, she looked around the two-bedroom bungalow she shared with her father, and at her most recent pay stub from the university. She gazed upon the photo of her boyfriend, Travis, who was a long-distance trucker with a wife and small children in Pennsylvania, and she looked in the mirror. She knew she was plain and that she didn't know how to dress. She recognized that kindliness and turning away from anger, two of her real virtues, had never carried her so far before, not once in ten years.

She stood up and turned a sober pirouette, then leaned close to the mirror. She whispered a word. The word was "Cinderella."

16

Earl Ponders

W H E N E A R L B U T Z leaned his bulk against the bars of his pen to better meet up with and enjoy the scratching he was getting from Bob, the orange steel bars bowed slightly outward, but Bob, whose life since meeting Diane had been a whirlwind of new experiences, didn't notice. He just scratched and scratched. Earl, for whom being scratched was a major source of pleasure, was asking no questions. If Bob wanted to stand there with his elbow on the pen and his chin in his hand and scratch and scratch and scratch, Earl's only responsibility was to stand there likewise and enjoy it. Nevertheless, the bars of the pen showed what the charts also showed but what Bob was too preoccupied to notice—Earl Butz was getting monstrous big.

Earl himself felt it in the effort it took him to heave himself to his trotters in the morning, in his increasing desire to lie around and have things, like cooling baths, brought to him, rather than going out to receive them. There was a suspicious bulge toward the center of the pen in the shape of Earl's toileting area—his characteristic fastidiousness was beginning to disappear. He still worked hard at his main occupation of eating. He couldn't help that, it was bred into him; but like any variety of genius, appetite was beginning to overshadow other, more individual traits of his personality. He no longer played with his toys, for example, though he often contemplated them from a recumbent position. And he did not only feel his growing bulk spiritually, he felt it physically, in the form of migrating pains in his legs and trotters. There was no persistent lameness—a limp would have revealed that to Bob and he would have noticed, he wasn't completely dazed, after all—no, the pains were sometimes here, sometimes there, sometimes sharp and sometimes mild, but never, anymore, absent. He could avoid them by lying down in his pile of straw, and so that's what he did whenever he wasn't hard at the trough.

For his part, Bob saw Earl so frequently that these signs of decline, if that's what they were, were hidden from him. In addition to that, he was remarkably fond of Earl—of his friendly, willing nature and the philosophical way that he made the best of his incarceration—and so he was not inclined to notice evidence of pain that would only give him pain, too. Whatever stirrings of unease that some subrational apprehension of Earl, some bodily response that came from a life of knowing hogs, might give him had not yet surfaced, and certainly would have a hard time doing so amidst the storm of feelings he now entertained for Diane Peterson, the girl he had met at the party.

In Bob's former opinion, girls had been generally unremarkable. Some future one had your name on her, but her likeness to your sisters or aunts or mother was major, and reassuring. He had long assumed a relationship to the whole realm of girls that was very similar to his father's relationship to his mother—respectful, with much understood, little actually declared. He had been subtly warned against anything else, for one thing. His father and grandfather spoke disapprovingly about boys and men who followed their dicks around; his mother and aunts reserved their most puzzled scorn for girls and women who didn't fit in, didn't ask for recipes, and thought themselves better than other people. It was easy to see the rational basis for all of this disapproval, too—that kind of man and those kinds of women made no one happy, least of all themselves.

Nevertheless, now there was Diane. All judgments he might have made about her character, all predictions he might have based on those judgments, were blasted away by her own sense of her future. "Make the best of it," his father's commonest and sagest advice, didn't even occupy a niche in Diane's brain.

It was also surprising to him how many different perceptions he had of Diane, after just Saturday night, and then another little date-like engagement Tuesday, when they studied in the library together. He had to spend all these extra hours mulling and scratching Earl's back just to sort through everything. Girls before had presented him with fairly uniform surfaces; Diane dazzled him with facets. Everything she said or did contained some bit of knowledge about her that he had to have, as if he were collecting jewels. His capacity for appreciating her astonished him. It was as if a whole new wing in the cottage of his inner life had suddenly opened up, revealing to him long unknown riches that he already possessed. He wasn't the dull guy he always considered himself to be.

Earl was a comforting and calming companion in all of this. The discipline of keeping the hog's snowy hide clean, his pen picked out, his trough full, of checking him for the odd parasite, the stray infection (for these, though there were no other hogs around, Bob himself was a vector, since hogs and people share certain diseases), of just easing his solitude (which Bob felt more poignantly now that he felt his own solitude more), was an honorable way to pass the time, Bob felt. He did it all for Diane, though she hated agronomy, was afraid of hogs, would certainly run from every activity that his family members did on a daily basis.

And it *was* an honorable discipline. Earl himself had no quarrel with that. It's hard even for a hog to know whether to blame others or himself, especially when the new afflictions seem ephemeral— possibly the product of some little mood swing or change in the zeitgeist.

17

A Vision of the Future

Assignment: Write a story based on the following situation: three people are in a room and something happens which at least one of them must react to. You may define the idea of "room" very loosely. Remember that it is not enough to set the situation up—a story doesn't *begin* until a character recognizes a dilemma and responds to it, and it doesn't *end* until no further responses can be made. A note on ambiguity: Please remember that most readers do not want to decide for themselves *what happened*, though they may like to decide how to interpret it. If you, the writer, don't know what happened, that is not ambiguity, it is a fault in the story. Just make something up.

Sept. 17
Monahan, FW 325

"The Boy"

a story by Gary Olson

The room was dark, even though it was nearly noon, because Lydia Karstensen had the shades drawn. Lydia didn't like the daylight, because it made her see too much. She had gotten into the habit, since the birth of the boy, of staying up late watching TV, then sleeping as long as she could. If she had to go out for groceries or something, she would try to get Lyle to do it on his way home from work. Lyle, though he had a good degree in electrical engineering from a well-known university, worked in a factory.

Lydia woke up and heaved her giant body over onto its side, then she laid there, feeling around on the floor for the candy box she had been eating from the night before. All the chocolates were gone. She yelled, "Brownie, get in here!" but the dog was afraid of her, and just hid under the kichen table. Suddenly, Lydia realized that her daughter and son were in the room. They were sitting very quietly in the corner, huddled together, holding hands. She said, "Why aren't you kids in school?"

The boy said, "Allison had a temperature, so Daddy said I could stay home and take care of her."

Lydia said, "I haven't got time for this. I'm going to take a shower." She heaved her pig-like bulk out of bed. She took off her nightgown. The children hid there eyes. Lydia said, "What a shit-hole this place is. I don't know why we can't have a house of our own."

She was waddling toward the bathroom.

The boy saw that the cord to the telephone was stretched between the bed and the wall. He didn't say anything. Lydia didn't see it. She hadn't seen her feet in years. She stumbled over the cord, which did not pull out of the wall. She fell down with a thump that shook the apartment building. The boy could feel it.

Lydia said, "Oh shit. Help me up." But her leg was broken, and try as he might, the boy could not get her up. Then Lydia began to cough. She coughed some blood up. She said, "Hand me the phone," but the phone was dead. The boy and his sister went back to huddling together in the corner.

Lydia said, "Something's really wrong with me. I think I'm going to die. Come give me a hug, you two." Allison got up and went over to her mother. She hugged her around her fat neck.

But the boy didn't move. He remembered too many slaps, too many times his mother had yelled at him. All he did was sit and watch. Pretty soon, a gurgle came from Lydia's throat and then she was dead.

When Lyle came home from his shift at the factory, he noticed that all was quiet in the apartment. He began looking all over the apartment.

He went into the bedroom.

The first thing he saw was Lydia's giant bulk lying lifeless near the bathroom. He shouted, "Oh, my God!" Really he had always loved her in spite of everything. Then he saw the children, huddled together in the corner. Allison was crying, and she jumped up and ran into her daddy's arms. He looked at the boy. The boy did not move. He looked back at his father.

The boy's hair, which had been almost black, had turned completely white.

The End

Gary—

I think this story needs some work. You seem preoccupied with Lydia's fatness. Does fatness itself make her unlikable? That's what you seem to be implying. What is her personality like apart from her fatness? What did she used to be like? What was it about her that Lyle fell for to begin with? How has she gotten the way she is? How does she feel about it? You need to explore her character some more. The boy needs a name. What is his personality like? Is he malevolent? I don't quite understand how you want me to take him. If you decide to rewrite this story, please see me first.

Gary finished reading the comment with some resentment. He himself had found the story both poignant and thrillingly scary. He had, in fact, stayed awake for some hours after writing it, thinking what a revolutionary combination it was of Stephen King and Charles Dickens. AND he had fulfilled the assignment exactly. Three people in a room, something happens, they react until they've used up all the possible reactions. He turned the paper over, looking for a grade, but there was none.

The press of students changing classes that had moved him to one corner of the corridor had thinned, and now he saw the door to the Spanish class open. Lydia came out with another girl. Gary's first thought was to shove his paper into his notebook and look away. He shouldn't have used her name, or Lyle's. Though it seemed easier, it was too dangerous. She and the other girl passed him and started up the stairs. She had a great pair of jeans on, tight, with red flats. Her thick liquid ponytail swung back and forth, and she laughed, suddenly, her musical laugh. They were talking excitedly about something. Gary moved as close to them as he could without attracting their notice, and began to listen in. The thing was, it was hard to remember what they were saying. You had to cultivate your memory, the way Professor Monahan was always telling them to. But there was no doubt about one thing. It was interesting as hell once you started paying attention.

18

A Soldier of the Revolution

LOREN STROOP DROVE an old John Deere tractor with thousands of hours on it and without a cab of any sort, much less an air-conditioned one, so he had found that keeping abreast of bulletproof vest technology really paid for itself in weight and comfort, especially for summer cultivating and hay harvesting. Every year he bought the newest model advertised in police magazines and wrote it off on his tax forms under "miscellaneous equipment." After a year's wear, a vest was pretty rank, but Loren passed it on anyway, to the local sheriff's troop or to anyone who asked. Loren's wife was dead and he didn't have any kids of his own, so he was known around the neighborhood as a generous old guy.

Loren liked to keep busy, and his interests took him out of the house, so the bulletproof vest was his best protection against the FBI, the CIA, and the big ag businesses, all of whom, he knew, wanted to get him out of the way before he perfected and marketed his invention, which was going to revolutionize American agriculture. This didn't mean that he was lax about residential security—he had a burglar alarm and there were plenty of dogs inside and outside the house. He saw on the TV once where they asked a bunch of convicted burglars what security system they would use, and they all said they would just get a dog, and he felt vindicated. He'd always thought you could rely on dogs, the more the better.

Loren himself didn't own a gun anymore. It was his opinion that a gun just invited you to use it. Every time you got mad at something, your thoughts started to circle around that gun, as if that gun would solve anything. No, his personal safety was of secondary importance. He put his energy into working on his drawings and plans. He thought it was a good idea to keep copies of them in various places, and make sure they would get out if he should no longer be around to do it, by composing letters to various officials, to be sent out upon his demise, even if the circumstances didn't seem suspicious. He intended to get around to that very soon. He was well aware that the CIA, the

FBI, and the big ag companies had plenty of ways of doing you in so that it looked accidental, or even like it was your own fault (the injustice of THAT really stuck in his craw). Wasn't there an old story about a man who was negotiating to change jobs from one big company to another—computers, maybe, or oil—and he was staying at a hotel out East, and they found him in bed with a bullet in his brain and they said it was suicide even though the gun was lying on the floor and the guy's arms were tucked under the covers? This was a clear example of how far they would go to protect themselves and, most importantly, their investments. If you were going to revolutionize American agriculture, which meant you were going to render obsolete billions of dollars of investments already made, then it was naive to think that they were just going to let you walk in and do it.

Nevertheless, Loren was a tremendous patriot from way back—he ran the flag up every day, and he followed the old rules about taking it down in the rain and folding it up in a triangle and never letting it touch the ground, and he also knew, with the same conviction, that his dean of extension, Dr. Nils Harstad, would eventually do the right thing and champion Loren's invention. The thing was getting past Dr. Harstad's secretary, who, like most women, didn't have a grasp of the principles involved and preferred filing her nails to forwarding American agriculture.

Well, a man like Loren Stroop, an experienced farmer who hadn't overextended himself financially and kept every part of his life in good order, was a man who had all the time in the world and could afford, even at the beginning of harvest, to wait patiently for an interview. Every weekday morning he fed the dogs, made himself an early breakfast, put the dishes in the sink, and went out and worked in the fields until about noon. Then he went inside for a sandwich and a glass of milk, changed out of his work clothes (but not his bulletproof vest, because they could pick out your car even if you had it painted every year, which Loren did, and wrote it off under "depreciation") and drove in to the extension office at the university (his university, founded under the Morrill Act to help him), arriving there at one p.m., and parking illegally for exactly an hour (the parking office was orderly, as well, and didn't send a ticketing van to that parking lot until after two). Loren had weighed the dangers of maintaining a routine, especially after they said on the TV that those people who were always getting kidnapped in those foreign countries left themselves open to that by doing the same thing every day, but how to vary his routine was something he hadn't yet decided and, he felt, had to be approached with caution. In his experience, when you varied your routine you tended to forget a lot of things, and more as you got older, no denying that.

Anyway, after one, he sat politely in his dean of extension's office for about forty-five minutes, always sending in his name and a reminder of who he was, written out in pencil so as not to inconvenience the secretary. These visits reconfirmed his understanding that the dean was an extremely busy man, and that sometimes people had to wait years to see him, as it once had been, they said on TV, with kings and princes over in Europe.

When he was finished with his visit, he went for a little walk in the garden beside that brick building with no windows and admired its succession of plantings. It was a garden he knew well by now, and approved of, and he admired what a good (and sweet-tasting) crop of peaches and apricots they managed to get every year even this far north, and he had taken the liberty of planting some of the peach pits and apricot kernels he had gathered, but they weren't near bearing yet, so he didn't know how they would do on his place.

The rest of the time he refined his invention, and his barn was often lit, late into the night, with the blue of his blowtorch, and often rang with the music of hammering. Being a generous man, he also found time to do repairs on his neighbors' equipment—he didn't mind going over to their places, and he always waved away payment with the remark "A piece of pie'd kind of hit the spot, though," and then he would go in the house and get the latest gossip from the wife and take a look at the kids and see how things were going, and then he'd give each of the kids a dime, and he could well afford it because of the way his invention was going to revolutionize American agriculture and make him a rich man.

Nils Harstad had a full file of Loren Stroop's letters, all written, or rather printed, in pencil, and containing lines like "I have to be careful because of those working against me," "Please please please do not communicate anything you hear from or about me to anyone in the AG BUSINESS," and "I first saw your name in a magazine when I was confined in the hospital." This last, Nils interpreted to be a mental hospital, but had in fact been the county hospital, where Loren was having his gall bladder out on the government's nickel. In Nils' view, Loren's schedule of visits was both further evidence of mental instability (didn't people ritualize their lives more and more as they got crazier?) and a signal convenience—he always took his lunch hour from one to two p.m., so that should the shotguns and automatic weapons come out, he, Nils, would be nowhere within the line of fire. He had, of course, invited his secretary to do the same, but actually having seen Loren, she did not estimate the danger very highly. And anyway, if no one was in the office at one, he would just find another time to come. That seemed clear. Nevertheless, she did attempt to be as polite as possible, and she always offered him a cup of coffee when he sat down. In the view of both campus security and the police, he had yet to do anything of interest. His letters were crazy, but never threatening. Nils' secretary felt herself to be living on the edge of danger, and, considering how dull life in this town was, she didn't really mind it.

It happened that by some magical synchronicity of spirit, both Nils and his secretary arrived at an inner conviction that they had had it with Loren Stroop on the same day. After a year and a half of receiving his letters and entertaining his visits, after apparently coming to terms with the strangeness and the inconvenience and the fear of it, they both could stand it no longer. Former worries of precipitating some crisis by acting fell away all at once, and they agreed it could go on no longer. This simple agreement had the effect of turning wish into resolution, resolution into plan. Nils did not know what the secretary was thinking, but he himself felt that he had to take this bold action for the sake of his six unborn children, as Marly Hellmich had agreed to marry him.

And so, when Loren got to the office that day, the secretary courteously took his coat and hung it up, though she seemed to lose her balance, because she fell against him (saying, "They always wax this floor so!"). Then he sat down while she went into his dean's office (where, unbeknownst to Loren, she reported that she had called security and they were standing by, and that she had felt nothing in his pockets when she fell against him) and then she came out and said, "The dean will see you now," and in he went, slick as a whistle. His dean looked at him pretty sharp, taking his measure, no doubt, the way a man should, and he looked back at his dean pretty sharp, but then they sat down and visited together, easy as you please.

Nils said, "I know you've been trying to get in to see me for some time, Mr. Stroop, and I apolo—"

"No need of that, Nils"—you could call your own dean what you pleased, Loren thought—"I know you are a busy busy man, and I'm a patient man, so no harm done."

"Good. How may I help you?"

"Well, I can't really say."

"Pardon me. I thought you had some particular business—"

"Oh, I do. But I can't really talk about it, you see. It's a secret."

"Well, then—"

"There are two dangers, Nils, and I'll be frank about them because it's my opinion that you deserve that, and if any of this gets out, anyway, I'll know how it got out—through you, you see."

"Well, let me assure you, Mr. Stroop—"

"Okay, I'll let you, because eventually, this has got to get out, and it's got to start somewhere, and a secret is no good to anybody, especially if it's this kind of secret."

"Perhaps if you would—"

"Now, the two dangers are these, number one, that they might steal what I've got and keep it quiet, or use it on their own, and get the money, though I'd give that up if I thought that was the price of this getting out, because, you know, I'm an old man, and I don't care all that much about money. You see that, don't you?"

"Well, of course—"

"The bigger danger, as I see it, is them just quashing this whole thing. Now I take precautions." He unbuttoned two buttons of his shirt, and Nils' heart began to slam against his ribs. He pulled aside the plaid fabric and revealed something shiny and dark gray. "You may not be in a position where you have to be familiar with these things, but this is a bulletproof vest, and if you ever want one, I know just the brand to get, I've read all the stuff about them." He smiled warmly. Nils took a deep breath. "I wasn't born yesterday, and I ain't no Commie, but I know how THEY think and that's their right as Americans to think that way, but I think another way, so I protect myself."

"Do I take it that you have produced some invention, Mr. Stroop?" Nils grinned and leaned back in his chair. Never had he known before with such perfect clarity what it meant to be reborn. A farmer with an invention! If there were three hundred thousand farmers, then there were two hundred thousand with inventions out in the barn. He grinned.

"I certainly have," said Loren Stroop. "You heard of McCormick?

or of John Deere? or of Garst? I'm too old for modesty. The men sitting in these chairs in fifty years'll know the name of Stroop just that way, unless they stop me. I'm a patriot and a good neighbor, but I know those things don't come into play when you threaten their investments."

"Do you have the plans with you?"

"I never carry the plans with me. Too risky. We'd have to set up a meeting. Not here. Not at my place."

"We can do that. Where would you like to set it up?"

"Then you want to help me?"

"Helping you is my job, Mr. Stroop."

"Yes, I know that, Nils. That's why I call you 'Nils,' because I know all about the Morrill Act and what your job is."

"Then let's set up a meeting."

"Well, when you come right down to it, I ain't ready for that just yet. I work slowly, and I got to make sure of every step. But I'll be back in touch."

"Good. Good. I'm glad of that." In the last fifteen minutes, Nils Harstad had regained, in every particular and every thread, the self-confident and doubt-free life he strove for. Why not extend a hand to this old guy, the last of a breed, the heart of the heartland? The essence of charity, he often thought, was not deciding what others needed and giving it to them, but giving them what they wanted. What Stroop wanted—an eye and a sympathetic ear—was well within Nils' power. As they parted at the door of Nils' office, he shook Stroop's hand with real friendship.

And Loren Stroop felt that, felt the sincerity of the man. Now this, he thought as he stood outside watching the parking van ticket his car, was a red-letter day.

19

The Worst Horse in the World

". . . THE EGGS incubate from two to six days, hatch on contact with moisture, then burrow into the tongue or the fleshy parts of the jaw. It is here that they molt to the second stage, are swallowed, and pass into the stomach. Please see the pictures and the chart on pages 634 and 635 in the text. Almost all horses seem to have bots."

Bob looked down at the chest and forelegs of the horse he was holding, but he didn't see any telltale eggs. He did, however, step back half a step. His horse didn't notice. She was standing with her head down, her ears flopped, and her lower lip hanging.

"Very important: strongyles. You only need to know about the main types, called 'the large strongyles.' These are bloodsucking intestinal parasites, and have been found in the intestines of the earliest known horses. The larval worms migrate through the organs and tissues of the horse, causing thrombi and emboli, that is, blood clots, that block the vessels. Many experts think that strongyles have parasitized the horse for so long that the horse has evolved elaborate sets of branching connections in the arteries of the intestine. Think of the strongyles as causing internal wounds in the tissues of the horse. Prevention is by far the best course of action."

Bob's horse was now clearly asleep, her eyes closed and one back hoof cocked casually, resting on the toe. As a specimen of horse flesh, she wasn't nearly as nice as the gelding on his other side. She had pan-shaped feet, short legs, a big hay belly, a swayed back, prominent bony withers, a thin mane that revealed a ewe neck, long ears, and a bony, nondescript head, neither boldly Roman-nosed nor pleasingly dished. Just a head with a dangling lower lip.

Miss Pfisterer cast her gaze around the group. She was very serious, and never made jokes in class. Bob thought that might be because she was so little—no bigger than a twelve-year-old, really. Whatever the reason, the effect was to make his horse class seem like life and death every meeting. "Pay attention, because I'm about to say something important. The prescribed worming regimen for horses is every two months, that's six times per year. As a result of this regimen, a number of strongyle species in particular are resistant to seven of the chemicals that have been introduced to control them, and five species of small strongyles are cross-resistant to five of the chemicals. In all cases, introduction of chemical controls breeds resistance in the target population of parasites. Relief through use of control chemicals is always temporary."

Some girl across the circle, holding a pretty Appaloosa, asked the required question, as she always did, with a self-satisfied smile. "What would *you* do, Miss Pfisterer?"

"Certain management practices, of specific control of specific infestations, of alternating horse grazing with cattle or sheep grazing, and of preventing infestation of foals, show some promise. A return to management practices of earlier days, such as tie stalls and absolutely no pasture, has been suggested. After all, the population of horses used to be much higher, so they must have had some means of at least inadvertent control."

The girl actually said, "Thank you," in a sort of preening way.

The horse to Bob's right lifted his head and pricked his ears forward. He was a bay, and looked very quarter horse-y, with a short, arched, well-shaped neck and that appearance of being shorter in the front legs than in the back. An idle interest in horses was something Bob shared with his father—not all that common in a farmer, and not pursued ever, except for the two ponies they'd pastured when Bob and his brothers were kids.

Now Miss Pfisterer had brought out some equipment, a plastic tube, a large syringe, and a small syringe. She said, "There are three methods of worming—through injection, tubing, and paste syringe. In a few weeks, we will go into the lab and try and decide which of these methods has been the most effective, through studying the feces of each of the three groups of horses."

They stood patiently, twenty-one horses and twenty-one students, while she moved between them, sometimes showing how to inject a shot, sometimes showing how to insert the long nose of the paste wormer through the toothless bars onto the back of the horse's tongue. When she came to Bob, she took the coils of plastic tubing off her shoulder, and said, "This looks bad, but Brandy, here, doesn't mind. Put your left hand under her chin and lift her head up with the lead rope." Brandy opened her eyes and stood up, but made no protest. "The esophagus is on the left side. You want to look for it, feel for it, and know that you aren't going down the windpipe. Now you look down her mouth and feel where the tube is going." Bob did so, while Miss Pfisterer ran the siphoning end into a bucket. Extraordinary lengths of plastic tubing seemed to disappear down Brandy's gullet. She stepped to one side and rolled her eyes, but made no other protest. Behind him, Bob heard someone go, "Yecch." Miss Pfisterer actually smiled. A few moments later, the horse had been dosed, and Miss Pfisterer was easing the tubing out of her mouth, rolling it up again. She patted Brandy, who seemed to go back to sleep almost at once, on the neck. To Bob, she said, "You know why this is the most valuable horse in the barn?"

Bob shook his head.

"Well, look at her. She's one of a kind. She defines the bottom. Every element of conformation that you wouldn't want in a horse, she possesses. Once a student has looked her over, has really concentrated on her, really seen her, he knows what he doesn't want to find in any horse he might ever buy in the future. It took us a long time and a lot of luck to find her, and we keep her very healthy. With all these breeders' associations and these breed standards for every little variety of equine, we might never be able to replace her. She's the worst horse in the world. She's my favorite, too." Miss Pfisterer now kissed Brandy on the nose and palmed a piece of carrot between her whiskered lips. Had she not been Miss Pfisterer, Bob might have thought she was joking. She turned on her booted heel and stepped over to the bay quarter horse, who curvetted and danced, trying to watch her as she prepared to give him a shot. She showed the girl holding him how to cup her hand over his eye, restricting his rear vision, then expertly injected him. When she smacked him with the flat of her hand and said, "Hey! King! Stop that!" it was without affection.

Joy Pfisterer was nothing if not methodical. She had begun the worming procedures with thirty minutes left in the period, and wound them up in time for the students to lead their animals into the stable and close them in their stalls. Once her father's pride (ready at any time to ride her pony standing up, ready to somersault forward or backward at any gait, ready to try any fence if someone assured her the horse could do it, ready to try any horse if someone assured her no one had been able to ride it), she was now her mother's surrogate (sober, thoughtful, mindful of consequences, her sense of responsibility mushrooming ceaselessly). She was perfect in her job, since

the university horse herd was a black hole of duties—feeding schedules, shoeing, worming, and inoculation schedules, exercise, turn
out, grooming schedules. She inspected them for evidence of accidents, ill-fitting tack, skin problems, foot and leg problems. She knew
the fields where they grazed blade of grass by blade of grass (there
was always the danger of poisonous plants or parasites), rabbit burrow
by rabbit burrow (broken legs).

Some sort of aversion therapy, probably education, had made gal-
loping, jumping, cross-country eventing, the very activities she had
abandoned herself to with such exhilaration at fifteen, psychologically
painful to her at thirty. After all, a trail-ridden horse who had the
benefit of steady slow exercise could live and work past the age of
thirty. Many jumpers were used up at fourteen, legs shot, joints swollen up. How could you act in the face of that knowledge?

But then, how could you act, period? A mushrooming sense of
responsibility, she had begun to think, soon overcame every pleasure,
every way that humans had devised to lose themselves for a little
while. Joy knew she had become the kind of person that people appreciate from a distance, but are uncomfortable in the presence of.
All except Dean, who loved her anyway and was too self-centered to
really pay attention to her mood. Living with him, which she had
until recently resisted, was not that different from living by herself.

She held her tongue when Dean crowed to her about his bovine
false pregnancy project. The fact that she was known for speaking up
meant that when she didn't, he assumed that everything was fine with
her. It was certainly fine with everyone else. It seemed like everyone
could see the virtues of artificially induced false pregnancy in cows,
if the false pregnancy could result in unending lactation. The fact was,
pregnancy added up to calves, and calves added up to danger and
inconvenience for the cow and therefore for the farmer. And supplying
the farmer with perfect heifer calves that he might otherwise raise on
his own added up to profits for the company, too. A dairy farmer,
in close cooperation with his supplier, of course, could maintain top
production year-around, could even keep his best cows producing
well past the current four-year average. Joy could appreciate that,
couldn't she? Joy certainly could.

There was a lot of money talk. You'd know how much a cow who
never calved was worth, right to the dollar, because you'd know ahead
of time how many pounds of milk such a cow was going to produce
over her lifetime. A little company now dabbling in semen and em-

bryos could get predictably bigger selling whole herds of predictable cows. Mysteries of the business would disappear along with the mysteries of reproduction. Businesses liked that. Unknowns would fly out the window as economies of scale came in the door. Right now, as an accompaniment to talking about future money, everyone was talking about present money—namely, what Dean could expect to get for his research. Every night, when they sat over supper chatting about their day, Dean rolled out heavy-sounding sums of money—a half million, three-quarters, a million, two million. This was not money, of course, that accrued directly to their household budget, but it accrued to his reputation, his stature in the university, his raise for next year, his experience of himself. Later, if (when) there were patents, well, that would translate directly. It was a rosy prospect.

Joy couldn't shake the picture in her mind of the cows AS money: green, falsely pregnant cows in a green field, crisp and crackling, like new dollar bills. One time she had hazarded the remark "Wouldn't that be boring? I mean, the only thing that keeps me going some days is that at least something new and interesting is going on."

He'd said, "Remember that Chinese curse, 'May you live in interesting times'? The dairy farmer's curse is, may you have an interesting herd of cows. The thing is, you, we, have a steady income. We can afford to cherish what's interesting." Though he laughed when he said this, she'd known how to take it. Her approval or disapproval seemed self-evidently irrelevant. Anyway, to be frank, the people Dean was talking to were mentioning such interesting sums of money that he hadn't even minded her remark.

The round of work continued through the noon hour. The horses who stayed in most of the time were hayed and watered. The rest, numbering thirteen, filed out to the near field, where the water tanks had been filled during the morning. Joy placed an order for oats and feed corn on the cob, which she liked to use because if you left some cobs in the feed dishes, it took the stabled horses longer to eat and gave them something to do, looking for stray kernels, in their all too abundant spare time. She ate a sandwich and drank orange juice from her thermos. The night before, he'd said, "You know, your own routine is the problem. You've been doing the same thing for five or six years, now. You haven't even taken a trip, except to buy horses or go to a show. No wonder you're in a bad mood all the time."

And she'd said, "Am I in a bad mood all the time?"

He'd shrugged a little shrug, to say, Yes, but I'm not going to mention it aloud, then he'd said, "Not bad, like irritable. Bad, like down in the dumps. It doesn't BOTHER me, but I worry about you."

But it did seem like the more doubts she overcame with regard to Dean's phantom pregnancy project, the more doubts she developed with regard to everything else. All those cows with the same pattern of black and white, all turning their heads at the same time, all mooing in unison (his first love was still cloning) and all feeling pregnant when they were not, didn't seem to be an image she could hold in her head along with the rest of what she knew about life. On the other hand, she seemed to be the only person Dean knew with this problem.

20

Who's in Bed with Whom

MARY, much to her surprise, is in bed with an extraordinarily handsome Palestinian named Hassan who is a graduate student—graduate student! Twenty-five at least—in plant genetics. She has known him for a week now. After meeting in the lunch line at the commons, they have seen each other every day and every evening. He has many virtues, some of which she likes to admit to herself and some of which she doesn't, but admits to herself anyway. Among the former—he is ambitious and hardworking. Five of their dates have been study dates, and he has, in a kind way, never belittling her, unraveled a good deal of the tangle she was in in her calculus class, while she has corrected the English usage on a paper he was writing. He is direct—he admits that he doesn't understand American dating customs, and his solution for this problem is to ask her what would be comfortable for her. He is cosmopolitan. Although new to America, he has lived in Beirut, Paris, Rome, and Algiers. His family had been importers-exporters in Palestine. Now most of them work for the Israelis. He is politically aware, though he doesn't push that on her, and she is a little afraid to investigate too deeply. She likes to think of his history and circumstances as apart from his self, just the way she likes to think of her own history and circumstances. A virtue she doesn't like to admit to herself—he is neither black nor white. When she tells her black friends and her white friends that he is Palestinian, both sets are impressed. Both sets suspend the judgments they would otherwise make. He is also good in bed, as she has just found out, relaxed with the relaxation of experience (Beirut, Paris, Rome). He has never slept with a black woman before, and now that she has slept with him, she thinks of herself as a black woman, not a girl any longer.

NILS HARSTAD AND Marly Hellmich are not actually in bed. They are two rooms from the bed, in fact, and will not, anytime soon, go near it. Marly wouldn't mind, except that she has just now discovered that Nils thinks she is a twenty-five-year-old virgin who has selflessly devoted her time to taking care of her elderly father, who will, Nils says, of course be welcome to live with them following the ceremony. He is talking right now, holding her hand and running the fingers of his other hand up and down her arm. Her elderly father. Nils, himself, now fifty-five but sooner than you think seventy-five. He is talking in a low soothing voice about their six imminent children—in vitro fertilization, embryo transplant, multiple pregnancy, pergonal, multiple birth, Jesus. Marly feels drowsy. He can have her pregnant by Christmas if they get on with the ceremony. A year from now! Just think. Marly can't think. The words, his hand ruffling the hair on her arm—it's all like a drug. But she holds the thought that she can talk him out of it once they are married. They have to get married. She has to get out from behind that steam table. It was one thing to work there year after year, expecting no change, dumbly following her round of duties. Now that she has seen the light, been inside the house and the Lincoln and the Pinetree Supper Club, the need to leave the steam table behind is a thirst that is killing her. After the marriage, after sex, she will wake him up once and for all.

BOB AND DIANE are in bed in the technical sense, though not yet in the larger sense, since they've agreed to sleep next to each other but not to "do anything," but they will be in bed in every sense in about five minutes, because Bob has just taken off his shirt. His chest and shoulders and abs, from lifting hay bales and feed sacks all his life, form a rippling, solid, and precise picture of maleness that seems to render abstract Diane's every doubt about him and every certainty about her goals. He turns around to hang up his shirt (he's very considerate of her—not the virtue it should be), and his back curves and the muscles fan away from his shoulder blades and the waistband of his jeans sits on his hips. He turns back. His smile is nice, too. It is not, after all, sex that distracts you from your goals. Diane takes the pill and carries condoms, one of which she will hand Bob, to his thrilled humiliation, in about seven minutes. It is marriage that distracts you, and just because Bob thinks that you always end up marrying the first girl you sleep with (or one of the first, anyway, this is almost the nineties, after all), that doesn't mean that everybody thinks that way, she is just a freshman and no one expects freshman relationships to last. She will think about that later.

It's just that when he slips off his jeans, well, the definition all the way down, quads, calves, ankles, even feet, well, it kills her. That's what she's going to tell the others tomorrow, that his body just killed her. But she won't mention, except maybe to Sherri, the long solid pressure she can see inside his briefs, which seems to represent and concentrate and present for her alone all the rest of his body. She says, "Oh, Jesus. Okay," and sits forward so that her shirt falls away from her breasts and his eyes get wide. And then he turns away just for the smallest second to make sure the door is locked.

HELEN SAYS, "Be careful," but Ivar always is. He always enters slowly and then slows down even more. It is a technique he learned in his thirties that transformed his sex life from urge to art. Like now. He is concentrating; he can tell that Helen is concentrating. Just slowing down expands every moment, every sensation, his very experience of her. And as his mind diminishes to a point, his body expands to a universe. His penis feels like any number of things: a man in a dark tunnel, a flood pushing through a narrow canyon, a hand sliding into a satin glove, a furry animal burrowing in the earth. The more slowly he goes, the more the images collect, all widening the simple act of sex into a cosmic sense of connectedness, which is what he likes best, which is what he feels with Helen more than he has with any other woman. Helen can concentrate as well as he can; it's the main thing they have in common.

In his ear, he hears a very deep groan, a creak in the foundations of her body, and he goes in deeper, imagining cracking those foundations with his power. She opens her legs and lifts them backward, inviting him, but he resists the invitation in an impossible way, like a man who has jumped off a diving board, but then, through force of will, lowers himself inch by inch into the pool. Another groan comes, a groan of such desire that it is as irresistible as gravity, but he resists it—the man creeps along the wall of the tunnel, the hand pauses, the furry animal hesitates. Then he moves forward again, forward and down. Though he wants it more than anything, the slowness makes him crazy—the tip of his penis is a hot coal. He feels her hands on his buttocks, pressing. He cups his own hands around her breasts and pinches the nipples, he is that cruel. "Ohhhh," she says, and her hands come up to push his away but instead squeeze the fingers tighter. Down and forward he goes, making his way, blind and huge, lost.

And then they are thrusting, slowly, more quickly, more slowly, and he is wondering, as he always does, why he put this off, it is so perfect a motion, so much what his whole body had been wanting to do all along, and just when he has relaxed into it, a surprising explosion comes and after that he is back in his head, sprawled on top of Helen, who is chuckling a deep chuckle that he can feel all along his chest.

THINGS AREN'T going as well for Tim, whose sex life is still compounded mostly of urges and, for all he writes about it, hasn't mutated into art yet. The trouble is that he has been consulting the wrong authorities—male novelists from Eastern European and South American countries. He has been believing their stories about fifteen-year-old girls desiring eighty-year-old men and mistresses who are uncritically insatiable year after year. He also takes as a guide his own erotic dreams, which he assumes show the royal path to his real needs—desires—what's the difference?

Cecelia seems to be enjoying herself well enough, but now that he has made it into her bed, he's less excited than he planned to be. He's only, say, 80 percent excited and, given the effort of wooing her over the last few weeks, he had planned to be 110 percent excited. Her body, which had practically made him come the first time he saw her, now seems more like a geographical task—he has to make his way from mouth to shoulders, to neck, to tits (nice tits—he hasn't lost his esthetic sense), to waist, to pubic hair, to labia, etc.

Those Latin American and Eastern European novelists aren't any help here. They live inside the mansion of female desire as if it is their right. Their own desire is a nice healthy dog on a string, ready to eat, fuck, fetch, piss on the bushes. Clearly Tim's desire is unreliable compared to that, and he hardly lives in a mansion of female desire. Cecelia, whose fault all of this must be, has made this simple act such a big deal that it's simultaneously demeaning and frightening. If she'd just let him fuck her when he wanted to fuck her, the way women in Eastern Europe and South America did—

But it is a mistake both moral and practical to stray into that sort of bad thinking. He likes Cecelia, he really does, as much as he likes anyone these days. She has virtues and charms where other people don't even have qualities. The fact is, he is happy to be with Cecelia right now. He just would prefer being somewhere else with her. She opens her eyes and looks at him. He brushes her hair out of her face and smiles at her with honest affection. She says, "Tim?"

He resumes thrusting.

EVEN THOUGH it's after midnight, and Mrs. Walker and her companion, Mrs. Lake (they know each other as "Loraine" and "Martha," of course, but everyone else they see, day in day out, from Loraine's coworkers to Martha's fifth graders, calls them "Mrs."), are wide awake.

Martha says, "So the twin is getting married? Unbelievable."

"Mark my words it won't happen. She'll call it off."

"Who is it?"

"Marly Hellmich. She works in the kitchen over at the Union. The father used to work in the machine shop until they fired him for drinking on the job. The mother was a nice woman. Of course she set herself to be long-suffering, just like it was a degree you could get."

"Dead?"

"Liver cancer."

"How did you know her?"

"How do I know anybody? I just did. She was around, I was around."

"What does Ivar think?"

"He was surprised, but he's so bound up in this other stuff that he hasn't reacted very strongly. I say good riddance. They've been twins long enough." Martha reaches over and touches Loraine's bare breast affectionately, and Loraine's gaze lingers over Martha's similarly bare breasts—similarly bare and similar breasts—they have come to look a lot alike over the years. Loraine loves the thin, stretched feeling of the skin of Martha's breasts, especially underneath. It is the most delicate tissue—living, pale, warm, as smooth as the way water looks pillowing over a rock in a stream. She smiles, thinking that the next day is Sunday and they can stay up all night if they wish.

Martha props herself up on one of their big fluffy pillows. "You never told me about HIM."

"He hasn't changed. Little guy with big ears. He spoke of me to Ivar as 'your girl.' "

Martha smiles.

"He's up to something. I guarantee you, he's in bed with Elaine Dobbs-Jellinek, Associate Vice-President for Development, 113 Lafayette Hall, right now, and he's getting ready to fuck the whole university this time." As Martha reaches around for the comforter, her legs spread a bit. Loraine gazes at the exposed pubis affectionately. She says, "I can't wait to touch you there."

"Here?" Martha touches herself.

"There." They smile at each other.

"Are you hungry at all?"

"Mmm, maybe," says Loraine, then, "Turn over."

Martha does so, slightly elevating her buttocks. They stare at each other for a long moment, until Loraine reaches across and begins massaging Martha's buttocks in big, firm, circular motions. Every so often, she lets her hand wander between Martha's legs. When she does so, Martha closes her eyes and sighs. She says, "I'm starving."

They sit up and head for the kitchen, but after she opens the refrigerator door, she is moved to turn and drop to her knees, to explore Loraine's labia and vaginal opening (they try never to use euphemisms about women's sexual parts) with her tongue. Loraine leans against the sink, her legs apart, her feet on a chair, her arms braced, her head back, her eyes closed. She can't see Martha's breasts, but she can remember and imagine them, silky and pendulous, waiting to be sucked.

Martha murmurs, "I'd like to put something in you."

"There's that dildo in my bedside table."

"Shall we go to it, or shall I bring it to us?"

"Don't stop." Martha doesn't stop. She grasps Loraine around both her substantial thighs and thinks how she loves this, finding Loraine's clitoris with her tongue and sensing it swell and throb. Loraine's odor rises around her head, making her own vagina feel open and hot. It is she who likes the dildo, both using it and receiving it. Loraine is partial to stroking and licking. Loraine groans and Martha can feel the clitoris contract and then the artery in Loraine's thigh, next to her ear, seems to pulse. Martha lifts her head. She says, "Don't fall!" At their age, they have to be careful.

"Don't stop!"

Martha doesn't stop.

Loraine doesn't fall.

A bit later, Martha stands up. Loraine helps her, and gives each of her nipples a warm kiss. Together, they turn toward the refrigerator. It is still open.

"Just a fingerful of guacamole for me," says Martha.

"Ready for bed?"

"Mmmmm."

CHAIRMAN X LIES on his back, his chin upthrust, snoring. Beth, next to him, has one foot on the floor, and she is listening intently. He lets out, or rather pulls in, because he has a habit of snoring on the uptake, a long, ruffling, intermittent bleat. She reaches over without looking and smacks him on the shoulder. He turns away from her at once and curls into himself. The snoring stops.

But does the coughing? After three nights, she'd thought Amy's croup was over with, but just as she was drifting off, she'd sensed the long cawing that portended another sleepless night. A fearful dream? The real thing? She wills the house into silence so that she can hear.

Nothing.

She brings her foot back into bed.

She is wide awake.

She thought they were going to make love tonight, but they didn't. It seems like a bad sign. Or rather, what seems like a bad sign is that their sex life has receded over the last two or three years, and now looks like a house a few doors away that they once lived in but no more. And the real bad sign is her equanimity about this. She does not actually seem to need to have sex. In the past she thought that she needed it; she even, in the early seventies, took defiant pride in a need that her parents, for example, didn't share. And now she doesn't need it and neither does he, and a good sex life looks like any other virtue that you half will and half enjoy—eating enough fiber, cooking only vegetarian meals. Her parents probably felt relief crossing sex off their list, but Beth feels a kind of cool guilt.

Now it comes, the cawing and the hacking, clear as a bell. She sits up. It's plenty loud enough to hear and she knows from that that her earlier suspicions were motherly foresight, a visceral knowledge, maybe from the way Amy's body felt when she put her to bed, that the child was still sick, though she seemed well and hadn't coughed all day. Don't go to sleep, her own body said, It's coming.

Amy is hot and mostly asleep, tangled in her knitted blanket. Her head has an acrid, feverish fragrance that Beth feels guilty relishing. They all smell that way only when they're sick, but it's such a delicious smell. The coughing subsides slightly as Beth sets the toddler upright against her shoulder, but it still sounds as if it is coming from a loudspeaker rather than a child. She cuddles Amy and carries her into the bathroom, where she turns on the shower, hot. The small room begins to fill with steam. Beth sinks down on the mattress they've carried into the bathroom, with her back and head against the wall. Amy's arms encircle her neck and her darling head shifts over to one side. The breaths she draws begin to quiet. Beth closes her eyes. Sometime later, she wakes up. Amy, too, is awake, and pulling at her nightgown. At fourteen months, she is still nursing once or twice a day. Beth unties the bow at her throat, and exposes her breast. Amy smiles. Her breathing seems normal. She finds the nipple and begins to suck. Beth settles herself into this profound relaxation and closes her eyes again.

DR. LIONEL GIFT IS in bed with Arlen Martin, billionaire, but only in the Washington, D.C., sense. Martin himself is back in Dallas, working late and pleased, when he happens to think about it, with the success of his brief trip to the university. Dr. Gift's dark, richly furnished chamber contains only his dream, but the dream is thrilling, and actually passes no more quickly than the sensual self-abandonments of the others.

His dream concerns just that word, "billion." In a normal waking state, Lionel Gift isn't much impressed by a single billion. In terms of things like the national debt, the budget deficit, the gross national product, the number of stars in the Milky Way, the net worth of corporate America, the debt load and interest payments of corporations that participated in leveraged buyouts in the eighties, and, his own special field, Third World development through the International Monetary Fund and the World Bank, one billion isn't much, and he would disdain it. But $1 billion attached to the personhood of Arlen Martin has unexpectedly moved him—the small, poignant mortality, the "poor, bare, forked animal" with the jug ears, the eager smile (Dr. Gift can tell that Martin has heard of his own work, and has been anxious to meet him), the deceased wife (though he has never married, Dr. Gift finds deeply romantic the idea of all deceased wives, women he pictures in their lost youth, reddened roughened hands deep in suds, wearing some rag of a housedress, staring down the long, say, Oklahoma vista toward the oil fields just for a glimpse of the ambitious young man with jug ears to whom they joined their fates until some early, sudden cancer or accident of childbirth took them away smiling and rewarded only by their own virtue, never to be corrupted by idleness), the shoes more comfortable than stylish, the belt high rather than low. How does a simple economist solve this mystery—the relationship between the hard, glittering sum of money and the soft, particular man? Dr. Gift feels that this spiritual conundrum, more than other allurements, is what secures his attachment to Martin's project, which after all is just a project like most others, where one thing in one place, currently without value, will be transferred to another place and endowed with value. Ho hum. But Arlen Martin himself as an object of contemplation! Well—

Dr. Lionel Gift's dream contains no actual human figures, only what, in Hollywood, is known as a voice-over, his own voice, it seems, counting. How many houses in Orange County, average price $10 million? (A hundred.) How many Maseratis, average price $150,000? (Six thousand.) Rollses? (Five thousand.) Apartments in Paris? (A thousand.) Apartments in Tokyo? (Two hundred.) In his dream, houses and cars and apartments and paintings parade by, all the ones he's seen over the years and coveted, a kaleidoscope of goods, goods to touch once, to contemplate for a few moments before something else comes up and takes its place, goods to know you own, whether or not you have time to actually use them. In his professional life, Dr. Gift has met many many people who know and control numbers, but somehow, until Arlen Martin (who clearly reciprocates his respect, on intellectual grounds) he has never met so Godlike a figure, either consumer-wise or production-wise. And his glad duty, thanks to Elaine Dobbs-Jellinek, will be to serve. How many times might Arlen Martin buy and sell Dr. Lionel Gift himself? Well, apart from the enigma of the worth of knowledge, exactly two thousand times. In his dream, the thought of being personally bought and sold by Arlen Martin two thousand times brings him to such a pitch of excitement that he wakes up and can't go back to sleep.

21

It's Ironic

IN THE TWO WEEKS since his extension dean, Dr. Nils Harstad, had agreed to do his duty and look over his invention and his plans, Loren Stroop had lost and gained his courage five or ten times every day. His self-confidence and exhilaration, for example, had drained away almost the very moment he had expected it to burgeon—the moment he returned from the university, went into the barn, turned on the light, and viewed his machine. He had not noticed before how patched-together it looked, how unshiny and low-tech it seemed. No longer was one of the machine's virtues that it climaxed Loren's life of making the best of things by making the best of every one of its parts. Now Loren looked at it and saw the harrows, windmills, tractors, bicycles, planters, corn pickers, pumps, automobiles, refrigerators, and disks that had supplied those very parts; the machine looked like a jumble, never mind that it worked. It DID work—Loren had used it himself on all sorts of fields.

And the plans, so carefully put together, were drawn wrong. Nils Harstad not only wouldn't understand them, he would be repelled by them, since they were stained here and there, soiled here and there, continued here and there on the back of the sheet. You could see, if your gaze were cold enough, and Nils Harstad's gaze WOULD be cold enough, that the enthusiasm that had motivated and thrilled Loren Stroop through every step had also made for carelessness.

What had impressed its inventor for what it had grown from now depressed him for what it had not turned out to be—something sleek and handsome, revolutionary impact evident in every line.

Which is not to say that Loren was disheartened or deflected from his goal. No no no. He merely did what he had done all his life— after every hailstorm, every gully washer that washed away the new, vulnerable seedlings, every drought that burnt them up, every breakage of machinery, every fall in the markets that erased his profits— he redoubled his efforts. This was his virtue and his flaw, a quality that may have been merely a habit, a quality that may have been imposed from outside, by farmer-peer-pressure, a quality that may have been something he brought to farming, that had enabled him to succeed (or at least survive) as a farmer where so many had failed (but Loren would never judge them—he would be the first to say that impossible circumstances got the best of them, or bad luck, or, most likely, the collusion of the USDA, Cargill, Iowa Beef Processors, Pioneer, Ciba-Geigy, Deere, IH, the Big Banks, the CIA, the FBI, and the Trilateral Commission).

The first thing he did was get a couple of friends to harvest the rest of his crop—he'd gotten enough in and sold it so his costs were covered, and he could always eat out of the garden and do a little hunting later in the fall. After that, he spent his nights and days in the barn, straightening this, fixing that, tightening the other thing, putting on a coat of enamel—off-white, because people seemed to like that. Most computers you saw at the computer store were off-white. Must be for a reason. He got out, but only when he was called out. It was harvest season, after all, and now that the nearest implement dealer was eighty miles away, lots of his neighbors had come to depend on him to repair their combines, so that's when he ate, when they offered him a meal. It was dependable enough. Anyway, he didn't notice when he didn't eat.

He wore his bulletproof vest night and day. He wasn't going to be gulled into thinking that the pressure was off. Quite the contrary, the pressure was more on than ever. They had ways of knowing when you were about to make your move. You could see that every night on TV—the closer you got to your goal, the harder it was to get there, and the more likely some big explosion, say, or a car wreck would intervene. Getting lost in your work tended to make you careless right at the time you could least afford carelessness.

He got the plans drawn on special paper he bought, the right paper, and he took them down to the copy center, where they said they had to keep them overnight. He didn't like to leave them there, but they insisted.

He weighed the likelihood of the copy center being broken into by the big ag companies, but he was almost certain no one had followed him and seen which copy center he had chosen.

He had purposely not titled the plans or indicated top and bottom. That was some protection. He gave his name as "Joe Miller."

He left the plans nonchalantly, just as if they were insignificant, as if no one would ever care about them. He told the boy behind the desk that he would be there first thing in the morning, when the doors opened. He saw the boy write that on the paper—"Joe Miller, 8 a.m., ASAP overnight."

He felt dizzy as he drove away, leaving them there.

Then he felt dizzy again, as if his vest were a little too tight, as he drove into the real Joe Miller's yard, where he'd promised to stop and look at the differential on the combine. He noticed that Joe was about three-fourths done with his corn. Then he noticed that after he turned off the truck with his right hand, he couldn't make his left hand take hold of the door handle. Then, it was the funniest thing, when he opened the door with his right hand, he couldn't put his left leg out, and when he pushed it out with his right arm, it didn't hold him, and he fell. And then when Sally Miller came running over with all those kids behind her, he wanted to laugh at how silly it was, but he didn't seem to be able to get a word out, and she ran off and here came Joe. And the little girl, whose name seemed suddenly far away and impossible to get a hold of, kept patting his hand and saying something in a language he couldn't understand.

Part Two

22

Trickle-Down Economics

State Journal, October 1, 1989: In a surprise move today, Governor O. T. Early slashed the state budget by more than $200 million, with cuts affecting many state programs and agencies, but not all. While some cuts had been foreseen for a number of weeks, the scope and depth of the final cuts took most observers by surprise. "This is a victory for the fiscal health of our state," declared Governor Early, "and will ease the tax burden on our citizens. I consider these necessary cuts the boldest and most courageous accomplishment of our administration so far, and I know that the citizens of the state will applaud them."

Most severely affected are social services agencies, education, health care programs, and public works programs. The cuts will go into effect January 1. In some agencies, whole programs will be cut; in others, a proportion of the personnel will be laid off across the board. The Governor's office will press a "last hired, first fired" policy, which may have the effect of gutting recent affirmative action gains. "Sacrifices are always painful," said the Governor.

The Governor went on to say, "I've been on a diet before, and I know how it feels. For the first few days, you think you've got to have those donuts and hot fudge sundaes you got so used to. Later, though, you know how much better you feel with a little salad and a piece of broiled fish for lunch. This state has been on a binge that we can't afford. I came into office with a mandate to end that binge, and this is the first, hardest step. There's going to be clamor and complaining, but I vow to the citizens of this state that I will be strong and resist. No more hot fudge sundaes!"

Governor Early has often been praised for the homely, down-to-earth way in which he communicates his ideas to the voters.

When asked specifically about health care, the governor remarked, "This state has some of the best doctors and hospitals in the world. It doesn't make sense to me to keep open, at the citizens' expense, a bunch of little hospitals scattered here and there, when folks are just going to have to go to the medical centers after a few days anyway."

Of education, the governor had this to say, "Education is an investment. The trouble is, they don't run it like an investment over there, with the students as customers, because that's what they are, you know. Now they run it like welfare, but I'm telling you, if they won't turn it around themselves, we've got to turn it around for them. This administration believes strongly in education."

Governor Early's office will issue more specific plans for how the cuts will be made before October 15.

One year ago, after the majority in both houses of the legislature passed a line-item veto, something the Governor had been working for for three years, Governor Early made some cuts in the budget by vetoing phrases, words, numbers, and even letters in the budget document. When those cuts were overridden by votes in both houses of the legislature, the governor declared, "They ain't seen nothing yet."

Sources in the legislature today expressed doubt that the governor's newly announced cuts would meet with much opposition. "The handwriting is on the wall," said state senate minority leader John Dealy (D-Rock City). "We can read it as well as anybody."

The World Trade Center, the Capitol Convention Center, the Governor's Program for Enterprise Development, the new maximum security facility in Sidekick, the budget for the state government, and plans to build a riverfront mall in the capital city are among those programs that will be unaffected by the cuts.

Memo
From: Provost's Office
To: All Departments and Faculty
Subject: Budget cuts

As some of you know, severe cutbacks will affect many programs in the spring. While our office had been expecting a budget reversion of some $7 million, the actual sum now demanded by the state is closer to $10 million. Nor do we guarantee that this will be the only reversion of this fiscal year. Each department is therefore required to supply, by October 20, a schedule of prioritized cuts, some or all of which may go into effect on January 1. In addition, no hiring is authorized for next year, even to replace departing faculty members. All searches must cease as of the date of this memo.

Memo
From: Chairman
To: English Department Faculty
The department can no longer pay for the following:

1. Long-distance telephone calls concerning professional business.

2. Xeroxing, copying, or dittoing of any kind, even for departmental business.
3. Office supplies not used by the secretaries. THE SUPPLY CABINETS WILL BE LOCKED. DO NOT ASK FOR THE KEY.
4. Faculty or student computer time on the university mainframe.
5. Travel expenses of any kind.

In addition, faculty offices will no longer by cleaned by the janitorial staff. Brooms, mops, buckets, and rags may be checked out through the secretaries from the janitorial supply room on the first floor. Trash should be carried to the Dumpster outside the east entrance.

Memo
From: Provost's Office
To: University Physical Plant Services
Subject: Old Meats

Please act as quickly as possible to find a suitable buyer or buyers for the interior equipment of Old Meats, and for the building material that will be generated by the demolition of the building. Please, also, take bids on the demolition itself. Application has been made to the state to remove Old Meats from the State and National Registers of Historic Places. Following action on these applications, demolition will begin immediately. As a personal note, Howard, I'm sorry the planned renovations are now out of the question because of these cutbacks. We can barely put together the funds for structural repairs to the dome of Columbus Hall, but we hope to do something through alumni. Unfortunately, alumni attachment to Old Meats isn't all that strong. Too bad, Ivar.

Memo
From: Office of Classroom Scheduling
To: Professor Lionel Gift, Economics

Please make a note of the new room for your Spring 1990 "Introduction to Economics," MWF 10:30 to 11:30:

Old room: Red Stick Lecture Hall #2, seating capacity: 450

New room: Clemson School of Art and Design Theater, seating capacity: 1,500

The range of video monitors attached to the ceiling of the theater, which you have indicated that you plan on using, must be run by a certified university engineer, Class 1 or above. Please contact our office for a list of names. You are reminded that under new university policies, faculty members using work-study engineers in the classroom are required to pay these students themselves. THE UNIVERSITY CAN NO LONGER PROVIDE THIS FREE SERVICE. Class 1 engineers are paid $8.50 per hour. Class 2 engineers are paid $10.50 per hour.

One more note—in your last memo to this office concerning your spring course, you referred to certain "customers." Does this indicate that you intend to seat more than the enrolled number of students? If so, these nonstudents will be billed a "seat charge" of $35.00 for the semester.

Memo
From: Dean of the Library
To: Acquisitions Department
Subject: Budget cuts

There will be no acquisitions until further notice. Orders should be withdrawn for any volumes that have been ordered but not received by the library.

Memo
From: University Computer Center
To: All University Personnel
Subject: Computer log-on fee

As of November 1, a computer log-on fee of $.25 per log-on will be charged to every user. Users' monthly accumulated fees will be added to their regular university bills. Please note that this log-on fee will be assessed EVERY TIME YOU LOG ON, EVEN IF YOU HAVE JUST LOGGED OFF.

In addition, charges for printouts will be raised from $3.00 per hundred pages to $.05 per page.

Memo
From: Helen
To: Cecelia

This is just a reminder that the number of students registered for your beginning- and intermediate-level Spanish classes in the spring will be thirty-two for each class, rather than the twenty-five that you have had this fall. Isn't this the worst? Roger had to let go all of the instructors, because the university lawyer told him he couldn't break individual contracts but "a bloodbath is legal."

Memo
From: Dean, University Extension
To: All Offices

All publications of Extension materials will now be charged at $1.00 per publication, plus postage, rather than being sent out free, as formerly. See attached schedule of postage fees.

Please be sure to inform callers of this change. Those desiring publications should send checks or money orders to Mary Logan, Office of Extension, etc. We are not equipped to accept MasterCard or Visa at this time.

Note
X,

They plan to tear down Old Meats, but they're keeping it very quiet. ASAP is the rumor, in spite of State and National Registers. Selling it off as junk, can you believe it? Even though I've always thought having an abattoir at the dead center of campus was only too revealing, I hate to see it go. And I know what it means to you. Good luck,

Garcia

Memo
From: Brown
To: All Administrative Offices

Please remember that our customers do not have a "right" to any particular services in return for their dollar, though they may think that they do. Sentiment against recent cutbacks may manifest itself disagreeably in your offices, but a short, informal workshop on maintaining positive customer relations directed primarily toward secretarial personnel should limit these unfortunate but predictable effects. I am at your service if you wish to consult with me about these concerns.

23

The Dusty Archives

ALL THROUGH HIGH SCHOOL, college, and graduate school, Cecelia's great belief about herself was that her heart was in research. In the midst of the passions, disappointments, conflicts, and noise of her family and her ex-husband, she had dropped her eggs one by one into a single basket, the life of the mind. Her mother's complaint, in Spanish, "Jorge! She's not listening! I'm talking right to her and she's not listening!" had segued neatly into her ex-husband's complaint, "Hello? Earth to Cecelia! Honey, you haven't heard a word I've said."

At UCLA, she had treasured up her days in the library, first in a distant carrel far from any entrance, deep into the Hittite and Sumerian shelves, where no one ever went. Later, she'd gotten her own little windowless office and filled it with books and journals about medieval Catalan literature and other books and journals about feminism that assured her that the development and expression of the feminine mind was in itself a daring, revolutionary, and responsible act, and as antisocial in its way as reserving her thoughts and her attention for herself in the middle of the demanding swirl of her outer life.

At the beginning of the fall, she had confidently found herself another distant carrel, this time amidst the Icelandic and Greenlandic collection, no volumes of which had been checked out in seven years. She had applied for a library office, too, but they were in short supply. This, however, turned out to be a lifesaving development, because had she been confined to her office, she might have slept forever, might have found herself locked repeatedly in the library. In her carrel, at least the occasional janitor or the occasional student on his or her way to the German Romanticism collection roused her.

The fact was, in spite of the cooler weather, her mind had no life. All medieval Catalan literature did for her was put her into a coma, and all feminism did for her was arouse guilt, which in turn made her drowsy. Scholarly endeavor, which had for so many years felt especially pure and enlivening, had felt exactly like exercise of the mind (stretching, lifting, pushing, straining toward a clear goal), now felt like hollowed-out willpower, emptied of desire or purpose. Nevertheless, she came to her carrel every day and sat down, opened her books and began. Somewhere in them, it seemed, she would find the golden seed. She imagined herself eating it, and desire rooting and blossoming once again.

As for Tim, well, that wasn't working out either. He was turning out to be one of those men whose interest diminished as they got to know you. You got into this pattern of trying to be interesting by revealing more and more of yourself, like a salesman unpacking his sample bag, but the man, though he looked like he was smiling and paying attention, was really shaking his head internally—not that, not that either, no I don't think so, not today. The temptation was to unpack everything, not exactly for that particular guy, but just to rise to the challenge, just to get the nod. Apart from the fact that Tim was still the only edgy, interesting person she knew, and still looked THAT WAY, the relationship, and probably the friendship, was moribund. Which meant that in two months she had made firm contact with no one—no colleague, no one in the feminist reading group, no student, no passing acquaintance.

And now, annoyingly enough, there was someone in her carrel, a man with an open book. In sixty straight days in the library, there had never been anyone in her carrel before, and the shock was almost more than the annoyance. She stopped short, and picked a book off the shelf. It was written in Icelandic: "Par munu eftir undrsamligar gullnar toflur—"

Chairman X, meanwhile, looked up, and saw the beautiful Costa Rican woman he had sat beside at Gift's lecture. Her coat was unbuttoned, revealing a long red sweater and black leggings. Her hair was pulled back in a thick ponytail, and she was absorbed in a dark, heavy-looking book in a way that seemed impossible to him, because his present state of distraction was clearly permanent, and all he could do was what he had been doing for the last week, carrying it restlessly all over campus and parking it in unlikely places.

After a moment, she slipped off her coat and pushed it through the stack, so that it hung there. He averted his gaze, not wanting to catch her eye, and only looked back when he was sure she had returned to her book.

What was not wrong? They were going to bulldoze his garden, rip the peach trees and apricots up by the roots. They were going to halve his gardening staff and cut the heat off to half his greenhouses. They were going to hand the campus over to the corporations; the hole in the ozone was growing; a thousand species a day were falling into extinction (Chairman X knew that one of his afflictions was that he could so easily imagine the blue and sunlit globe of the world, its fragility and variety. Too many treks after specimens had exposed his sight to too many unique microenvironments. He had appreciated the adaptive mechanisms of too many plants—how such mechanisms combined utility and grace. He had appreciated too many vistas, small and large, had been struck by each as if each were an event. And each discrete appreciation that his memory contained was painfully twinned with others in his imagination that he was fated by mortality and the wideness of the world to miss. Gift and Nils Harstad were unburdened by such an affliction because, Chairman X thought, they knew so little about what was out there that they assumed whatever they might substitute for it would be good enough.)

The Lady X was fed up with him and his older children were embarrassed by his increasing eccentricity. Just this morning, the oldest little X had spoken unequivocally at the breakfast table. She had said, "Daddy, the junior high is going to call you about Career Day, about coming and giving a talk." She caught his gaze. "No matter what they say, turn them down. I mean it. If you don't, I will never forgive you." She didn't have to say that she meant that, too. Her hair and her one cherished Benetton outfit were perfect. The Lady X had tried to save his face, saying coolly, "Your father doesn't have time for that anyway, and you should be more courteous, young lady."

A toss of the head. "Please, then."

"That's fine," he had said.

He closed his book, and thought of another place to carry his unease—the university cemetery, where he could spit on the graves of those who had hybridized corn and tea roses and double chrysanthemums.

The Costa Rican woman said, "Oh, are you leaving?" and she said it as gladly as you could say something so cool and impersonal. Then she said, "I remember you. From the lecture." She came closer. "He was an awful man, wasn't he? So complacent. Are you feeling better now?"

"No."

The unexpected anguish in his tone transfixed them both. It was the most naked expression of emotion Cecelia had heard in two months. She snapped awake just like that. She stepped forward.

It was hard for the Chairman to grasp how large she became as she moved toward him. Such largeness was unique in his experience. Her red sweater loomed, thick and reassuring. She tossed her head, and those same hammered silver earrings seemed to twirl like moons against her neck. Pheromonic radiance lifted off her in clouds, compounded of her serious look and her half-smile and her unconscious grace as well as the usual biological operations that Chairman X had occasion to explain to his classes every fall and spring.

He turned his chair suddenly toward her, with a squeak, a noisy scrape against the floor. Now he was awkwardly close to her all of a sudden, but she didn't step back. Maybe he didn't give her time to step back. Maybe he just grabbed her and buried his face in that red sweater, smelled her wool and Jergens fragrance and put his arms, just as if he had a right to, around her hips. At any rate, this unorthodox greeting was followed by a momentary pause the largeness of which sank deep into the Chairman's very flesh, and then her hands found his head and neck and back, and she was kneeling and they were kissing, and Cecelia felt the fog blow out of her brain as in a stiff wind and as she lay back on the cool floor, each book on each shelf looming above her achieved perfect distinction from its every neighbor, and the acrid archival dust billowed deliciously around her.

His hands came up under her sweater as she pushed her leggings smoothly down over her hips and somehow every man she had ever known came to seem by comparison to this man, who didn't look THAT WAY in any sense, hesitant, reserved, doubtful. She closed her eyes.

The Chairman was mostly filled with shame. Here he was, at it again, doing just what he had promised the Lady X and himself that he would stop doing, "fleeing to the woman" (her words), "driving over a cliff, dick in hand" (his). Even when you really just wanted to bury your face in a big warm red sweater, once you got inside those pheromones, you went on and on as if (but only as if, said the Lady X, and he did agree with that) you couldn't stop.

No one happened by.

They lay quietly, their faces turned in different directions, until she could no longer stand the hard pressure of the floor against her backbone.

They sat up, their backs against the stacks. She remade her ponytail. He successfully refrained from burying his face in his hands. After a moment, he said, "I want you to know that my wife works for the STD and HIV Campus Information Hotline, and I am completely infection-free."

"Me, too." She paused. "I guess I should say, me, too, as far as I know."

"Transmission is a lot less likely female to male."

"I've heard that."

Their breathing slowed.

He said, "I'm getting too old for this. I'm exhausted."

"I always nap here anyway." Today, however, Cecelia didn't foresee any naps. Truly she could say that the future of days in the library and the classroom that she had possessed only minutes before had vanished without a trace. Now she had a hard time foreseeing anything. She said, "You know, your sweater is on inside out."

He looked down. He hadn't taken it off, so he must have put it on that way before leaving the house. He said, "I'm a little distracted lately."

"Me, too."

They smiled at each other.

He said, "Do I understand that you're from Costa Rica?"

"Well, not exactly—" Watching him, as Cecelia now felt compelled to do, she saw the searchlight of his gaze dim just a few watts at this reply. In spite of herself, really without any volition on her part, she continued, "But of course, yes, I am."

"How interesting," he said, and leaned irresistibly toward her.

24

Picking and Choosing

DR. DEAN JELLINEK'S great grief, and one wholly shared by his son, Chris, was that the university had never fielded a winning basketball team. Dr. Jellinek and Chris had been to every home game in the last five years, and they had tickets just behind the bench, but as the season approached, he wondered if he would be able to get through it without a heart attack or a stroke. It was so frustrating to look down from his seat at Coach Rawlings making his pissant little drawings of anally retentive little plays, circling his pointer on the floor of the gym in tighter and ever more introspective spirals while the players looked on in hopeful confusion.

The cannon fodder who played for the university had come to seem to Dr. Jellinek like ranks of willing soldiers freshly recruited for a long war that they were already destined never to win—the Thirty Years' War, the Hundred Years' War. Coach Rawlings, with his tragic worldview and his rueful half-smile, sucked the heart out of every freshman class drop by drop. Dean Jellinek was the coach's enemy, and put his own name in every year for the Faculty Athletic Council, just so he could lead the fight to fire the parasite, but they never put him on it.

This is not to say that he had learned nothing from his years as a basketball fan. Now, for example, that seventeen companies were vying to fund research into calf-free lactation, he called on all that grace-under-success he had witnessed in the NBA if not at the university, and, calling upon it, found it was there. He made himself, for example, as happy-to-be-here as Magic Johnson, as coolly sincere as Michael Jordan, as grittily determined as Charles Barkley. Were he actually tall, black, and electively bald rather than short, pallid, and unwillingly balding, he could not, in his humble estimation, have handled his recruiters with greater skill.

First of all, he let his research record speak for itself, the way they let their ball-handling talents do the same. He no longer felt quite the same way about the Nuclear Transfer thing—he was willing now to see his own role as more in a making-it-to-the-finals-but-losing-in-the-last-game sort of light, with an added stolen-by-the-refs bit of color (when he inserted this idea into the conversation, he always did it with a maybe-maybe-not-some-people-seem-to-think sort of shrug). Second of all, his career scoring record, both in percentages and totals, was plenty impressive; grant money, like points, seemed to enjoy its own company and this was reassuring to those who were friends with money. Even so, he allowed it to be known, as those basketball players did, that money was one thing, the game another. He played the research game purely for the love of it, though, of course, winning was an important part and not to be undervalued. Mostly he learned from those players the myriad ways of saying "I don't know" so that he could diddle and dandle their curiosity. Not "I don't know" about the project—you could never make that mistake—but "I don't know" about what was best—for the project, the university, himself, the companies in the running.

What was really best, everyone knew, was gobs and gobs of dough, simoleons raining down in torrents, choking great wads of cash that would give everyone confidence just by its presence, but that kind of cash was pretty shy and only displayed itself after everyone's desire had been forced to bloom in the hothouse of delicately managed rivalry.

Sometimes these days Dean felt like picking up the phone and calling his buddy Michael Jordan and chortling with him over how he'd played Continental Dairy Industries off against National Milk, but of course he didn't have Michael's number.

He did have a sense, however, that the last exquisite days of courtship were coming to an end, that soon the phone calls and messages would cease, that he would return to being himself again, and on top of that, he'd have to develop this herd of calf-free lactating Holsteins that he'd thought about so obsessively that he was now a bit bored with them. Soon they would devolve from potential money to real money, from an image of bovine paradise to years of probably laborious and discouraging work. Soon, in fact, he would have to once again call on the resources of his character that had been put on hiatus by the very exhilaration of this courtship, and he was superstitious enough, and midwestern enough, to harbor the occasional thought that his character might have gone terminally flabby from success.

Even so, he could still sit in his office, in silence, with his feet up on the desk, and stare at the phone thinking, Ring! and have it ring.

The fact was that he was so greedy for these moments of being sought, desired, courted that no future payback seemed too large.

The phone rang. Joan in the office said, "I have a transfer call for you, Dr. Jellinek," and Dean said, "I'm here," and it was Samuels, the R and D man from Western Egg and Milk Commodities, who said, "Well, Dean, Richards at Purdue and Isaacs at Iowa State say this deal of yours is impossible."

"For them, I'm sure it is."

Samuels laughed. "They say—"

"They say false pregnancy in cows isn't well enough understood. They say that PREGNANCY in cows isn't well enough understood. They say vet science isn't far enough along for that, not to mention biotechnology. They say we don't know enough. It's true. They don't know enough. But you read my proposal."

"It's a wild proposal."

"Out there is where you want to be, right?"

"That's what the boss tells me."

"Look, Hal, there's a lot of things money can't buy. We both know that. But there's a lot of things it can buy, and one of them is technology and the time to develop technical know-how. You get in on the process early, and this is what you get, you get a patent not only on the product, but on every process that leads to the product. That means that the others who come later, like Isaacs and Richards, end up having to take the back roads, or having to pay the toll. You own the patents, you get the tolls."

"True enough. I've got to tell you that this proposal has gone all the way to the top, not just of Egg and Milk, but to the top of the top, to Martin himself. That's where they REALLY like it. The old man fancies himself a lifelong innovator."

Dean didn't know who Martin was, but Richards' tone was reverent. Dean pretended he didn't notice, adopted his own tone of casual but superior knowledge. "Hal, let me tell you a story. You know the story of the invention of the computer?"

"No."

"You should ask Isaacs. I bet he knows."

"So tell me."

"Well, the short version is that the guy at Iowa State who invented the computer in the late thirties never patented a thing—not the memory bank or the digitizing system or the application of binary numbers to the problem of computing. Not the drum or the switch, nothing. And the university over there didn't take enough notice to do it for him, even in their own name, even as a crazy idea that might go somewhere. They forgot about the old machine, and threw it out, but when it came down to a court case about ten years or so ago between Sperry and Hewlett-Packard concerning who owned the patents, it turned out that nobody did. Now, that's nice for us computer users, wouldn't you say? But is that where Egg and Milk wants to be in twenty years?"

Samuels was silent for a long moment in which Dean could sense him adding up numbers. Finally, he said, "I think, Dean, that that's a story the boss would like to hear. That's true, right?"

"Call your friend Isaacs."

"Naw, I'm going to call Martin himself. Then I'm going to call you right back." He chuckled. "I don't want to get a busy signal when I call you."

"You can't always get what you want, Hal. I got students calling all the time, asking for lab help and deadline extensions."

"I'll bet."

"Betting takes money, Hal."

They both laughed, and after a moment hung up. Dean leaned way back in his chair and stretched until each of his vertebrae seemed free and mobile. Then he let his head drop until he could see upside down out the window, and thought, Ring! The phone rang. It was Lawrence, a V.P. at Consolidated Embryo. Dean said, "Look, Bill, let me tell you a little story—"

25

A Revision of the Future

Assignment: You are to take a single paragraph of one of the stories that you have written so far this semester and expand that one paragraph to the length of the original story. The goal of this assignment is to excavate your knowledge of this situation or these characters much more deeply than you have, or, preferably, to learn to imagine them more complexly, more fully, in more detail, etc.

Gary—

I have decided since our talk to let you revise the Lydia and Lyle story, since you seem far more committed to that one than to the mass murderer-execution story. Your specific assignment in this revision, though, is to find some redeeming qualities of character OR personality in the Lydia figure.

Oct. 19, 1989
Monahan, FW 325

"Waking Up"

a story by Gary Olson

Lydia woke up and heaved her giant body over onto its side. She wondered, as she did every morning, how had she gotten like this? In college, only ten years ago, she had been thin and stylish. She had worn a size six with ease. And all her hair had fallen out, too. In college, she had had long thick blond hair, the envy of all the other girls. Now she was nearly bald. Actually, what had happened to her made her very sad. She couldn't help blaming the kids, who she thought were at school. She laid there. Then it came into her mind that she hadn't finished the box of candy she'd been eating the night before during the Johnny Carson show, so she felt around on the floor for it. They were gone, though. She decided to blame the dog. She yelled, "Brownie, get in here!"

What happened was that she had gained lots of weight with each of her pregnancies. She couldn't help that. Her mother always said that it was glandular. With the boy, Frankie, she had gained eighty pounds and with the girl, Allison, she had gained over a hundred. Being pregnant gave her a big craving for junk food. She would eat five or six Big Macs at a meal, and a couple of McShakes, and then come home and have a big bowl of popcorn. She said to Lyle, "Well, I just can't help it," and it was true that she couldn't. He knew that from college when they would argue about her weight. Lyle thought that maybe it was his fault for talking about it all those early years, and so he felt guilty and that's why he stuck with her.

The boy, Frankie, weighed five pounds at birth and Allison weighed four. Nothing made a dent in what she had gained. Now everybody was afraid of her, even though she didn't want them to be, and was really a rather nice person underneath. What she really wanted was for Lyle to make love to her again, but Lyle had seen what could happen, and didn't want to take any chances.

She thought about how she had been in college—she had been very sexy. She wanted to be that way again.

The dog was afraid of her, and just hid under the kitchen table.

Suddenly, Lydia realized that her daughter and her son were in the room. They were sitting very quietly in the corner, huddled together. She thought that the worst thing that could happen would be if the same thing that had happened to her would happen to Allison. She felt tears come to her eyes at the thought and then run down her cheeks. She said to herself, "I wish I could die." The children were holding hands. Lydia said, "Why aren't you kids in school?"

(Even though he had come to the end of the original paragraph, Gary added two paragraphs to fill out the length demanded by the assignment.)

She made herself sit up. She could not help looking down at herself, seeing her giant breasts cascading over her giant stomach. She said, in her own mind, "Inside this big body, there is a thin, nice person trying to get out. When it gets out, then I will be able to take better care of my children and be more attractive to my husband, Lyle, who had lots of promise when he was an engineering student in college, but now works in a factory and is downtrodden and depressed."

Frankie came over to the bed. He said, "We're hungry, Mama."

The End

Gary took a meditative handful of popcorn, then a sip of his McShake. Truly he felt that Lydia was a much more rounded character now. For one thing, she was sad about being fat and she really wanted to be a good mother. He wasn't really sure about the glandular thing, but he had heard his grandmother and her sister say that about one of the neighbors. He could always change that part if Monahan didn't like it.

Just that evening, Lyle and Lydia had had a big fight, right in the apartment, and Gary had tried to figure out a way to fit that in, somehow, but it hadn't been about weight, it had been about the sheets on Lyle's bed, which were filthy because he hadn't bothered to send his laundry home in four weeks and he had forgotten the sheets the previous time anyway. Gary more or less agreed with Lydia that all the solutions Lyle proposed (sleeping on top of the blankets with his sleeping bag over them, ignoring the dirt, wearing some clothes to bed, all solutions that Lyle considered sufficient for himself) were both disgusting and revealing of deep character flaws. He also agreed that Lydia shouldn't be asked to wash them and knew what Lydia suspected, that Lyle had said two or three times, while taking swigs from the milk carton, that when the sheets got black enough she would break down and do them—it was a test of their relationship. Gary, himself, had even offered to show Lyle how to do the laundry; it was especially not hard to do the sort of laundry Lyle had, everything at least 50 percent polyester, even his jeans, and guaranteed not to shrink or bleed.

It was exactly this sort of thing, in Gary's opinion, that was so hard to deal with in a story. It was bad enough that Lydia was neither fat nor ill-tempered, bad enough that Lyle's transformation from engineering student to factory worker could probably only be accomplished by brain transplant. What was worse was the way his personal loyalties seemed to shift around in this slippery way, confusing his narrative line. And worse than that was that he now couldn't stop paying attention to Lyle and Lydia. Avoidance had turned into obsession. Was it just by chance that he listened to all their conversations, noted what they wore and ate, had Lyle's daily routine (not an edifying one) down pat? Of course not. He could say that the obsession was Professor Monahan's fault—he was always harping about details and paying attention, but he also knew that if Professor Monahan and English 325 dropped over the edge of the Earth, he would still keep teasing this scab.

And it wasn't as if he were getting an A, either. The worst of the worst was that he knew the story was bad and he still couldn't leave it alone. He pressed the "Save" and "Quit" commands on his computer, and here came Lydia. She ruffled his hair and said, "Whatcha doin'?"

"Writing a story about you? How's that?"

"Better not."

"Okay."

"Okay. Listen, have you read *Lysistrata*, that play?"

"Yeah."

"Well, explain that to Lyle when he comes in. Explain that's why I've taken my stuff back to my dorm. I'll see you around."

"Really?"

"Really."

"Really and truly?"

"Lyle Karstensen is history."

He looked at her. She didn't look upset. She looked the way girls did when they were shooting out of the known universe and had no fear. This capacity was something he had seen only in girls, and one of the reasons he liked them so much, but how could he fit that into his story? He said, "I would like to see you around."

"We'll see, Gary, okay?"

"Okay."

She picked up her bag and opened the door. After it closed behind her, he opened his document again. He just couldn't help it.

26

Clutter

THE NEXT MORNING, just before seven, Lyle arrived at his job at Auroch Copies, as he did every morning between Tuesday and Saturday, his white bag of donuts clenched between his teeth and his eighteen-ounce cup of black coffee in his hand. Everything was as usual except that, as far as he understood, Lydia had dumped him because of some play that he'd never heard of that she and Gary had been reading together although they weren't in any of the same classes.

This eventuality confirmed suspicions about Gary that Lyle'd harbored all fall, that he was after Lydia's ass and had been working covertly against himself, Lyle, while his, Lyle's, back was turned. This thing about the bedsheets wasn't convincing at all—it was too sudden.

The overnight manager left, and as soon as he was gone, Lyle laid out his six donuts in order—maple nut, powdered sugar, cherry, chocolate frosted, glazed, and plain. Breakfast, he knew, was the most important meal of the day.

Nevertheless, while he dismissed Lydia's specific point about the sheets, he couldn't help acknowledging that the shit all around him was getting deeper, and it was time to shovel some of it out. Here at Auroch Copies, for example, the bins were full of unclaimed originals, books from libraries public and private, and unclaimed stacks of copies. Rules handed down from the main office in Ann Arbor were clear—every week, send originals back to their place of origin, put coursework booklets in the stockroom for the duration of the semester or quarter, and hold private materials for twenty-one days, calling the client each week, then discard. Adhering to these rules was point three in Lyle's job description, but his own rule was simpler—after a couple of months, throw everything out except books from the university library or the public library. If a disgruntled customer happened to appear during Lyle's shift, the rule was to say that he'd just started working here in the last few days. If the customer recognized him (this had happened once), he liked to say that he'd been out of work, in the hospital, and had only just gotten back (and, of course, found the place in a royal mess).

Today was the day.

You had to admit it was pretty invigorating, and socially conscious, too, to heave those stacks of office paper into the giant recycling bin out in the back, to rip the brightly colored covers off, to empty the cubbies of Keats poems and papers about ag economics and fisheries biology, to box the books and address them to Circulation, University Library (they were always grateful). It felt like getting younger again, as if that state of unmarked whiteness, of waiting reams and copiers with their counters at zero, of full staplers, of passing that first dollar (on the wall, laminated, dated September 1, 1982), was being regained.

Lydia should see him now. She'd have those sheets off the bed in no time.

He came to the "oversize" cubby and pulled out some plans for a guy named Joe Miller, no phone.

He had a respect for plans, having drawn some up for engineering classes over the years. But these, you couldn't even tell the top from the bottom—the words were turned in all directions, there was no scale, no title. Weird. Some kind of machine, maybe. He rotated the paper and scrutinized the drawing. A bicycle wheel. A compressor fan. A network of hoses. When he rotated it again, more familiar objects appeared—a couple of fan belts and a gearing mechanism, a big drum.

The bell rang above the door.

Lyle dropped the plans back into the oversize bin. They were maybe the only intriguing thing he had ever seen at Auroch Copies. As he stepped to the counter, he felt the cleaning urge dissipate for another month or so. That was okay, too. The customer took her hat off and smiled. Red hair fell in a wave over the shoulders of her jacket. She said, "I'd love for you to copy a whole book for me."

He gave her his most serious look. "Do you have publisher permission, miss?"

"Why, no, but I've just got to have it. I'm flunking this course because the teacher is so unrealistic! There's all this reserve reading and it's so hard to get to the library. But I managed to get the book for a couple of hours." She unzipped her backpack and pulled it out, then set it on the counter. Clearly marked on the cover were the words "Two-hour reserve, do not remove from reserve room." They read them together.

It was a thick book, probably three hundred pages or more.

Lyle said, "The whole thing?"

"Yes, isn't that awful? When she told us we had to read the whole thing, I'm, like, gagging!"

"You can use that machine by the wall."

"But I have to go to class! I am just in such trouble. I'd be so grateful! I can't tell you. Please?"

Her lips were perfectly lipsticked and glossed. They lingered in a smoochie way over the "p" in "Please?" then stretched around the "ee." Lydia's lips had been a little on the thin side. The girl lifted her red hair off the back of her neck. Lyle said, "Come back after your class. We'll see." He hadn't cracked a smile the whole time. Smiles were for later. She put her little gloved hands up to his cheeks and he felt their soft wooliness. She said, "Ooh, thanks. You are sweet."

"I said, 'We'll see.' " He thought, what we will see. He thought, if he mailed his laundry today, he might get it back by Saturday.

EVEN SHERRI had to admit that almost two months of making up for time lost back home was beginning to tell on her. Midterm exams, for instance, were speeding toward her like a brick wall, ten days away. At this point, though, she was still just clutching the wheel and gazing at them in horror, enthralled by coming failure. She wondered if they made you leave right away, or if they let you stagger around with your injuries until the end of the semester, but she was afraid to ask anyone, because anyone she might ask would encourage her, buck her up, stiffen her spine, and then she would have to start in on all that work she had to make up, and it was somehow easier, however frightening, to career through each day alone in the knowledge of how badly she was doing.

On the other hand, she looked great. Kids from her old school didn't even recognize her. She who had been big was now little. She who had had straight light brown hair was now a curly redhead. She whose face had been terminally round now had cheekbones, along with collarbones, hipbones, ankles, insteps. She who had once taken a boring call from Darryl every night at exactly nine o'clock now never knew who was calling, and they didn't call to complain, either, as Darryl had; no no, they called to tease her and flirt with her and entice her to go out with them, and never on study dates to the library. The thing was, Mary had fixed on that Palestinian guy, and Diane was gaga for some reason over Big Bob, who was just like every guy Sherri knew back home, but Sherri had fixed on a life and she loved it as deeply and romantically as the others seemed to love their boyfriends. Its virtues were minimal sex combined with maximal attention, swirling variety in friends and party associates, lots of activity of the sort your parents were always restricting—not drugs and drink and sex so much as running around just because you felt like it and screaming and singing and cultivating high spirits.

She didn't go to class, as she had told Lyle, but went back to her room at Dubuque House. If you shirked all your responsibilities you could have this in college, too—privacy, a nice little nap. She wrapped up in Keri's afghan and fell onto her bed. Soon her deliciously favorite sensation of abandonment was diffusing through her.

27

Call for Papers

THE FOUNDATION FOR BLACK ENDEAVOR didn't do anything on the cheap, Margaret Bell noticed as she inspected the envelope she had just gotten in the mail, and she was immediately suspicious. From pamphlets to smudgy Xeroxes to dittoed newsletters, the literature of the organizations she trusted was *always* produced on the cheap, always announced itself as marginalized and therefore trustworthy— the crackpot was openly crackpot, the sane and the profound were honestly sane and profound. But a letter from the Foundation for Black Endeavor, an organization she had never heard of, was proof that she had gotten on some unfortunate mailing list and now IT would commence. In America, it was the most common form of betrayal. As soon as you accomplished something, anything, that caught their attention, they started trying to raise you out of your natural milieu. Of course her betrayer was certainly the university, which must have given out, or sold, all the names of those newly promoted to the rank of full professor.

The letter was a personal one, on bond stationery, a call for papers to be delivered at the Foundation for Black Endeavor Conference at the Stouffer Orlando Resort in March. Her airfare would be paid by the foundation, as would her room expense. Right at the top of the board of directors column was Thomas Sowell. After him came a cast of characters out of her worst nightmares—Linda Chavez, Arch Puddington, twenty others as bad, all of whom, she could imagine, had a secret password such as a derogatory remark about Toni Morrison, whom Margaret considered a goddess. Her eye caught the words "per diem," then the words "I am familiar with all your work, and feel, along with the board, that your contribution would make this year's conference a particularly special event, a marvelous way to inaugurate the activities of our organization." Though she was immune to it, of course, the flattery combined with the bribery did make her just a bit angry. "Please do let me know that you will consider giving a paper." Margaret spoke aloud, a withering "Ha!" "I heard your paper on intersecting political and literary continuums in minority literatures at MLA last December and was enormously impressed." Here Margaret got up from her desk chair and walked across her office and back.

She could feel herself soften, O death! soften because she had loved that paper herself, had felt that idea ripen so sweetly, been so proud of it, her first MLA paper, and felt so overlooked after she gave it, because of course it turned out that there were too many papers on too many topics at too many conflicting times by too many self-absorbed English professors. She had been reduced to doing what she had vowed never to do, count the number of questions asked (four) and use that as some index of the interest she had aroused.

"I have read both your books, the second one twice. Do come. We need people like you to give this conference the edge we are looking for."

Margaret licked her lips.

Florida. In March. The Stouffer Orlando Resort. She picked up her phone and dialed an outside line, then used her credit card to call the Stouffer Orlando Resort. A voice answered that was accustomed to curry favor. Room rates? High season? Why, of course. Double rooms, $425 per night; suites, $595. Will that be all? Margaret put on her Negro-est, most Arkansas voice and asked whether rooms were available in March, the second week. The young man didn't miss a beat. "Certainly, ma'am. May I make you a reservation? Yes, please do call back. We look forward to welcoming you. No, thank *you* for calling."

Clearly the color line at the Stouffer Orlando Resort was green rather than black.

Margaret read her letter again.

Margaret was not fond of recent fashions in literary theory, fashions that delighted in finding formal or(and) stylistic contradictions in a piece of writing (text), and used them to prove that the text had no meaning. The idea that because words in a language developed meaning only in relationship to one another, therefore the meaning of all aspects of the piece of writing (text) existed only in relationship to each other, sounded a lot to Margaret like equally specious proofs-by-analogy that she had grown up with: God the "Father," black men as "boys," the man as the "head" of the house. She did not think it any coincidence that ideas denigrating literary authorship had taken center stage simultaneously with the emergence of formerly silent voices for whom the act of writing, and publishing, had the deepest and most delicious possible meaning, simultaneously with the emergence of an audience for whom the act of reading and thinking was an act of skeptical anger, sometimes a transitional act to violence.

A *book*, she had emphasized in her paper, was a negotiable commodity. Above a certain level of obscurity, the public paid for it in either money or praise, rarely both. All American writers of books (makers of films) considered themselves artists, because they defined artistry as the creative manipulation of materials. Through accidents of heritage, upbringing, psychological profile, and temperament, every artist found her(him)self more or less in conflict with the prevailing cultural norms and forms. Choice on this score would be as impossible as choosing one's own fingerprints. Artists from the mainstream of the culture would locate themselves on a single continuum, and if they were in agreement with cultural norms and forms, their reward would be money and no praise (Danielle Steel), and if they were in conflict with cultural norms and forms, their reward would be praise and no money (Ishmael Reed). The restlessness of American cultural norms and forms was well known, however, and any but the most hermetically sealed writer could hope(fear) that the ever-darting spotlight would one day focus on her(him).

The minority complication of this model, Margaret had said, was that the writer sat on at least two continuums in relationship to the mainstream culture, and these two(or more) were already at odds. Every book (cultural and commercial act) affected the writer's position on both continuums, and as the writer became less and less generally obscure, the information communicated to her(him) by the only two cultural means of money and praise became more intense and more contradictory.

Margaret had not portrayed this effect as a conspiracy of the culture against minority writers, but as an inevitable result where one culture was dominant and many others were semi-incorporated into it and partly in conflict with it.

Three of the four questions asked after her paper had been hostile ones, and had implied that she took a destructively benign view of the culture in power.

Her advisor from Harvard had advised her to receive this hostility as praise rather than money, and later, over dinner, remarked that the Midwest seemed to have "smoothed" her.

She had not known he had considered her "rough."

Now she was sought as a speaker for a manifestly conservative group.

She looked out the window of her office, feeling that she had passed through a doorway that she had never realized was there. Or that the very thing her model predicted, that in its restless flitting and focusing, a cultural spotlight (one of the very smallest and dimmest, to be sure) had landed on her.

She sighed. Of course, it was always one thing to know something, and quite another to act upon that knowledge, and refuse an all-expenses-paid trip to a resort in Orlando.

Across the campus, in a building Margaret could see but could not have identified, Dr. John Cates, professor of chemistry, a man who had never read any literary theory, was also looking out his window, but he was talking on the phone. He was saying, "Yes. Yes, of course. I have a very interesting paper almost ready. Oh, and my wife and son will be accompanying me to Orlando. Your offer of airfare extends to them, I'm sure. And we would prefer a suite. Terrific. Thank you. And if you would have their tickets to Disney World at the desk on our arrival—great. The three-day package should be enough for even him." Cates laughed cheerfully. "Well, in fact, there is another conference right then, of the Societá Italiana di Fisica. In Rome. Yes. Oh, yes, all expenses paid. I had intended to give my paper there, but I hadn't gotten around to sending off my confirmation. Good. I knew you'd understand. This would be a relief, actually. I do hate that jet-lagged feeling, but—" He spun his chair once around, once back, listening, then smiled and said, "We're all set, then. Good-bye. Oh, oh. One last thing. Sea World. Three one-day passes to Sea World. Perfect. Thank you, you've been very cooperative."

28

Networking

OVER THE YEARS, Mrs. Loraine Walker's vision of the campus had changed. The collection of stone buildings had evolved, in her mind, into a web of offices, where secretaries sat under bright lights and near them, much more dimly, sat administrators whose grasp on things was tenuous at best. Once the filaments connecting the secretaries had been phone lines, and making connections had taken that minimal effort of picking up the phone and dialing the extension and moving the mouth through greetings, well-wishings, and idle chatter to the gist of the call. No longer. The only people who talked on the phone anymore were the administrators, whose whole lives, like those of chimps, were made up of nit-picking, stroking, and jockeying for dominance. The secretaries were connected by computer. Mrs. Walker and her colleagues inhabited a universe of information as pervasive as air, and Mrs. Walker was careful to keep abreast of the weather systems moving through that atmosphere. The stony walls and concrete paths, the closed windows and doors, the trees and shrubs, all the elements of the campus that seemed to separate people, had become permeable membranes undetectable in the wafting currents of information.

Now it came to her from several directions that Arlen Martin and the TransNationalAmerica Corporation were, or would soon be, present on the campus after all. She saw that she had misjudged the purpose of his meeting with Ivar. Optimistically, she had assumed that Martin had been seeking Ivar's cooperation because it was necessary. She saw now that it had only been desirable, perhaps even less than that, a matter of form, or simply a signal. The fact was that no faculty member needed Ivar's permission to seek or accept a grant. The provost's office maintained the university guidelines on intellectual property and ethical research standards, and if there were a scandal, the provost's office would have to take the lead in handling it, but faculty members were officially assumed to be knowledgeable and responsible in these areas, and, Mrs. Walker had to admit, Ivar was well enough disposed toward the world to believe the official assumption. He was also a strong believer in academic freedom, which, in Mrs. Walker's view, was rather like accepting the precepts of supply-side economics and industrial self-regulation.

Over Mrs. Loraine Walker's eyes the wool could not so easily be pulled. Her own guidelines on intellectual property and ethical research standards were rather strict and geared toward preserving her office from crises that could result from incompetence, negligence, or venality on the part of a professorial population that was, in general, insulated from the consequences of most of its own actions by tenure, mandated salary raises, and other perks of university life.

In these days of fiscal crisis, it was also true that Ivar was far too relieved by any good news on the financial front and far too panicky in his focus on the actions of the board of governors and the state legislature. His thinking was clouded by both fear and desire. However, as a state civil service employee of long standing, an official in AFSCME, a fully vested member of her pension plan, and an owner of a six-unit apartment building near the campus that was entirely paid for and always rented, Mrs. Loraine Walker could afford to eschew both fear and desire in favor of propriety, moral standards, and long-term damage control.

It was also true that she resented the way Elaine Dobbs-Jellinek had sought Ivar's compliance, then ignored him when she didn't get it, and, in addition to that, the way she had circumvented Mrs. Walker's authority. Elaine was a royal bitch to her own secretary, who was witless enough to be intimidated even though she held Elaine's entire information system, the font of any administrator's power, in the palm of her hand. Were Elaine to successfully bring in many millions in grant money, her manners, thought Mrs. Walker, would certainly deteriorate even further. Mrs. Walker did not think that she would like to see that.

It was clear that, as she did so often, Mrs. Walker would have to act on her own and in some secrecy. There were many areas, all of them located in the principle of academic freedom, where the provost's office could not be perceived to be treading, even lightly.

As she said to Martha, "You wonder what there is about the place that is even worth saving. You wonder, why not just let them stumble around the way they seem intent upon doing. But it offends me. It's too disorderly. And in the end, all that disorder would land right in my lap. That, I am too old for now."

While it was too soon to act, Mrs. Walker did suggest to Ivar that he hadn't staved off the Arlen Martin threat. Ivar said, "Well, he has a lot of money."

"Do you mean that he carries a big stick, or that he carries a big carrot?"

"What's the difference?"

"Well, none, I suppose, since they both make me angry."

"We'll see."

"We'll see?" She expressed pointed disbelief.

"I'll talk to some people."

"That will be an interesting first step."

"There's not a lot we can do."

"Academic freedom?"

"Well, of course."

She could see that he was defeated already. She said, "I thought you should know."

"Thank you."

She turned briskly and strode out of the office, clearly communicating disagreement. As soon as she sat down at her desk, though, her phone rang. It was Ivar. He said, "Mrs. Walker, I know you'll be careful in all matters."

She said, "Well, of course."

And she was.

All she did, when she had time to do it, was access the Poultry Science files for recent outgoing communications having to do with unorthodox (what, anymore, though, could be unorthodox?) poultry feeding systems. Or poultry breeding systems. Or chicken processing systems. There was nothing. You could say, she thought, that the files were clean as a whistle, or you could say that poultry processing had devolved as far as technologically and humanly possible, and therefore no longer interested Arlen Martin. Mrs. Walker herself always bought local free-range chickens from a farmwife co-op in the next county, so when she accessed some data about potential links between growth hormones in factory chickens and the early onset of menarche in selected populations of American girls, her interest was fairly abstract.

Anyway, chickens were the leading edge of the past. She had accessed chickens mostly for tidiness' sake, so that she couldn't accuse herself of overlooking the obvious. But there was no activity in poultry.

Under her own version of Ivar's signature, Mrs. Walker had, over the years, authorized the library to buy as many available databases as they could. She had actually transferred funds out of the athletic budget into the library budget from time to time, possibly her most dangerous covert action. The result was, though, that she could now, bit by bit, during breaks and minutes of free time, track Arlen Martin and the TransNationalAmerica Corporation through the *Wall Street Journal* index, *Facts on File*, *Commercial and Industrial* blah-blah, *Acquisitions and Mergers International*, etc. There were plenty of articles about Martin. He had allowed himself to be interviewed by everyone from USAir's in-flight magazine to *Life* magazine to *Business Week* to a weekly newspaper from the suburbs of Amarillo, Texas, to *Der Spiegel* and British *Vogue*. At the same time, his holdings were a secretive and complex web of interlocking companies, some apparently just names and boards of directors, others actual businesses. Tracing his ownership and influence amounted, at first, to recognizing recurrent names, then intuiting relationships and duties from the positions and companies attached to them. After a while, she could track his restless interests. One of them, and an odd one compared to the others, she thought, was mining. Around Christmas, the TransNationalAmerica Corporation, through two intermediaries, had acquired the Seven Stones Mining Corporation, home office, Denver, Colorado. And Martin had paid a lot for it. She turned back to the *Wall Street Journal* index, and found an article headlined "Once Powerful Enough to Topple Governments: Mineral Industry Now in Doldrums." She transferred herself to university E-mail, and left a note for Library Media: "Please send a copy of the following article to provost's office." She cited the article. Her instincts, which were not only naturally good, but muscular from use, told her that, speaking of mining, she had found a very productive seam. She logged off and stood up. Out in the living room, the clock read 1:24 and Martha had fallen asleep on the couch. Loraine stood her up and guided her into the bedroom.

29

Midterm Review

THE THING that Keri had noticed over the last seven weeks in Dr. Lionel Gift's beginning economics lecture class was how happy he seemed. He bounced around the podium, full of high spirits; his smile beamed everywhere in the large room, as if his teeth were strangely iridescent. He made lots of jokes, most of them not that funny, but he was in such a good mood that the students laughed along with him anyway. The students were mostly boys, and they seemed to enjoy classes very much. Keri felt more at a remove. She felt, in fact, as if Dr. Gift were telling rollicking tales about an entirely alien planet, the Bizarro Planet, home of Bizarro Superman. She also felt that today, with "Midterm Review" on the syllabus, was her last chance to assimilate Bizarro World and thereby pass her midterm. She came into the hall and set out her pens and pencils, her notebook. She WOULD write everything down, and if she couldn't understand it, she would memorize it.

The usual glances from the mostly male lecture audience followed her entrance. In fact, it was she who put most of them into a receptive frame of mind. Gift presented the task, but Keri, the life-size Barbie with a voice like the reassuring low hum of insects on a summer night, represented the reward. Sometimes, one or the other of them offered to help her with her homework, but she shook her head. Reassuringly like every dream-girl, she acted self-contained and re-mote, bestowing smiles and friendly nods out of a sort of impersonal good cheer, clearly signalling that she had no preferences of her own—the best candidate would win the prize, and his very accomplishment would be enough for her. In the words of Dr. Gift, "pure competition would lead to an optimal allocation of resources." The boys, who in economics classes tended to be self-confident and to look forward to lives of wealth and power, licked their lips at the thought. It all agreed reassuringly with every myth and fairy tale. Reality-girls might have preferences—that was a result of their fallen natures, as represented by their imperfect looks and unpredictable demands. But if you could get beyond THEM to THIS one, well, every vibration of every boy's desiring soul promised him a paradise of total love, respect, and acceptance.

Nor did it occur to any boy to empathize with the desire of any of the other boys. Dr. Gift said not to, said, in fact, that such empathy was impossible and even sympathy was an illusion. The only possible response to any other individual's good or bad fortune, according to Dr. Gift, was indifference. To feel this indifference, or even to cultivate it as a way of avoiding illusions of sympathy or envy, was every individual's duty toward the truth. And it was true that cultivating indifference was a reassuring discipline against the envy that seemed to the boys to have plagued them all their lives.

Just to show them who they were, early in every semester, Dr. Gift administered a test. He gave them all tokens worth $100 to an investing individual, but returning $220 when invested as a part of the group, though that larger sum had to be divided by all members of the group, with individuals who did not invest receiving as much as individuals who did. The investors could also choose to invest as individuals, in which case the return would be more modest—only $110 per $100—but the sum would not have to be shared out among the group (which would also include noninvestors). Dr. Gift made clear to all, even the most confused, that an individual's greatest return would be on the group investment, IF the entire group chose to invest with the group. Then he polled them—how would they invest? Almost uniformly over the years, 20 percent of them chose to invest for the group, 80 percent chose to invest for themselves. When he announced the results of the tests, they looked around. It was pretty clear who was in the minority—students who weren't doing very well in economics.

Dr. Gift, himself, had noticed the correlation between doing well in economics classes and choosing, even hypothetically, to maximize one's own profits at the expense of the group. Just another piece of evidence, he thought, about the nature of success.

Keri knew she was one of those who fell into both undesirable categories—not doing well in economics and choosing to invest for the group. It had seemed so clear to her on the day of the test—if they all invested for the group, everyone's return would be 120 percent greater. If even one more than half invested with the group, they'd get more than they would as individuals. The math seemed to be absolutely clear—she was convinced she had grasped something and the conviction bolstered her confidence. When Gift announced the results, smiling as always, the Bizarro Planet seemed to float completely out of her ken, and she was embarrassed, to boot. She had blushed. All the boys around her thought it was charming.

The midterm review was mostly of relevant mathematical models, which Keri understood fairly well. As with all mathematical models, the sides of the equations balanced each other, and therefore seemed pure and true, irrefutable. She wrote them down carefully.

Dr. Lionel Gift was well aware that he could teach this class, and even entertain and please the customers, with no thought whatsoever. What he was saying to them now was like a television program on another channel that he could switch to whenever he wanted, just to see that it was still on, just to see that he, the talking head, was still adhering to the script. Somewhat more often, he checked the audience. Heads down, pencils moving, the occasional nod, all the way back to the last rows. It touched him, it really did, the imparting of knowledge, the initiation of a whole new group of customers into the domain of truth.

The enlargement of his class in the spring by three times was satisfying for so many reasons. In the first place, market demand had been recognized, even by the bureaucrats in the administration. In the second place, the larger amount of tuition money soon to be flowing in his direction would be good grounds for a raise, no matter what the legislature decided to do for the faculty at large (as a matter of principle, Dr. Gift was indifferent to their concerns). And in the third place, there was this intangible. As little attention as he liked to pay to intangibles, this sense in the room of knowledge pouring out of his mouth and being soaked up by their eyes and ears and note-taking hands was intoxicating. How much more intoxicating, how loaves-and-fishes-like it would be when the same amount of knowledge poured out and was soaked up by three times as many customers! The thought brought him right back to that nagging question of the value of information. Once he had his report done about the Arlen Martin plan, he would get back to the joy of that sort of pure economics.

Every class period, Keri discovered that willpower was not enough to keep her attention fixed on the material Dr. Gift was delivering.

Her own experience in economics, extensive and gained on her father's farm through the farm crises of the eighties, did not, for example, teach her that the workings of the market unerringly produced the general good. When her uncle Jack, having done well in hogs, bought out her uncle Dwight at a farm auction when Keri was in sixth grade, and then farmed the land himself rather than giving it or renting it to Dwight ("He owes a lot on a new combine, *he says*," said the relatives), forcing Dwight to commute to a chicken processing job two hundred miles away, Keri's father, Sam, had been caught in the middle, as had her grandparents—her grandfather sided with Jack and admired his success, her grandmother sided with Dwight and said that it was just like Jack, always had been, he had no more family feeling than a cat. Jack and Dwight were certain never to speak until they died, every family holiday was wrecked, her cousins lived on hand-me-downs and envied everything Keri had or did, her father, once playful and fun, now hardly ever spoke at all, her mother said he was impossible to live with (and Keri knew what that could portend), the whole township knew their family business and had an opinion of it. She did not understand what general good Dr. Gift was smiling about.

Nor did her experience teach her to value consumer insatiability above all other virtues. She clearly remembered from her early childhood what life on the farm had been like when her grandfather and father and uncles were farming together on the original 400 acres. They farmed and fished and farmed and hunted and farmed and went to the state fair. Half her relatives sat on the PTA and were hand in glove with her teachers. Her father played Hank Williams songs on the guitar, and her mother sang, and her grandfather played the harmonica. Someone was always available to help with the 4-H projects—even the worthless pony and those crazy goats. Later, when her grandfather farmed the original 400 by himself, her father had 600 of his own, and Jack, the most insatiable member of the family, farmed his and Dwight's 780, they were in the fields day and night, every planting season and harvest was a nightmare, the family debt load soared to astounding proportions, all the money from the farm went back into the farm, and her mother and grandmother had to get work in town to pay for food. Her grandmother would say, "If this is success, you can have it."

It *was* true, as Dr. Gift said, that the land itself had no value except as a market commodity, but that fact did not cause Keri the mirth and good cheer that it seemed to cause her professor. The rocketing and plummeting of land prices that she had known as long as she had known her name had meant unexpected and mysterious indoor weather, unmanageable cycles of surprise and anxiety, constant repetition of one ritualistic phrase, "the bank, the bank, the bank," year after year. Then there was the valueless land itself. Her father fretted about it as if it *did* have value, as if he cared whether he planted on steep slopes, as if corn after corn after corn in the same fields was actually bad, as if he cared about cutting down windbreaks and filling in stream courses, as if he didn't know about land the very thing that so thrilled Dr. Gift—that land was inexhaustible, and fertility was, too.

And then there was that word, "market." Dr. Gift intoned the word "market" the way her minister back home intoned the word "Creation." All the goodness in the universe, Dr. Gift seemed to say, was contained in the market. Well, it was clear from one single detail of her childhood and adolescence that she would never pass economics, because she had learned early to leave the room when her father turned on the market reports. She hated that word "market," whether attached to hogs, feeder cattle, corn, soybeans, or any other word. "Market" was synonymous with "impending doom."

Every class period, she ended up sitting transfixed, gazing wanly at the spectacle of Dr. Gift on the podium. He spoke emphatically, jestingly, seriously, informatively, for all she knew, well-meaningly. The boys around her were caught up, though surely some of them had backgrounds in practical economics similar to hers.

Dr. Gift LOVED them. You could tell that by the way he let them know every day in all sorts of little ways that in America, a boy, a girl even, could always succeed by hard work and a little knowledge of the market. Though world-famous, he let them know he was personal savior-consultant to each of them. All they had to do was pass the test, see the light, believe. But Keri simply had no capacity for faith, willing though she was, deeply though she felt that faith in economics, though it might not lead to good works, would surely lead to goods.

He wound up, startling her once again with how quickly the hour had passed and how depressed she felt as a result.

"Bring your own blue books," he said. "Exams will be returned in exactly one week after the date of the midterm. I remind you that exams are graded on a strict statistical curve, so seven percent of you will get F's, no matter what. You may not thank me for that now, but I hope you will later, when you have attained greater wisdom." He smiled to show that this was meant as a joke. The customers laughed as they were intended to, and in the hubbub, the mysterious blond beauty vanished from the hall.

30

A Celebration

ON THE OCCASION OF his engagement, Dr. Nils Harstad felt it appropriate to spread his benevolence as widely and deeply over the campus as he could. To this end, he invited everyone he had ever known to witness his happiness. On the one hand, he was a little disappointed that Marly invited only a few people from the church, plus her brother and sister from the north-side splinter. On the other hand, he liked the idea of her mysteriousness. He asked her to wear something long and dark, to put her hair up. She complied. He liked that, too.

In the month or so of their acquaintance, he had found no reason to regret his choice. She had confessed that she wasn't quite as young as he thought, but he didn't blame her for that. In all fairness, he was willing to admit that the misapprehension had been his, and the person who had disappointed him was himself, not her. If he thought of her slightly differently as a thirty-five-year-old than he had thought of her as a twenty-seven-year-old, well, it couldn't be helped, and the blow to his vanity was probably deserved.

The father, too, had turned out somewhat differently than he had expected, not so wise and upright, a little more cantankerous and rigid, especially in regard to doctrine, frivolous amusements (like drinking—he had insisted that no liquor would be served at the engagement party and Nils had reluctantly agreed), and the respect due him by Nils himself. He did not seem at all impressed with Nils' résumé or his position at the university, proclaiming all such things as vanity every time they happened to come up in conversation. It had become clear that the father would be living with them (something Nils hadn't quite had the courage to tell Ivar yet) rather than staying harmlessly in his own bungalow on the south side of town, a convenient, in Nils' opinion, 4.2 miles away.

However, Marly seemed at least receptive to his childbearing plans, and there Nils pinned his hopes. He could not feature either Father or Ivar comfortable in the same house with six children under, say, three years old. He was confident that they would move out.

He had not actually told Ivar the extent of these plans, all the better to leave him unprepared as well as to avoid arguments. Father undoubtedly had no idea of them at all.

Nils, himself, was surprised by the power of those six children (three boys, three girls). As he guided the caterers in their last-minute preparations for the party (250 guests, nine dollars per person for hors d'oeuvres and soft drinks, and no liquor or wine or beer), he could see them everywhere—a dark-haired boy under the table, a sweet girl reading in the window seat, two boys on the stairs, soberly chatting, two girls in the kitchen, helping, glad to help, and all of them looking up as he passed, with admiring and affectionate regard. Now every time he went to church, they marched in front of him, heads down, perfectly behaved, handsome and always dark, never pale, as he was. The girls would wear glasses and look studious. The boys would reveal a contained fire—boyish spirit reined in for the Lord's sake.

Swedish meatballs in a chafing dish. He said, "Rather than having those on the dining table, let's set them up with some napkins in the living room. I don't like it when all the food is in the same place, don't you think, dear?"

Marly nodded. This was her first cocktail party, and she had no actual opinions of her own.

Tiny sausages in barbecue sauce. Spinach puffs. Cheese toasts. Miniature quiches. Garlicky stuffed mushroom caps. Nils went around after the caterers, straightening things, spying his children everywhere. There was a creak on the stairs. Nils looked up to see Ivar surveying it all in a charcoal gray flannel suit with an expression of such obscurity that Nils, even after fifty-five years and more of life together, couldn't begin to penetrate it. Ivar glanced toward Father, who was reading his Bible in the sunroom. Nils shifted uneasily from foot to foot, an old habit from the days when Ivar seemed to accrue some sort of authority from his extra six minutes in the world. Of course Nils felt nothing of that now, at his age.

Even so, he had yet to tell Ivar about his one significant conversation with Father. Father had issued a number of instructions, to wit: He expected to have his breakfast served promptly at eight a.m., no matter what. He preferred to be the first one in the house to look at the mail, read the afternoon paper, and do the crossword puzzle. He watched

"NBC Nightly News." He did not eat pork and any sort of beans made him gassy. He would not sleep on the second floor. There would be no television watching or radio listening on Sunday, and only a cold dinner on Sunday and Wednesday. These were all, said Father to Nils, rules that he lived by and was too old to change. Furthermore, to be perfectly candid, he thought Marly and Nils were both too old to get married, and so he disapproved of their plans and, since he disapproved, he didn't feel obliged to change his style of life to accommodate them. When Nils' hopes had begun to rise just a degree at this last remark, Father had dashed them again at once: The one good thing about the whole deal was, in Father's opinion, that he could sell his little house that he'd paid twelve thousand dollars for twenty-five years ago, and the realtor fellow said he might be able to get forty or even forty-five for it.

The doorbell rang. The old house looked terrific—festive with sunlight and an abundance of good food. What could go wrong, really?

Ivar mastered his impulse to answer the door, even though he was nearer to it than anyone. Nils practically leapt for it, but then one of the catering people smoothly intervened, and Nils stepped back, to the side of his fiancée. The door opened to reveal two agronomists and their wives, with a soil scientist and and a plant geneticist and his wife close behind them. More guests were coming up the walk. The catering woman stepped aside, and they came in with something of an avid look that Ivar saw was satisfied as soon as they laid eyes on Marly. There would be a big crowd, all of them curious. Ivar experienced a little moment of embarrassment, then mastered that, too. He had drawn the conclusion years before, almost in childhood, that though they looked uncannily alike, Nils' orbit was to be far more unorthodox than his, and that to probe the sources of this would be both fruitless and frustrating. He knew that in some way he had early accepted the mystery at the heart of their twinship, far earlier than Nils had, and in accepting it he had smoothed their relationship and his own course through life. But then he looked again at Old Man Hellmich, and his lips tightened. No matter what they said, and they had said it each of them already about a hundred times, he did not intend to call the old bastard "Father." The door opened, and Ivar smiled. It was Helen in her reddest suit, red like a California poppy, or an ash berry, vividly alive and full of promise. He stepped forward and took her elbow. Her squeeze of his hand was discreet. After five years, discretion was their habit, and a monumentally pleasant habit it was.

Chairman X could not figure out why he had been invited to celebrate Nils Harstad's engagement. How much hostility did you have to display before even the most resolutely forgiving person got the point? For a week, since receipt of the invitation, he had been telling the Lady X that of course they wouldn't think of going, so when she came into the bedroom and found him taking an ironed shirt and a sport jacket out of the closet to wear with his jeans, she seemed a little surprised. He said, "You don't have to go."

"You don't, either."

"Yes, I do."

"Why?"

He looked at her. She had the baby on her hip and a banana in her hand. He said, "I don't know. Because Communism is collapsing all over Europe and cocaine is the ultimate cash crop and I can't figure out an alternative, and my whole life is a failure and I just want to SEE."

"See what?"

"See THEM, the winners."

The Lady X sighed and let Amy take a piece of the banana, which she did with delicate precision. She said, "Do you want me to go?"

Chairman X thought Cecelia would probably not be there. He said, "Yes, but only if you want to. Garcia might be there. He could restrain me."

"More likely egg you on."

Now they were inside the big brick house and the odor of professional courtesy wafted everywhere. The Lady X was issuing him instructions in a low voice—you do not have to defend the idea of communism, or insist that mistakes were made and that it could have succeeded if capitalism hadn't destroyed it; you do not have to make audible comments about the meat dishes, you can just avoid personal intake of them; you do not have to lecture anyone about perennial polyculture; you do not have to talk about blood money at any time. Chairman X nodded and nodded. She was only reminding him of social niceties that he preferred to conform to. Keep smiling and don't say much, she advised. Don't let them draw you out, and be thankful they aren't serving any booze. As an alternative to offending anyone, Chairman X took a large glass of mineral water and sat down beside an elderly man who seemed to be ignoring the party and reading. The man paid no attention to him, and Chairman X sipped his cooling drink. The Lady X, who was wearing a rather nice blue dress, had joined some friends. Garcia wasn't there.

Well, it was a blow that Cecelia wasn't here, either. He could have quietly tormented himself by watching her and the Lady X circulate through the same rooms, creating patterns like the pattern a cigarette coal fluttering in the darkness made on the retina, patterns that only he could see, since he hadn't actually told the Lady X about Cecelia and hadn't actually broken off his acquaintance with the Costa Rican woman yet, either. Since this option was unavailable, he got into mischief by noting that the elderly man was reading the Bible, the actual Book of Revelation. Chairman X remarked, "I think the world is so screwed up because so many people ignore the visible in favor of the invisible."

"What's that?"

"Well, if you're always thinking about the afterlife, then you can ignore this life. If you're always thinking about something you call spirit, then you can destroy the physical, both in yourself and in the world, without caring about the consequences. It's just a kind of self-evasion, if you ask me."

"I didn't ask you anything."

"I admit that."

They sat in silence. Chairman X knew that if he were to stand up right there, he would avoid an argument and refrain from embarrassing himself. He knew that if he continued to sit there, the old man would not be able to resist a reply, and that neither of them would ever ever see eye to eye with the other. He sat there, twisting his glass in his hand. At last the old man said, "There is peace here." He tapped the book. His voice was warm and knowing, as if he could have as easily tapped Chairman X's head and said, "but none here."

Chairman X, taken by surprise, did not immediately reply. Finally, he said, as gently, "That's the peace that costs the Earth."

The old man looked at him. After a moment, the corners of his eyes creased, and he suddenly laughed. Chairman X found himself laughing, too.

Two rooms away, Beth heard the laugh above every other sound, the way she heard all the noises, large and small, that her family made. Relieved, she laughed suddenly herself, even though Ivar was just then lamenting the budget crisis right into her ear. She caught herself when he looked at her quizzically, and said, "I'm sorry. Please go on."

In a corner of the dining room near the kitchen, within touching distance of the other guests, but totally cut off from them, Dr. Bo Jones had Elaine Dobbs-Jellinek all to himself, and he was quizzing her about available funds for something she did not quite understand. She said, "Really, Dr. Bo, if you'd just look into what the swine breeding companies are interested in—"

"No, ma'am. No, ma'am. I know what they're interested in and you do, too. I'm interested in something different. I'm interested in HOGS."

"Isn't that what they're interested in?" He was standing so close to her that the only way she could get a sip of her, what was it, tonic water with lime? Why *wasn't* there any gin? was to sort of slide it up her front and introduce it into her mouth from below. And then he moved a half step closer. He said, "No, they're interested in what you do to hogs, with hogs. I'm interested in who hogs are."

"Who are hogs?"

"See, now, nobody knows that."

"No, I meant, is that what you're interested in, who are hogs?"

"You bet."

"Oh."

"You see, you're stumped, aren't you? Give me a hog fact."

"What?"

"You been around here long enough to know one little thing about hogs. Just say what it is."

Elaine turned her shoulder into Dr. Bo's chest and gave a tactful little shove. She felt as though he were pushing her down a hole, as though she should raise her hand and wave for help.

"Just one."

"Uh—" She took a deep breath. "Uh. Let's see. Well, I know they go for slaughter at about nine months old, or two hundred and thirty pounds or so." Her shoulder blades grazed the wall. She felt a little panicky.

"You need to get some money to save Old Meats."

"Physical plant matters are out of my purview."

"That's a truly historical building. Fittings in there could go into a museum. You could make that place into a museum."

"The university does have a museum—"

"All they got over there is pictures. In this museum, they ought to get old farm implements, some educational displays about corn and beans. Something for the kids. You could have some real good exhibits, like stuffed farm animals in characteristic groupings and activities, or a diorama of typical hog behavior, if anybody knew what that was. Kids like taxidermic displays. You ever been to Cabela's, out in Kearney, Nebraska? They got grizzlies and mountain lions, and everything you can name. No hogs, though. You could get money for that."

To Elaine, now inwardly gasping, it seemed as though his moving lips were saying, "You *will* get money for that." She did have a distant perception, like the vision of stars up a chimney into which you had been wedged, that Dr. Bo might actually have a good idea, but she would grasp that later. Now it only mattered that he move back, that she escape, if necessary through his legs. She said, "Fine. Yes. I have some ideas."

"I'll call you Monday."

"Please. Do."

"You know where the bathroom is? I got to piss in the worst way."

Elaine lifted her little hand in a gesture of last resort and signalled limply toward the back of the house. At last he moved off. She came out of her corner as if out of a dark closet, and moved to the center of the room, where the light was good, the air was clear, and she could keep her eye on Jack Parker, who, all the time he was schmoozing with people, also seemed to be making mental notes on who was flirting with whom, so that he could later follow them to hotel rooms and take their pictures in flagrante delicto. It did not escape Elaine's notice that, as often as she found herself at a social gathering with Jack Parker, he had never given her the once-over. He didn't now. When he caught her looking at him, he turned away immediately and went over to the coffee urn, where he refilled his cup.

As usual, everyone in the room was aware of Jack Parker. As she drifted to the table and balanced a shrimp between her fingernails, Elaine heard a zoologist say to a botanist, "To look at him, you'd never know that Jack Parker made the University of Michigan what it is today."

"Really?" said the botanist.

"Single-handedly," said the zoologist. "Ask anyone at NIH."

In the living room, Elaine's former husband and coparent, Dean Jellinek, was basking in the even bolder glare of public attention. A million over five years was the rumor that Dean refrained from

confirming or denying, instead allowing to play over his features just
the merest complacent smile. The well-known reluctance of midwesterners to talk about actual sums of money worked in his favor, since
refusal to talk about it made it the unspoken subject of every exchange,
and yet he didn't really have to explode any fantasies, including his
own, just yet. It was amazing to him in this succulent moment of
rumor just how friendly they all were—the President, Ivar, Dean
Harstad, the chairmen of a whole catalogue of departments, from his
own, Animal Science, through Economics and Statistics all the way
to Zoology. Since the subject was money, of course, all their congratulations were hushed ones, but, after all, all the more welcome for the
implied reverence.

Joy had come in with Dean, but taken her headache, now permanently implanted just above the worry line between her eyebrows,
into the dining room to feed it. It absolutely hollered for a drink, but
there were no drinks. Joy had never before been to a university party
where there were no drinks, and her immediate reaction was that she
just couldn't find it, that there was a bar somewhere in the house
where a nice young man in a white jacket was pouring out Bloody
Marys, but that no one would tell her where it was.

The only other relief from her permanent headache lately seemed
to be tears. Every time Dean updated her on his calf-free lactation
project, which was hourly, she went away and burst into tears and
the pain was gone for about fifteen minutes. Now, when a reliable
source (the catering woman who was replenishing the sausage rolls)
told her that there was no liquor at the party, she did the only thing
she could, which was to burst into tears. She turned away, quietly
dabbed her eyes with some napkins, and began poking melon chunks
into her mouth.

As if by radar, Helen Levy was immediately at her side, asking
what was wrong.

Joy gestured that her mouth was full.

Helen enveloped Joy with her motherly arm and said, "You know,
I feel like I see you less than before even though you're right next
door now."

Joy thoroughly chewed every last atom of the melon, swallowed
every droplet of its juice. She saw that people were glancing at her.
She said, "No drinks. It just surprised me." Now Helen would think
she was an astounding drunk.

Helen said, "Well, I suppose that's the first honest response we've had to that situation. Everyone else pretends to be relieved. Nils' fiancée's father wouldn't allow it."

"Oh." Joy snorted and wiped her eyes. The tears had dried up and the headache was gone. She said, "If you have a headache that's pretty constant, but it goes away if you have a drink or, say, cry about something, could it still be a brain tumor?"

"I don't think so. How long have you had it?"

"Seventeen days. Advil doesn't touch it, neither does Tylenol."

"Good Lord, Joy."

"I know. Let's talk about something else. Is that the fiancée?" She cocked her head toward Marly.

"Yes."

"I've seen her somewhere."

"She's been a server in the commons for years."

"Isn't she awfully young?"

"Old enough to know better, I think."

"How did they meet?"

"He picked her out of the other virgins at his church."

Joy cast Helen a surprised glance—Helen hardly ever spoke in a catty way. As if in response, Helen softened her tone. "I like her. She's sweet, and when Nils starts in about the Lord's intentions, she has sense enough to look embarrassed."

"When are they getting married?"

"Before she has a chance to come to."

"Oh, Helen, you never approve of anybody getting married."

"Not for love. Love is a general emotion. Marriage is exactingly specific. Bad mesh. Anyway, a singleton can never understand an identical twin, and Nils, since he doesn't understand himself, won't be able to guide her. And all they are armed with ahead of time is some biblical precepts." Helen shook her head gravely. "Precepts are worse as a basis for marriage than love is."

"What does Ivar think?"

"He never judges anything Nils does. Never has. I wish I could say the effort was reciprocated."

Joy put a hand to her head. It was coming back the way it always did, as if it had a right to be there.

Helen said, "Come upstairs. I'm going to do something to you that looks weird in a crowd, but it might help."

Joy had never been upstairs in the big brick Harstad manse. She was not in such pain that she failed to notice the decor of the upstairs hall—swirling green and gold flowers, avocado carpeting just a shade off. Turquoise shag in the bedroom, a white chenille spread on the bed with orange pillows. Helen took off her red suit jacket, went around behind her, and said, "Close your eyes."

Given the decor of the room, Joy didn't have to be asked twice.

Helen began at the base of her skull, seemingly with fingertips, but also with something sharper—the point of her elbow? Her hands seemed to go in a number of directions, and to press in particular spots, the painful ones. She said, "Rise up on your toes." Joy rose up on her toes. Helen worked on her for what would have seemed like five minutes, if they hadn't been five minutes of remarkable migrating pain. Only Joy's customary reticence prevented her from crying out or asking Helen to stop.

Helen stopped.

Joy opened her eyes. She was just about to shake her head in discouragement when she felt the pain in her head drain away and her whole self, body and spirit, lighten and seem to lift off her feet, out of her spine. Helen said, "Did it work?"

"Yeah! Yeah, it did! What did you do? How long will it last?"

"About twelve hours. Shall we go back down?"

Later, Joy remembered that Helen didn't tell her what she had done to her, or, in fact, what were actual good reasons to get married.

Tim Monahan was working the room entirely out of habit. In his experience, technocrats like these could not actually be "worked," as, say, publishing or magazine people in New York could be, and expected to be, but his heart wasn't in it anyway. Though he was smiling and complimenting and making connections, it was pure hackwork, not real careerist art, and he would have stopped if he had known what else to do at a party. Anyway, his promotion had been recommended by the department, 11 to 1 (he thought he knew who the one holdout was), and faculty around here were remarkably touchy about even the appearance of the beginnings of the shadows of an attempt to influence the college committee. The uncomfortable result was that he barely spoke to Helen. Gift, Cates, and Garcia were not at the party. A note from Margaret in his mail, just "Dec. 1," had let him know the date of the committee's consideration of his material. He believed that was all she actually knew, but it was hard to talk to her these days, too. Those words he could not avoid saying, "my promotion, my promotion, my promotion," rolled out in a self-absorbed donkey bray and intolerably offended his own ears. But it had been ever thus—my book my book my book, my story my story my story, my review, my article, my work. At least in the East there was a kind of uneasy fellowship of narcissistic whiny bragging that it was both necessary and semi-pleasant to be a part of, but here, he knew, the preferred mode of stoicism extended beyond failure and even success to any form of publicly expressed self-regard.

In the days when Cecelia still paid actual attention to him, they had laughed about this, but now something simultaneously so distracted her and so enlivened her that she didn't seem to be quite the same person she had been. It wasn't a mystery to him—she was sleeping with someone—but it did offend him that she hadn't the courtesy to sustain her usual personality in the teeth of this secret passion—clearly a married man—but indulged in adolescent mutability that a woman her age, and once married, should have grown out of.

"So," he said to the hostess, Marly Something, it had said on the invitation, "what are our duties and pleasures if we want to properly celebrate your engagement?"

"What?" She looked surprised and dismayed at being spoken to. Tim's interest perked up instantly. He moved closer and smiled. He had a practiced, global perception that under these wrappings she called clothes there was a good figure to go with the thick, burnished oak hair and the deep-set, heavily lashed dark eyes. Thin lips, big hands a woman could do nothing about, and they were minor flaws, really.

He said, "What do you do at a university party if you're tired of jostling for status and promoting your career? If you want to actually attain delight and selflessly celebrate the good fortune of others?"

"Have you had anything to eat?" She sounded nervous.

"A little of everything."

"You aren't having a good time?" She sounded as if this were a personal failure on her part.

"Well, it's been a long while since I've had a good time, especially without any artificial stimulants. Maybe since I was eleven or so, before girls and ambition set in."

"Is that true?"

He chuckled. "Sure. What about you?"

"Well, I don't count on having a good time very often."

"Are you having a good time here?"

"I'm too worried about everyone else having a good time. Anyway, I've never been to this kind of party before. I guess my best times are at church suppers, you know, afterward, when all the women are cleaning up, and we start laughing and can't stop."

"What do you think makes you start laughing and unable to stop?"

"Well, no men around, for one thing." She looked at him. "Though I shouldn't say it. But it's true. If men see you acting silly, it's their obligation to ask you to stop. And the kids are funny, even if you know they're being a little naughty."

"I would like to be able, right now, to laugh without stopping."

"It would be fun."

"Too many men around."

"Anyway, everyone's too dressed up to laugh. We go to church suppers in our regular clothes. That's important, too. On Sundays, when we wear good clothes, I don't think I've ever seen anyone laugh once."

Well, the conversation saddened him. When some old guy in a black suit beckoned to her and she apologized and moved away, sadness rose in him like a low-grade fever, and it wasn't depression and it wasn't despair and it wasn't alienation—nothing respectable like those psychological, artistic, and sociological feelings. There was not the usual invigorating admixture of anger, either. He looked at her in her bun and her long wool dress and her flat shoes, bending respectfully toward the old guy, and he thought of her saying, "I don't count on having a good time very often," and he thought, She can't take care of herself, and his sadness deepened. Time to go home, he thought. He was in the perfect mood for grading papers, because the one emotion his students could narrate without any coaching was sadness.

At the table, picking out some savory bits and pieces for Father, Marly was sorry she had let down like that. There, that man she had been talking to, was leaving already. He had come to celebrate, and they hadn't celebrated yet, and he looked just like she felt. Was it too self-centered to think that she had done that to him? She hadn't meant to say what she had said. The women at church, who had been giving her all kinds of advice about getting married, had all said, "Don't let them know what you're really thinking. It scares them." One had even said, "It scares them and he'll get back at you somehow, even if he doesn't want to. He can't help it." She put the last of the shrimp on her father's plate. She had been skeptical, but not anymore. She sighed. Marly did not choose to look forward to marriage in this sad and lonely way, but it seemed to come to her without her bidding, even against her will. Even so, she went toward the wedding day by day. The old life had, after all, ejected her, and there was nowhere else to go.

Dr. Garcia passed Tim Monahan as he was hurrying up the walk, and carefully mastered his temptation to stop and chat. What was there to chat about besides the very interesting way Tim's hopes, aspirations, and personality structure meshed with those of the tenure committee, the very thing Garcia could not possibly chat about? And even the most idle conversation would reveal—

Tim glanced at and obviously recognized him. Garcia felt his left eyebrow, the conspiratorial one (his right eyebrow was the disapproving one) arch upward. He made his face into a mask and kept going. The exchange took a nanosecond, and after it, Garcia paused and turned to look at Tim's receding back. He didn't kid himself into thinking that the exchange hadn't registered—the ability of primates to interpret even the most subtle facial expressions of other primates was so highly developed that even chimps could, with 99 percent accuracy, pick the friendly expressions from a series of slides of other chimps flashed upon a screen for a tenth of a second apiece. As Tim was a novelist, Garcia thought, his skills in such interpretation, whether learned or innate, would be all that much more acute.

He stepped up onto the Harstad porch and rang the bell. The door opened. You know, he thought as he made his greeting, you could get a bunch of novelists together and run all sorts of tests. They were not an especially well-studied group—

He went into the house and the big red door closed behind him.

31

He Tells Her He's Not Married

IT WASN'T a very nice day—rainy and chilly, too cold for Cecelia, and only in the thirties. What in the world would she do when the temperature dropped into single digits, and the windchill factor (a frightening concept) into the double digits *below* zero—fifties and sixties below, she had heard.

Her thermostat sat magically on seventy, where the landlord had set it before locking it in, but the air temperature seemed to gyrate wildly anyway, at least between frigid (when she was sipping hot tea) and unbearable (when she was grading tests, homework, and compositions). She had on a heavy undershirt and three sweaters and was contemplating her third hot bath of the day when he knocked. She discarded two sweaters as she walked to the door.

Of course it was Chairman X, even though it was Sunday, and after four, and he and the Lady X had promised the children a movie at seven as a reward for the last-minute baby-sitting that had allowed them to go to that ghastly engagement party.

He looked, as he often did, as though he was just going to say one thing and then leave, but no. As soon as she had shut the door, he had his hands under the sweater and the undershirt—that she had no bra on was not a coincidence—and she had hers on his face, and he was kissing her all under her ears and down her neck as he eased her onto the living room carpet and pulled off her slippers, socks, more socks, corduroy slacks, and tights and shouldered them aside in heaps. She arched toward the tropical warmth of his need for her, and in about two seconds she was naked and sweating, a girl at the beach, her eyes closed against the glare.

The only married man Cecelia had ever slept with had been her own husband; it seemed clear that marriage produced a more volcanic effect on Chairman X than it had on Scott. He showed up every day or so. His need to go to bed was as constant as the sun, but his desire to do so was as erratic, and dramatic, as the loop of a comet through the solar system. One day he had made up his mind that he could not, would not, today or ever again. The next day he had to, no matter what. But in fact, his convictions had nothing to do with it. He would assure her, in a voice full of tragic feeling, "I have a choice, you know. If there's one thing I've learned, it's to take responsibility for my own actions." Cecelia would nod with her eyes closed, nearly unconscious with the desire that his tone of voice aroused in her. If there was one thing she had learned it was that, right now at least, she was irresistible.

They got up off the living room carpet and moved into the bedroom. He covered her tenderly with the bedspread, then hung her clothes fondly over the back of her desk chair, pairing her socks and slippers in a row on the dresser.

He didn't look THAT WAY, or any way that Cecelia had ever been attracted to he was small and wiry, though years of outdoor work had hardened his hands, forearms, and shoulders. He was much older than she was—his hair was thin on top, and graying, and badly cut. Most of the time it looked like he had been pulling it, or that it had just stood up on its own out of an excess of feeling. Even though he was thin and muscular, his body looked used and uncared-for. Apparently he had solved the problem of what to wear by always wearing the same thing—jeans, a laundered shirt, a threadbare cotton sweater, crew socks, brown boots. But she took this and everything else as a true sign that he was altogether different from her standard, a true sign that she had dropped to a deeper, more genuine and powerful level of feeling, a true sign that even deeper levels than she had ever imagined existed were available to her if she had the guts.

He said, "I didn't mean to stay. It's almost five, and I promised my kids they could go to a movie. I've got this bean loaf in the oven."

"What?"

"It's my day to cook. I made a bean loaf and a salad."

These clues about his domestic life were tantalizing and strange. She sighed with appreciation at his uniqueness. In this area, she had little to offer—sometimes a soup on the stove that he wouldn't eat if it had meat in it, sometimes just a jar of Skippy peanut butter and a loaf of Roman Meal bread or a bowl of popcorn.

He lifted her hand, which he was holding tightly in both of his, to his cheek. She spread her fingers and he pressed into them. He said, "I really have to go."

She said, "I was thinking about my uncle Carlos, well, he's really a cousin, but lots older than my father, and at one time he was a rich man, so we all called him 'Uncle Carlos' out of respect. When I was little, we would go to his farm every summer. He was the only one in the family with both a house in the city and a farm in the country. The farm was mostly orchards that his father had planted—"

Chairman X put his feet on the bed and looked at his watch. He said, "Ten minutes at the outside."

Cecelia hid her smile with the bedspread and said nothing, only went on about Uncle Carlos. "Lots of familes live on the farm to take care of the orchards. I don't know that they were profitable, but Uncle Carlos had some other businesses. All I know is that there seemed like there was always plenty of food. And this other thing, too. I don't know that the fruit actually did give off much fragrance, but it always SEEMED that the air was full of sweetness—not overpowering—just enough to make you want to inhale and inhale." Cecelia felt that although this bit about the fragrance was a lie, that in fact this whole tale was a lie, it should have been true.

Chairman X said, "Just a minute." He got up and walked over to the phone on her desk and dialed with his back to her. After a moment, she heard him say, "Honey, did you take the bean loaf out? Good. Listen, I'm tied up right now. I'll try to be home in time to go to the movie, but I can't guarantee it. Maybe I'll meet you there. Okay." He hung up and came back to the bed. When he sat down, there was a silence between them, and Uncle Carlos seemed to have receded into the distance. Chairman X said, "You know, twenty years ago, I would have said, 'Honey, I'm over at Cecelia's, and we decided to get it on, I'll be home when I can,' and she would have said, 'That's cool,' but we can't do that anymore."

"Your wife is unfaithful, too?"

"We're not married, technically."

"Excuse me?"

"We forgot, in a way."

"You forgot to get married?"

"It was low on our list of priorities. Now my daughter's in the eighth grade. I don't know. It seems like if we turned around and got married now, it would lower my daughter's opinion of her mother too much." He sighed. After a long, pensive moment, he said, "You know, I've got to say that twenty years ago, I didn't expect to be living in the world I live in now. If I had, I might have been more ready to embrace political violence." He shook his head, the way

people in L.A. did when they talked about how they wished they'd
bought into the Orange County real estate market in 1965.

Then he said, "Tell me what was planted."

"What was planted?"

"In those orchards."

"Oh." She returned to the story she was making up, taking her
usual pleasure in seeing him turn away from his past and toward
hers. "Almonds. Apricots. Avocados. Some peaches. I don't know.
Grapefruit. Lemons. Probably oranges."

"All those together?" His eyes were closed, but he sounded skeptical. Cecelia licked her lips, caught. There had been an Uncle Carlos,
and he had had a farm, but Cecelia didn't actually know anything
about it. Even her mother had only been there once or twice. "Well"—
she drew the word out, as if delving carefully into her memory—
"the farm was large, and on the side of a mountain. I guess there were
lots of different elevations."

"Microclimates can vary considerably, even in a rather confined
geographical area." He put his hands behind his head and made himself
even more comfortable. Although he wasn't touching her, his settling
in felt like an actual embrace.

"Hmmmm," she dared, "I think there were grapes, too."

He nodded. The lies Cecelia kept telling felt to her like a net that
she was throwing over him. She glanced at the clock. It was almost
six. He wouldn't be meeting his family at the movie, that was for
sure. The quiet exultation of this knowledge was possibly the most
astonishingly selfish feeling she had ever known. But she felt no re-
morse. As she talked about Uncle Carlos, she unbuttoned the Chairman's jeans and opened his zipper so slowly that she could feel its
teeth separate one by one.

32

It's Always Something

LOREN STROOP WAS making a remarkable recovery from his "brain attack." His doctor didn't like the word "stroke," which he said made a medical accident sound like an act of God, of which there were none. His doctor was particular about the niceties of brain attacks, and he was careful to inform Loren that his recovery was in the eighty-fourth percentile of male patients of his age group (65 plus) in speed of recovery and in the seventy-ninth percentile in scope of recovery. Loren couldn't talk yet, so the doctor anticipated his doubts by advising him not to think of these percentiles as if they were grades (a B and a C−), but to think of them as representative examples of the law of averages. Loren had escaped, by thirty-four percentage points and twenty-nine percentage points, the law of averages. The doctor was pleased with this, and in his daily conversations with himself about Loren, which Loren listened to as much as he could, since they were taking place in his room, Loren tried to find as much satisfaction as the doctor in these numbers. If Loren looked depressed, the doctor would fill him in on the progress of Mrs. Gruber, down the hall (age group—45 to 65, percentile rankings—thirty-two and thirty-four), who wasn't doing well at all. Loren knew this clandestine information was supposed to buck him up, possibly to make him feel lucky that he had gotten away with some of Mrs. Gruber's rightful points (although, according to the doctor, no one had any rights in the law of averages), so he did his best. The nurses all liked his doctor very much, and approved of his manner with his patients, which was to set an example of determination and good cheer that they would feel obliged to follow.

He could use his right arm and his right leg. He could recognize objects on his right side. He could use his left leg and arm if he could manage to keep his right eye on them, which made walking with his new cane possible but not easy. He could understand what people said and read the right side of a book page, but he could not produce language of any sort, either by speaking or writing.

He woke up in the morning thinking about his main problem, which was how to get his plans to his extension dean Harstad, and get his dean out to his machine. Sometimes he thought about his other problem, which was how he was going to live with these "functional deficits," as the doctor called them. They did not fit in very well with the solitary farming life that was the only life he knew.

The nurse came in with his breakfast and put it on his right side. He recognized everything except one thing, but when he turned his head a little, he saw that what he hadn't recognized was cantaloupe. He kept his head cocked, and remembered, all of a sudden, an old cow he'd had, blind in one eye, who cocked her head like that. You had to milk her from her good side, but he'd liked her, liked the deliberate way she'd gone about her business, the habits she'd developed to compensate for her disability.

After breakfast, they made him walk around the halls. They wanted him to go faster than he wanted to—it was taxing to have to ignore the way everything on the left sloped away to confusion. It was like walking on the edge of the known world and he had to protect himself against the fear it seemed always to arouse. It was easier to lie in bed with his good side up, but they were bound and determined not to let him do the easy thing. The walk lasted forever, and made him forget about his future, but never about his machine or his plans. He could picture both perfectly in his mind, but no matter how receptive his pretty and sweet speech therapist looked, no matter how softly and encouragingly she said, "Go ahead, try it. Say it," still, the sounds came out like mooing.

He did not doubt that the big ag companies, the CIA, and the FBI had introduced some sort of selective brain poison into his water supply in order to disable or, more probably, kill him. He did not doubt that he was lucky to be alive. He did not doubt that he would overcome this mooing problem and prevail in the end. But it seemed unfair, after a life of hard work and patience, that they would get him at last.

The Millers came before lunch. They brought a sack of apples, their Haralsons that he liked so much. They sat on the right side of the bed, and the nurse told them he had walked four circuits of the hospital today. They were thrilled. Sally did most of the talking. She and Mary Hutton had been over to his place, cleaning. Mary's dad, Linc, had had a little accident with his truck, but Linc had beaten the dent in the hood out with a hammer and it looked as good as new.

Mary wasn't speaking to her sister in Chicago, still. Sally's own girls were back on the basketball team at school. Practices had just started. Weren't the apples good-looking this year? And crisp! Just wait until he tried them. Sally smiled and smiled, and stroked his right hand so that he didn't want to pull it away even though he did want to find each of the girls a dime.

While Sally talked, he stared meaningfully at Joe, until finally Joe said, "Well, I told you about how we sold your beans? Got a good price on them, too."

Loren shook his head. That news was weeks old.

Joe went on uncertainly, "Corn's in the bin. It had about seventeen percent moisture. Pretty good, I thought. We dried it down to about fourteen. Just waiting for the price to go up a bit to sell it. That's what I'm doing with my own."

Loren shook his head. Though Joe would have been dumbstruck by the thought, Loren didn't care at all about the corn.

Loren looked at Sally, who fell silent. After a bit, she said, "You want to tell us something?"

He nodded.

"Not about the corn or the beans or the dogs? The dogs went over to the Christensens. You mind about that? They like dogs."

Loren shook his head.

"The house?"

Loren shook his head, though doing so made his worlds, the known and the unknown, swirl painfully together. Nothing quite took it out of him like shaking his head.

Joe said, "The machinery? Lyle Hutton and I put it away in the machine shed the other day."

Loren shook his head.

Joe said, "Now, we ain't been in the barn except to turn out the lights. I know that's your secret place, and we don't want to get into that, so your secret is safe. We haven't been a bit nosy, if you're worried about that."

"That's right," said Sally. "You can count on us. We stopped the mail at the post office and had the phone turned off, but we thought it was better to leave the electric on, and some lights on in the house. But believe me, we haven't gone into your private things."

Loren nodded vigorously, to indicate that they COULD go into the barn, they COULD investigate his private things, because he was convinced that if Joe did that, he would be impressed enough with the machine that he would take care of it, preserve it. Preservation would be, well, might be, enough. Somewhere, a few points up in the percentile rankings, he would find language again. The mooing would turn into persuasion, and there he would be, back in the office of his dean, showing his plans; there his dean would be, out in the barn marvelling at his revolutionary machine, and that would be IT for the CIA, the FBI, and the big ag companies.

But the Millers interpreted his nods as approval, and assured him again that they wouldn't get into his private things, and pretty soon they had told him the rest of the gossip and gone home to their dinner. His own dinner was meat loaf, which he ate because there was nothing else to do, and then he turned his good side up and tried to doze off in spite of the sense he had of the strange unknown place beneath him, over which he lay suspended. He substituted knowledge for feeling, making himself think, over and over, I'm just in bed, I'm just in bed, I'm just in bed, but the fact was, if you went with that, substituting knowledge for feeling, then you had to admit that, maybe, probably, that machine would never get out of his barn and those plans would languish at the copy place until after he was dead, and then they would throw them out. If you substituted knowledge for feeling, then you had to admit that the FBI and the CIA and the big ag companies, especially them, were likely to have their way, with him, Loren Stroop, as with everything else.

33

Why?

THE PERPLEXITY of Mrs. Loraine Walker at the acquisition of the
Seven Stones Mining Corporation by TransNational turned out to be
shared by the *Wall Street Journal*. Although the *Journal* devoted to
Seven Stones only a single paragraph toward the end of a long article
about the decline of the great mining corporations, that paragraph
made some interesting observations, in Mrs. Walker's view. Pre-
viously, as noted by the running-dog-lackey-of-the-imperialist-class
writer, TransNational had been known for acquiring small companies
just as, or just before, its innovative techniques or products gained
general corporate acceptance—TransNational owned more than twice
the number of patents owned by the average conglomerate of the
same size. Arlen Martin was well known for his disdain of "stumbling
white elephants," into which category he consigned every company
from Exxon and IBM to Reynolds Tobacco and General Foods. He
had been quoted as disdaining someone he knew who ran Jell-O.
"There's a guy," he had said, "who spends his time thinking up salad
recipes and telling folks that canned pineapple in green Jell-O won't kill
them. Me, I'm not in the maintenance business. I'm in the revolution
business." But the Seven Stones Mining Corporation was an old and
top-heavy company, doggedly working nearly played-out seams in
the teeth of declining, you could say collapsing, profits. Its main
feature of interest, detailed by the writer with typical *Journal*-style
covert admiration, was a colorful history of stealing land, buying
elections, possibly arranging the death of a UMW official, intimidat-
ing government inspectors and agents, and resisting mandated safety
measures.

In addition, according to the rest of the article, there wasn't much
of a future in mining, at least in the U.S. The Mesabi Range, the
Upper Peninsula, the Mother Lode country, Wyoming, Montana,
what with reduce, reuse, recycle, even the biggest companies were
saying, "Why bother?"

Of course there was Kennicott. Mrs. Walker's lips thinned to a disapproving line. Digging a lead mine in Wisconsin. Hmm. Right on the Flambeau River. Hmm. Though Mrs. Walker had spent her childhood rather east of there, outside of Shawano, she knew the Flambeau River, the pristine, immaculate, one-of-a-kind, dark deep teeming chill delicious avenue through the forest Flambeau River. Lead was something Mrs. Walker preferred bound up in ore, safe in the ground. She didn't like it in paint, in trash, in soil, in the air. She certainly did not like it seeping into the Flambeau River. Kennicott. Her eyebrows lowered and approached each other. She made a note to call one of her cousins, who still lived on the reservation.

But the riddle at hand was Arlen Martin. She accessed the computer files of the geology department. She found no outgoing correspondence addressed to any of Martin's companies, no reference at all to Seven Stones Mining. With some reluctance she admitted that she was, at least for the time being, stumped. To console herself, since it had taken so long for the library to find and print out her article, she accessed the athletic budget and transferred enough money out of there to the library budget to pay for two more two-thirds-time work-study students in Reference.

Part Three

34

Why Not?

AS HE FINISHED up his report for the TransNationalAmerica Corporation (he always got down to contracted tasks right away, another of his virtues), Dr. Lionel Gift reflected upon how satisfying it was, once again, to do a good job for a good cause. Of course the report, as Dr. Gift well knew, was only one of the services he had contracted for. They would hardly have approached a man of his intellectual and moral stature for a mere report. Once he was finished with the report, then the real work of wheedling, persuading, and setting a good economic example for his friends and admirers in the Costa Rican government would begin. And it would have to begin soon. Seven Stones Mining was toppling faster than Martin had foreseen, and it was costing the other branches of TransNational a fortune to keep it out of bankruptcy. Martin had a thing about bankruptcy, one of those unsophisticated Depression-boyhood things that Dr. Lionel Gift found poignant and vulnerable in the man. And anyway, he was right that if the banks took hold, there was plenty of costly equipment that Martin might not be able to transport out of the country to, say, Costa Rica.

And if you wanted to dig a gold mine under the hemisphere's last primeval cloud forest, you couldn't do it without costly equipment.

In Dr. Gift's considered opinion, there was no rational case to be made AGAINST such a gold mine, and a significant case to be made in its favor. He had spent the last two weeks accumulating that case grain by grain, point by point, and as a result, he himself was convinced. It was a pleasant feeling.

On the other hand, Dr. Gift had weaknesses of character just like any other man, and he knew that one of these was that he could not have made so persuasive a case for, say, a molybdenum mine, a cobalt mine, a manganese mine. Even a silver mine. Precious as these minerals were to the world of modern technology that Dr. Gift revered, what had sustained him through the composition of his report was the thought of that hidden thread, that filament of sunshine and prosperity

running through the lightless depths of ore—GOLD! It reminded him
of the universe, how rare and priceless light was in that vast blackness,
how humans, who lived upon that light, had to seek it or die. Now
geologists at Seven Stones Mining had discovered a golden seam at
the very top of the South American granodiorite intrusions, an unlikely and unlooked-for offshoot of those legendary lodes now dug
up and abandoned. The land around the cloud forest that International
Cattle, another TransNational subsidiary, had quietly bought up surrounded the seam but did not contain it. This ray of light and life
ran under the forest, rising to the surface here and there, producing
for the birds and monkeys and snakes golden-flecked streams, sparkling soils, glittering motes on the floor of the forest. It was inspiring
in a painful, anxiety-making way, the thought of that gold going
unclaimed, unpossessed. It mocked consumer insatiability. Dr. Lionel Gift couldn't stand contemplating it for very long. Neither could
Arlen Martin. It was a bond between them. Better not to know
about it.

But they DID know about it, and knowledge demanded action.

It was also better that no one else know about it. The deposits
contained duller metals, molybdenum, for one, and the forest, of
course, had other profit potential in its medicinal plants, wood products, and tourist allure. For the preservation of these, sound management demanded that the sort of low-level rush of individuals possessed
of an insatiable but inconvenient desire for gold, as well as of sieves
and pickaxes, etc., that California and Alaska had seen be avoided at
all costs. As a man of the nineties, Dr. Gift made these environmental
points a prominent part of his report.

In fact, very few persons were on a need-to-know basis in regard
to Dr. Gift's report. The grant money, of which the university would
get half (10 percent less than the university's usual take, a perk that
recognized Dr. Gift's unusual contribution to university life), would
go through Elaine Dobbs-Jellinek's office directly into Dr. Gift's
G-account. Had he written this report as a paid consultant rather than
a grantee, Dr. Gift would have received more money, but, of course,
it was Elaine Dobbs-Jellinek who had set them up and circumvented
Ivar (Dr. Gift perfectly remembered the chicken feed controversy).
Dr. Gift would never cheat a middleman or middlewoman. The market, in fact, the divine market, was the inspired creation of middleper-
sons everywhere who had nothing to offer but reliable intuition about

what prolific producer needed what insatiable consumer and vice versa.

Nevertheless, as a grantee, Dr. Gift had to supply a copy of his report (and later a summary of his persuasive activities, especially if he planned to travel on the university expense account, which he did) to Elaine Dobbs-Jellinek's office. The importance of secrecy was great enough, Dr. Gift felt, that once he had composed it on his word processor, once he had printed out three copies—one for himself, one for Martin, and one for Elaine Dobbs-Jellinek—he erased the file (what a chill that gave him!) and stored the copies in his fire-proof, theft-proof, tornado-proof, and flood-proof household safe. It was scary, in a way, having only printed copies. It reminded him of ephemerality, human mortality, the transience of objects. How quickly he had gotten used to the safety of storing his documents all over the campus—in the computer archives, on his own hard disks at the office and at home, on a backup disk, as printout, and, finally, in journal articles. Storage itself enhanced the perceived value of information, didn't it?

He made a small note to that effect for his knowledge and information paper.

35

The Consequences

MARY HAD a fever of 102, and every time she tried to stand up, it felt as though chills were cascading down her body. So, she was lying in bed, covered up to her chin, with a cool washcloth on her forehead that Keri had put there as some sort of rural folk remedy. Nor would Keri allow her to take aspirin, hadn't she heard of Reye's syndrome? Only Tylenol, but they didn't have any Tylenol, so Keri had gone to get some.

Otherwise Mary would have left the room and gone to the lounge, in order to avoid listening to Sherri whine over the telephone to her mother and father, who had just received her midterm grades.

She whined, "It's really hard here. I wasn't exactly prepared."

She whined, "I did learn things. I haven't been wasting time."

She whined, "I know it costs a lot. Geez, I know exactly how much it costs, for Christ's sake."

She whined, "I'm sorry. No, I haven't learned to talk that way from my roommates." She looked over at Mary, and made a face. "I'm just frustrated, is all."

She whined, "I know it's a privilege you and Daddy didn't have. Well, I am sorry."

She whined, "I am. I really AM. I thought I sounded sorry. I tried to sound sorry." A pause. "Because I AM sorry!"

Mary's grades had not gone home, because she had gotten no F's or D's. She had even gotten a B − on her calculus test, which meant that statistically (in her calculus course, the computer grading system spit out a merciless curve) she was above the fiftieth percentile, which meant that more than 50 percent of the students had an even more tenuous grasp on calculus than she did, which was, in its way, almost frightening. At least it was if you had a fever of 102 and discrete, unpleasant ideas were rolling around in your head like steel pinballs, making a lot of noise and lighting up various feelings, all of them negative.

Sherri whined, "Well, it's hard for everybody. Nobody did great, not even Diane. I don't see why you're so mad. Daddy isn't that mad, and he's the one who's paying."

She whined, "I know. I'm sorry. I AM sorry. I know. I know."

Sherri had gotten two F's and a C−, which meant that her grade average was .94, not even a D, and that if she didn't bring it up, didn't in fact double it, she would be out at the end of the semester.

Sherri whined, "Yes, my hair is red. I dyed it. Can we talk about that another time?"

She opened her little refrigerator and took out a pack of cigarettes. Then she brandished a mineral water in Mary's direction, but Mary shook her head. An open one that she hadn't been able to finish sat on the desk beside her bed.

Finally, Sherri whined, "Well, I AM going to do better, okay? I promise. I PROMISE. Okay, then. Okay, bye." She hung up and went over to the window, where she lit her cigarette. Between puffs, she held it out the partially opened window. When Mary assayed a little cough, she said, "I know, I know. Tobacco is bad for the soil, bad for the workers, bad for the public health, and bad for the body. I'm a sucker." This litany, made up by Keri, was something the other girls had employed to persuade Sherri to stop smoking, but so far it hadn't worked.

She whined, "God! She just went on and on."

Mary felt like her bed was rocking, or her head was sloshing. One or the other. One or the other. One or the other.

Sherri said, "You going to throw up again?"

"I don't know."

Sherri stubbed out her cigarette and ran for the bucket in the maintenance closet in the hall, where Diane had left it to dry after washing it out from the last time. She set it by the bed, then she felt the washcloth, which had heated up, and carried it over to the sink and wrung it out in cold water. She seemed to share this belief in the efficacy of the washcloth. She and Keri had been faithful and firm about keeping it on Mary's forehead.

What with Mary's virus and Sherri's grades and some kind of snit Diane was in about Bob, the girls had been spending more time together and it hadn't been so bad, really. Okay, Mary admitted, they were taking the opportunity to hide out in their room, to not go forth in the various ways that demanded bravery of them, or at least fortitude. They were eating chicken soup made on a hot plate, and popcorn, and Cheez-it crackers, and tortilla chips with salsa. They were doing their hair and their nails and their laundry. They were turning down dates. Mary had even told Hassan not to come see her—he could give the stuffed grape leaves somebody in married student housing had made for her to Keri.

Keri had turned into the mom, and that was okay, too. She made the soup and the popcorn, picked dishes off the floor and washed them, took Mary's temperature, called Student Health for advice, set the example of how to huddle in close quarters by keeping her bed made and her clothes folded and put away. She had bought the mineral water. Soon she would be back with the Tylenol. The cocoon was warm and comfortable and private. Outside it was chilly and gray. Mary closed her eyes.

Sherri went over to the window and lit another cigarette. She held it out as far as she could, but it was starting to rain. She bent down and put her nose to the crack of the open window. The moist, cold air felt good on her hot cheeks, but she didn't want to go out into it. She didn't want to do anything but smoke and sit around. That was her problem. She could see that Mary was falling asleep. It would be a perfect time to go over to her desk and at least read her English assignment, a relatively painless activity compared to the others. But she couldn't move, except to bend down from time to time and feel the outer chill. She knew this sloth was a sin, a sin to match all the others she had committed since coming to school—lust (she had slept with three different near-strangers, one of them twice), gluttony (she had gained at least five pounds going out for pizza after supper), covetousness (one of the guys she had slept with was going with a girl from her high school, and she'd only gotten interested in him because Doreen had always dated the cutest guys and made a big deal of it, which pissed her off), anger (every time her mother called), envy (she kept it quiet, but it circulated—Keri could eat anything, Mary had great clothes, Diane, at least until lately, had fallen into this great sex thing), and pride. Well, pride. Pride was what kept you from admitting you had any problems, even when everybody knew you did.

The thing was, whether or not virtue was in fact its own reward, it did seem like sin was its own punishment.

It wasn't as if she didn't think about changing her ways. She did.

But the thoughts came to her idly, without conviction. Just as now she thought idly about reading her English assignment, she often thought idly about stopping smoking, which she had, in fact, just started, and didn't like all that much, she thought idly about going to classes, she thought idly about going to the library, she thought idly about going to her computer station and accessing her geology problems. She thought idly about not taking two desserts when she went through the dinner line. The food in Dubuque House was good—everyone helped cook and one of the rewards of multicultural-ism was a spicy and delicious diet. The thing was, she had let down completely. The thing was, every thought of her family served to show her a way to let down even further than she had suspected was possible. It seemed like every brick wall that she ran into, that was supposed to hurt her enough to shake her up and give her some conviction, just turned into a door and she passed through it into deeper inertia. She stubbed out her cigarette and lay back limply on Diane's bed.

The thing was, one day last week when she'd gotten to her English class, the teacher and some of the students who always sat in the front row were laughing about a memo the teacher (whose name Sherri still wasn't quite sure of) had gotten in which the students were called "customers." Now it was true that Sherri had come in late, and also true that she owed the teacher two papers, so she hadn't wanted to attract the woman's attention any more than necessary, but she'd found the laughter confusing at first, then aggravating. When the teacher tried to widen the discussion by asking what the others thought about the difference between "students" and "customers," Sherri had maintained the same appearance of benign ignorance and noncommit-tal good will that the other freshmen had, but that didn't mean that she didn't have an opinion. In fact, they all had the same opinion, which they expressed to one another after class—if they were paying all this money, then they must be customers, and if they were custom-ers, then why was that particular English teacher so bo-o-o-o-ring? Factory reject? Candidate for manufacturer's recall? Obsolete model? Was the total tedium of their class due to mechanical failure or pilot error? Well, it had made them all laugh afterward in the hall outside of class. But now, limp on her bed, Sherri decided it wasn't funny. The fact was, she wasn't getting what she was paying for, which was—what? She couldn't define it, exactly. But she knew this limp, irritable feeling well enough. It was the sensation of consumer dissatis-faction, and it was soooooo annoying.

The sound of Mary rustling and gagging roused her. She jumped up and ran across the room, managing to catch the washcloth before it fell into the bucket. She held Mary's forehead and patted her back and tried not to look at the bucket.

36

Another Point of View

Assignment: You are to rewrite the story you have chosen to revise from the point of view of another character in your story. It is risky to choose (1) a pet's point of view, (2) the point of view of a piece of furniture or a fly on the wall, (3) the point of view of one of your character's alternative personalities. These and other tricks have been tried before and have, invariably, failed. Your goal is to enrich your portrait of both the old point-of-view character and the new one. You have a certain amount of leeway in changing the plot of your story, but it should be recognizably the same story.

Oct. 25, 1989
Monahan, FW 325

"The Boy," version #3

a story by Gary Olson

Although he kept quiet about them, and he was only eight, Larry had some extra powers that he didn't really understand. For example, he could see around corners, and he could remember his whole life, all the way back to being born. He didn't let himself remember the early part of his life very often, though, because it made him too sad. That was when his mother, Lydia, had been younger and prettier and thinner and happier. That was when his father had come home every night right after work to have dinner with her and play with him, Larry. They were a happy famly then, and Larry missed that now. The extra powers seemed to make him see things that made him sad rather than happy.

"Lydia and Larry"

a story by Gary Olson

Larry knew he had lost his mom—she had been taken away one night by the police, and an enormous fat woman who didn't love him had been supplied in her place, a real screamer. They had also supplied another child, his supposed sister, Allison, but in fact Allison came from another family entirely. Larry thought it was very weird that his father, Lyle, hadn't noticed the switch, but Lyle was very busy in his job, and often worked two shifts, so he didn't notice much of anything.

Some days, Larry tried to get the new mom to admit that she wasn't Lydia, and he never really did, but she always started screaming at him, and that was a dead giveaway. His real mom had never screamed at him, and he could remember many times when he would be lying in her arms, looking up at her, and she would be smiling down at him, and he knew he was going to get to suck her breast

"Lyle"

a story by Gary Olson

Lyle Karstensen often wondered whether it was him who was really to blame for what had happened to his wife, Lydia. He knew now, looking back ten years to their years at college, that he hadn't really appreciated Lydia, and that she had stuck by him in spite of the many ways that he had ignored or belittled her. For example, he remembered how he would make her sleep in filthy dirty sheets until she made up her mind to wash them. He remembered how he had let the pizza boxes stack up in his room, even though his roommates had thought it was disgusting. And he remembered how jealous he had been of his roommate Larry, whom he thought Lydia was paying too much attention to. That was why, after Larry was killed in a terrible accident, trying to save some elderly people in a fire, Lyle had named his firstborn son after Larry.

The fire had taken place in Los Angeles, where Larry was directing his first movie at the lowly age of twenty-five. He had written the script, too, and everyone was very excited about the project. But he lived down the street from a group home for elderly people, and when, in the middle of one night, the faulty electric wiring started to burn, Larry had thought nothing of

Mr. Monahan—

I have worked very hard on this paper. I really have been working every day, like you said, for forty-five minutes or an hour, and rewarding myself for it, trying to build good habits. But I am not getting anywhere. Here are my beginnings, just to show you that I *HAVE* been working. I hope you will not grade these. I will try again for next week.

37

Earl's Opinion

EVEN THOUGH Bob Carlson was of absolutely no use to her, Diane found that she was taking a surprisingly active role in pursuing their relationship. This was clearly not a good idea, since it implied a certain attachment on her part that did not conform to her plans. This did not mean that she didn't date other guys—she had dated a Theta Chi, a Sigma Chi, a TKE, and a DKE. All four had taken her to fraternity parties where she had witnessed her future made present, and honed her social and flirtation skills. All four dates had been big successes, but each of the four boys she had gone out with had been a trial. They only wanted to kiss when they were drunk, and then their kisses were overabundantly wet. They didn't want to actually talk to her, just to have her on hand while they talked to their fraternity brothers. Worst of all, when she resisted getting particularly drunk herself (in the interests of further study), their attention shifted to other girls in the room who were moving more rapidly toward unconsciousness.

The thing about these guys was that they had no secrets. Their high opinions of themselves, and their sense of entitlement to things like sexual favors, nice clothes, good cars, and a future in which everything would go their way, were fully on display. What you saw was what you got, and she did not believe, as some of the other girls said, that the boys at the parties were separate from some sober incarnation of the same boys. The boys at the parties were being who they wanted to be, and while at one time she had harbored illusions about who they were, and while she had lost some of her enthusiasm for them, she still didn't doubt that their world was where she was headed. Now she just thought that forewarned was forearmed.

Bob, though, was full of secrets. The plain face with the great body constituted one secret. The sexual inexperience with the big dick constituted another. The way he wrote letters to girls all the time was mysterious (she hadn't quite brought herself to rifling his things to see what they wrote back to him—that guy Gary was always in the apartment, working at his computer). The way he disappeared five times a day, including every night at eleven, no matter what they were doing, supposedly to do his work-study job, was one of these mysteries, though not, in the end, the biggest one. The biggest one was how, in contrast to the Theta Chi, the TKE, the DKE, and the Sigma Chi, he had developed a personality of his own, while they seemed to partake of a group personality, which, admittedly, varied slightly by fraternity—Thetas studied a little more, Sigmas preferred Miller to Bud, TKE was a real animal house, and DKEs were especially resentful if you didn't go along with their sexual plans.

During that week when all the roommates had hid out together (thank God that weirdness was over and she was back on track), she'd tried not seeing Bob at all. Mary said, "Why don't you just admit that he's a nice guy and go with it?"

Sherri said, "I knew ten guys in my high school that were just like him."

Keri said, "It's been a couple of months. Don't you think if you liked him, you'd know it by now?"

They hadn't seen what a crisis this was for her, because they didn't understand the seriousness of undergraduate corporate life, Diane thought. The fast track, for a girl, was more like a high wire. You had to take every step with care, and you also knew there were going to be sacrifices. In the end, though, she hadn't been able to go on not seeing him, and had decided to pursue a more creative management strategy. When he stood up from his statistics problems and came around the table to give her a kiss, she said, "Don't distract me."

His feelings were hurt. He went back to his own side of the desk. His section was two chapters behind hers. When he struggled, she sometimes helped, as a way of pulling him onto the fast track with her, but not tonight. Her plan was that when tonight he closed his books, kissed her, and headed off across the campus, he would be so wrapped up in perplexed depression that he wouldn't even raise his eyes from the contemplation of his shoes.

Yes, it was ruthless, but even aside from the fact that ruthlessness in general was a quality to be cultivated, he had brought this upon himself with his secrecy about wherever it was he went five times a day. She glanced at her watch. Ten-thirty. She focused on Rules of Apposition. Almost immediately (when you were determined to succeed, even the time reading grammar rules tended to fly), Bob stood up and pulled on his jacket. He came around the table. Diane saw that her books were sitting on his hat, so she pulled it out and handed it to him, also handing him a smile. He looked a little more depressed than she had planned, maybe a little too much on the it's-not-worth-the-grief side. She reached into his coat sleeve, which was too long because he was always forgetting gloves and hunching his fists up into his sleeves for warmth, and gave his big, muscular, and incredibly sexy hand a squeeze. She felt the squeeze in her own vis-cera—God, if he knew, if *anyone* knew, how exposed and embarrassed she would be!

"Well, good night," he said. "Are you sure you don't want me to come back and walk you to Dubuque House? I hate you walking across campus alone."

"Sherri and Keri are up on the fourth floor. We'll be okay. I'll see you tomorrow. Come over to the house for breakfast after your early class. It's Muffin Day." One place where he had her was this no sex on Sundays, Tuesdays, or Thursdays, because he hated to go to his statistics class (7:30 a.m.) in a state of exhausted tristesse (that was not what he called it). He nodded, then turned and slumped across the atrium and out of the library into the night. She had positioned them at a table by the east windows, so she watched until he rounded Lorman Hall, and she was on her feet, into her jacket, her gloves, and her own hat at once. Keri, who had been alerted earlier, had agreed to pick up her books on her way out of the library.

The campus walks were well lit, but as soon as she rounded Lorman Hall herself, Diane saw that Bob wasn't sticking to the walks. She had to stop and sweep the area for signs of him (why hadn't she surreptitiously stuck a piece of fluorescent tape across the back of his jacket? He would never have noticed), losing precious steps while she tried to pick dark movement out of the dark trees planted everywhere. There he was. She ran through the frosty grass, soaking her shoes but making up time, then halted behind a tree, gazing again. It was true that she did not feel safe, especially in these darker spots—those axe murder rumors, said her anthropology professor, were just mi-grating legends, perennials on every campus since the beginning of higher education, but they were potent all the same. It could be that she had thrown Bob into such a revery that he wouldn't even hear her dying screams—

There he was again, heading for Davis Hall, but no, he passed that one, too. She scurried to keep him in her sights. He was darling from behind—bowlegged, small-assed, broad-shouldered, his walk a little shambly and a little springy, and if Sherri knew ten like him, then what was she doing dating some of the graceless clods and squirrelly yahoos that she kept bringing back to the room like trophy heads?

He slowed, probably to look at that garden, he was a sucker for that stuff, and Diane almost got too close, but that turned out okay, too, because then, when he went beside the loading dock of that dark building behind the garden and unlocked the door and threw it open, she was just close enough that with a burst of silent speed, she could grab it before it latched and hold it while his footsteps receded down the echoing hall. She'd have bet everything in her checking account ($611.37, minus a $1.05 service charge) that he had no sense of her pursuit. She stood and held the door. As he walked away, he turned on the lights, his trail of bread crumbs. She waited. At last there was the ringing sound of a heavy metallic door, then silence. She slipped inside and let the door she had been holding latch behind her.

Pursuit had made her hungry for him, no doubt about it. Though she knew he had no idea she was following him, it still seemed that he was getting away from her, and she was having second thoughts, probably inevitable and not ones she should pay a lot of attention to, about how she treated him, how she *was*, which was often irritable and cool, withholding of her time and her patience and all promises about even the most immediate future. She knew he thought she might sever relations at any moment—without prior experience he had no way of valuing the one thing she offered freely and even gladly—sex. Her own prior experience told her that her response was right out of a male fantasy, and exactly the sort of response those TKEs, DKEs, Sigmas, and Thetas thought they were entitled to and never got. But Bob was a little afraid of it. That put her at a disadvantage. And being at a disadvantage was against her personal rules of business.

So she made her sneakers quiet on the concrete floor. Lights led her, with only two wrong turns, to a large metallic door, newer than the others in the building, and sealed all around with dark gray rubber: that would be the door. The handle turned. The sealers sucked a little as they released, and before she even had a peep inside, a strong, acrid hog smell poured out of the opening, and, in spite of herself, she said, "Yuck."

But softly. When she could see inside, she saw that Bob hadn't heard her, though the hog had. It was lying on its side, trotters toward the door, its head lifted, its eyes dark and curious, its ears perked. Bob was inside the pen, picking up straw with a pitchfork and throwing it into a wheelbarrow. Diane paused for a moment, then said, cheerily, "Well, I caught you!"

Bob whirled around.

"You refused to tell me. I don't think that was very nice."

He didn't look pleased.

"You didn't have to make such a mystery of things. Lots of people have unpleasant work-study jobs."

"How about if I talk to you later. I've got stuff to do."

Diane closed the door behind her and walked over to the pen. She said, "What's its name?"

Earl, breaking his nighttime routine of many months, heaved to his feet and moved toward the far end of the pen.

Diane said, "God, that's a big animal! How much does it weigh?"

"Almost six hundred pounds. His name is Earl. Earl Butz."

"He's really white, isn't he? I mean, really white. I thought pigs were pink or something."

"He's a Landrace. They're white. He's a very fastidious hog. Lots of times they are. Anyway, you're making him nervous. Your voice is too shrill."

That wasn't the half of it, in Earl's opinion. Lifelong solitude had made Earl an especially sensitive hog. An inborn preference for calm had blossomed, absent the hurly-burly of other porcine companions, into a decided disinclination toward any noise or disruption whatsoever. Diane carried disruption on her person. Her actions were quick and harsh, her voice was shrill, her very being was excitable. Earl was as sensitive to body language as any animal. It seemed important to him to put as much distance between himself and her as possible. And he didn't want to look at her, either. He looked at the wall in preference, and also let down a pointed stream of urine. Diane said, "Yuck," just as if an intelligent animal like Earl couldn't hear and understand her distaste. He grunted.

"See," said Bob. "He's acting very weird."

"God, he's so fat. I mean, look at the rolls!"

"You don't have to insult him."

"I don't have to insult a pig?" She laughed. That, Earl did not like at all. The most mirth he had ever heard was a deep guffaw from Dr. Bo Jones or a chuckle from Bob. He twitched his tail and grunted again.

"Hey, Diane. PLEASE go out and wait for me. You're making him nervous, and I'm annoyed that you followed me without asking.

That's probably bothering him, too. He's a valuable hog. He's my responsibility. I'll be finished in ten minutes."

"Well, I'm just leaving." She turned and walked toward the door. As she put her hand on the handle, he said, "Don't cross the campus. Just wait."

"I can't stand that protective shit!" She opened the door and let it slam behind her.

Earl turned and walked across his pen, then turned again, and walked back in the other direction. He felt in his own tissues that he didn't have the vitality to throw off this disturbance. Bob finished picking out his pen, then wheeled the barrow away, coming back with more straw. Earl stared at him. He saw that Bob gave him some extra straw. Then Bob picked up the scratching stick. But Earl didn't go over to the fence. He didn't want to. All he wanted to do was stand there staring, like a dumb animal. Besides, the shooting pains he tried so hard to avoid were starting in his forelegs. He sighed.

Bob sighed. After a few minutes, when Earl still refused to move, he stood the scratching stick against the wall, said, "Okay, Earl, I'll leave you alone." Then he turned out the light and went out. Earl stood there in the dark. It occurred to him to visit his feed trough, what he would normally do when he found himself on his feet, but for the first time in his life, he didn't feel like it.

She was sitting on the loading dock when he came out, and she wormed her hand into his as they started across the campus, but all he said between Old Meats and Dubuque House was "He really is fat, isn't he?"

Diane didn't reply. It was possible, she felt, that she had made a mistake that she was going to regret. What that felt like was a thick, seeping coldness in her limbs. But that was not what she THOUGHT. What she THOUGHT was that the exigencies of competition often required bold action, and if Bob truly understood that, then he would feel admiration rather than annoyance.

38

An Unbelievable Coincidence

MRS. LORAINE WALKER DID NOT normally eat in the commons. She preferred to bring something leftover and delicious from the previous night's meal, but there weren't always leftovers, especially if the previous night's meal had been especially delicious. Eating in the commons, she thought, was a good punishment for gluttony. You didn't have to choose the taco bar (odd-tasting tortilla shells, blackened ground meat that had been steaming for hours, orange cheese, white tomatoes) in order to regret eating there. You could regret any entrée at all.

She went through the line, speaking in a friendly way to Marly Hellmich, who didn't seem to have quit her job yet, and choosing the broccoli quiche, the scalloped potatoes, and a soft roll. There were a lot of people she knew here, another reason to avoid the place. She had found it a wise policy over the years to cultivate her personal mystery.

All of the tables were occupied, and she found that she had to join some blond woman in a corner of the nonsmoking section. The blond woman turned out to be Alison Thomas, Elaine Dobbs-Jellinek's secretary. Mrs. Walker sat down with more enthusiasm.

"Hi, Mrs. Walker," said Alison Thomas, in her what-did-I-do-wrong-now-I'm-sorry voice.

"Well, Alison!" said Mrs. Walker. "I haven't talked to you in a couple of weeks."

Alison sighed. "There's been a lot to do." She had a forkful of barbecued beef close to her mouth, but she allowed it to sink to her plate. Alison, Mrs. Walker knew, had an M.A. in linguistics from the University of Michigan. Her husband taught in the vet school, and she actually drove to work in a certified, though elderly, Mercedes. Rumor had it that these very claims to academic respectability were what goaded Elaine Dobbs-Jellinek, once a mere faculty wife herself, into the irritable, demeaning way that she treated Alison. Having not found a better job in spite of everything she had going for her must have convinced Alison that she deserved such treatment. But there was nothing Mrs. Walker could really do about it, except recognize the fact that some people didn't have the sense to come in out of the rain, and Alison was one of them. She said, "Well, that's always true this time of year. You have to be firm about what they are going to do for themselves, and, of course, realistic about what they CAN do for themselves. Sometimes they look more competent than they are. On the other hand, they like responsibility if you shift it to them gradually."

"Oh, Mrs. Walker, you have a much more organized sense of it all than I do. All I know is, she's always jumping out of her office, wanting this and wanting that. She likes to think she's just a paragon of order, but she's terribly disorganized. We're a match made in hell, frankly. And she doesn't listen. I can tell her something three times, and she'll come back to me a day later and get on me for not telling her. The thing is, and the others in the office have noticed it, too, she only really listens to men. Even when she KNOWS it's vital to listen to me or some other woman, she just can't do it." Alison sounded as close to anger as Mrs. Walker had ever heard her. Mrs. Walker came to the crust of her quiche, which hadn't been too bad—apparently they'd drained the broccoli this time before introducing it into the pie—and cut it carefully into four parts. She put the first part slowly, encouragingly, into her mouth. Alison watched her, then, encouraged, went on. "And she's obsessed with Jack Parker. Every day she comes flying out of her office asking where Jack Parker is, is he in Washington again, are they putting him up at the Hay-Adams again, why don't they put him up at the Ramada? That's where they put her up!" She sighed. "Now there's this lost document. She had it last night, and she put it in her briefcase. I said to her right then, 'Let me Xerox that before you take it home,' because, you know, her house is worse than her office, things stacked on chairs and the floor. I've had to actually go over there and find things for her, and they're always mixed in with underwear and slips and stockings and stuff. And let me tell you, that kid of hers is neat as a pin. I don't know where he gets it." Mrs. Walker shook her head in the soberest manner, even though inwardly she was laughing.

"So, of course when she got to the office this morning and looked in her briefcase, the document wasn't there, she didn't remember taking it home, and she didn't remember me offering to Xerox it, and when I told her the exact sequence of events, her eyes sort of glazed over. I could tell she wasn't listening to me at all, she was just waiting to find out whether Jack Parker was on the campus and then to tell me to look through all the file drawers, because that must be where it is, so I had to put aside all my other work and go through all the file drawers. Oh, she is imPOSSible!"

"I've been telling you for a year to apply for another office."

"She's not going to give me a good reference. And she filed a bad report on me last winter. AND we both know not every office gets to have someone at my salary level. With these cutbacks, it'll be fewer still. I did call. But Personnel said there just weren't any openings."

Mrs. Walker tried an idle tone. "What sort of document was it?"

"Oh, something from Dr. Gift, in Econ. They've got their heads together."

"Why don't you just call Sophie over in Econ and have her print out another one?"

"It's not on the computer. I tried that. Sophie hadn't ever heard of it."

"That's odd. He's one of the worst for dumping work on the secretaries over there. He's got a permanent request in our office for his own personal secretary. I might authorize it the day before he retires." Mrs. Walker smiled.

"It's some kind of grant report or consulting thing. If it's coming through our office, it must have to do with this grant he's got from Horizontal Technologies." She sniffed. "It's not that big a grant. The university's share was twenty-five thousand. SHE acts like it was ten times that much."

"Horizontal Technologies?"

"Isn't that a funny name? That's why it stuck in my mind."

It had stuck in Mrs. Walker's mind, too. Horizontal Technologies, she knew from her investigation of databases, was one of Trans-National's holding companies—no business, no assets, only a board of directors. She sat calmly at the table, scraping up the last of the atomic yellow sauce from her scalloped potatoes. Finally, she said, "Did she ever find it?"

"Well, what do you think? Of course not. She's got it at home. It's probably under the bed, with all that old popcorn, those apple cores and candy wrappers and wadded up Kleenexes." They looked at each other and laughed.

This, Mrs. Walker knew, was the document she was looking for. Briefly she imagined herself and Martha heisting this document from

Elaine Dobbs-Jellinek's house or, possibly, from Lionel Gift's house—the secrecy, the excitement. Instead she looked Alison Thomas right in the eye and said, "If you send me a copy of that document, I will find you a job in another office."

"Can you do that?"

Mrs. Walker looked at her.

"What if she can't find it? It's just for the file drawer. She wasn't going to do anything with it. Usually she only exerts herself to find things if her butt is on the line in a meeting or something."

While Mrs. Walker considered it demeaning to address these particular mealymouthed fears on Alison's part, she did say, "If I find you a job in another office, Alison, you have to take charge right away. The worst thing you can do is allow them to develop some habitual way of thinking about you that undercuts your authority. This is your test. If you can find a way to take charge of this one situation, then you will have demonstrated that you can handle another position."

"I can see that."

There was a juncture in every enterprise that Mrs. Walker savored. It was that moment when the success or failure of her plan seemed to move out of her control into the much more tenuous grip of someone else, like Alison, like Ivar. For some duration of time, her plan teetered upon the commitment, the competence, or the honesty of another person. This moment, these moments, always exhilarated her, and not only because, most of the time, she had judged correctly, asserted herself tactfully, and would know success. Another sort of exhilaration—a ghostly reminiscence of her elopement with Mr. Walker when she was seventeen and he was nineteen—came from the risk itself. She would never again live her personal life according to such an unreliable breeze, but there was a little more play in her life at the office.

Across the room, she saw Just Plain Brown carrying his tray and looking for a table. He had a glass of milk, a humble brown bag, and his everlasting smile. As if by magic, three students stood up and vacated a table. Just Plain Brown set down his tray.

Alison said, "I'll see."

"Good," said Mrs. Walker. She looked at her watch.

"At least she's got a meeting until three."

They walked companionably out of the commons.

39

Off Campus

UNFORTUNATELY FOR Chairman X, the autumn work of mulching
beds, taking up bulbs, pruning, composting, harvesting, and sorting
and preserving seeds, scions, grafts, rootstocks, forbs, and all the other
natural and unnatural reproductive material of the plants he was in
charge of was pretty much over, and teaching classes and tending to
administrative work left him plenty of time to contemplate the end
of Communism in Europe. To his own disadvantage, in this case, he
had trained his group (department, constituency, cell) to work with
such revolutionary enthusiasm that they did everything with dispatch.
The enemy was across the campus, in Agronomy, the war was played
out in terms of row planting vs. bed planting, monoculture vs. polyculture, mechanical cultivation vs. human cultivation, fertilizer vs.
compost, feed crops vs. food crops, and a thousand other antitheses,
and the horticulturalists really believed that gardening would save the
world that agriculture was destroying. "How do you think everyone
was employed for thousands of years?" he would rage. "In growing
food and fiber! Is idleness on the streets actually BETTER?" They
loved his lecture on how agriculture actually promoted starvation
by first promoting overpopulation. They would surge out of the
classroom, electrified by the passionate vision of agriculture as a
catastrophic historical mistake—he could produce fifty new revolu-
tionaries every semester without any classroom preparation.

For years that had been enough for him. Well, almost enough. But
now, every day, after reading *The New York Times* and the Chicago
Tribune, after watching CNN on a little TV he had brought to the
office, after thumbing through *The Nation* and *The Progressive*, he sat
staring out his window, tapping a pencil on his desk, and mulling
over the triumph of consumerism, selfishness, technology, leisure,
meat eating, localism, competitiveness, and appetite. In the exhilaration on every face in every picture or videotape from Eastern Europe,
he saw the self-defeat of Communism, and even though he'd disagreed
with forced collectivization of the peasantry and had worried about

the Cultural Revolution and had, in general, been filled with doubts about all sorts of specific policies for years, he couldn't help sighing at the departure of certain ideals—work, rationality, cooperation, brotherhood, altruism.

Those who saw the world as inherently cruel, and didn't mind it, who saw people as inherently materialistic, and didn't object, who saw capitalism as natural, and shrugged off the inherent inhumanity of it, had won. And they were thrilled to have won, as if cruelty, materialism, and inhumanity were benefits. Well, maybe they were. In Chairman X's experience, most of the self-doubt was on his side, almost none on theirs. That was true in this case as in all others. He sat back until his chair creaked, stretched his neck to one side, then the other, and went back to tapping his pencil on the desk.

IN HIS OWN HOME, though unbeknownst to him, his life's companion and the mother of his children was herself feeling the pall of twenty years of Marxism lift, and she was feeling it with almost the same exhilaration as the people on TV. It was true that for years they hadn't hung the four-foot-by-four-foot silk tapestry of Karl Marx that Chairman X had ordered from China; it was true that the Chairman hadn't voted for Gus Hall since 1972; it was true that their subscription to *Challenge* had run out in 1971, and all issues had gone out in some cleaning frenzy around the time the eldest was born; it was true that their early habit of Left-speak—"a worker student alliance," "a good struggle relationship"—had fallen by the wayside. Steady employment, the birth of the eldest, the purchase thereafter of their own washing machine and dryer (from Sears, on credit) had raised them almost without their own efforts into the middle class.

But over the years he had greeted every purchase she proposed— a NEW car, a food processor, an attractive winter coat, a microwave oven, a VCR, an automatic garage door opener, air conditioning in the house—with a look of deep betrayal and hurt. "Fine, if you really want it," he would say, but she knew he was thinking something else, thinking that these desires showed how shallow she was, how weak; she knew he was wondering if it was inherently feminine to want things, to live one's ideals in such a wishy-washy way. Couldn't the money go to better causes? For everything that they would *like*, there were a hundred things that other people *needed*, he reminded her.

Now she could look at the people on TV, at their wild happiness, and say, "Nobody *likes* drabness! People like to feel some money in their pockets, and to have the power to choose! A little desire isn't equivalent to greed! Beautiful objects grow out of the love of craft as well as the exploited slavery of the workers." At least, she said it to herself. Chairman X was so depressed lately that she didn't have the heart to say it to him.

HAVING READ Milan Kundera and Václav Havel and Witold Gombrowicz and seen the films of Andrzej Wajda, Timothy Monahan could claim that he was hardly surprised at the fall of European Communism. In fact, when people shook their heads and said, "Isn't it amazing?" he shrugged and replied "No" with a startling (he thought) and rather knowing air. Socialist realism had never been a popular or expressive art form, and really, you had to look no further for an answer than that.

What surprised him, on the night they had their final argument, was Cecelia's attitude.

It was almost Thanksgiving vacation, and Tim was leaving in two days for the East Coast, where his agent had set up a meeting with the editor at Little, Brown. The editor, she said, might or might not. He wanted to sound Tim out on the changes he thought the book needed, which might be, probably were, certainly were pretty drastic. "I don't know" was what Tim said to his agent, but "almost anything" was what he said to himself, albeit with a familiar feeling of shame.

He took Cecelia to Drake's, his favorite bar, and the only nonstudent bar in town that didn't have a theme, the only one whose decor had simply accumulated over the years instead of being designed at corporate headquarters to evoke some brand of alcoholic nostalgia.

Their conversation had moved crabbily from one topic to another. Her classes were not going well; the semester was too long here; she couldn't get warm; the pipes in her duplex banged all night long. He wanted to know who she was seeing, but they didn't seem to be good enough friends anymore for him to ask. They fell silent, but that got uncomfortable. She said, apparently annoyed, "Those people in eastern Europe are in for a big surprise. They should send a fact-finding mission to L.A. before they do anything drastic. That's what I think."

"Well," said Tim, in his usual way, "I'm not surprised at what's happening. If you read Kundera, it's easy to see what sort of profound alienation—"

"Why is your tone always so cold? It's like you've put all of this in a box already, and you don't even care."

Tim looked around, then said, "What?"

"That really annoys me about you."

"What does?"

"Well, you'd think a writer would have uncontrollable passions, or would be seized by events or feelings or *something*."

It was clear that she was comparing him to someone, probably the unknown lover. He said, "I don't happen to be seized by this, is all. I can't make myself surprised if I'm not. Besides, that's a very romantic view of writers." He smiled, trying a little joke. "I specialize in irony, anyway."

"Well, I think it's very detached. No wonder you're always so depressed. If you can't get excited about this, one way or another, then I think you need medical help."

Tim sensed that his jaw had dropped, and consciously closed it around the rim of his glass. His beer had warmed. He caught the eye of the bartender and signalled for another. Then he said, "You think I need medical help because I've read a lot of Eastern European litera- ture and seen a lot of films and I'm not surprised that the alienation from the political system they uniformly express has finally emerged?"

"You make me sound ridiculous, but it's all a part of one thing."

"What thing?"

"How cold your writings are, how cold you are, the way you talk about your career and the way you contain it all with some funny remarks. You're a nice person, but look at your life. There's nobody in it, you're not excited about anything." Her voice was rising.

Tim's first impulse was not to be offended, but to be surprised. He said, "Why in the world do you care?"

She just looked at him. Tim had a feeling that she knew what she wanted to answer, but she didn't dare. After that, though, the feeling of offense hit him all of a sudden, as if in the back of the head. He felt his face heat up suddenly, and redden with anger. He said, "I think I'd better take you home."

"Me, too."

He dropped her in front of her duplex and drove off without waiting to see whether she got in okay.

The irony was that two nights later, when he saw they were running

Doctor Zhivago on Cinemax, and watched it just because there was nothing else on, he did start to cry. He did feel the breathless clamping down of the Communists; he did find the ever-renewed hopes of the characters pointless and sad; he did regret the three generations and more that would be lost to a failed experiment; he was moved in a new way, as he had never been moved by the film when the system was firmly in place.

The further irony was that on the plane, in the office of his agent, across the table at the City Cafe from the Little, Brown editor, he could summon up even less feeling for his own little book, less feeling, in fact, than the editor, who was surprisingly enthusiastic and whose idea of "drastic" was scandalously respectful. Tim agreed to the changes without any sense of self-betrayal. Was that the final irony, and the final proof of everything Cecelia had said?

No, the final irony was when the editor said, "Well, I think we have a deal. I'll mention some numbers to your agent," Tim thought, Well, that's nice.

WHAT INTERESTED Loren Stroop about the fall of Communism in Europe were the pictures they had once in a while of farmers in their fields, with their hoes and shovels and half-broken wheelbarrows. Few of Loren's new companions at the rehab facility showed even that much curiosity. He would sit with them in the lounge, one of a semicircle of damaged people in chairs and wheelchairs drawn up around the screaming television, and sometimes he would look at them instead of the television, slumped down in their seats in spite of the straps, many of their faces (like his, he knew) oddly skewed by their "brain attacks," and almost all of them much farther down in the percentile rankings than he was. That woman was there, the one his doctor had always talked about, but young as she was, she never appeared in the lounge, she wasn't up to even that. If it hadn't been for his plans about revolutionizing American agriculture, Loren would have regretted how the chips had fallen, him so old, and with so much potential. Her so young, with kids and everything, and without much of a future at all.

On the television was Eastern Europe, especially since Loren himself was mobile enough to change the channel and nobody else seemed to care. He used to like those quiz shows, "Wheel of Fortune" and them, but no more. Now he sat willingly through the business reports and the "Hollywood Minutes" and the sports updates, just waiting for a glimpse, not of buildings or happy faces, but of fields, animals, and machines. He didn't mind what sort of machines—cars, factory equipment, levers, pulleys, wedges, tractors. It was like looking far far into his youth, when he himself had been surrounded by such machines, before everything was sleek and painted bright colors. Looking at the machines was how he understood how old he was. He actually was eighty now, seven years older than the Soviet Union, thirty-five years older than the Eastern European Communism that was falling apart to such fanfare. He was old, old, old. When he was discouraged, it seemed like he was too old, no matter what, to revolutionize American agriculture. But when those machines came on the screen, those farmers who farmed with shovels and hoes, it seemed like they were calling out to him, telling him that his real destiny, if only he could find his tongue, was to revolutionize world agriculture, and that the CIA and the FBI and the big ag companies would never stop him, and he opened his mouth and spoke back to those people, trying with all his might to mold his mooing into words, until the nurses came and begged him to be quiet.

ONE THING Dr. Bo Jones knew about hogs was that the chances of their still living as their ancestors had lived were far greater in Asia, and even in places like Hungary, than they were anywhere in the West. Therefore he was more excited about the fall of European Communism than he had been about anything in years. He wrote letters to every conceivable ministry in Russia and Eastern Europe and Washington, begging for visas, begging for permissions, begging for information. Decades seemed to fall away, and he was thirty years old again, planning treks into a wilderness that part of him knew was as vanished as his youth. But only part of him. Every letter he wrote evoked scenes in his own mind that were irresistible—a native companion, some dogs, the glimpse of a boar flashing through the underbrush—a lean boar, black, bristly, fast, and mean. Upthrusting tusks, rippling shoulders, as ugly as a hog should be. And then there was himself pressing onward—no shortage of breath, no aching in the joints, no fatigue, the native companion barely able to keep up. Every letter he wrote convinced him that these possibilities had not been lost, that history hadn't actually claimed his youth and strength, or the habitats of the boars and sows. Even as he typed Earl's statistics into his computer, he was beginning to lose interest in the experiment, and he found less and less reason to go over there, lean on the fence, and dote. Of course, the hog was in good hands with that Bob fellow—Dr. Bo had no qualms on that score. Really, it was marvelous that politics had moved aside just at this moment, almost a miracle, really, almost divine intervention. Dr. Bo Jones licked his lips and started another letter, this one to Cabela's, ordering some gear—and that would be something, too, to bring back a trophy boar from central Asia. The boar would be stuffed just as its head lowered and its eyes focused on the quarry and all its fury flowed forth, and the little plaque would say, "Donated by Dr. Bo Jones."

DR. CATES WASN'T nearly as interested in the fall of Eastern European Communism as his wife was. What she did was, she sat there in front of the news, and she nodded and said, "Ah. Ah. Ah." Or she shook her head over the newspaper and made a sound in the back of her throat that her mother and sisters back in Ghana made when they were deploring something.

Cates himself didn't really see what there was to deplore. Although you probably couldn't rely 100 percent on their findings, there would soon be new scientific hypotheses and theories to consider that had been secret for many years. New minds would come into the field, with new perspectives and maybe even some new methods. That could only be to the good. Dr. Cates didn't see how science could fail to benefit from the fall of Eastern European Communism, but his wife kept nodding and shaking her head and making little noises and deploring.

Finally, one night after their son had gone to bed, and they were sitting in front of the late news, he said, "What's wrong with this? We won. We're closer to peace than ever before in my lifetime."

"Is that so?"

"Well, yeah."

She smiled.

"Why not?"

She shrugged.

"You've been muttering about this for weeks."

"Well, now, you see, John, all the tribes will get themselves stirred up now."

"What tribes? You mean in West Africa?"

She shook her head, gestured toward the screen. "Those Czechs," she said. "Those Slovaks. Now they can fight. Now they can turn to their neighbors they've been living beside for years and say, 'I want what you have. I want you out of here.' "

"Why should they do that?"

She threw her head back and laughed out loud. She said, "Because they are people. People are all the same. You give them a little of what they want, and then all they do is want, and all they see, they want. And some of them, who don't have much to do, they want to fight, just to fight, so they bring everything else into the fighting."

"Well, maybe."

She laughed again. She said, "You white people"—Cates shifted in his chair; he knew she meant, You Americans, but he didn't correct her—"are the only people in the world who are surprised when people are people."

40

Dissemination

THE BOX that said "UARCO Trimedge@" sat next to Mrs. Loraine Walker's desk for two days after it came up from the copy center, a bit of disorder that the other women in the office knew Mrs. Walker wouldn't tolerate from them or from Ivar. It therefore aroused curiosity, but it took Mrs. Walker's colleagues a while to overcome their respect for her privacy and ask what was in it.

She was surprisingly forthcoming. She opened the box right away, saying, "Oh, you might be interested in this. I thought it was quite something." She handed a copy to anyone who asked, suggested only that when they had finished with it, they hand it on to someone else who might be interested.

Otherwise, she spent a fair amount of time on the phone with Patty Malone in Personnel, arranging Alison Thomas' transfer from the development office to another part of the campus. In this she was more prudent than Alison herself. Whereas Alison said, "Anywhere," Mrs. Walker said to Patty, "As far as possible from Elaine Dobbs-Jellinek's chain of command, preferably with someone predisposed against her."

"How about the horse barns?" said Patty.

Mrs. Walker felt that she herself had served as Alison's inspiration, and took some pride in the way Alison had marched into Elaine Dobbs-Jellinek's office and said, "Pardon me, but I've had it." When Elaine, startled and offended, looked up, Alison had smacked her hand on the desk and said, "My files are a mess. Every drawer has a substantial number of folders missing part or all of their contents." She raised her voice authoritatively. "We can't work like this. You have to go home right now and find everything that's been lost in your house and bring it back to the office."

"I have a meeting—"

"I cancelled it. You have three hours. I will keep cancelling things until you do this."

"Now just a minute—"

"Fine." Alison Thomas turned on her heel and started out of the office.

"Well. Well, all right. I suppose it's about time." And Elaine Dobbs–Jellinek put on her cashmere coat and her alpaca scarf and went out. Two hours later, she returned, saying, "Someone's going to have to help me carry this stuff from the car."

Alison continued to sit in her seat, continued to work at her computer. Without even glancing up, she said, "There's a dolly in that closet."

She found the report for Mrs. Walker an hour later, far down in the mess, held together with a bobby pin and smudged with what looked like foundation. She carried it over to Lafayette Hall herself.

Well, it was a good story, thought Mrs. Walker, and a good omen for Alison's future, but when the report got out, and a stir was created, no amount of personal power would protect Alison Thomas from Elaine Dobbs-Jellinek. She herself was not wholly safe. Truth to tell, it was one of those moments. Invigorating. She shook herself energetically, and said to Patty, "Where is that man now, the one who's been so much trouble, what's his name, Bartle? William Bartle?"

"The one who won't do anything?"

"Yes."

"He's in Fred Raymond's office."

Fred Raymond was the university lawyer. Mrs. Walker said, "They've put up with him long enough. Why don't you switch them?"

"I'll see. He might prefer not to move."

"Do what you can."

"Oh, I will."

Meanwhile, Mrs. Walker left a copy of the report on Ivar's desk, right where he couldn't miss it. But so far, he hadn't said anything about it.

Martha, though, had plenty to say. The first thing she said, after reading the very first page and then holding the report away from her and turning it over the way you would turn over a piece of tainted fish, was "Who is this guy?"

"He's an economist. Quite famous, actually. He's won two teaching awards and he's the highest–paid faculty member. He goes to Washington all the time."

Martha read on.

After a few minutes, she said, "But he's promoting digging some gold mine under the largest remaining virgin forest in Central America."

"I saw that."

Martha read on.

She said, "This is crazy."

She said, "I've never heard of anything like this."

She said, "What is he thinking of?"

She said, "Listen to this, 'While gold mining is admittedly stressful to the environment in a number of ways, it is the opinion of this writer that environmental impact assessments will show that it should take a hundred years or less for the area in question to recover from the necessary impacts of mining, especially if the historically disruptive migrations of peoples to areas where gold has been discovered are prevented by adequate security. While such security precautions may be out of the financial reach of the Costa Rican government at this point, there are alternative avenues for meeting this expense, possibly through public moneys raised in the U.S. as a result of lobbying Congress to prevent the dissolution of Seven Stones Mining, which employs a substantial number of people in areas already economically depressed. Such a lobbying effort on the part of Chrysler Motors had a very favorable result in————.' My God!"

Martha read on.

She said, "This guy goes on the assassination list."

Mrs. Walker said, "It isn't his idea. It's Arlen Martin's idea. Gift is just fleshing it out for him."

Martha read on.

She said, "I can't read any more. It's giving me a stroke."

Mrs. Walker took the report out of her hands. She turned to the last page. She said, "Well, just listen to this. 'Gold, even more than petroleum, holds a hallowed place in the human psyche. It is both useful and beautiful. It could perhaps be said that the search for new sources of this precious life substance has fueled human history and the rise of civilization itself. As the old sources are played out, few new ones have been found. Does this eventuality define the end of human civilization, perhaps the end of human history? While such speculations may seem far-fetched at this point, it is well to weigh in the balance the meaning of this ever-precious, ever-vanishing source of human wealth against the readily renewable, not to say relentlessly burgeoning, natural abundance of the forest.

" 'One could also speculate that now that gold has been found in the forest, the SAFEST thing to do is to remove it with the best possible methods, thus forestalling future uncontrolled depredations. It would perhaps have been better that the gold deposits had not been found, but now that they have, it is the opinion of this writer that the findings are best acted upon.' "

Martha fell back on the couch.

"And listen to this," said Loraine. "I called a guy in the geology department, and said, 'What's the latest, most state-of-the-art way of extracting gold from ore?' and he said, 'There is no state-of-the-art way. You dig it out, crush it to powder, treat it chemically so that the invisible flecks of gold concentrate into a solution and run out of the ore, then you neutralize the solvent. Of course, a fraction of the solvent always escapes. That can be a problem.' And I said, 'Why?' and he said, 'Well, you know, the solvent is a cyanide compound. You don't want that to get in the groundwater, but of course it does. And then there are these enormous mounds of powdered ore, because the high-est-grade ore still only carries one ounce of gold per one ton of ore. Then the ore oxidizes and sulfur compounds dissolve into sulfuric acid, and THAT runs into the groundwater. Very problematic.' "

"Lord, I guess."

"I said, 'What would be state-of-the-art?' and he said, 'Well, maybe to stuff that powdered ore back down the mine shaft to keep it from collapsing. Some states require that. That's why a lot of mining com-panies are moving to the Third World. They don't have to adhere to so many environmental regulations.' "

"What did you say?"

"I said, 'I'm sending you a document through campus mail that I think you'll find very interesting.' "

Martha smiled. Alone of all their acquaintances, she found Loraine hilarious.

The next day, Mrs. Walker called Ivar into her office when the rest of the staff was on break, and she said, "Did you read that document I gave you?"

"Mrs. Walker, I am not going to ask you how you came to have that document."

"But did you read it?"

"I did."

"It is my personal opinion that something should be done about the contents of that document."

"Dr. Gift was consulted as to his views on the project. If those are his views, then there's nothing the university can do about them."

They looked at each other. Ivar saw Mrs. Walker's face settle into her most disapproving and impenetrable Menominee visage, and he wondered if she would actually quit over a matter of extremely, in his view, abstract principle. It made him nervous. Mrs. Walker saw Ivar's countenance turn pale and stubborn, a mask of apparent bland-ness that deflected her most resolute determination. Simultaneously, they said, "Academic freedom." Ivar then said, "Well, yes. It would be very dangerous for the university to act. Or," he pressed on, in the teeth of his growing nervousness, "for anyone in this office to act. No one in this office acts solely in his or her own behalf, but always as a representative of this office." Now he could barely utter the words, but he forced out, "I do hope you understand that, Mrs. Walker."

She didn't say anything.

He knew she understood.

He also knew that wouldn't necessarily make any difference.

He should have taken control years ago.

She had her hands on the keys of her, their, computer. He would never have control now. He went back into his office and sat down in the desk chair.

As the door to his office closed, the door to the hallway opened, and Just Plain Brown glided in on a smear of eternal congeniality. "Ah, Mrs. Walker," he said. "Just who I'm looking for!" He glanced down at the "UARCO Trimedge@" box with evident delight. "Here they are! May I?"

He bent down just a fraction of a second before she nodded, and lifted up one of the reports with apparent reverence. Their eyes met. He leaned over the desk, turning the full force of his good will upon her, and said, "Thank you for this!" A second later he was gone.

In his office, reading reports from the promotion and tenure com-mittee, Ivar noticed when Mrs. Walker's extension lit up. Very care-fully, he picked up the receiver. She was saying, "Hello, Dorothy. This is Mrs. Walker. Would you transfer me to Professor Levy, please?" Moments later, Helen's warm, loved tones announced, "This is Helen Levy, hello?" Ivar carefully replaced the phone, and smiled.

41

Harvest Home

THANKSGIVING WAS Helen's favorite holiday, and for at least five years Nils and Ivar had spent Thanksgiving with her, along with an assortment of lonely, overworked, or impecunious faculty members who she happened to run across in the course of the fall. She tried to seat twelve or fourteen. This year, however, the lonely, overworked, and impecunious were out of luck, and she was preparing a rather small dinner for Ivar, Nils, Marly, and Father.

Small didn't mean that she couldn't go all out, but it did mean that most of her kitchen equipment, from her Bosch food processor to her Calphalon turkey roaster to her Viking oven, was just too big. The ingredients she measured out seemed to sit in little puddles at the bottom of large vessels, and there were things she would never use again that she actually had to go out and buy—an eight-inch pie plate, a three-quart casserole.

Ah, but her yard, her root cellar, and her freezer were abundant with provisions.

For Thanksgiving, Helen liked to pursue a western hemispherical theme. Banished from the table were some of the Italian and French flavors she loved—truffles and tarragon and crusty bread, lamb and pork roast, olive oil, lemons, oranges with cloves, pears poached in wine—but for Christmas, she always put on a large buffet with an Old World, semi-Mediterranean theme.

Everything about the preparations pleased her—the setting out of ingredients, the measuring and mixing, the trips to the root cellar and the freezer, the view out the window of her frosted garden under its winter mulch and all of chill nature alive in the wind, the darkness that because of thick November clouds never really lifted. Around her, in the kitchen, the bowls and pans glowed and auspicious fragrances rose and mingled. Dinner was scheduled late, at six-thirty, so that Helen could savor as much of the day as possible.

At noon, just as she was setting the cranberry mousse in the refrigerator to cool, Ivar showed up, and he followed her around the kitchen with a spoon, tasting a bit of everything. "Mmmm," he said, "Mmmm," in a reflective way that showed he would have said the same thing if she weren't in the room. After he had savored all, he sighed and said, "Mind if I watch a little of the football game over here?"

"Of course not."

"Did you hear from Tia?"

Tia Mathilde was Helen's twenty-six-year-old daughter with her former husband. She was an archaeologist working in Greece. "She called. She's spending the day with an American couple in Delphi."

"Good. I should have stopped for a six-pack of beer."

"You left two Heinekens in the refrigerator."

"That's a bonus." He put his arm around her and pulled her solidly to him. She had pinned up her hair, but it was coming down, and she smelled spicy and delicious. She had a big French vegetable knife in one hand and a head of garlic in the other. He kissed her hungrily on the lips and let his hand drop to her large, firm buttocks, which he could feel in delightful detail through her silk slacks and her silk underwear. All the silk she wore was another thing he liked about her. Really, in fact, there was nothing about her that he didn't like, including the innate independence that prevented him from ever approaching the marriage question, even the living-together question. Where would they live? He was a welcome guest in this world, but always a guest. It reminded him of the old saying "Take nothing but photographs, leave nothing but footprints." He sighed.

"Nils?"

"Oh, I suppose."

"Frankly, Ivar, I don't think it's going to work out the way he thinks it is." She said this mildly.

"Well, since his heart is set on the marriage, one'll be as bad as the other."

"For him, maybe, but not necessarily for you." She said this even more mildly. She always tried to uphold the fiction that Ivar and Nils really were two separate individuals, since she didn't know, even now, how deeply the identification between them ran. Nils had always resisted any closeness to her, and that had been fine with her, since some instinct made her distrust him—his very good will and desire to do the right thing at all times seemed dangerous. He was a classic example of aggressive beneficence, which meant, in her opinion, that he often interfered when he might have more productively left things, or people, alone. And she had been around when he found religion and gave up all doubts (to be honest, he had had few enough to give up). She had, in fact, once known his Ceylonese wife, who had always seemed to be carrying the doubt load, who had, in fact, died of doubt. Her appendix burst because she doubted whether it was important enough to bother either Nils or the hospital emergency room about the severe pain in her side. Nils (this was when Helen was still married and didn't care one way or the other, really) had hardly seemed to grieve, the woman seemed for him just another Third World development project that didn't work out owing to the inherent frailty of the native stock. Not caring for Nils was just like not caring for your best friend's husband—Helen was careful never to criticize Nils, never even to listen to Ivar's occasional complaints with a sympathetic ear. When pressed, she defended Nils. That seemed to be fine with Ivar.

She began to feel a kind of fleshly eagerness for Ivar to leave her kitchen domain, and stepped out of his embrace. She turned and brought the handle of the knife down sharply on the head of garlic. It fell apart into cloves. "Would you like a sandwich?" she said.

"No, not right now." He slapped her gently on the buttocks and strode into the living room invigorated. When he turned on the TV, the football game was just beginning. His beer opened with a satisfyingly effervescent crack. He settled into one of Helen's leather recliners. It was easy, when he was with her, just to sink into the present moment, the physical moment. When he was not with her, it was nearly impossible.

As soon as they walked into Helen's house, Marly could tell that Father was offended. She could see his eyes flick from chair to painting to flower arrangement to oriental rug and stamp each, "Worldly pride, worldly pride, worldly pride, worldly pride." Almost immediately, he sat down in the plain wooden chair beside the front door and reached into his pocket for his worn Bible. Marly said, "Please don't embarrass me," but he just let the Book flop open and then began moving his lips. She said, "I know you can read without moving your lips, so please stop making this fuss." He didn't look at her.

Nils walked right in, past Father as if he weren't there. This seemed to be Nils' strategy for dealing with Father, and Marly rather admired it, or at least envied it. She herself thought the house was beautiful.

That didn't mean that it didn't make her mad. Almost everything did, these days, starting with Father, going directly to Nils, and then expanding outward to encompass family, church, work, her car, the weather, passersby, everything on television, including the Christian Broadcasting Network, and nearly every encounter that involved the smallest amount of money. It was as if, for the past decade, she had been storing her anger rather than, as she thought, disposing of it, and now the storage tank had sprung a leak and turning away with a soft answer just didn't cut it anymore.

The beautiful house made her mad because she hadn't ever been anywhere like it before, hadn't even imagined that houses like this existed. It was not ornate and enormous and movie-like, the sort of house anyone could buy with enough money, it was the sort of house that you loved to be in, but could never have or reproduce, unless you were Helen herself, and since you would never be Helen herself, you were cut off forever from inhabiting this house, and from feeling, moment to moment, the pleasures of these colors and shapes and aromas. She said to Father, "Oh, for goodness' sake. Get up and be polite." He threw her a warning look, but he got up and moved to an unpleasantly comfortable sofa near the fireplace.

She sat next to him, entertaining herself with the idea, which of course she would never act upon, of pinching him hard in the leg the first time he annoyed her. She stared across the room out the big back windows overlooking Helen's yard.

Except that it was hardly what you would call a yard. The thick hedge enclosed a deep double lot. To the left, the black leafless limbs of neatly pruned fruit trees twisted in a sort of Japanese-type sculpture, like those little bitty trees in dishes, only full-size. To the right was the garden, but it wasn't square like most people's—it ran here and there in curves. Right now it looked from the house like a big mound of leaves and dead grass. In the middle of it was a little screened building, and she could also see, near the building, a little bridge. In back of the garden and the fruit trees was a wilder-seeming spot, with some dark evergreens and the white trunks of birches curving gracefully against them. This was not a yard with some tomato plants and a deck like most people had, it was an outdoor extension of the house, as if the house represented the world that people made, and the yard represented the world of nature, and with windows and doors and terra-cotta patios and paths and stepping-stones, you could easily move between them.

Which Marly knew you could not, or, at least, you should not. It was better for your soul to see the world of plants and animals as a hard, thoughtless place, and the man-made world as seductive but empty. She knew that.

The reason that it was harder for a rich person to get to heaven than for a camel to squeeze through the eye of a needle was simple— even the most well-meaning and guiltless rich person gave in every day to the temptation of creating his or her own world in his or her own image, and then, of course, came to love that very mingling of shapes, colors, textures, tastes, aromas, musical sounds. A careful soul had to prefer a drier, harder life, one more or less impossible to love. The trouble was, Marly was not sure she did prefer what it was prudent to prefer.

Helen invited them to the table. She had Ivar sit at the head, which Nils noticed, but which did not actually OFFEND him. She put Father at her right hand, and Nils and Marly across from each other. Nils strongly approved of Marly's behavior on this occasion. She was soberly dressed, a little alienated, he thought, from Helen's house, which he had always considered to be overdone. She was respectful of her father, about which, lately, Nils had found her a little lax. She was pleasant toward himself, but not talkative. He liked that. One of the ways Helen and Ivar had sometimes made him uncomfortable was how they would sit with their heads together, and you could see Helen doing most of the talking, and Ivar just nodding. That arrangement was cockeyed, Nils thought, and just the opposite of the way it had been with their parents, and the way it ought to be, period. Now that he was close to getting married, he had a lot of thoughts about the way things should be, and he had started writing them down in a little notebook.

A feast, Nils thought, was a good occasion to make some important announcements, and after dessert, he was going to make some. There would be some surprised faces around the table, no doubt about that. But a surprise attack was the best kind. You got your way while they were scrambling around trying to figure out how to react. Father, Ivar, Marly: throw 'em off balance now, Nils thought, and none of them would get (or manage to keep, in Ivar's case) the upper hand. As the courses were served, Nils could barely taste them for the anticipation he felt.

Now this food, thought Father, was mighty strange. First there was some tomato soup, but it was cold and had green stuff floating in it. Then there were the sweet potatoes, but they turned out to be regular mashed potatoes, even though they were yellow. The beans he recognized, but then beans gave him gas, so he didn't have any. The turkey, which he thought he could rely on, was too rich-tasting, and the stuffing burned his mouth—it had chili peppers in it, who'd ever heard of that? Then instead of a nice cool cylinder of jellied cranberry sauce sliced into disks, there was some kind of cranberry junket. Then there was blackberry sherbet—that was okay—but after that there were two more desserts, pumpkin pie, but with a strange cornmeal crust, and chocolate cake, but with cranberries in that, too. Frankly, there was hardly a bite of food at this table that Father recognized, and he knew that he was going to get up hungry. Even so, he minded his manners and kept his mouth shut, and every time this woman who'd made the food looked at him, he smiled. He wasn't blind. He knew the pale one who wasn't marrying his daughter—good thing they didn't dress alike, or he'd never tell them apart, every time they were all together, he had to ask Marly what Nils was wearing, and then memorize it—was fornicating with this woman, and he wasn't surprised.

Fornication never surprised him, he had fornicated himself before truly accepting Jesus, and he had drunk intoxicating liquors, and he had laid blows upon some of his fellow men—he was a man, wasn't he? You couldn't be a man without knowing what a man was. Fornicating late in life surprised him a little, though. He always thought that fornicating was something you got through on the way to other, better things. But look at King David, a good man whose mind was set on fornicating. Father knew he wouldn't be thinking about all of this if the food had been regular food—and then his son-in-law-to-be sat back in his chair and said he was going to say some things, so Father took his mind off King David and fornicating, and all the rest of it; afterward he always said he knew something was coming.

Marly herself liked the food, and tried not to show how unusual it was to her. What she didn't like was the way Father grunted and snorted at everything, and every time Helen spoke to him, he leered at her like he was thinking about fornication—it was a good thing Helen didn't know him as well as Marly did, and couldn't read his mind the way Marly could. And then Nils cleared his throat in that way he had, and Marly knew that what he was about to say was important, and also that it was just for her, so she licked up the last bite of her pumpkin pie with some regret, and looked up at him.

Helen was passing the coffee around, a nice Colombian blend that she thought they would like, when Nils cleared his throat and said, "Well, this has been a lovely dinner, thank you, Helen, for your effort, as always it's a true occasion for thanksgiving here, and I remember the bounty of the Lord and the way our ancestors came onto this continent, and I feel thankful for that. This is a good day for me, because I feel that on this day, our national life is truly joined to the Lord the way it was in the early days, and of course that gives me hope for our national future. In my earlier life I devoted myself to exporting not only our know-how and our technology, but also our national ideals."

Helen realized he considered this a self-evident good, and shifted in her seat, trying to maintain her smile. She vowed not to say anything just now about her view that Americans took a great deal too much credit for creating wealth, when most of the time they had really just been living off natural bounty unprecedented in the history of the world. She glanced at Ivar. He was looking up at the ceiling.

Nils went on. "Frankly, I thought my life was over, or at least winding down. I'm fifty-five now, and I was looking forward to a future of watching others do what I used to do, or what I didn't think I would ever have the chance to do. But"—he beamed down at Marly—"I was wrong. I see my life starting over now, with a special, good, Christian woman, a woman with all the womanly virtues of kindness, care, selflessness, Christian love, trust, faith, modesty."

Marly smiled, Helen thought with some embarrassment. And what a prescription, anyway. She glanced at Ivar, who was looking at her this time. His eyes rolled discreetly upward and he gave a little shrug.

"You may not know that Marly and I plan to have six children—"

Ivar's gaze landed on Nils with an almost perceptible thud. He said, "No, I did not know that!"

Nils went smoothly on. "I have never been one to reject the marvels of technology. Best to accept them and turn them to the Lord's purposes. Right, my dear?" He beamed at Marly.

Father said, "You're going to saddle my daughter with six kids at your age?"

Nils, in accordance with his new policy, ignored this interruption. He did say, though, "The Lord has revealed his plan to me piece by piece. Lately he has revealed another important piece, and that is our future in Eastern Europe."

"Excuse me?" said Marly.

"Yes," said Nils, "the Lord has borne it in upon me that as His

Word comes as a revelation to those unfortunate sufferers, in exactly that way there will be a great need for experts such as myself to show them the way to a more secure agricultural destiny."

"You should have asked me first," said Marly, pushing her chair back from the table.

"The Lord didn't ask me," said Nils. "He told me."

Father said, "Let me get this straight. You're planning on having six children and moving to Poland or someplace? What about me?"

Nils beamed upon Father. "It isn't always comfortable to do what the Lord asks, but I have no doubt that as we all pray over these changes, we will all see how positive they will be. Marly and our children and myself will be an example to people over there of all facets of righteous and productive living." He cleared his throat, a touch embarrassed at the personal defeat he was about to reveal. "My, um, failures in certain overseas endeavors were due, in part, I've come to believe, to the pressures to, as it were, go native. Although I loved my wife, of course."

There was a long, uncomfortable pause.

"A family such as ours will be is the best model and, perhaps, the best protection against, ah, temptations of all—"

Father came to the nubbin. He said, "I don't want to move to Poland."

Nils' smile broadened. "I never thought that you would want to."

Father and Nils looked each other right in the eye.

Ivar said, "Nils, maybe you're going too fast on this. I think one step at a time is a better bet."

Nils intoned, "The Lord didn't ask me. He told me." Then, after a weighty pause, he said, "A vision is a whole. You can't take it apart and choose to act on bits of it and not act on other bits of it. It doesn't work that way."

Helen said, "Nils, you can't just do what you want and say that God is telling you to do it—"

"With all due respect, Helen, and I do recognize we are guests in your home, this is really not your business." He beamed. He said, "The Lord has returned my youth to me for a reason. I have prayed over and pondered what that reason might be. The fall of Godless Communism in Europe is the answer. I have wandered in a wilderness of meaningless activity for all of my adult life. I studied to bring enlightenment to developing nations, but people who were supposedly on my side worked against me, and the people I was trying to help failed to see the light. My wife died. I fell into despair. Only then did I find the Lord, and only then did I find Marly and our future together. Only NOW do I understand what I was sent here to do. The Lord's message can come through CNN as easily as in a glorious cloud." He fixed his gaze momentarily on each member of the party, then said, "If you pray ardently and earnestly, you will understand that we will not be balked, and that for all of us here, embracing this vision rather than resisting it will lead us forward into the light." He sat down, grinning.

Helen realized that when he used the word "we," he meant himself and his coconspirator, the Lord.

42

Leben und Arbeit

EVERY DAY, Dean Jellinek had to dig a little deeper to haul up the remaining glow from his courtship by the Final Four corporations who had vied for the privilege of granting him not exactly, or even close to, the million dollars everyone on the campus thought he had gotten. It was a habit he got into—when he sat down at his computer in the morning, the first thing he did was run his hands over the keyboard (it was a new computer, one he had bought with much of the first installment of the money, a computer powerful enough to crunch all the numbers he was contracted to generate in the next year, five months, two weeks, and four days). Running his hands over the keyboard reminded him how enthusiastic all four corporations had been, and that reminder gave him enough confidence to call up the program he was modifying to receive his data. He did not have any data yet, which was okay, because he hadn't perfected his program. He spent many hours every day perfecting his program. Had it not been for that remaining glow, Dean Jellinek would have been in despair: As a longtime computer nerd, he knew that, for him, perfecting programs was what watching television was for others—a mindless activity that promised pleasure, lasted for hours, and left him feeling like an old cigarette butt. He knew this because when he went home at night, he watched everything on the TV from the nightly news with Tom Brokaw to David Letterman almost without looking away from the screen.

Dean Jellinek was a hard-working, hard-playing, hard-driving sort of guy, outwardly balding but possessed of an internal crewcut stiff as the bristles on a wire brush. Only once before in his life had he endured a period like this one, and that was in the early months of his marriage to Elaine Dobbs-Jellinek, when he was beset by second thoughts and he knew she was, too. The signs were all the same: Every morning, sometimes late, sometimes early, but always whenever he could no longer resist, Hal Samuels, the R and D man from

Western Egg and Milk Commodities, would call him up and ask him how it was going, and he would say that it was going fine. "Give me some idea," Hal would say, "something I can tell the board," and Dean would give him some idea—zero to sixty in five seconds, a line drive to deepest center field, a sky hook from the center line, a double eagle over the water hazard, a seventy-yard touchdown run, a slap shot between the goalie's legs. After trading enough sports analogies, Hal and Dean were both reassured, and both felt, in some obscure way, that information had been exchanged. But really it was just the same as it had been with Elaine—honey, I've been thinking about you, honey, how are you, honey, have you been thinking about me, honey, last night was great, didn't you think so, too, to which he would answer, good, fine, yes, and yes, as warmly as he could.

Ah, but, as with Elaine, how had he gotten himself into this? Ah, but, as with Elaine, how had he invested so much—the computer had, in fact, cost as much money as that house they'd bought—so quickly? Ah, but, as with Elaine, how was he going to, day after day, month after month, year after year, endure this commitment? Ah, but, as with Elaine, how was he going to find some breathing room, with Samuels clinging to him all the time, his expectations, like Elaine's had been, unvoiced but ever-present? The great irony was that he had been priding himself on what he'd learned about relationships—one of the reasons he was drawn to Joy, one of the reasons he'd pressed her to move in with him, was that she didn't give him that breathless, closed-in feeling. He'd heard somewhere that one thing about horsewomen as girlfriends was that they almost didn't have time for you. That had suited Dean right down to the ground.

The frightening thing was that a corporation wasn't like a girlfriend or wife, or like the federal agencies he'd gotten earlier grants from. This time he'd signed a contract. There would be no going to Samuels and saying, "Gee, honey, it hurts to say this, but I just don't think it's working out." This time he had to learn to live with that suffocating feeling of commitment. He had to renew his faith in calf-free lactation, faith that had faded another degree with every step toward realization. These days calves looked GOOD to him. How else could a farmer so cheaply replenish his herd? What farmer would go for a life of dairying without calves? But he had to embrace Samuels, Western

Egg and Milk, and those Holsteins anyway, without reservation, with desire and enthusiasm and hope and joy. He soothed his doubts with the same arguments he would use to soothe Samuels' doubts, should Samuels express them: "Hey, marketing is YOUR end. I'm just here for the technical breakthroughs." All things considered, it was easier to perfect his program.

"Joy," he had said this very morning, "Joy, honey, you aren't helping me here. We've got ourselves into a big project, the biggest, and there can't be any drag. The slightest friction, the least little wind resistance, and I'm afraid this airship isn't going to get off the ground." He then pursued his point. "I have to admit, Joy, and I only admit this to you, that the ship is bigger and the engines smaller than ever before. Not as much *thrust*, not as much *thrust* as we've been able to count on before." Remembering her doubts, he added hastily, "The idea's good, don't get me wrong, the idea's great, but it's big, Joy, it's so BIG! I can't help being daunted. Anyone would be, so the least little, I don't know, failure of cooperation, of, yes, *teamwork*, that's a problem. I can't help but think of this as our project, because it's a project that we both have to live with. I can't do a project like this at work. The immersion has to be total. I have to eat, sleep, and dream this project, and that's where you come in, because I feel a small but decided spiritual space between us, like a crack in the tail assembly. I don't want to crash, Joy, I don't want to, and I know you don't want to either."

He went on and on, buttering one slice of toast after another, and listening to himself spout this unbelievable bullshit while she sat across the table from him drinking a cup of coffee, no, sipping it one milliliter at a time, wrapped in her robe as if she were freezing to death, a statue of misery, and when he should have been saying something like "Joy, what's the problem, how can I help you, let's take a vacation, I'm right here, and I want you to talk to me," he felt too deeply the wedge of anxiety driven into his soul by the four-hundred-thousand-dollars-over-four-years grant from Western Egg and Milk (God forbid any more than that—a real million might have killed him) and could not say what he should have said, but could only say, "We've got to get rolling on this, Joy, we've got to buck up and buckle down, turn this team into a victory machine, and I know we can do it, it's only a matter of getting with it and getting on with it." Go go go, fight fight fight. And then he ate all that toast, just folding each slice in the middle and shoving it into his mouth and gulping it down until he could tear himself away from the kitchen table and make himself go to the lab.

THERE HAD BEEN a time, Joy thought, as she opened the gate to the indoor riding ring, when nothing stood for anything else, when the world around her was literally meaningless and her activities were essentially mindless.

When the gate was all the way open, she went through, then turned and pulled gently on Frenchman's reins. The rangy bay four-year-old gelding ambled through the opening calmly enough, but once in the ring, he pricked up his ears and cocked his head and arched his neck as if all around him invisible stallions were challenging his authority. He let out a long, imperious squeal. From far in the back of the barn, his great and good friend, Tillie, let out a muffled but distinctly needy reply. Tillie was a seven-year-old Connemara pony mare, very much on the stocky side. They were a mismatched pair, but given the choice, neither would have moved a step without the other. Joy had tried three times to separate their stalls, knowing that continuing companionship only exacerbated their dependency, but the callings out and squeals of despair and clarion challenges and pledges of undying faithfulness on both sides had reechoed for days on end, until Joy had given up her principles and put them back together.

Frenchman was a good-looking thoroughbred with some real talent for dressage, but love had made him distinctly less useful—he was always distracted by his attention to Tillie. He was bad enough when she was out of sight and far away. He was almost impossible if she were nearby.

Joy pulled down the stirrup and mounted with an athletic little spring. While she was settling into the saddle, the gelding brought himself to frozen attention, and then squealed again. Joy nudged him with her heels, but he wouldn't move off, so she smacked him hard on the rump with her whip. His pattern was to move eagerly in Tillie's direction, and sluggishly away. Usually, Joy had to smack him very hard with the whip and use spurs to get his attention. He had been gelded late and Tillie had been bred twice. Both, therefore, had known sin, through the carelessness of owners who did not take equine virginity seriously enough as the foundation of a useful and productive life. Nor did it help that when the two were out in the field together, Tillie liked to back her round and lowly hindquarters right up to his nose, flop her tail over to the side, and offer herself, to his eternal frustration. It was a bad situation, and Joy couldn't see a solution short of selling one or the other.

Two years ago she would have sold Tillie without a second thought, briskly diagnosing the problem and efficiently solving it. Now she saw things more or less from their point of view, with results fatal to her own usefulness.

She asked, then demanded, that Frenchman move into a trot. Tillie called out. The gelding's ears swivelled, but he maintained his gait. Joy squeezed him a little harder with her legs, but held him firmly in with her hands. She felt the tension in the reins increase. His neck and back rounded as he went onto the bit and his trot settled into a bright, easy, swinging two beats. She felt the pleasure of it all through her thighs and hips, into the small of her back. This is what he could have been without Tillie. She guided him through some small circles, then some figure eights. On the serpentine, he curvetted out of his line and arched over the bit, testing her. She pushed him forward with her legs and then with the whip, making him do it again until the half-circles and straight lines he cut in the tanbark of the ring were as crisp as she knew he was capable of, then she brought him down to a walk and let him stretch out his head. He immediately issued a challenge to all the invisible stallions and a reassurance to Tillie that he would protect her. She neighed supportively back. Had they been human, their single-minded devotion to each other would have aroused admiration, or envy. As horses, their obsession was just another example of how simpleminded they were.

She herself was simpleminded about Dean. Now that their paths seemed to be inexorably diverging, she was a little surprised at the power of her attachment to him. It was not as though she didn't know what Dean was all about. In their five years together he had come up short morally or spiritually any number of times. He was devoted to Ronald Reagan, for example. The two of them could sit side by side, watching the same speech, and Joy would find herself so irredeemably appalled by the vacancy she saw in all the actor-president's looks and gestures that she assumed that this time, at last, even Nancy Reagan could see it, but at the end, Dean would turn to her and say, with real enthusiasm, "God, that was great! What a great man! Not since Abraham Lincoln—" Another one of Dean's habits, so transparent that Joy winced every time, was to buy something expensive whenever he felt anxious or unconfident. When they were first together and didn't have much money, he had even gone from reconciling the checkbook and lamenting how low their funds were directly to the mall, where he would buy a new stereo component or a Shetland sweater purely out of the fear of being broke.

She lifted Frenchman into a sluggish canter on the wrong lead, stopped him, got his attention with her whip. The next time, he took off at a livelier pace, and she settled into the rocking motion, circling the ring four times, then turning diagonally across it and asking for a flying change of lead in the center. She could feel his doubt, but then he did it. She smiled, and let him extend himself down the long side. One of the great pleasures of her early life had been long easy canters, sometimes mile after mile, down dirt roads in Oklahoma, where she had grown up. Her pony would be so fit from a summer of exercise that in the cool of the fall he seemed like he could go without stopping. She'd ridden mostly western then, or bareback, no goals and no pretensions.

She had never wanted to marry Dean, but now, perversely, considering how deeply she disapproved of calf-free lactation and how firmly convinced she was that their couplehood would cease sometime soon, she wished they had gotten married, so that their life together would go out with a bang, rather than passing away in the vapor that now seemed inevitable. Partly she wanted this so that the surprising pain she felt at the breakup would be publicly marked and noted. Partly she wanted it because in retrospect her whole life seemed mostly vaporous, undifferentiated by events—no children, no marriages, no advanced degrees, not even any big-time championships, many pretty good horses that she'd brought along well enough, but no great one. Okay, and no grand love for an extraordinary and unique lover, either, just many days and years with Dean, an ordinary man of ordinary tastes who was terribly afraid of seeming ordinary, itself a characteristic that Joy had noted in almost every man and most of the women she had known.

Down the center of the ring, six black and white poles raised by crosspieces six inches off the ground lay in a grid. She turned Frenchman toward them—cavalletti—and pressed him into an extended trot. The extended trot was Joy's favorite gait, because of the bold way the animal's forelegs shot forward, and the proud arch of the animal's neck. The goal was not speed itself, though a certain amount of speed was a by-product of the longer stride. The goal was the balletic ideal of a long line, full display, and an extreme degree of dynamic tension achieved and controlled. They were going away from Tillie, so the horse was reluctant and lazy. She turned him out just before they reached the cavalletti and went back to the track. She raised her whip-hand high over his rump and brought it down hard, simultaneously maintaining a tight grip on the reins. His rump tucked. She applied her spurs. He was young enough and unsure enough of himself to wake up right then, right when she asked it. They came around the end of the ring, and she turned toward the cavalletti again. This time he was looking ahead, preparing himself to spring over each pole without breaking stride. They came to the first pole. She drove him on with her legs. She felt his muscles work, and then they were through. She brought him around and did it three more times, each time as well or a little better than the first time. Then she let him walk. He let out his neck and dropped his head. When Tillie called out, he was too tired to reply. Joy smiled.

DEAN WENT to the commons for lunch at 11:30, right when it opened. He always hated it if one of the entrées was gone when he got there, because it would have been the best entrée and he would have missed it. Today he chose the bar-b-qued beef w/ sesame bun, carrot sticks on the side, cherry pie w/ whipped cream squiggles, and lettuce wedge w/ ranch dressing, $3.72, though perhaps he should have gotten the hamburger stroganoff w/ dairy sour creme and egg noodle bake. On the way to his table, he spoke with pleasant authority to everyone he should have, but he made it clear that he needed to be alone by pulling out his notebook and a mechanical pencil as soon as he sat down. As the recipient of a rumored million-dollar grant, he did get to sit alone while all the tables around him filled up.

In his notebook, he sketched a Holstein cow—he'd always had a knack for drawing—who was standing by a fence gazing into the distance. Her udder hung heavy and full almost to the ground (120 pounds a day) but she wasn't mindful of that. She was looking at the distant hills, which he then sketched in, and sniffing the fragrance, carried by the wind, of the unseen ocean beyond them. She was wondering. That was all, just wondering. Then he flipped over the page and began a list. The first item on the list was "Talk to Joy about her concerns ten minutes a day, increasing two mins. a week." The second item was "Chris, this wkend, McDnlds and computer store." Then he began to do what he should have done weeks ago, which was to break down the procedures he was going to have to employ in completing his project into smaller and smaller components. As he did so, it became clear which ones he could assign to his graduate assistant, which ones he could put off, which ones he needn't do at all if he didn't want to ("Write up daily report"), which ones he could do easily ("Make backup copy of number-crunching program"), and which ones would take some thought ("How does embryo signal its presence to cow?"). By the time he had gone back and gotten a serving of hamburger stroganoff w/ dairy sour creme, the list covered seven pages, and his future no longer frightened him. He licked the last of the dairy sour creme from his fork and saw by the commons clock that it was 12:39. He saw that he could get that program copied by 1:00—it really was good enough for now, and he wouldn't know what else he needed to do to it until he had some numbers to crunch—and then he could go on to the next item on the list—"Call Suzanne (grad. asst.) and set up meeting Wed.?" and so on and so forth all the way down to the bottom of page 7—"Apply for larger grant."

JOY, too, was ruminating over her plans while eating lunch, and her goal was not dissimilar—passage through the current difficulties and into a more relaxed and spacious life. She unwrapped the elements of her repast and set them on her desk. She had a meat loaf sandwich, a nice pear, two Chips Ahoy!, a cranberry Sundance, and a small bag of sour cream and onion potato chips. Five items, five goals: Find someone who would marry her. Have at least one child. Move back to the West, preferably the Southwest. Vacation in Alaska. Save enough money to buy a Swedish Warmblood—European-bred with big sturdy hooves. Dean was not an item on her list, but even so, when they got home that night, she was happy that they seemed more easy and pleasant with one another. It was not something they talked about—Dean thought that now that he'd gotten himself on a schedule, the details would work themselves out, as they always did, and Joy thought that now that she had given up focusing her inchoate desires upon Dean, who clearly couldn't handle them, she could relax until her inevitable departure from his big, pleasant house. They even went to bed together for the first time in a couple of months, and once there, it seemed both possible and fun to make love, so they did, and so they fell asleep, and so they found a way to go on together for a while longer.

43

Up or Out

DR. GARCIA DID NOT mind the thirty hours or so of reading articles like "The Tractatus Humorus of Antonius of Cesena: Notes Toward an Arrangement of Extant Fragments," or "Folding and Unbinding Transitions in Tethered Membranes," or even "The Use of Strain-Specific Monoclonal Antibodies to Model the Field Spread of Soybean Mosaic Virus." There was a free-floating quality to his sojourns into these disciplines and their codes. Some ideas emerged from the murk like answers in those old black "Eight Balls" he and his friends once had—"The answer is no," "Ask again later." Others did not. It was not his responsibility, anyway, to judge and interpret the articles—that would have been done in the department and those judgments and interpretations were passed on to the college committee in each chair's recommendations, which Garcia did understand. But he read the articles anyway, at least one per candidate, just to get a global apprehension of who the candidates were, of how their self-presentation differed from the department chair's presentation of them. The reading was quiet time, investigative work in the mysteries of the mind, in this case, the intellectual mind, of the sort that he enjoyed.

But the meetings were a trial. The five of them had suffered through two so far, each four hours in length, each voting on and discussing eleven or twelve cases, each expressing, with every remark and every vote, the fact that this particular committee/family was dysfunctional in the extreme.

And now they had to take up the promotion of Timothy Monahan, one of the few candidates whose work Dr. Garcia could actually understand. Margaret left the room. Garcia sighed.

Gift said, "I have a communication from the department chair." He looked over his glasses and read, " 'Professor Monahan's third novel has been accepted for publication over the Thanksgiving break. The publisher, the well-known and highly respected house of Little, Brown, has agreed to provide a letter confirming that the novel needs only minor editing work, and should be out in about a year. This letter is coming by overnight mail, and should arrive in a day or so. It is my opinion and the opinion of the departmental committee that this acceptance should clinch Professor Monahan's promotion to the rank of full professor.' "

Dr. Gift cleared his throat. He said, "This is the book, I believe, that we read selected passages of, and part of which has been published in—yes, *Playboy* magazine. I believe one page of the selection ran alongside a picture of a nude young woman."

"That's the one," said Cates.

Garcia wrote down in his notes, " 'That's the one,' said Dr. Cates."

Dr. Gift said, "I am not sure I see how the mere publication of salacious material renders it superior to what it was before it was published."

Helen said, mildly, "Lionel, I've told you before that I don't consider the selections from the novel salacious."

Dr. Garcia wrote, "Dr. Levy objected to the characterization of Professor Monahan's work as salacious."

Cates said, "I think 'trivial' is a better term for what I read."

Dr. Garcia wrote, "Cates characterized the work as trivial." Now they were all looking at him. He put down his pen and worked up a meditative look. He paused as long as he thought he could. Then he said, "I would not say that Professor Monahan is writing great literature, but I also would not say that this university is positioned financially, geographically, or culturally to attract or keep a writer of great literature who might simultaneously be, let's say, a drug user, an alcoholic, a victim of bipolar disorder, addicted to sex with younger female students, or given to any number of other problems that can accompany remarkable creativity."

He jotted down, "Dr. Garcia remarked that such a second-rate institution as this one probably was doing well to have attracted Professor Monahan in the first place."

"Frankly," said Helen, "I don't think that any of you has the literary experience to judge Professor Monahan's work. Just because you read *Crime and Punishment* in college doesn't mean you have any discernment."

Dr. Gift gave an audible sniff.

"Okay, Lionel," said Helen, "how about this. A magazine like *Playboy* gets thousands of submissions in a year. They pick twelve or eighteen. Professor Monahan's excerpt was one of them. That means that he's succeeding in a tough market. The same with his first novel, the same with his second novel. Thousands upon thousands submitted, a few hundreds, at the most, accepted. And, this should appeal to you, Lionel, he gets paid for his work."

"How much?" said Dr. Gift.

"I believe the advance on the first novel was around twenty-five thousand. The average for a commercial publisher is under ten."

Garcia thought Gift looked a little swayed. Gift said, "Can we find out the advance on this novel? How it ranks nationally on the scale of advances?"

Helen said, "Oh, for God's sake, Lionel."

"These factors are relevant, in my opinion."

Cates said, "Does that mean we aren't going to decide this case today?"

Garcia wrote, "Discussion arose of whether Professor Monahan's candidacy should be discussed at a future meeting." Then he said, "That WOULD entail a special meeting. This is our last scheduled meeting."

Helen said, with thrilling decisiveness, "I don't want to meet again. Lionel, this is a candidate, maybe the only one we've discussed, who has a direct relationship to your favorite institution, the market, and who does fairly well there. He's the only person we've discussed who's actually engaged in FREE ENTERPRISE! Stick by your principles, Lionel!"

Garcia could see that old Dad was torn, and that he was offended, too, at having Mom speak to him so sharply in front of the children. On top of that, there was the way in which she had attacked him. Garcia had once written a paper called "Patriarchal Privilege and Its Relationship to Principle in the Nuclear Family," in which he had demonstrated that in over 90 percent of traditional families, the father was given considerable leeway to diverge from behavioral norms, even those that were clearly defined and upheld by that particular family. Father, in short, did not HAVE to set an example. What was interesting was the different ways that the two parents excused the father from adhering to professed norms: the father almost always declared that hard work outside the home and consequent earnings gained privileges (one reason many men were resistant to women working outside the home—they knew that extending such privileges to another family member might put at risk the moral life of the family); the mother almost always offered the opinion that men were inherently wayward, and could neither control themselves nor be controlled by women or by abstractions. Thus, Dr. Garcia had suggested, a wife's conflict strategy of holding up principles that the husband failed to live by could be an especially volatile one, depending upon whether the husband saw her move as a power play, a reminder of his failures as a man, or, positively, as an opportunity to embrace the common life of the family.

He watched Dr. Gift.

Dr. Gift said, "I suggest that we vote."

The voting was done on a scale from 1 to 10. The candidate could squeak by with a 6.5, but a 7 or 7.5, for promotion to the rank of full professor, was a much stronger recommendation, and would surely pass through the provost's office with no trouble. Garcia, as secretary, opened the slips of paper. "4"—that was Cates. He was almost never swayed by discussion. "5"—that would be Dr. Gift: his answer to Mom. "7"—Garcia himself. There *had* been stronger candidates, with three books actually published; you had to consider that. "8"—Helen, who often argued in extreme terms, but then voted rather conservatively. Dr. Garcia said, "Well, we've recommended him with a six."

Dr. Gift said, "In my opinion, that's realistic."

Cates said, "Generous, if you ask me."

Garcia sighed.

Helen was rummaging around in her briefcase.

Dr. Gift settled his body into his chair with perceptible self-satisfaction. Garcia opened the door and motioned Margaret, who was sitting on the bench outside the door, reading a book called *Feminism Without Illusions*, to come back in. That'll be the day, thought Dr. Garcia. Cates went over to the coffee machine.

"Here," said Helen. "Let's take a break and discuss this." She pushed a stapled, typewritten document across to Dr. Gift and then passed copies to everyone at the table.

Dr. Lionel Gift could count on one thumb the number of times he had been taken by surprise, and even that surprise, the stock market crash of 1987, he would have foreseen if he had been in the country, but he had been in Costa Rica, calculating the costs and benefits of his then brand-new vacation home. Nonetheless, he was surprised at the sight of his confidential report on Seven Stones Mining sliding across the table toward him. It was as if Helen could reach into some magic bag and draw forth whatever she pleased. His first thought was that he should have gone ahead and voted his principles rather than his instincts with the Monahan fellow. That was a lesson to him—any divergence from principle was a mistake.

He said, "Where did you get this?" And he saw that there were five other copies, too, as if his copy had magically spawned. He said, "This is confidential."

"Not anymore," said Helen.

Elaine Dobbs-Jellinek. Dr. Gift stood up, and said, "I'm going to make a call."

"Good," said Helen. "That will give the others time to read this."

"They can't read it. It's confidential. It was never meant to be read." He sat down again.

Dr. Bell, who had been skimming the first few pages of her copy with her eyebrows lifting ever higher, said, "That's an interesting point you raise, Dr. Gift. There is actually a significant body of literary theory that proposes that the ultimate power in any writer-reader transaction lies with the reader. The writer may persuade, attract, or lure the reader, but it's the reader who chooses how to interpret, and even whether or not to read. One critic says that giving up control over material by writing it down is analogous to having an orgasm. Both frightening and *thrilling*." She gave Dr. Gift a covert glance, then allowed herself a private little smile. She went on, "Of course, I think that's a very masculinist interpretation, but it may have some validity."

Dr. Gift was staring at her, but not, Garcia thought, as if he was listening to her, more as if he were weighing his next move. Helen said, "Wondering whom to sue, Lionel?"

"There are certainly university regulations protecting the confidentiality of a faculty member's papers."

"No doubt there are," said Helen.

"Well, then, I shall pursue that course."

"On a Saturday morning? Does your lawyer wear a beeper to the golf course? I happen to know that the university lawyer is in St. Louis this weekend, at a large family wedding. You could try and reach Provost Harstad, of course. He's driven to Kansas for the basketball game and should be back by midafternoon tomorrow. Even if you can reach him, I doubt whether there's anything he can do until he meets with the university lawyer on Monday." She smiled.

Dr. Gift tried to reach across the table and grab Dr. Garcia's copy of the document. Dr. Garcia instinctively snatched it out of his reach, then saw that he had committed himself. For once he had inclined to

Dr. Gift's point of view, but Dad's graceless attempt at bullying revealed a disrespect for himself, Dr. Garcia, that he resented. He pushed his chair back from the table a foot or so and leafed through the report. He felt joy in doing so. He felt principles vanish from the room and simple desire take over, first in the form of curiosity, as each of the children partook of old Dad's secret.

Outside of his discipline, Dr. Garcia was just a citizen. He did not profess special knowledge, or even special interest in environmental concerns. For as long as his friend X, in Horticulture, had been ranting at him about the ozone layer, biodiversity, endangered species, the disappearance of the rain forest, and overpopulation, he had been attributing X's overinvestment in global issues to long-standing psychological stresses typical of the high-idealism, low-tolerance personality type. The patterns X conformed to were all well known—he had the instability, the anger, the deep self-doubt, the background alcoholic, the charisma, too. Garcia was very fond of him.

But despite Garcia's manifest indifference to most extrapsychological issues, he did feel a little clang of shock at the proposed gold mine beneath the largest remaining virgin cloud forest in the world. He even felt a sense of unpleasant surprise at the knowledge that the forest was entirely ringed by land owned by this company, International Cattle. The images were primitive, and all the stronger for that—the ring of private land like a noose, the tunnels of the gold mine literally undermining the forest's attachment to the earth.

Cates said, "You know, Seven Stones Mining is an interesting company. About ten years ago, they were taken to court to prevent them selling off a company they owned called Appalachic Coal, that was being sued to provide compensatory damages to the residents of a town that sat on top of an old mine that had caught fire underground. I believe that fire's been burning for twenty years, anyway. As the judgment neared, and it looked like it was going to go in favor of the town, Seven Stones made plans to sell off Appalachic so that Appalachic could go into bankruptcy and not pay any damages. As it turned out, the Kentucky court in the case did allow the sale, and no damages were paid."

Helen said, "Where did you see that? I would love to have a reference." She picked up her pencil.

"I'm sorry, I don't have a reference. I have some cousins in a nearby town. I always thought it was an interesting case, though."

As always, Garcia thought, Cates was cool, almost indifferent. The chemistry professor went on, "Actually, my relatives didn't suffer until Appalachic went out of business. Then they lost the little store they had."

Dr. Bell was scowling at him. She said, "Now isn't that just typical?" Garcia didn't know if she was referring to Cates or to the situation he had described.

Dr. Gift bestirred himself. He let his gaze rest upon each of them in turn, then said, "Perhaps the best policy is to finish our work here, as we only have four candidates to go, and their cases are fairly clear-cut."

Everyone nodded. After all, it was always a relief to take refuge in routine, thought Garcia. It gave you something to do while you were getting ready to do the next thing that you desired to do but knew deep down that you shouldn't. In his case, that would be a little ride over to X's house, where he would drop off Gift's report. X, he knew, would commit it to memory on the first, fiery reading. Then, who knew? In Dr. Garcia's experience, this matter was unprecedented. He smiled to himself. That was exciting, too.

44

Some Research

GARY WAS well aware that one of Professor Monahan's favorite sayings was "Fear no research." To that end, and solely as an exercise for intellectual growth, he called Lydia and invited her out, careful to do so when Lyle was at work, so as not to arouse his roommate's entirely unjustified suspicions. Lydia had not seemed especially enthusiastic about their date, and seemed even less so when he assured her that it was no big deal. That was an annoying thing about girls—if they weren't especially interested in you, and you tried to reassure them that you weren't especially interested in them, either, they just got offended. Guys were not like that. Living with roommates, for example, depended on everyone's conviction that they were almost totally indifferent to one another.

He had never finished any version of "The Boy" or "Lydia." He had made a gallant effort with other material—a man in a spaceship hearing a voice that he finally realizes is God playing dice with the universe, and a crazy Vietnam vet who blows himself up because he can't take it anymore. Professor Monahan had not cottoned to either story, and to tell the truth, Gary himself had found them a little boring to write. So, when the teacher reiterated that research for stories did not necessarily mean going to the library and sifting through primary source material, Gary returned to the theme of Lydia's tragic future with renewed enthusiasm, and called her up.

They met outside the Black Hole but walked up the street to Down But Not Out, an undergraduate hangout that catered to both men and women. It was cold, and Lydia was wearing a matching scarf and mitten set of vibrant blue and purple mohair. When she took off her coat, he saw that she had a sweater to go with the scarf and mittens. They sat at a table, and with both hands, she reached behind and tightened her ponytail, which Gary knew she knew also lifted her breasts and separated them just for him. Gary slouched down in his chair and stretched out his legs. They both smiled, exchanging the information that these gestures were impersonally meant, impersonally recognized. Now they could get down to business. Lydia said, "I didn't see you at that party at Berkeley Hall? It was an unbelievable crush."

"I heard they had four kegs."

"They had everything. It was like the sixties."

"Lot of people passed out?"

"And major puking."

They fell silent for a moment, appreciating the good time had by all in Berkeley Hall.

"So what's Lyle doing these days?"

"Nothing. Work, school, you know."

"I saw him at that party." She tried to make it sound casual.

"Oh, yeah?"

"Yeah."

He got up and went to the bar, then returned with a pitcher of PBR. She said, "The thing is, I need a Diet Coke. My roommates and I agreed we were going to stop drinking for a week, from that party."

"Major puking?"

"Too major."

He got up and fetched her a Diet Coke. They took thoughtful swigs from their drinks. Gary had the strangest feeling, one he did not recognize. After a moment, though, he remembered it from the earliest days of junior high school. He felt uncomfortable, and with a girl! Amazing! He didn't know what to say, how to flirt! Astonishing! Gary Olson, the boy with five sisters, ill at ease! He said, "Well, it's too bad you don't come around anymore."

"Why's that?"

"I miss you."

"Oh, yeah?"

"Well, you know Lyle and Bob. They don't have a lot to say. And that girl Bob was seeing, that's cooled off, so he's moping a lot."

"I didn't know about that. Who was she?"

"Diane Somebody. Just a freshman."

"Oh."

"Want another Diet Coke?"

"Sure."

He went to the bar again, then trudged back to Lydia. The thing was, it was frightening to imagine how fat she was going to be, how bitter, how unhappy. Here she had this great hair, this beautiful voice, this pleasant face, and this deep ignorance. She thought she was going to be a college girl forever, buying mohair sweater sets on her parents' charge card with the absolute assurance that she would always turn every head in the bar. If she thought of marriage and a career and children, and what girl in this university didn't—a couple of years ago in his English class Professor Bell had asked how many of the girls expected to have high-powered careers as well as large happy families, and every girl had raised her hand; when she'd asked the boys how many expected their wives to work, only three had raised their hands ("Who do you expect to marry, then?" she had remarked)—if Lydia thought of the future, then she was seeing this self, this slender, fluid, fleeting beauty striding around in it as around a stage set. She didn't see the future entering her, reshaping her, as Gary did. It tied his tongue because now that he'd written those stories, that was what he knew about Lydia, and instead of doing his usual thing, which was getting the girl to tell *him* about herself, he wanted to do something very strange, which was to tell *her* about herself, and really, what had Lydia done to deserve this? She had been in the wrong place at the wrong time—in his roommate's room, talking—just when he was supposed to be writing down some dialogue. Now she was doomed. Her own little boy would be terrified of her. Gary sighed at the unfairness of it.

Lydia, meanwhile, was looking around, and across the large room of bar tables she saw the redhead who had been talking to Lyle at the Berkeley Hall party. Even at this distance and in this light, she could see the girl's dark roots. She sniffed. She was heavyset, too. Wasn't that always the way? That's what had happened with her father. Before her parents' divorce, he worked all the time and never even picked his own clothes off the floor. If he wanted more food, Lydia's mother or one of the girls got up and served him some. He had so little patience with his children that the only time he would willingly be in their presence was driving in the car with at least two of the four sleeping. In his second marriage, however, and Lydia was a witness, so she knew whereof she spoke, he changed diapers, dandled infants, washed clothes, learned to cook a repertoire of northern Italian special-ties, and frequently stopped to smell the roses, which meant taking off plenty of time from work to be with his new wife and the two babies, while often remarking to Lydia or Holly or Roxanne or David during their visits that children were only young once, and he thanked God he had realized that and he hoped that they would never make the mistakes he had made. Every time she or one of her siblings mentioned the sorts of things their father now enjoyed, Lydia's mother would go bananas. Once she said, "You know, I've gotten over the divorce and I like our life together, but the idea of him making BRUNCH and eating PANCAKES drives me crazy!" Lydia had never mentioned that her father took especial pleasure in *serving* his new wife, Mary Beth, her pancakes, which he shaped into Mickey Mouse faces, just the way Mary Beth liked them.

Lydia looked again at the redhead, and realized that she had seen her before, in her Spanish class, early in the semester. After a week or so, the girl had either dropped or stopped coming. She had a flamboyant way about her. Lydia thought she was a little trampy-looking. She sniffed. Well, that wasn't surprising, either.

Gary was saying, "So anyway, that's why I'm thinking of switching my major."

Lydia smiled with all sorts of apparent interest, and trilled, "I do think you should major in something you're really interested in."

"So did I, but now that I'm almost a senior, I'm beginning to think that's impractical."

"Oh, really?" The thing was, everything about Gary was impractical. He was good-looking and nice and could be lots of fun and a lot of girls she knew had had crushes on him for a while, but in Lydia's opinion there was some little hard thing missing inside. There wasn't enough friction with Gary, which meant, she thought, that he didn't have any character. He was like the second edition of her father, a nice smiley face, compared to the first, an actual person that daily life brought you right up against.

". . . law school," he said.

"You want to go to law school?"

"No, Lydia, I don't." He looked amused. "What I said was 'I'd do anything but go to law school.' "

"Oh."

"Well, if you aren't paying a lick of attention to me, what are you thinking about?"

Lydia wasn't in the habit of revealing her thoughts, but she had been impolite, she decided, so she said, "Oh, that girl over there. I saw Lyle talking to her at that party. She's fatter than I am, and her hair is dyed, too. And my dad and mom since the divorce. My dad's always, like, 'I'm a new person, don't you think, aren't I great?' and then he points out some little thing on one of his new children, like her belly button or something, and starts raving about the miracle of life.''

Gary laughed.

''Mark my words, Lyle's going to turn over some new leaf.''

''Well, he stopped drinking straight out of the milk carton.''

''I told you—''

''No, Bob trained him. Every time he saw Lyle drinking out of the carton, he took the milk away from him and poured it down the sink, almost whole gallons. I think he showed him some slides of what grows in milk, too. Even Lyle got disgusted.'' They laughed again, then Lydia said, ''You know, I kind of miss you, too. Why don't you kick Lyle out and find another roommate. Then I could come over and hang around.''

Gary settled in his seat. She was smiling now, relaxed. This was more like it. And he didn't have to write down what she'd said about her parents, either, since he'd trained himself to remember. If he took her home by midnight, he thought, he could put at least a couple of hours in at his computer.

45

Privileged Information

WHEN THEY PASSED in the halls or paused by the coffee machine, Tim Monahan seemed to have forgotten about his promotion. When Margaret said, "Congratulations," the Monday after hearing about the sale of his book, he actually said, "For what?" He meant it, too. She said, "Why, on your book, of course," and he said, "How did you hear that?" and then, "Oh, right. Well, thanks. It's great." A little smile. So she invited him to dinner.

He hadn't been over, except for a Christmas party, since the end of their little affair years before. As he came in, he said, "Where's everybody else?"

"I didn't invite anyone else."

She headed for the kitchen and he followed her. They passed the refrigerator, and he opened the door and took out a beer. She said, "Would you like a beer?"

He looked at the bottle in his hand, and said, "Got any Beck's?"

"I might. Why don't you check?"

They laughed, and Margaret realized that she had been just a little nervous about this evening. But after all, you could always rely on Tim to keep the conversation going at a superficial but entertaining clip. He said, "I know, you told people that I was coming, and they all turned you down."

"Only the women."

Instead of laughing, he sighed.

He didn't tell her the price of the wine he brought. Nor, she realized, had he remarked upon her new carpeting—"Is it wool? Nylon? Olefin? How much was it? What else did you see? Was that more expensive? Pad and installation included?"

She shrugged. "Well, you know, it's been so long since we talked, and I've been so distracted this fall, that I said, why not, I don't have anything better to do that night."

He smiled. "Hey, since I'm not getting any ego boost here, what's for dinner?"

"Veal. Veal medallions with artichoke hearts and lemon, parmesan potatoes, and braised string beans."

"Okay, then! I'm here, you're here, fuck 'em if they can't take a joke!"

"Yeah!"

"Yeah!"

She turned to the stove. Everything was ready except the veal medallions, which were a last-minute dish. She picked up a pale round of meat and began dredging it in seasoned flour. A mixture of butter and olive oil sizzled in the skillet.

Actually, Tim had been looking forward to some spicy black beans and red rice, ladled over cold orange slices, something Margaret had cooked for him three or four times because she knew he loved it. He was a little shocked at the veal, a dish he could have gotten from anyone who had a subscription to *Gourmet*. From Margaret, he expected principled food, nourishing, cheap, and delicious, food worthy of someone whose greatest monthly kitchen expense was olive oil rather than meat. And she had carpeted the living room, too, in the sort of closely woven and subtly colored plush that would run thirty dollars a yard from the sort of flooring place that charged extra for carpet and pad. He resisted a disapproving nod and called upon his most tactful tone of voice. "Remember that dish you used to make, black beans and rice, really spicy, and you would lay a big slice of cold orange in the bottom of the bowl before ladling up the beans?"

"Sure."

"I loved that. You got a recipe?"

"Are you going to start cooking?"

"I might."

"Why?"

"Well, I was teaching Kafka in my class a week or so ago, and I realized that the reason Gregor Samsa is redeemed by being turned into a bug is that he learns to live in the physical world, and take pleasure in simple actions like running over the walls of his room or hanging from the ceiling and rocking back and forth. Being turned into a bug is a step UP for him. So I think it's time for me to start cooking. I don't know. To start eating everything with a big spoon. Simple pleasures. I stopped showering."

"You what?"

"I mean I started taking baths instead of showers."

Margaret dropped six floured medallions into the fat, and the delicious fragrance of browning meat rose around them. "See," he said. "Time to stop and smell the MEAT." He sighed.

Margaret turned and looked at him. "As I remember, you always said that self-improvement should be a writer's greatest fear."

"This isn't self-improvement. This is spiritual redemption."

"Pardon me for getting the two mixed up." She moved the browned pieces of meat to one side of the pan, and poured in the artichoke hearts, the lemon juice, and some white wine.

"See," he said, in a tone Margaret found irritatingly informative. "The body, the mind, and the spirit don't form a pyramid, they form a circle. Each of them runs into the other two. The body isn't below the mind and the spirit; from one point of view it's between them. If you reside too much in the mind, then you get too abstract and cut off from the world. You long for the spiritual life, but you can't get to it, and you fall into despair. The exercise of the senses frees you from abstraction and opens the way to transcendence."

"Did you make this up?"

"Well, of course. Though I'm sure there's all sorts of bits and pieces of things I've heard and read. All unattributed, needless to say. Novelists never have to footnote."

"Am I to infer that you have fallen into despair and you are making your way out of it with hot baths and black beans and—"

"Jogging. But not for reasons of fitness or vanity or health."

"God forbid." On each plate, she laid three golden rounds of veal and ladled over them some of the artichoke sauce. Beside them, she set two parmesan roasted potatoes and some beans. They carried their plates into the small dining room and Tim went back for the wine. Though he hadn't bragged about it, she noticed that it was a white pinot, her favorite. She estimated the cost on her own—fifteen to twenty dollars.

He didn't even turn over his saucer and check the label on the bottom.

She said, "I don't think you've seen what I've done to this house."

"New carpeting, new deck. What else?"

"I remodelled the bathrooms."

"Great."

That was all. After a moment, she prodded him. "I got a terrific deal on the carpeting."

"Good. You know, this veal is excellent."

"You want the recipe?"

"Well—"

"Well?"

"Well, spiritual redemption is in beans, not veal."

Margaret felt herself taking offense.

"You know, Margaret, I'm glad you're interested in all this, because—"

"Honey, I'm not that interested."

"Oh." He returned glumly to his dinner.

Now this was alarming. The old Tim would have given her six reasons, all of them invasively personal, about why she SHOULD be interested. It was then that she did what she shouldn't have done. Probably if he had shown any more curiosity, let's say, curiosity remotely approaching what he had shown early in the fall, Margaret would not have been tempted. His naked urging would have pushed her toward high moral ground, and that's what she had expected, urging of the most naked sort. Probably she would not have been tempted if he had not sprung so suddenly from the veal to the moral high ground himself. "You know, we had our meeting."

"I figured you would have by now."

"Don't you want to know?"

"You would never tell me."

She looked at him. She said, "It was good." She thought about him dismissing the veal again, veal she had felt a little pride in presenting. She added, "But not really good."

He didn't say anything.

"Not good enough, maybe—"

He actually shrugged.

It was Margaret who exclaimed. "Monahan! What is the matter with you? Where is the careerist lowlife, the money-grubbing, arrogant, narrow-minded, narcissistic, sexy, exuberant, happy guy I used to know?"

"So, tell me the number, then."

"I can't tell you the number! But, lower than seven, higher than five!"

He shrugged again.

The old Tim would have leapt out of his chair at how weak his recommendation was, how iffy its passage through the provost's office would undoubtedly prove. She would have been treated to a tirade against hidebound so-called scholars, hacks in suits, the corruption of the intellectual life, the bankruptcy of the American campus and all the soldier ants who scurried—

"I can't believe this."

"What?"

"The way you are."

"What way am I?"

"Sadly well-meaning." She thought of the old Tim, then said, "Unsparkly."

"Not fun?"

"Well, no. Not fun."

He pushed back from the table, but not without running his finger around his plate, picking up the last of the sauce and then sucking it thoughtfully. He said, "I was too much fun. I was relying on that for everything. Remember that woman at Helen's party in September?"

"Cecelia?"

"Yes, her. She and I, we got fed up with me."

"How so?"

"Oh, you know how I am. Things were going well with her for a while, but the more that I was the way I was, the less interested I got in her, even though I liked her more and more, and then she met some mysterious person around the campus who sort of transfixed her with passion, and I realized that I have never transfixed, nor been myself transfixed . . ."

His voice tapered off, and Margaret got up to get the pie, but then he said, thoughtfully, "You've read my work. Look how relentlessly I've mined every romantic feeling and sexual desire for profit or career advancement. Look how carefully I've studied other authors for ideas about how to rework that material over and over for more profit and career advancement. Now everything I do reminds me of something I already wrote."

Margaret laughed, though Tim did not.

Then she brought out the lime chiffon pie and set it on the table. It was a good one, high and foamy-looking, but firm. The palest, coolest green. It was an old-fashioned sort of pie, one her mother had taught her to make, but her favorite. She cut him a wedge and set it in front of him. She said, "Well, Monahan, what can I say? You're probably right on all counts."

"Vindicated at last."

They thoughtfully ate their pie.

Finally she said, "One thing I have to ask. Have you given up snooping through other people's things?"

"Not at all."

"I thought you were having a moral rebirth."

"Jesus! No. Besides, snooping isn't immoral, it's just impolite. It's like looking at people's cards if they don't hold them up. You're supposed to do it."

"Say," said Margaret, "you know, I was thinking of Cecelia just the other day. She is Costa Rican, isn't she?"

"By way of L.A., yeah."

"I bet she would be interested in something. Where did I put that?"

And that was how Margaret supplied Tim with an excuse to call Cecelia. It was not that she hadn't complied with Dr. Lionel Gift's memo/request that she return her copy of his report to him, it was just that she had happened to Xerox it first.

46

So Soon

NORMALLY WHEN Elaine Dobbs-Jellinek bore good news, she bore it coolly, over the telephone, or in a memo. As a rule, the manner in which she delivered the news depended on the size of the grant. Only once before had she delivered it personally, and that was early in her career, when a proposal she had guided and helped write had won the university her first $250,000 grant. To mark that turning point in her fund-raising career (during the late, lamented days when SHE went to Washington, when Jack Parker was just a name attached to the University of Michigan) she had marched straight into the office of the president (who was gone now, to the University of Minnesota, fat lot of good that did her) and carolled, "A quarter million from NIH!" Later that very afternoon she had called the grant recipient and informed him.

Since then many six-figure sums had rolled through her office, and the receiving of grants had come to feel very much like buying new clothes—briefly invigorating, and certainly necessary, but never as thrilling as that very first Donna Karan with the Ferragamo pumps that matched perfectly, uncannily, as if they had been made for each other.

Nevertheless, Elaine was making her way across the snowy campus to Storrs Hall, where Dr. Bo Jones had his office, or, as Elaine preferred to think of it, his pen. Elaine was glad she had worn her SPF 15 moisturizer that morning, because a sudden blue sky, dry and brilliant, domed the campus and the thick, sugary covering of new snow on every building and branch, every cornice and curb and telephone wire and bicycle rack reflected and elaborated the sunlight until Elaine was almost blinded. After four or five steps, she took out her sunglasses with the UV protection coating and put them on. That was better. Now she could really appreciate how scintillating and lovely the world had become since she'd picked up her telephone twenty minutes before and heard the always exciting voice of Arlen

Martin's personal assistant say, "Miz Daubs-Jallanak? Mr. Martin on the line for you, honey."

It was the last day of classes. Although Elaine was on a twelve-month appointment, she was not quite immune to the combined fatigue and excitement of that fact. Indeed, the high point of Elaine's life had been her four years of college at the University of Iowa, where she had divided her time between the Pi Kappa Phi house and the music building (her major had been voice). Her college career had come just on the heels of two years of student unrest, but the only thought Elaine had given that recent history was regret that the windows of the college bookstore, which had been repeatedly broken the year before, were so small that they couldn't mount attractive displays. Elaine's college world had been a smaller version of the world of the fifties Big Ten—parties, classes, Greeks, football games, and nice clothes. There were many people on the campus who wore rags, went barefoot, played the recorder in front of Old Capitol, handed out leaflets, and drove VW buses with slogans about sex painted on the sides, but Elaine had done them the favor of ignoring them, and now they were gone, and she had a perfectly intact and entirely positive college experience to look back upon: pajamas, popcorn, and dance-marathoning for charity in the sorority house, a yearly round of tutoring, classes, choir concerts and recitals over at the music building, the choir tour to Belgium and Norway, and, of course, her courtship by Dean, which had been better by far than the ensuing marriage. As Elaine crossed the campus, she bestowed her UV-protected gaze most frequently on undergraduate girls who reminded her of herself—careful of their appearance, feminine, hopeful, attentive to details like the cut of a collar, the size of an earring. These girls, she knew, had unexpected futures before them, but they were well equipped to handle the unexpected. A girl who made no mistakes about the right shade of lipstick would always land on her feet.

Dr. Bo's pen was on the second floor of Storrs Hall, and the doctor was in, his back to the open door, pounding away at his computer, seemingly with his fists. Elaine raised her voice, as always with Dr. Bo, and shouted, "Dr. Jones! Dr. Jones!"

WHAT SHE looked like was a cardinal, the way a cardinal stood out red against the snow as it flitted from branch to branch. Dr. Bo was fond of snow, preferred cold weather to hot, preferred ice skating and skiing and snowshoeing in a nose-biting wind to any summertime sport. In fact, he had already begun the winter conditioning program that would prepare him for his trip to Tadzhikistan, Azerbaijan, Uzbekistan. That was a sentence he'd lately included in his letters of application (still unanswered): "I am in excellent physical condition and have embarked upon a training program guaranteed to fit me for any potential hardships." Just last night he had skied six miles to and from the campus after his wife had gone to bed.

Elaine took off her sunglasses and pulled off her leather gloves finger by finger. Dr. Bo pushed himself away from his computer, and she opened her red coat. Her suit was electric blue. The two together, the red against the blue, vibrated. When Dr. Bo looked away, at the white wall behind his desk, he saw an afterimage of her in green and purple.

She was grinning. She sat down on some books in a chair, grinning, and said, "Listen to this. Old Meats is saved! I found a donor who loved your idea about the museum, and is willing to fund the entire project, and all we have to do is name the museum after him!"

Without warning, rough tears came into Dr. Bo Jones' eyes. He hadn't been thinking much about Old Meats lately, having travelled far beyond that place already, but really, he was one of the few people on the campus who remembered Old Meats when it was bustling with activity, with white-coated, bloody-aproned meat science instructors who formed a tangible link between the animal on the hoof and the meat on the table. They were men of great strength and specific physical skills, who could fell an animal and bleed it and gut it and skin it, then show you the layers of fat and meat, the marbling that distinguished Grade A from prime. All the time the blood was flowing, they'd be talking. What to look for in a slaughter animal, signs of disease, the effects of various feeding regimens, breeds and varieties, even cooking techniques for different cuts of meat. They had no illusions, those men, about the cost of human life—it was high, and the fate of domesticated animals and plants was to pay it.

She said, "I knew you'd be excited!"

And he was! The displays leapt full-blown into his imagination— razorbacks hidden in the undergrowth, their tiny intelligent eyes glittering, the dark stinking hold of a Spanish galleon, crated sows squealing (there could easily be sound effects), the display of his own trophies, carried back from Tadzhikistan, Uzbekistan, Azerbaijan—

". . . chickens," she said.

Dr. Bo said, "What did you say?"

"I said, 'I don't suppose there is another museum in the country devoted to the history of chickens.' "

"The history of chickens?"

"Why, yes. That's what the funding's for. Old Meats is going to be turned into a chicken museum. I suppose that the plan is to celebrate the natural history of the chicken as well as the glory of modern chicken processing technology. The nation's foremost chicken historian is coming this week to look over the proposed site."

"That wasn't our idea. Ag technology, with some hog dioramas—"

"Oh, Dr. Jones, I remember that! That was a very good first thought! And I surely did emphasize that when I wrote the proposal, but things have evolved since then."

"You call a chicken museum 'evolving'?"

"I do." She tapped him on his tweed vest. "I do because that's what we got the funding for. It happens to a lot of proposals. There are good ideas, lots of them, and then there are fundable ideas, fewer of those. Fundable ideas are better ideas. In this case, chickens are fundable, so chickens are a better idea, you see?"

No, Dr. Bo thought, he did not see.

DR. LIONEL GIFT WAS all set. His summer-weight suits were packed, as were his Egyptian cotton dress shirts, undershorts, and socks. He had a spare pair of glasses, a swimming costume, a silk robe, a hat with a wide brim. He had his laptop, his modem, his internal communications program. He had his tickets and his money.

As usual, his exams would be given out by his graduate assistants and graded by the university computer. These grades would then be added to those already on the computer from the midterm, tallied according to a statistical curve, and reported to the students. By then, Dr. Lionel Gift would have been in Costa Rica for over a week. Let it snow let it snow let it snow: He would not be here to see it, and that suited him perfectly.

He looked at his watch. The limo to the airport would arrive in ten minutes. He decided to make one more last-minute check of the premises. All electrical cords were unplugged. All faucets were turned off. The furnace was set at fifty-five degrees. Two lamps and a radio in the living room were set to turn on around dusk, and one in the bedroom was set to go on at 9:30, his customary bedtime. All the lamps and the radio were set to go off at 11:00 (what was more revealing than lights that stayed on all night?). The burglar alarm, with its digital recording of a pair of furiously barking rottweilers, was armed. In other words, all was well and good in the Gift manse, all the goods well protected against the insatiable desires of those who had not prospered in the legitimate economy and had cast their lot with the illegitimate one.

Everything considered, this was a semester that Dr. Lionel Gift was glad to see pass. While he himself had performed with his usual excellence and probity, the same could not be said of his colleagues. The entirely unauthorized dissemination of his confidential report, while it had not damaged his prospects for success (nothing ever did that) had hurt him, had perhaps hurt him deeply, for it had revealed on the part of his colleagues what Dr. Gift could only interpret as abiding envy of his success and importance. As indifferent as he meant to be to the opinions of others, he found that he was not. Of course he would never show such a thing, but—

Even Cates! Even a chemist so successful in receiving grants as Cates had read the report with unseemly interest rather than just handing it back without being asked! And Helen! Many years ago, he had served on the committee that granted Helen tenure, and he had judged her an intelligent and personable young woman, pretty but not too pretty, French but not too French, Italian but not too Italian. Why had she turned on him? he wondered. And she was rumored to be involved with Ivar Harstad himself, so perhaps her behavior reflected some sort of opinion Ivar shared? Ah, Dr. Gift could hardly bear to think about it, it shot so full of holes his long-standing estimation of how he was generally beloved on the campus.

Even though it had no effect on the larger picture (his meetings were already set up, and the TransNational and the Seven Stones people would be there to follow up on everything he said and did), the shock was still with him, the shock that so few of his colleagues, all men and women of the finest educations, lived in so unprincipled a manner. He, who himself upheld the most scrupulous indifference toward others' fates, had not been able to quite overcome it, and so he felt doubly fortunate that the end of the semester afforded him the opportunity to get away. Down in Costa Rica, in his house there, he would certainly feel once more the pleasant knowledge that he was appreciated, and after all, that was enough for him.

As for his project, he had not allowed himself to underestimate the benighted forces who would, under the cover of "environmentalism," advocate a retrograde localism, express a knee-jerk conservationist ethic, and resist the inevitable embrace of the market and the future. There were a few radicals who could not be moved. That was always a given. Most of the others felt real fear. While this was more a psychological problem than anything else, practical considerations made it imperative that such fears be soothed, and he had worked up a sympathetic manner for dealing with the fearful. Fear was contagious, though, and there was another, more pivotal group that had to be protected from it. This group was inclined to move forward, and simply harbored a few doubts. He had an argument for them that they could understand: All transitions are difficult, and progress sometimes does look very much like deterioration, but that is an illusion caused by not fully embracing progressive ideas and methods. The solution is to redouble efforts and commitment. A fourth group he didn't have to worry about, though regrettably smaller in Costa Rica than in other places, they were entirely on his side already. This group fully understood the bottomest of the bottom lines—with revenues from forestry, fisheries, cattle, and tourism inexplicably gone, declining, or levelling off (Dr. Gift's own projections were proving rather optimistic, though he attributed that to the mistakes of geologists and forest and fisheries experts), growth could not be sustained without the exploitation of something new. This gold seam was an unlooked-for bonus that would keep that line on Gift's graph shooting upward for some undefined period of time, and really, that was what mattered most to those with the firmest grasp on reality.

He saw the limo round the corner up the street. Though the pavement had been plowed, it was still icy, and the vehicle fishtailed a bit as it entered Dr. Gift's street. Actually, it was not a limo, it was merely a minivan. Somehow these two things coming together—the sight of the van fishtailing on the ice and the recognition of the disparity between what the van was called and what it was—infused Dr. Lionel Gift with the sense that really he need not return to this place, that, if he chose, he could be walking out of his house for the last time. It was a remarkable thought, most importantly, a principled thought—he had spent considerable time and money on his house, and yet he was more or less indifferent toward it. He turned before picking up his bag and surveyed the front hall and the living room. Comfortable, masculine, decorated to resemble an exclusive men's club, but what attached him here? He smiled. He picked up his bag and his computer and stepped out onto the porch, careful to stay within the exit parameters allowed by the burglar alarm.

WHEN KERI OPENED the door, she saw Bob's neck crane to look around her. She knew then that he saw the empty room behind her, the made beds, the picked-up floors. But he said, anyway, "Diane here?"

"Hey! No, sorry." After a pause, Keri felt herself whine, "I know she'll be sorry she missed you."

"Well, I just brought by some stuff. You know. She left it. I figured she'd want it sometime."

He dropped the bag of stuff by the threshold, and Keri picked it up and set it inside the door. She couldn't help noticing that the stuff wasn't all that important—no clothing or underwear or anything personal. A toothbrush. A notebook without much in it. A novel. A package of blank computer disks. Bob sighed. Considering that he was the one who called it quits, Keri thought he looked awfully depressed. He said, "I guess you don't have any classes right now?"

"No, I'm done for the semester. I mean, except for exams." She continued to smile. They both knew that there had been plenty of those gab sessions that girls get into, and that therefore she knew plenty more about him than she was letting on. He interpreted her smile, which she meant to be encouraging and sympathetic, as amused.

"Well," he said.

"I'll be sure she gets this stuff," she said.

"Okay."

"Thanks."

"Yeah. Thank you." He turned.

"You want to come in and wait for her?"

"Sort of."

She stepped back from the door.

He said, "What do you think?"

"About what?"

"About what I should do next."

"Go home for Christmas and ask some girls out."

"Oh. I'm not going home for Christmas."

"You're not? Why not?" Now she felt genuinely sorry for him.

"Oh, my job, you know."

"Then get somebody to do your job for a day or two and go home. That's what I think."

The funny thing was, he'd always noticed how pretty she was, but only after a while. He said, "Okay, well, there's the stuff. Bye."

"Bye."

He turned.

After four steps, he turned back. She was just shutting the door. He said, "Say, don't tell her how weird I'm acting, all right? I mean, I broke up with her, and I still think it's the best thing to do."

"I won't tell."

And she wouldn't. But she knew that he wished that she would.

DR. CATES DID NOT, as a rule, develop personal relationships with his undergraduate students, which was why he was surprised to see one of them, or someone who said that he was one of them, standing outside his office when he came in about noon to pick up his mail. Dr. Cates was taking a rare day off. His son, Daniel, wanted to go sledding. Finding himself on the horns of a familiar dilemma— sledding was dangerous but Dr. Cates did not want Daniel to learn fear from him—Dr. Cates resolved it in his usual way. The sled was in the back of the car and Daniel was waiting for him in the front seat. Dr. Cates estimated that his way of safeguarding Daniel by going along with him whenever there might be a risk would last at most another year—Daniel was eight, and already beginning to chafe under Dr. Cates' restrictions.

The undergraduate student approached him as soon as he got off the elevator. "I'm Lyle Karstensen, sir?" he said, and he held out the portfolio he had under his arm. "I'm leaving school? I'm going to work for a year or so and come back? It's not like I'm flunking out or anything? It's just so expensive, you know?"

Dr. Cates said, "Is there a problem with your grade?" He pushed the key into the lock of his office.

"No, sir? You gave me an A? See, that was the only A I've ever gotten here? Because I really liked your course? So when I was thinking of someone to give these to, I thought of you?" He pressed the portfolio into Dr. Cates' hands.

"What is this?"

"Well, I don't know, sir? It looks like a cross between some kind of plans and one of those drawings where you find the hidden pictures?

I don't know what it's for, but I couldn't bring myself to throw it away?"

"What do you want me to do with it?"

"I don't know, sir? But just have a look before you throw it away?"

Dr. Cates had always thought that his special talent was focusing, and over the years he had learned never to be distracted by other people's business. Nevertheless, as he opened the portfolio, the elevator bell rang, its doors opened, and there was Daniel. "Dad! What are you doing? I'm cold!" he barked.

Cates caught himself in the act of flinching and smiled patiently. "I'm speaking to a student, Daniel. Please wait for me a minute."

"It's always a minute!" said Daniel in exasperation. "A minute isn't as long as you think it is, Dad!"

Lyle reflected that "please" was not a word that his father had ever used to him. But, of course, exasperation was not a feeling he had ever expressed to his father, either.

Cates made a show of looking at the plans, but really he didn't see them. He was too aware of Daniel's darkening mood and, also, too aware of the treat he had promised himself—the sparkling brightness of the day and the prospect of flying down that giant hill, Daniel or no Daniel. He closed the portfolio with his customary dignity, though, and laid it on his desk.

"Thanks?" said Lyle.

"Come ON!" said Daniel. "Here's the ELEVATOR!"

47

Joe Doaks, Young American

AFTER MARY HAD passed through the line at the cash register, she saw that the only seats available in the commons were at a large table right up front that was already occupied by a white kid, maybe a sophomore or a junior, kind of blondish and largish, the sort of person she had a hard time distinguishing from most of the other white kids on the campus. She hesitated, as much out of habit as anything else. Had she been with her own group, the other black students she ate most of her lunches with, she would have immediately looked elsewhere, but today she was eating lunch with Keri, Sherri, and Diane. If she didn't sit down, but passed by on a fruitless search for an unoccupied table, Sherri's exclamations would be loud and embarrassing, attracting everyone's attention to the sight of her conspicuous self turning around and scuttling back as ordered. Her hesitation lasted only the second it took her to summon her most opaque manner. She set her tray down at the corner farthest from the white kid and pulled out the chair.

Joe looked up from his meditation upon his lunch (two quarter-pound burgers with cheese and an order of fries, plus a large Pepsi) and leaned back in his chair. Without even thinking, without actually feeling unusually hostile, and without losing his ingrained feeling of innocence, Joe said, "Hey, nigger, you can't sit there."

In fact, this was the first time since coming to the university that Mary had heard the word "nigger." None of the black students here used it in the teasing way men used it in her neighborhood at home, and the white students and professors were very very careful, at least around her. So more in surprise than anything else, she said, "What?"

Now Joe looked around, just to see who was watching. Detecting a large and potentially sympathetic audience at the other tables, he leaned expansively even farther back in his chair. "Hey, nigger," he said.

Really, Mary thought, I could not pick this guy out of a crowd.

Average height, average clothing, average coloring, average hairstyle, average looks.

"You can't—"

Average voice, average build, average blue eyes, average straight teeth.

"—sit there!"

In embarrassment, Mary could not help staring at her tray, her croissant sandwich, her lettuce wedge w/ one-quarter tomato and Russian dressing. That was why she didn't see the look on Keri's face, only heard, "Oh, here you are," and then a heavy thudding clank as the edge of Keri's tray rammed the base of the white kid's skull and sent him sprawling into his burgers and fries. "Geez!" he exclaimed. "What the fuck!" He sat up, grease and ketchup glistening on his chin. Mary saw that he was rubbing the back of his head.

Keri looked as she always did, smiling and bland. She said, "Oh. I'm sorry. I must have not been looking where I was going."

"You practically fucking decapitated me!"

"I am sorry. I'll sit here." She sat next to Mary.

"You can't fucking sit here."

Now Sherri came up. She said, in her brassy voice, "Why not? Nobody else is. You can't save the whole table. It's not fair, and anyway I think it's against the rules." She set down her tray, and began taking off plates. She had her usual oddball lunch—two slices of cheese, some baked beans, a box of Rice Krispies, a glass of orange juice, and a large peanut butter cookie, each on its own plate. Pretty soon her lunch, her books, and her outerwear were spread all over the table. Joe Doaks said, "What the fuck?" Sherri gave him a look, then drew her books two or three inches closer to her plates. Diane sat across from Sherri, looking to Mary as though she were poised to hire, to fire, and to acquire large companies. Since the departure of Bob, she had redoubled her commitment to the executive demeanor. She said to Joe, who was sitting to her left, "Pardon me, but you have ketchup on your chin. It isn't very attractive."

It was impossible for Mary to gauge whether her roommates had or had not heard the white kid's remark. On the one hand, he had spoken in a loud voice. On the other, noise in the commons of eating, conversation, and clanking trays and dishes usually drowned out any solos. People at other tables had not really looked up as a group, whether because they had not heard him, or because they didn't care, or because they were embarrassed. Keri, across from her, was eating peaceably, as if no crisis had been weathered, as if no adrenaline were shooting through her veins, as it was through Mary's. Mary didn't seem to be trembling—her hand was steady as it raised her fork to her mouth, but even so, she felt as if she had passed through some kind of electrical field and been transformed—magnetized? polarized? had her ions reversed? Something profound like that but detectable only with specialized instruments. At the same time, the profundity of her response surprised and dismayed her, because she had assumed that she was ready for anything like this. She was from Chicago, for God's sake. Her high school had seen plenty of racial incidents. She glanced at Keri again, who was beginning, easy as you please, on her canned peaches. When Mary caught her eye, she sighed, and said, "God! I don't know how I am going to study for my econ exam. I know I'm one of the seven percent that gets flunked."

Mary said, "When is it?"

"Wednesday."

Joe said, "Hey! What SHIT is going down here?"

This time, people at surrounding tables did look up. Sherri said, "What's your PROBlem, man?"

"You've got your hairy mitten in my French fries!"

"Well, SORry! I didn't see them, okay?"

"They've got fucking white hairs all over them now!"

"You want a piece of cheese or something?"

"Nah. Fuck this." Joe Doaks stormed away, leaving his chair on its back and his tray on the table.

"God!" said Sherri. "What WAS his problem?"

Diane took a sip of her Diet Coke. "No future," she said. "He obviously knows that someone like him hasn't got a chance of even approaching his parents' economic level, education notwithstanding. Too bad, huh?" She smiled.

They had lulled her, all three of them, them and the professors and the other students in Dubuque House. They had drop by drop oozed around her defenses. They hadn't gotten to be her friends the way other people on the campus were friends, the way kids back home were friends, but they had gotten familiar, and even comfortable to be with. The way they were polite all the time—not just with her, either, but with each other because yelling, confronting, conflict of any kind upset them—had gotten easy and pleasant. They ignored the fact that she was black the way they ignored the fact that Keri was beautiful or Diane was ruthless or Sherri was flunking out, all so they could get along, and now this incident was ready to disappear because they would never be the ones to bring it up and discuss it. What she had to say, what she felt, might wreck the comfort they had achieved—that was the unspoken danger. And after only four months, she had come to enjoy that comfort.

And yet, the white kid had been punished—bruised, admonished, and humiliated by mere girls, and in public.

Maybe she should be the one to bring it up and discuss it? Some of her black friends, if not all of them, would say yes, absolutely, make an issue of it. Many, if not most, of her relatives, would say it was not quite big enough to bother about—hold your ammunition until you really need it. Hassan would tell her to follow her instincts, and act on her feelings, but she didn't know what those were. Mary looked at her lettuce wedge and quarter tomato. Actually, it didn't seem fair that she should have to work her way through the ins and outs of all this right when exams were upon her. Here it was, the old friction, the drag that slowed her down, coming up again. She felt her cheeks grow hot, and it seemed to her right then that her place in this world, which had been small enough to begin with, had suddenly grown smaller, had gotten to be just a pinpoint that she could balance on for a while until it disappeared completely.

48

"Lydia"

a short story by Gary Olson

THE ROOM WAS dark, even though it was nearly noon, because Lydia Henderson had the shades drawn. One ray of sunshine [Gary looked out the window of his bedroom] was glinting off the crusty, brilliant snow, passing through the crack between the two curtains, and lighting up Lydia's hair, which was spread around her on the pillow. All over the campus, brightly clad students were hurrying along the cleared walks to the rooms where their final exams were being held. But Lydia was asleep, deeply asleep, and dreaming of her future.

Strangely, she was married to Lyle Karstensen, a kid she had briefly dated the year before, who had since left school and gone back to Indianapolis, and whom Lydia hadn't thought of in months. She seemed to have two children, and in the dream, Lydia sensed that they were present in the room, but she couldn't see them; she could only hear them [Gary inhaled] breathing. In the dream, their names were Larry and Angela. The sleeping Lydia turned from her back to her side. She always slept without any clothes on, so as she turned and stretched, her left hand slid over her flat stomach and her lean hip, and came to rest on her thigh [Gary ran his hand down over his T-shirt and pants to see if this was possible]. The Lydia she was dreaming about did the same thing, and someone, somewhere, some Lydia that was viewing both the dreamer and the dreamed, felt a sense of surprise, because in the dream Lydia had a hugely fat stomach that fell in rolls onto the sheet [This was really good. Just that evening, Gary had been watching something on PBS about people who could make themselves conscious that they were dreaming but not wake up]. Now the Lydia in the dream woke up and saw that it was noon, but the dreaming Lydia did not wake up, though she was aware that it must be noon or even later. The dreaming Lydia said, "You two kids are in here, aren't you?" and two little voices replied, "Yes,

Mommy," but Lydia couldn't see them because the room was so dark.

Oh, thought the third, intermediate Lydia [Professor Monahan always said that you shouldn't let a good idea go to waste], what a nightmare this is, being married to Lyle and being enormously fat, and it being noon, and not being able to see my children, who must be hiding. How did I get into this nightmare?

Lydia the dreamer groaned, and her head tossed on her pillow, tangling her sun-streaked hair.

In the dream, the enormous Lydia heaved herself to her feet. She saw that there was a light on in the bathroom, and she thought that she would certainly like to look in the mirror. "Kids?" she said. "Where are you?"

Tiny voices said, "Right here, Mommy." That word struck her to the heart, that little "Mommy." She staggered two or three steps forward.

In Lydia the dreamer's room, the door opened, and Lydia's roommate came in from his chemistry exam. He saw that Lydia was still asleep, and heard her say something like "Kids?" and then give out a long, frightened groan. He put down his books.

In the dream, the enormous Lydia stumbled, reached out to regain her footing, but fell anyway. She felt her knees, then her palms, then her hip meet the floor. Then, just as she felt her head slam [that was a good word, Gary thought] into the chest of drawers, the third Lydia exclaimed, "This IS a nightmare! All I have to do is wake up!" And Lydia woke up.

Her roommate was opening the curtains. Light poured in. Her roommate said, "God, you were thrashing around! I thought you were going to study for your history exam this morning."

Lydia rubbed her eyes. She said, "I fell back asleep. God, I had the weirdest dream. I was so fat. I was married to Lyle. Remember him?"

They looked at each other and laughed. [Gary sat back, staring at the screen. Now what? Earlier in the semester, when that little short girl in his class, Ellen her name was, had put a dream in a story, Professor Monahan said that the dream had to relate to the real life of the story somehow. Gary got up and paced around the room. It was three a.m. by the kitchen clock. He had to have this in by noon. He thought of something and sat down again.] Lydia pulled her tangled hair back from her face, and twisted it together. Then she threw off the covers and stood up. Her roommate looked on in deep appreciation. When she went into the bathroom to brush her teeth, he sere-naded her with his favorite song: "Lydia oh Lydia, oh have you seen Lydia, Lydia the tattooed lady?" She put her head around the door. She said, "Gary, I do love you." [Gary blushed and pressed the delete key four times, then instead of "Gary," he typed in "Rick." He sat back. The other thing was, he wanted to get something in about the real Lydia's father, say, about his raving over his new babies' belly buttons, but that didn't fit, either. It was amazing how SMALL this story was, considering how LONG he had been working on it. But it was good enough, this late in the semester. And then, even though the class would be over, he might rewrite it over the Christmas vacation.]

Part Four

49

Feliz Navidad

AFTER THE COMMENCEMENT of her passion for Chairman X, Cecelia had given up her plans to return to L.A. for Christmas. She
decided to stay in her duplex and, as it were, force it to rise to the
Yuletide occasion. She WOULD be warm there, she WOULD feel
at home there, she WOULD make the place feel colorful and lively
by playing music and buying pillows and inexpensive but bright art-
works. It WOULD become a warm, welcoming nest for their sudden
moments together. As soon as she had turned in her grades, she went
shopping for transformative items. After that, she baked a batch of
sugar cookies and some cinnamon bread. That night, she went to bed,
late, with the baking aromas still wafting through the rooms. Her
effort seemed to have succeeded. With all the lamps on, the duplex
looked like a place you (he) might actually want to walk into, a place
where you (he) could sit down and have a warm conversation in the
living room, or where you (he) could follow your friend (Cecelia)
into the kitchen and eat hunks of fragrant sweet bread and laugh.

In the morning, not so. Twenty-eight gray days were still possible—on the weather report they were always talking gleefully about
the kind of record that included the most snowy weekends in a hundred years or the longest period that a Canadian air mass had remained
stationary over the city. She picked up the phone and bought tickets
for L.A., leaving the next day, full fare, departure time 6 a.m. This
decision, made on impulse without regard for Chairman X, seemed
eminently sane.

As soon as she bought the tickets she regretted it. Now the vacation
stretched before her as an infinite series of opportunities for passionate
abandon that she had thoughtlessly foregone. She hunched more
tightly over her teacup. She did not expect to see X before her departure—the thrill of the unforeseen was the root thrill of their affair,
and the one she had been unable to give up. One of these days—
maybe even tomorrow afternoon—he would come knocking and find
her gone, the windows dark, the walk unshovelled, the *Weekly Shopper*

yellowing on the porch. Cecelia gave a deep shuddering sigh at the thought.

She made herself look out the window again. The scene was unchanged. It could be any time of day, any day of the winter. She, in fact, could be any one of the three people she saw sliding along the sidewalk, bundled up to the eyeballs in dark, puffy wrappings. She tore herself away from her teacup and began to pack.

When she got off the plane, Cecelia realized that she had never in her life come to L.A. from any place cold. She was not in the habit of finding delight there, but the palm trees outside the airport, which she had hardly ever noticed in the past, now struck her as a positive marvel. Of course there was grime (she thought as they turned east out of the airport) and the air was yellowish with smog, but it wasn't gray and low and permanent. In fact, the salient characteristic of the Midwest, uniformity, was precisely what L.A. had the least of, had nothing of, to tell the truth. There were shocking spots of color— ragged bougainvillea draping scarlet over a sagging fence, hibiscus big as stop signs at the corners of porches. In her parents' backyard, she strolled among the lemon, orange, and grapefruit trees, inhaling the sweetness and palming the weighty fruits. Her father's avocados were black on the glistening jade branches, too numerous for the family to eat.

She kept meaning to mention to her father what both Chairman X and Tim Monahan had told her—that some big corporation with one of those bland megalomaniacal names was planning to mine gold in the Tierra del Madre forest, but between his work schedule and all the Christmas preparations, she didn't get it said. And he was in a bad mood—there was something going on between him and her mother, one of those periodic angry times, where they seemed fed up with one another and willing to fight on the smallest pretext. Perhaps as a result of her quiet life, Cecelia's tolerance for conflict was lower than it had been. Why add fuel to her parents' conviction that their lives—and the world—were steadily devolving? There was nothing they could do about it except take it out on each other. They would learn about this latest example from the newspaper or from relatives back in Costa Rica soon enough.

But what about her? Didn't she care about the largest virgin cloud forest in Central America? Tim expected her to. He'd brought her Gift's report practically on a platter, eager in a very un-Timlike way, and she hadn't responded as he'd expected her to, and she'd felt guilty, the way she'd felt once when her ex-husband gave her a black lace teddy for Christmas instead of the dictionary of medieval Catalan that she was expecting.

Well, it was not clear what she did care about anymore, was it? Now that she was back home, it was easy to see how she'd once directed her life, and easy to see how she'd fallen away from that, too. Here was her room, with her pink bedspread, her white walls, her white furniture, her sax in the corner, her New York City Ballet poster of pink toe slippers on the wall. Collections of books from every phase of her childhood since she'd learned to read at age four filled the bookcase. *Don Quixote*, for example, was well thumbed. She had read it five or six times. When she took it down now and opened it to the adventure of the knight of the mirrors, she could remember reading the words, and remember a sense of being lost in pleasure, but she couldn't imagine how her seven-year-old, or even her fourteen-year-old, self had understood it, either in Spanish or in English. Now it seemed that all she could remember was an effort to establish her virtue, to transcend her circumstances, to be the daughter her doctor-father-turned-gardener and her accountant-mother-turned-bookkeeper relied on her to be. Elevating herself had been both her virtue and her reward.

Now it felt like she had dropped to all fours and was roaming the old locations nose first. The house was full of smells—cinnamon and allspice and cloves, not to mention peppers and garlic and limes and oranges and the apple blossom soap her mother favored in the bathrooms. Oil frying. Emilio's wife's perfume, which was an alien whiff of Nieman Marcus suddenly presenting itself. The house was full of flavors, too, because she was always hungry, and went from room to room eating cookies and chocolate and pieces of fruit, or drinking juice. Always something. If she wasn't eating, she was wondering when the next meal was coming, or helping her mother to prepare it. The hardest thing was to lift herself out of these present moments and actually think of anything. Or rather, to think of anything other than having sex with Chairman X. She was thinking about that so fully and so constantly that she might as well have been having sex with him. How could she pursue the transcendence and virtue of the intellectual life when her mind had disappeared into her body like a sponge into a basin of ink?

Which did not mean, apparently, that Chairman X had imprinted her with his convictions. If he had, she would have told her father weeks ago about the gold mining plan. Chairman X's fervor on this subject was not like anything Cecelia had ever experienced before. He was already talking about it as he walked through her door, and continued talking without cease, with only a pause like a musical rest when he orgasmed, until he left. Every day, sometimes more than once, he called her, and without saying hello, he would begin, "They have scarlet macaws there, did you know that? The only other place in the world that serves as a habitat for scarlet macaws is in New Guinea, and that habitat will be gone by 2005 if the Japanese don't stop cutting down the hardwoods there. Have you ever seen a scarlet macaw?"

Her reply didn't matter, really. He was continuing, "And forty-eight species of toads and frogs! and 123 species of butterflies!" Then he would hang up, only to call later about the tapirs.

Once, just once, she had said what she knew her father would say to her—"It doesn't surprise me. It happens all the time," and Chairman X had nearly imploded right in her apartment. He had said, "Are you on their side, then?"

"Well, no—"

"If you think they can't be stopped, then you're on their side!"

For the sake of her own safety, she had soothed him. But did he go on like this at home, over the bean loaf? While bathing the toddler? Cleaning out the closets? Did he exclaim and exclaim, an ever-surging, never-ebbing tide of outrage? If so, how on earth did SHE, the nonwife, stand it? Over the years, he must, Cecelia thought, have turned his nonwife into an unfeeling stone. That's the only way you could live with someone like him. Cecelia herself had no illusions—there would be no living with Chairman X, no making a future together. There would only be fucking (she glanced at her father across the breakfast table as she thought this word. Well, that was another reason she hadn't told him, wasn't it? That she was afraid of her father knowing how this man had made an animal of her), only fucking, only fucking. She got up from her chair and went into the bathroom and splashed her face with cold water.

All the presents under the tree were for Emilio's and Carlos' children, mostly Barbies for Kelly and Ninja Turtle equipment for Derek, Danny, and Alex. Cecelia had ordered her mother a silk robe from Victoria's Secret and bought her father an expensive book that her mother said he wanted on the theory of Zen gardens. Emilio and

Carlos had nothing for her—their wives were too busy with the children to shop. But then there was something after all, way at the back (Cecelia's mother was grinning). Kelly, who could read her name and not much else, crawled under and pulled it out. She read the tag and said, "This isn't for me. Who's this for? Is there anything else for me, Grandma?"

Cecelia's mother said, "Kelly, that is for Tía Cecelia," and Kelly, who admired Cecelia and wanted to be her friend, presented it with a grin.

It was an album. Before Cecelia even opened the cover, her mother was discounting her own care and thoughtfulness in her usual fashion—"This house is so crammed, I had to get something out of here. You have your own place out there now."

The photos had been lovingly pasted in and labelled: "Cecelia, aged fourteen months (Christmas, 1964), with Tía Luisa, Grandpa's farm"; "Cecelia, aged two, and Tía Norma, 1965. The pony's name was Paco"; "Mama Juana, Tía Luisa, Tía Norma, Tía Angelita, Easter, 1956, with Grandpa, on the porch of the hacienda. Hats from DIOR!"; "Grandma and Grandpa, just married (July 1934), with their first car, a Ford from the U.S., downtown San José."

Her mother said, "I had those old photos copied for each of you, but the ones just you are in, those are the originals. Each book goes up to when you were twenty-one. I gave Emilio and Carlos theirs on their birthdays, but you weren't here then."

"Mom! This must have taken forever!"

"Well," said her mother, "sorting through all the pictures and finding ones without the heads cut in half, that took forever!"

Cecelia laughed. She turned the first pages deliberately, looking at the faces, but also at the indistinct gray backgrounds, trying to divine the greens, yellows, reds, and purples of her imagination. She said, "I can't remember a thing about being there! I wish I could." Her mother sighed. The photos of L.A., of this house, of grammar school and high school were without mystery—she could remember, in fact, every hideous and outdated dress she was pictured in. She leafed through those pages until she got to the end of the book, then turned back to the beginning again, to Grandpa and Grandma standing in one of their orchards, which was flowering. In the small black and white photo it was impossible to tell the variety of the trees, but the young couple looked confident and strong already, even as young as they were, much more confident and strong than Cecelia's parents or any of her aunts and uncles had ever looked. They looked at home, and strengthened by that knowledge.

Cecelia glanced at her mother, who smiled back at her, pleased that Cecelia was pleased, but Cecelia wasn't thinking precisely of the album. She said, "Mom, why did you and Tía Norma ever come to L.A.?"

"Oh, well, your father and Uncle Emilio . . ." Her voice trailed off.

"What?"

"They had big hopes. Or they said they did."

"But what?"

"Oh, the real thing was, there wasn't much going on there." She shrugged.

Cecelia felt a third presence enter the room, a presence she recognized. It was her mother's unspoken disappointment. She made herself sit calmly with it, something she had never been able to do before. And she let herself think a thought she had always avoided, that all their lives would have been better if they had stayed at home rather than coming to L.A. If their homes had been worth staying at. And then she felt a fourth presence enter the room. It was her own sadness. She closed the album and looked up. The rest of the family could be heard outside, flying the radioplane Emilio had given to Alex. Cecelia's mother began picking up wrapping paper and smoothing it over her knee. Cecelia said to her, "Say, you know what I heard?"

"What?" said her mother.

And Cecelia felt the story bubble up, as unobstructed as a fresh spring. "Listen to this," she said.

50

Away in a Manger

EARL'S REAL PROBLEM was how sudden the change was. One night Bob was forking dirty straw into the wheelbarrow and Earl was gazing at him through half-closed eyelids, and the next morning the door was slamming shut (Bob never let the door slam) and an entirely new person was unceremoniously dumping feed into the trough. Earl contained his usual impatience for the morning feeding and stood back in the corner. "Hey, Sooie," this guy said. "Wanna eat?" The feed mounded higher than usual in the trough, and the guy said, "I ain't hauling my tail over here five times a day, that's for sure. Two is what I got time for, and since it's Christmas Eve, you're lucky to get that. So here's enough to get you to dinner." Then, without even waiting for Earl to approach his trough and sample the day's offering, the guy wheeled the barrow into the pen and started flinging rather than laying the dirty straw into it. Earl found the noise disturbing and the sight of his products flying around rather embarrassing. The guy did a haphazard job, too. Earl could have pointed out any number of spots that he'd missed, but clearly the guy was anxious to be off— he set the pitchfork by the door rather than hanging it in its place, and he forgot to clear Earl's automatic waterer. No scratching, no fellowship, no conversation, no radio, which Bob turned on for him in the mornings. Abruptly, Earl lost his struggle against depression, and instead of beginning at the trough, which he had been all set to do, he went over, kicked his straw into a mound, and lay down.

Recently, Earl's reasons for getting up in the morning had gotten rather less compelling. At bottom, he was still the hog he had always been, the hog he was bred to be, and he was bred to eat. That was his genius and his burden. Whether or not he was hungry before Bob's arrival, the sight of feed in the trough was guaranteed to stimulate his appetite, and he was thereafter guaranteed to eat to capacity. He experienced this as a deep driving need, and he accepted it. Sometimes, even if his stomach felt full, and almost achy, his mouth just kept on going. Well, okay. But other than eating, he mostly got up to greet

Bob. He was happy to see Bob. It went beyond the eating, and the care, and even the scratching. To tell the truth, Earl Butz had gotten attached to Bob, almost dependent on him. He appreciated his relaxed and considerate ways, and he appreciated the respect and fondness he sensed that Bob felt for him. These were quiet virtues, to be sure, but the debacle of the morning had only redoubled Earl's gratitude.

But it went even beyond that. Pundits (of course there were none of these, since Earl's very life was largely a secret) might have doubted Earl's capacity for sincere feeling, given a hog's naturally sociable disposition combined with an unusually isolated upbringing that could have given him sociopathic tendencies, but actually, his isolation deepened Earl's pleasure in his and Bob's relationship. There was little he could do anymore to show Bob how he felt—he was too big and maybe too old to play with the toys Bob had given him. With his bulk, he couldn't get around the way he had done. Getting up in the morning and then going at his job with apparent enthusiasm was all he had to offer, and every morning he offered it, full of the assurance that though Bob didn't say much, he did understand.

Not this morning. Earl resisted jumping to conclusions. But that didn't mean he would exert himself today the way he did other days. Today he would give in, lie down, doze, let the ugly mound of feed just sit there.

And then he didn't wake up again until that guy was back, with another slam of the door. Earl stared at him through slit eyes, but maintained his deep breathing, as if asleep. The guy said, "Off your feed, eh, Sooie? No shit, either. You sick? Well, it's Christmas, and I'm not hanging around to figure this out. I suppose you can hold it till tomorrow, can't you?" And then he left. Good riddance, thought Earl.

The trouble with sleeping all day, though, was that then you were up all night. Earl, a hog of preternaturally regular habits, had never been up all night before, and he would have been the first to agree that it was not an experience he was likely to repeat.

First of all, it was completely dark, because that guy hadn't left even a single light on. Second of all, it was unusually quiet. Though it was always more or less quiet in Earl's pen, the total darkness seemed somehow to amplify the silence. If Earl simply lay there, hardly breathing, hardly rustling his straw, the silence flowed around him, seemed to pour into his eyes and mouth and nose as well as his ears. Seemed to wash over his hide like the warm baths Bob gave him every so often. But it didn't put him to sleep. The thing was, eyes open or eyes closed, he saw the same black screen no matter where he turned his head, and on it, after a bit, little flashes of color began to appear. At first they were mere dots, then larger dots, then streaks. As a hog, Earl didn't wonder much about the future, but in his experience, most odd things that happened were followed by pain, so the dots and streaks made him uneasy, until it was clear that they were just dots and streaks. He lay there and enjoyed them, not really analyzing them too deeply. What a mood he was in! Lost somewhere, it seemed, but neither anxious nor frightened, hardly aware of his bulky body and the discomfort, pain, and effort that were its daily lot.

Then, inside and contained by the darkness, he saw light and he sensed activity around him. He made himself very still, and the activity grew more intense. What it felt like was being about to open his eyes and stand up, stand up and run around, as if standing up and running around were the most automatic thing in the world. It felt as though, if he were to be just a little quieter, he could hear something, but he didn't know what it was. And no matter how quiet he made himself be, he could not be quiet enough to hear what it was, but whatever it was was reassuring and familiar. Earl gave out a deep sigh.

Then the feeling changed again, as if he had moved past the earlier feeling into something new. The something new was a sense of antici-pation, rather like the feeling he got every morning when he heard Bob outside the door, but this was a hotter and more eager anticipation, the passion of a younger hog, and then Earl could place what was happen-ing to him. He was remembering.

Of course it was all there—he had a brain the size of a grapefruit after all—and while it was somewhat lacking in the cerebral cortex division, Earl, like every other brain-owning individual, usually only bothered to use a small percentage of its intellectual capacity.

Earl did not surmise why he hadn't ever remembered more than the most daily concerns—mired in routine? or possibly denial? Now, however, sunk in darkness, he sensed the mundane fall away, and he distinctly remembered what it was that made his youthful self so excited. It was the out-of-doors.

As a well-bred hog, Earl had been gestated and born in an ultramod-ern confinement complex. Not for him the hurly-burly of the tradi-tional muddy hogpen, or, God forbid, a half-wild youth among pin oaks, nosing all the time for acorns. He was born to be air-conditioned and heated, to lie on a smooth grate and drink from an automatic waterer, to eat milled food laced with antibiotics, wormers, and growth enhancers. Nevertheless, it had happened that around the time of Earl's birth the farmer who bred him found his complex rather lightly booked—only three or four of the sows had litters, and it was a late Indian summer—and so he had amused himself by letting the animals out in the yard every day, they were so lively and cute.

The brown crackling leaves lay on the sunlit, moist grass, and the black branches of trees laced against a sky that day after day poured forth a light that Earl had never seen before or since. All the piglets gambolled and frolicked in the yard, and the farmer sat nearby, his yearly work of planting and harvesting done, remarking to his wife that the grandkids should see this. The sows enjoyed the air and the late-season warmth, and rooted around here and there for some sharp-tasting morsel or other, the farm dogs wandered over and barked in their official capacities, the farm cats looked on from a distance, and the days, five or six of them, passed in a rare dream of mammalian amity. Crows cawed in the trees, the wind blew, and Earl stored up a treasure of memories that only now, having set his work aside, he found the time to sift through.

They seemed to play themselves out on the screen of darkness that enveloped him whether his eyes were open or shut. That green, that blue, that brightness. The impact of one of his siblings barrelling into him, rolling him against the cool earth. His own trotters sinking into softness as he jumped about. Most important, all the scents and odors that mingled everywhere, all of them distinct, but none of them strong—much unlike the confinement building, where the odor of himself and his companions was overpowering.

He gave himself up to his memories, and lay in a half-stupor on his bed of straw, unsleeping but remote from his trough and his ventilation system and his toys and his duties, and also from the pains in his legs and his back.

When the guy came in with his usual slam the next morning (well, it was almost afternoon, but how would Bob ever find that out?), his conscience smote him at the sight of the still hog, and he panicked—dead, for sure, and this was some kind of unique experiment—and he ran out and called Bob, who was having Christmas breakfast with his family after opening presents. Bob thought first of Dr. Bo and second of Earl and jumped in his car without finishing his waffle, just putting a peanut butter sandwich and two pieces of sausage in his pocket, and by the time Bob got back, Earl was on his feet at the trough going at it as if nothing had ever happened and that guy was talking fast about how often he had come over and when he had last checked him the night before and first checked him that morning, and Earl pretended not to notice the quarrel. Bob felt him all over while the guy was standing there, and said, "Well, he seems okay. You're lucky. I'll pay you for two visits, is all." And after the guy left, Bob picked up the scratching stick and sat on the bars of the pen and scratched Earl on the back WHILE he was eating, a highly unusual and indulgent procedure to which Earl didn't object at all.

51

Merry Christmas

CHAIRMAN X COULD NOT help getting Cecelia mixed up with the last remaining virgin cloud forest, which that pompous, bombastic, cretinous imbecile from the economics department was doing his best to destroy, and so every thought of Cecelia, which would normally be at least a little soothing, a little refreshing to his spirit, was now infused with anxiety and rage. It ran both ways. Because he had not as yet happened to mention to the Lady X that he had been having an affair with Cecelia, he could not quite bring himself to mention the cloud forest and seek her advice about what to do about it. If he brought up the cloud forest, then that would lead straight to Cecelia, and that would lead straight to confession of the affair, which would lead straight to discussion of their sex life, which would lead straight to self-doubt and self-blame on the part of the Lady X, which would lead to a discussion of their relationship, which would bring on a crisis, which would force them to make a decision about the future, which, as he was in no condition to be making decisions, would fall to her, and God knew where that would lead, but Chairman X did not want to risk it, so he sat through all the Christmas festivities in an agony of silence, because, as the Lady X had always said, he didn't know the first thing about discretion.

Every year, to open the season of celebration, they went through their belongings and chose the best of what they had ceased to play with or wear and boxed it up for Toys for Tots. This year, he didn't bother to cajole them. If they wanted to hang on to outgrown items for no good reason except habit, he let them. They began giving him funny looks and making their arguments anyway. He shrugged. When they went to the grocery store to buy food for the can drive, the eldest tentatively chose two cans of roast beef hash. He didn't say a word, didn't steer her toward bags of dried beans and masa harina and un-sulphured dried apricots. She grew uneasy and on her own chose a box of raisins. He himself was too glum to be selective. He chose four jars of Skippy peanut butter. At the Christmas tree farm (on marginal land, rows of live Christmas trees planted in turf did an excellent job of holding the soil) he settled on the first Scotch pine he saw, instead of whipping and goading them all the way to the back of the acreage in search of the fullest, most symmetrical and fragrant balsam. He showed no interest in making cookies or molding the bean loaf into Christmassy shapes. When they asked for what they wanted, he didn't harangue them with his usual good cheer about the Siamese twinship of Christianity and capitalism as perfectly represented by the so-called Christmas spirit, which was really just a sensation of culturally permitted greed. In fact, Chairman X didn't interfere at all in the Christmas joy of his family, and while they were all obscurely grateful, it did make everyone secretly uneasy, but nobody said anything because to bring it up was to risk reminding him, and then he might start in again.

The eldest went so far as to mention it to her best friend over the phone. "My dad is so weird," she said with her habitual disloyalty, but then she did not feel the usual relief, and she let it drop. As weird as he was, it occurred to her, she did not actually want him to change!

Meanwhile, Beth was distracted enough with Christmas preparations to merely be grateful. When she did think about it, she thought that it was the fall of Communism in Eastern Europe that was affecting him, and even that he had arrived on his own at an interpretation of that event much like hers (communism was a nice idea but it didn't work and you couldn't actually live in such an extreme way. Even Christmas wasn't so bad if you exercised moderation and care for others). As for his unwonted silence, well, however you INTER-PRETED an event, there were still feelings to deal with, and let him deal with them on his own for once. She herself was going to bake lots of cookies and buy a few manufactured ornaments for the tree and maybe have a party, which they had never done before. When she told him that, he just said, "Oh. If you want to, okay by me."

Beth, who had grown up in a normal American family (which Chairman X had characterized frequently over the years as a purely commercial enterprise fatally corrupted by the capitalist need for a cheap workforce and an ever-expanding market), had envisioned some kind of consumerist profligacy on the part of the children, but they couldn't do it. Great conservatives, they opted for the homemade ornaments, the whole-grain cookies, the traditional donation of food and time to the homeless shelter, the stringing of the tree in the front yard with popcorn and cranberries for the birds. When Beth pulled out the MasterCard to charge a present for Amy, the eldest stopped her with reminders of mailing lists she would then get on, business and probably government files their names would subsequently appear in. The usual Christmas. And they didn't have the party, either. Too much work.

It was not until the afternoon of Christmas Day, the first ebb of the season, that Beth realized that something else was going on. The older children were out sledding and Amy was taking a nap. X was sitting on the couch, admiring the Christmas tree, or so Beth thought. She flopped down beside him with a happy sigh, and said, nestling under his (unresponsive, but she wasn't going to notice that) arm, "Well! This is nice. The tree looks good this year."

He said, "Does it?"

"Well, look at it!"

"Mmm."

She sat up and turned to look at him. He looked glum and his skin, usually flushed as an effect of pumping adrenaline, looked gray and chill. She said, "Are you all right?" She felt his forehead with the back of her hand.

"Oh, sure."

"You look blue." Actually, he did. Blue. She kissed him lightly, affectionately, on the nose, the way a wife does who's wary of attributing neediness before the husband has indicated that such an attribution is allowable. She said, "The kids were great this year. I think your policy of leaving a lot of decisions up to them was just right. They're old enough now—"

He put his face in his hands.

She pretended not to notice. "—to make up their own minds about the consequences of their actions. Did I tell you that when I pulled out that old MasterCard—"

He said, "Oh, God," but it was muffled by his hands. She pretended that he said, "Oh, good." She said, "Did you like the vest? I think those Seventh Generation sweaters and vests are terrif—"

He seemed to sniffle.

"—ic. And not expensive, considering. You can wear it with anything. If you add up all the times you wear something like that, it turns out to be a bargain—"

She tried another tack. "I did like the flower-embroidered blouse. I was just surprised because it's not the sort of thing I usually wear, but I'm sure it'll look better when I've lost a few pounds, you know

I'm amazed at how much longer it takes to lose it all after the baby's born when you're in your forties compared to before—"

"Shh," he said. "Shhhh." Well, that's what she should have done, she thought afterward. She should have shrugged her shoulders and stood up and gone into the kitchen and done the dishes, and then gotten Amy up from her nap and served Christmas pasta (broccoli and sun-dried tomatoes) for dinner and kept her mouth shut and her mind closed. But her mind opened up at the sight of his unusual distress, became first a great vacuum that sucked the story right out of him, and later—well, that was later.

Of course SHE was a great beauty. Of course SHE was very young (just born for the assassination of JFK, hardly out of diapers when *Sergeant Pepper* came out, in fifth grade when Beth and X sneaked out in the middle of the night and spray-painted "4-23-73: U.S. OUT OF VIETNAM, WE WON!" on a long brick wall in Lawrence, the most dangerous thing they ever did). Of course SHE was intimately involved somehow (this was not clear) with some lost cause in Central America (Costa Rica? Belize? Beth wasn't sure).

Unfortunately, Beth did not remain as cool as she would have liked, nor as cool as she had in the past (SHE would have been a mere seven-year-old when X cheated on Beth the first time). She thought she was going to stay cool at first, when she said, "For God's sake, just tell me what the problem is, we can handle it," in a light tone of voice, and even a few minutes later, when she said, "Well, I'm not surprised, though I did think you had stopped that sort of thing. It's very danger-ous. You know that." It was the way he kept repeating, "She's so unusual, Beth. You'd have to meet her and get to know her and see that. She's just very unusual and different," as if she, Beth, and all their children were not. As if he were saying, Now on the one hand we have you, Beth, and the children, and you are very ordinary, and on the other we have HER and she is remarkably unusual and different, so she said, in a voice dripping with sarcasm, "Oh, I suppose on the one hand you have US, your family, and we are so ordinary, and on the other you have HER and she is so very different and exotic and unUsual . . ." and she knew this would be insulting and it was, so that he said, "Goddamnit—"

And Beth said, "GodDAMNit? GodDAMNit? You tell me you are sleeping with some bit—someone else, and then YOU get mad?"

Then he said, "You didn't used to be like this," and she said, "You mean I used to just lie down and take it whenever you came home and told me that you were balling someone else and that it was just so great you wanted to share it with me, but that didn't mean I actually liked it—"

"You slept with other people. You slept with Simon Harris and Ben Holiday and that Olivia woman—"

"Okay, three. That compares to, what—"

"Now we are counting? Counting old betrayals? We always said we wouldn't do that, that that was the last thing we would do—"

He had her there. But really, he had her everywhere, in a way that she'd thought she would never be had. They shared too much, they had been together so long, through everything, their lives completed each other's in a way that seemed mythic, that was what she had told herself, but now it occurred to her that really she had been relying on her looks, just like everyone else, and as long as she had had them they had done the trick, but now she was forty-one and her once waist-length hair was short and graying and she hadn't had the energy or the time to whittle her waist (and besides she had relied on his difference from other men, on the fact that he loved her for her inner beauty, ha!).

And then there was a cry from upstairs, and while she was getting Amy, the others came in from sledding all cold and flushed and carrying the fragrance of the outdoors on their skin, and when she came down with the baby in her arms, she realized that she did actually love them more than she loved X, if love was an ever-renewed desire to see someone and a constantly flowing pleasure in their presence, even when they were crabby and unpleasant, and if love was an index of the number of times you looked at their faces and smiled in spite of yourself at how charming they were.

That night, the children took forever to go to bed. X said that they were just agitated from Christmas, but Beth knew that they sensed a crisis in the house, and they felt instinctively that they could stave it off if they stayed up and kept watch, kept, in fact, their parents from talking to one another. But finally even the eldest had keeled over, and Beth and X sat on the couch by the tree, and they spoke calmly, and what he said over and over was "I know I didn't have to. I know I could have resisted. I did make some attempts to resist. But I just wanted to. I just wanted to. Okay, you probably won't believe this, but I just wanted a little. I wanted it a lot, but I only wanted a little bit, just SOMETHING, not everything. That's why I didn't tell you."

Well, he had her there, too, because it was just like Christmas and the fall of European Communism for her. All the arguments in the world were on the side of mere subsistence, of altruism, of giving till it hurts, of to each according to her needs. But after twenty years, she very much desired a little more than that, a little more than what he defined as her needs, and all fall, while he was distracted (by HER, of course), Beth had taken a little leeway here and there, to buy this or that, full price, with no regard for where it came from, who was paid five cents a day to make it, what chemicals were used in its production, what corporate thieves and villains profited from it. She wanted to. It was that simple.

After he went to bed exhausted, she sat in front of the tree, staring at it. The dishes from dinner were still to be washed, and it was nearly two (Amy would be up by six), but Beth sat, anyway, without moving, and she thought long and hard about what else she wanted, and how she was going to get it.

Meanwhile, Chairman X had come wide awake as soon as he got under the covers, and he lay in bed looking at the framed nineteenth-century botanical prints between the two windows across the room. In the darkness they were too dim to see, but he knew them by heart (*Linaria linaria* and *Myosotis scorpioides* and *Echium vulgare*). He knew that downstairs Beth was thinking furiously about him, and that wherever she was (no doubt L.A.), Cecelia was thinking furiously about him, too, but even tonight, even with his future in the balance, even knowing that this room, where he had slept for seventeen years, could disappear in the (possible? probable?) slow explosion of his life with the Lady X, he couldn't seem to fix his attention on either of those women. It was as if he didn't know them at all, had no memory of Cecelia's fine, heavy breasts, unruly dark hair, and sudden smile, or of the way the Lady X's shoulders and muscular back tapered to her waist and her lowered, thickly lashed eyelids looked dark and dramatic over her large, deep-set eyes. He couldn't envision what he did know, but he could see perfectly what he had never known, the mountainous terrain of Costa Rica, the thin, moist soils, the living cloud forest floating there, ever so tenuously gripping the earth, but really making its home in the air—leaves and flowers and ferns and inflorescences, of all the trees and vines and epiphytes and shrubs, drinking in the humidity and taking nourishment therefrom. He could see the twisted threads of paths that the tapirs, jaguars, and anteaters made through the brush, hear the cries of the scarlet macaws, see the king vultures and white hawks riding thermals high above. If he closed his eyes, he saw the flashing disappearances of the howler monkeys and the white-faced capuchins through the great leafy *Peltogyne purpurea* and *Brosimum terrabanum* trees. He could even smell the myriad perfumes that rose all about. And he could see that slinking fat-faced low-life bloodsucking lickpenny from the economics department striding here, striding there, ever smiling, ever calculating, ever buying low, ever selling high, everlastingly trampling rare glass frogs underfoot, and he wondered if he was too old to take up radical violence after all, and he felt his fists open and close with the desire of it.

52

Happy Holidays

HER SISTER Carol had more opinions about Mary's activities than Mary had herself. So far, she had made it clear that Mary should not have come home for Christmas break (Mary had let it out that Dubuque House was open through the vacation and a few students stayed, studied, cooked, and cleaned), that Mary should not have bought expensive gifts for Carol's sons, Malcolm and Cyrus, that Mary should not help their mother bake ten varieties of cookies for the church, because those women shouldn't be snacking on pure butter and sugar like that, even at Christmas, that Mary should major in engineering or computer science or become an actuary, too bad if she liked art and English, that Mary ought to change the orientation of her bed so that it ran north and south rather than east and west. Nor was Carol shy with opinions about her own life—on every front it could be a lot better, and her only reason for expressing what might have been left unsaid was to prevent Mary from Making the Same Mistakes, most of which, in Carol's opinion, had to do with men.

Mary had, therefore, not mentioned Hassan. Nor, until now, had she mentioned what had since come to be present in her mind as THAT TIME.

The fact was that Mary dreaded receiving her grades, because her grades would show exactly how THAT TIME had affected her. Before it, she had taken one exam, calculus. She had been pulling a B+ for the semester, and she had gotten a B+ on the exam. In Western Civ, though, her A, laboriously gained with a fifteen-page investigation into the Dreyfus affair, had certainly dropped to a B+. Her B in first-year French was lost, and her A− in History of Art survey, too. Fortunately, she had already finished her last English paper and turned it in—her A− there was safe. When she added up the grades she would have gotten if THAT TIME had not happened, she came out with a better than 3.5 cume. If she added up her probable grades as a result of the incident, she came up with just over three points. And the loss was not just an ego loss—certain sections wouldn't be open to her, now, not to mention certain honors. Wasn't it Carol herself who always said, "Now, girl, you got to have the numbers on your side. Affirmative Action and all that other stuff can go for you or against you, so you always want to have the numbers right in your corner"? THAT TIME had cost her 14 percent outright, and who knew what else in terms of lost opportunities and additional effort to be made in the future?

Anyway, she couldn't get it out of her mind. The bland, innocent look on his face, the distinct, rounded tone of his voice as it separated itself from the background noise, her own response—how she had heard it the first time, but not heard it, and so asked him to repeat, so that now she had two enunciations of the same remark to keep in her mind. And they did stay in her mind, never dissolving and then dissipating, but as it were encysted, self-contained, unchanging, hard, permanently possessing a niche, like some types of parasite. She knew that were she to tell Carol about it, she would be in a prime position for another of Carol's favorite responses, the What-Did-You-Expect? response, complete with Look of Astonishment and Snort of Disbelief. All the same—

So she was standing in Carol's little kitchen. Her mother was at choir rehearsal at the church. Cyrus was watching a movie on Cinemax in the other room and Malcolm was reading in the bathtub. Every so often, they could hear him turn on the hot water for a minute or so. Carol was putting dishes away from dinner. The kettle was boiling for tea, and Mary said, "I'm sure my grades are going to be here tomorrow."

"They'd better be good."

"They'll be okay."

Carol shot her a sharp look. Instantly exasperated, she said, "Now, I've explained the train to you before. You are the engine, Malcolm is the boxcar, and Cyrus is the caboose, and that train is going to pull me right out of this apartment and this city, so you'd better tell me right now why those grades are going to be okay and not good."

"Well, they might be good."

"If those white teachers do you some favors?"

"No! I did work hard! There was just something that happened."

"There is always something that happens."

"I know that."

"Well, then, you get the numbers on your side and less happens."

"Don't you want to know what happened?"

Carol turned to look at her and put her hands on her hips. She said, "No, I don't, because I don't want you making a story out of it, because as soon as you make a story out of it, then it keeps happening every time you tell it, and if you make a good story out of it, then you're gonna want to tell it, so don't bother."

"I thought you'd be sympathetic." Actually, she hadn't, but it was worth trying.

"Me? You thought I'd be sympathetic?"

"Well, I guess not. I hoped."

"Hope again, girl. Hope that I'm gonna kick your butt, because that's what I am gonna do." She turned back to the stove. Mary watched as she turned off the burner, then bent down to sniff it. After that, she lifted the range top and checked the pilot lights. These precautions were so much second nature that Mary bet she did not even realize she was doing it. After that, she went to the bathroom door and shouted, "Malcolm, that's enough hot water. You been in there for two hours now!"

Malcolm's thin yodel came through the door. "I just got one more chapter, Mama."

Mary knew that Carol's fantasy was a small but particular one, nothing as grandiose as their mother's vision of heaven, just a nice big kitchen like the ones in the kitchen-and-bath magazines she collected, with an inset marble slab for baking and a six-burner stove and a restaurant-type dishwasher adjoining a bathroom with a whirlpool, two sinks, and a separate shower with two heads. Exactly where this kitchen-and-bath combo would be Carol left up to Mary, Malcolm, and Cyrus. Trees? Lawn? Countryside? Okay for looking out at, but not necessary if you had some nice track lights. Mary sighed and sat down at Carol's tiny Formica table. Carol went back to the stove and poured two cups of tea. A moment later, she plunked one of them down in front of Mary. She said, "Here. Don't look back. Just fortify yourself and keep going." She smiled, a rare event that Mary fully appreciated. She said, "Okay, girl, just to show how sympathetic I can be, I'll kick your butt later, after those grades arrive."

53

Season's Greetings

BEFORE CHRISTMAS, Tim had wangled invitations to a *Paris Review* party for Michael Ondaatje, Norman Mailer's publication party at Random House, and a Poets and Writers party in celebration of Václav Havel and the changes in Czechoslovakia. On Christmas Eve (always a touchy time), there was, fortunately, a huge party at ICM's New York offices that his agent took him to, and from there he went to Smith & Wollensky's with Richard Bausch, Phil Caputo, and T. C. Boyle. That meant he didn't get back to the apartment he was borrowing (no tree, no decorations, no Christmas carols, no women, no children) until nearly dawn. At six on Christmas Day, he called his mother on the Cape and asked if she got the basket he'd sent from Williams-Sonoma. She had—she was just going out the door, she would call him tomorrow. He lay back in the bed and pulled the covers up to his chin. That night he was on for drinks and dinner at a restaurant in the Village, and then there was MLA, which started the next day, and really got rolling on the twenty-seventh.

There was nothing actually wrong with his schedule of events. Most of the people at the parties recognized his name, and when they asked how he was, he was able to say that he had a book coming out from Little, Brown, a sign of good health if ever there was one. Tom, Phil, and Dick had been lots of fun. They didn't mind that he was younger and less famous than they—in fact, that was exactly the right combination for them, and they had offered bits of advice here and there. Phil's, not to give in to the temptation to buy a big house with his advance, would have, if he had actually been getting a big advance, been better than Tom's, which was never to wear mismatched socks on television. He did not disclose what he might buy with his advance when they disclosed various things they had bought with theirs. Instead he got up and went to the bar for more drinks. As gentlemen, they allowed that. Later, however, when the conversation turned to golf, which all of them had recently taken up, he did disclose that his college golf handicap had been 2. "I haven't played in ten years, though," he said. Conversation stopped while they all contemplated the size of his handicap. Almost immediately, the subject returned to advances. At the end of the evening, Dick had muttered to him in the silken Virginia voice that Tim could only aspire to, "Just never let them know the size of your advance."

All things considered, though, Tim had scared up very little in the way of writing assignments—nothing but an In Short for the *Book Review*, and when he was introduced to Robert Silvers, an event he had always imagined as a kind of greased chute directly into writing long think pieces for *The New York Review of Books*, Silvers had very politely, but unmistakably, looked over Tim's shoulder at someone across the room. Then, when he asked where Tim taught and Tim told him, Silvers had looked almost puzzled. Tim had been forced to fill in—"Well, admittedly, the place is famous for hardware rather than software"—a look of even greater puzzlement on Silvers' part— "you know, engineering rather than great literature—" Had Silvers then given him a pitying smile? Or had the look been merely the last rag of a conversation that the man had already forgotten? Tim knew that he shouldn't lie in bed and contemplate these things, especially on Christmas, but the apartment was cold—the guy he'd borrowed it from had locked the thermostat at sixty-two.

Across the room, on the windowsill, was the robe his mother had sent him, his only (wasn't he too old to care about that?) Christmas gift. The robe was black, a color that his mother seemed to associate with his lifestyle—she always gave him clothes, and they were always black. That was, in general, fine, but just today it seemed like she might have chosen, say, red, to give the room a more festive air. He did not feel like getting out of bed in this frigid apartment and putting on a black robe under the gaze of the framed poster the guy had by the window, of Sid Vicious and Nancy Spungen. Across from it, there was a companion work that included the rest of the Sex Pistols. These were the only decorations in the bedroom. Tim put his head under the covers, but then had a moment of unease—he had to be at the restaurant in the Village by eight—and looked at his watch. It was nearly seven. On any other day of his life he would certainly have leapt out of bed in a panic—he hated this feeling of his career leaving him behind at the wrong station, only to stop down the line and pick up some guy who would then have the career that should have been his, a free ride all the way to—Ah, to where? That was the great golden question. Even Phil and Tom and Dick didn't know the answer to that one.

He rolled over, keeping the covers up. A breezy gap opened behind his back, and he squirmed to close it. Really, there weren't enough covers. This guy didn't believe in big feather beds that you sank into and thick down comforters that you pulled over yourself, what they believed in in the Midwest. These were light, thin covers that kept you half awake most of the night mulling the next move in your career. Actually, the cold made him think of Cecelia, who was always cold. The thought of such female fragility usually gave him a little frisson of pleasure; now it just gave him a shiver. Was he really going to skip the drinks and the dinner?

He had slept with Cecelia twice; he recalled that both times he had felt a feeling of dissatisfaction, almost of boredom. He recalled that he had felt these feelings, but he couldn't in fact recall the feelings. Instead, he recalled how warm her body had been. Her skin had a silky alive feel that pressed on your awareness the actuality of her circulatory system. With some women you felt mostly muscle; with others, even thin ones, that layer of subcutaneous fat they all had. With still others, there was a hard, bony quality. Cecelia was the only woman he'd ever touched where you felt, not the fluid itself, of course, but the heart's force, the energy that drove the fluid. How could that have left him dissatisfied?

Well, she'd been lonely—that had been an undercurrent of the whole autumn. Loneliness in women always scared him. Getting close to that loneliness felt like getting close to the edge of a subway platform. Even if you didn't lose your balance, someone could accidentally on purpose push you over, and while you recognized this fear as paranoid, or at least wildly exaggerated, you still got in the habit of casually standing back from the edge. Still, the rareness of Cecelia! And then a voice, a voice he recognized as Margaret's (clearly the voice of his conscience), said, "What earlier rareness did you fail even to notice?" and he had to squirm again.

By his watch it was seven-thirty. He should be getting into a cab right now.

Instead he turned off the bedside light. The windows across from the bed lit up.

One of the reasons this guy's apartment was so cold was that these very windows overlooked the Hudson, and received the full bore of winds from the west. They rattled in their frames, unshielded by the most routine storm windows, unmuffled by the simplest drapes. Irresponsible windows in the extreme, the sort you would only find in New York, where heat was included in the rent and flies and mosquitoes stayed close to life on the street. But all the same, you could lie here for hours staring at those windows, at the interpenetration of light reflected from below and darkness pouring in from above. The whole sky, a rare view for Manhattan, and the stars, when you could see them, no brighter in the glow of the city than motes of dust, but no less beautiful for all that. Something about the windows was peaceful and mesmerizing, and after a few minutes, Tim felt his anxieties quiet a bit.

In that lull, he fell to contemplating Cecelia's reaction to the report Margaret had given him for her. Tim had, of course, read it. The envelope Margaret had put it in had been clasped, not sealed, and she had only said, "Well, this is for Cecelia," with no explicit instructions not to take a peek. And their discussion of his snooping could easily be construed as permission as well as disapproval. Freud and all the others were entirely clear on the mixed intentions of any communication. The report had not shocked Tim. Shock would imply surprise, and this late in his career and this late in human history, nothing surprised him. His first reaction had been that he wasn't into eco-fiction and, as potentially interesting as tunnelling a gold mine under the last remaining virgin cloud forest might be as a theme or motif, he didn't see how you could make much of it as a main subject, unless, of course, it had already happened and you were a writer native to that country reflecting upon the destruction wrought upon your land by the impersonal forces of capitalism or, perhaps, by the age-old universal of human greed. All things considered, denouncing capitalism was rapidly becoming outdated, so it wouldn't be wise to go with that unless you also denounced the Communists and your novel pointed the way toward a newer theory of the individual vs. the collective. Tim didn't feel that he was quite up to that. Human greed he had done already, though admittedly under the guise of desire, and under that guise, he had treated the issue rather favorably. For all the irony that Cecelia found distancing, he had upheld the standard of freedom, passion, immoderation, appetite, etc., that all writers got from Hemingway and was more or less de rigueur for a manly fictioneer. At any rate, since he was not a native of Costa Rica and the mine had yet to be dug, he had passed the document on to Cecelia without even making a copy.

Now, though, the other half of the writer-reader exchange recurred to him, and he thought of Dr. Lionel Gift. You could not work at the university for any length of time without coming to know Dr. Gift by sight and by reputation. By sight, he was an unimposing round man with a disproportionately large head. He looked as though the first thing he had spent his money on after getting some was custom-made suits, and Tim had had occasion to admire both the flattering cut and the distinguished fabrics of Gift's duds. In addition, the university was always promoting itself through Gift, so his face regularly appeared on brochures, flyers, university publications, alumni bulletins, in the student paper, you name it. If it was printed by the university, it was guaranteed to carry a photo and thumbnail bio of Gift once every academic year. Tim knew how they did those things—the public relations office always called you up and asked you what you wanted them to say about you. It would be the same with Gift, and Gift's sketch of himself was always chockablock with fulsome self-praise and -congratulation. Distasteful, Tim thought.

And then he thought again.

He remembered the night Margaret had told him how the committee had voted for him. He hadn't been much interested, and strangely, that indifference had lasted, but he had heard her—he wasn't THAT indifferent—and he now realized that his dangerously low number (6,6,6, it stung a bit) was attributable to someone, and it wouldn't be Helen, and it wouldn't be Garcia (who had once complimented him on a story of Tim's he'd read in *Harper's*), so it had to be the other guy whose name Tim couldn't remember and it had to be Gift. Gift was working against him.

He sat up in bed, baring his chest to the elements.

So, it was the pet project of this nasty man to blast a gold mine under an innocent cloud forest. Tim knew nothing about mining, but it was easy to imagine bulldozers uprooting the trees, stripping back the soil. It was easy to imagine large explosions and innocent plants and animals of all kinds shooting skyward in surprise and pain.

It all made him think of Cecelia again, her female fragility. But now that presented itself in another, more exciting light. He got up and put on his robe, then took a pack of cigarettes and a book of matches out of the pocket and stood under the gaze of Sid and Nancy looking down upon the white of Riverside Park and the black of the wide, as yet unfrozen river. Cecelia had taken the paper from him without opening the envelope, and he hadn't been able to urge her to do so without revealing that he had read her mail. Besides, she was still angry with him. So that had been that. But she would have read it by now. He went to the phone and called her, thinking, Well, it would be nice to talk to her, and to be known to have thought of her, too, on Christmas night. But he only got her machine, and her customary message inviting him to leave his name and number after the beep. No clue whether she was at home, at a party, or even, maybe, gone somewhere.

He gave it up, along with his dinner plans, and went into the kitchen, where he got out some leftover black calamari pasta with nut sauce that he'd bought down at Balducci's the day before, as well as a bagel and some lox and cream cheese from Zabar's. Before he had even assembled his meal, he was too impatient to eat it. He tied his robe more tightly around his waist. This rain—no, cloud—forest thing was too interesting not to talk about, and he had let a whole week and some four or five parties go by already. People in New York were always looking for things to talk about that no one else knew about, and clearly this Gift thing was a secret—Margaret had said as much—and of course it was a shame, no, a sin, no, a crime, no, a tragedy, no, a disaster, in its own right.

He could already voice what he would say about it. Of course, tomorrow was MLA, and he could talk about it there, but people at MLA were so distracted by their own greed for professional notoriety that they hardly listened to what you were saying, and who could blame them. Damn! He had spent a whole week with people like Toby Wolff and Robert Silvers and he had overlooked his real entrée. "They've got to have it all," he would say. "The Arctic National Wildlife Refuge, the Tierra del Madre cloud forest! Did you hear about that?" An article! He could have buttonholed Silvers with a real idea for a real think piece about whether capitalism, now that it had won or was winning, could, structurally, leave any resource unexploited. The possibilities there were timely—

But he hadn't. All he had was some little In Short about a first novel of growing up in Indiana somewhere.

But he did have that editor's name.

He took a chance, since the editor's name was Pearlman, of calling the *Times Book Review*. The editor answered on the first ring. Forty-five minutes and two intermediate *Times* reporters later, he was talking to an environmental reporter who was filing a New Year's story about lobbying efforts by oil companies against required use of double-hulled tankers in the Arctic even in the wake of the Valdez oil spill, and there he was, promising to deliver, in two or three days, Gift's report for whatever that company had been, though he didn't know where Cecelia could possibly be and who would have another copy of the report, since Margaret had sent the original back to Gift.

Finally, it was a nice way to spend Christmas, on the phone, cooking up the downfall of Dr. Lionel Gift and all his allies and minions.

54

Happy New Year

As a way of greeting the New Year, all the authorities (Medicare, the insurance company, the state health care authority, and the board of regents of the rehab facility) in charge of Loren Stroop's recovery had let it be known to him that they weren't going to wait forever for Loren to rise in the percentile rankings and walk out of the facility. Finally, his bad luck in being genetically predisposed to high blood pressure, and his bad judgment in failing to faithfully safeguard his health belonged to him alone. If, as of January 1, he did not begin making timely payments for his care, well, he was out. Each agency noted in its letter that he was possessed of considerable assets in real property. Sale of these assets and placement of the proceeds in a trust would take care of his financial and health needs for the foreseeable future. The insurance company informed him that they were prepared to oversee every aspect of this process, from the real estate transaction ("Our brokers are uniquely equipped to find you the best buyer. We specialize in bringing together enterprising investment groups with valuable real assets like yours!") to the setting up of the trust ("Whether your needs are income, growth, or high-yield, our brokers are uniquely equipped to manage your precious nest egg!") to the distribution of payments ("Save yourself from the complex and time-consuming chores that rob you of the time you would prefer to devote to your passions. Our brokers are uniquely qualified to act as your agents in all fiscal matters!").

It was readily apparent to Loren that the CIA, the FBI, and the big ag companies had found him at last, and that they had him in a tight spot that it was going to take considerable ingenuity to get out of.

They had gotten to his doctor, that much was clear as day. His doctor's former chivvying manner, telling him he had to do that walking, had to work hard with the speech therapist, in general just stirring him up and getting him going, had relaxed. Now he was suspiciously reassuring—yes, there were many patients who regained significant function after the first months. Only last year, one man he had treated—

One, thought Loren, wasn't enough. It wasn't until your percentile rankings were in the nineties that you could pay attention to one man last year.

The nurses, too, were always telling him now to take it easy. Even his favorite, a thick blond woman who would have known just how to treat the prisoners in a Soviet work camp, had been bought off. How else could you explain the fact that one day she was scowling at him and demanding that he eat with his left hand, then chastising him for spilling, and the next day she was smiling and setting his chow on his right? Nope, those agents had gotten in and bought everybody off, and no doubt the doctor had cost them a pretty penny, that was Loren's only consolation (though they had all the money in the world, the CIA, the FBI, and the big ag companies). So, the long and the short of it was that they could write him all the letters they pleased and he would pretend that he didn't understand them, and they could come talk to him, and he would pretend that he couldn't hear them, and they could take him to court and bring papers for him to sign, and he would pretend that he couldn't work his hand, though he could, well enough to scrawl on dotted lines.

He didn't care about the farm for itself. It was good land, and he would have liked to see it go to Joe Miller, but he didn't have much sentimental attachment to it. His dogs were gone, and though he would have liked to see them again, they were better off where they were, where there were some kids to play with. The thing, of course, was his machine. As long as the farm was in his name, Joe Miller wouldn't let anybody trespass there. As soon as the farm went out of his name, they would come in and dismantle that machine and make it like it had never been, like Loren's brain had never borne fruit, like his life had never happened and they had won forever—forever into the past as well as forever into the future.

Nevertheless, he knew from the letters he got that he was in pretty dire straits and he had to come up with an idea right quick because it was a far cry from sitting up in his bed, happily ignoring everything on the left and willing himself to speak rather than to moo, to cooking, cleaning, plowing, planting, cultivating, harvesting, drying, and selling, activities you needed a fully operational left side even to contemplate, much less to perform. It was clear from the letters that all the authorities assumed he would never perform these activities again, and that once he had taken care of the detail of payment, they were prepared to make sure that he never had to.

Here was where he saw the telltale hand of the CIA, the FBI, and the big ag companies. It was one of their long-standing policies to screw you, but to always make sure that whenever possible you paid for it. That was federal farm programs all over.

The nurses were all aware that New Year's was his last day. Darla gave him an extra muffin for breakfast, and buttered it for him before setting it on the right side of his plate. Not a word about cholesterol or sugar or any of that stuff she tried telling him about other mornings. Darla and Samantha, an aide, tied some balloons to the foot of his bed that were from a New Year's party they had gone to the night before. They were black and white, which Loren did not think was especially festive, but he smiled anyway. They let him watch CNN for an hour, all through the protests of the others, who wanted to watch football, or at least listen to it, or at least be in its blaring presence. Football, Loren clearly saw now, was meant to distract you from what they were doing to you, and he did not intend to watch football anymore.

In the afternoon, he had to struggle out of his chair and into the hallway with his cane, just to show that he was going to take his walk or else, and when Darla said, "Oh, Mr. Stroop, I thought you might like to take a little vacation today—it's a holiday!" he saw that though she may have regretted being bought off, she was going to follow their orders anyway. He shook off her hand and walked by himself, up and down the corridor, the green wall on his right side and the Void on his left.

For dinner, they brought him a little cupcake with some sprinkles on it and pink icing, and there was a card, too, one of those big ones, signed by all the nurses, saying what a great guy he was and how they would miss him, and Darla said that her second cousin was actually the visiting nurse who would be coming by to look after him every few days, and so she would hear about him, and send him messages, but she had tears in her eyes, and so did he, as it turned out, because even though they had all betrayed him and gone over to the side of the CIA, the FBI, and the big ag companies, what choice did they have? Underneath they weren't bad people, and surely they knew not what they did.

After supper, he had to admit that he felt kind of down. All during his time in the hospital and then his time here at the rehab center, a little softness had crept in, a willingness to let things be done for him after a whole life of doing for others. That must have happened, because it was the only explanation for the way he felt—a little fearful of what he would find in the new year and a little hesitant to leave. Even his roommate, a real old guy who had never said a word, took on the patina of affection as Loren looked over at him. His name— Leo Gift—was all Loren knew about him other than the sound, smell, and timing of his bodily functions. He never had visitors, he didn't seem to have a doctor, he couldn't speak. Half the time his eyes were open, half the time his eyes were closed. Once Darla told him how old the old guy was. Turned out he was eighty-six, five years older than Loren. He looked a hundred, though Loren would never have told him that, had he been able to speak instead of moo. Loren did not feel that they had a relationship, since old Gift hadn't ever acknowledged him, but he was a presence, and Loren would miss him.

What he would really miss, though, was how simple everything was here. The residents and the nurses all gathered here like passengers on a train, and all they carried was a suitcase or two. You could open any cupboard or any chest and you would find everything in there laid out, one two three, pajamas, toothbrush, bedroom slippers. They had escaped from their former lives with only a few pictures to show or to look at, if they could make out the images. All sorts of things had fallen unregarded from their grasp—knitting needles and crochet hooks, books and checkbooks, tools and musical instruments, paintbrushes and the keys to cars and trucks and houses and offices. Now they lived in the television or in their own heads, and there was soil, yes, the remains of the body, but there wasn't any clutter.

Clutter was the name of the game back home, though, and after getting used to the swept surfaces and well-lit corners of the rehab facility, moving back to that clutter wasn't going to be easy. And it was the middle of winter. The way he thought of it was, that clutter would be lit by a few sixty-watt bulbs, and it would weigh upon him, and because he had less strength than he had ever had in his life, he would make less headway against it, and before spring it could very well eat him alive.

His late wife had always said, "Clean as you go, you won't regret it," and he had always honored her opinion, but the flesh was weak.

And getting weaker.

It wasn't so rare in his neck of the woods, a solitary old farmer or a lonely old woman disappearing one day, then at church or at the gas station in town, people starting to wonder, and then, the breaking down of the door, the calling out, the piercing odor, the strange spectacle of the corpse among the clutter.

All things considered, old Gift was better off than Loren, far gone as he was.

Well, these were thoughts that came to you when you were down and got you even farther down, and Loren made up his mind to throw them off. He pushed back his covers and grabbed his cane and pulled himself up by the bed rail. He saw on the wall clock that it was 10:45, late by rehab center standards. Old Gift was snoring. Loren made his way out to the corridor, and looked to the right, then, carefully, by turning his whole body, to the left. The dimmed lights and the closed doors were peaceful and relaxing. Loren turned left and began making his steps. First he cocked his head to the left and with his right eye made sure that he set the black tip of his cane against the floor molding. He had found out that that would hold him up even after he had turned back to the right and lost the sense of his left side. Then his right leg swung forward, reliable and trusty. After that, there was a moment of fear that he had learned to ignore, and then the surprising sight of his left leg swinging into view, and the conscious effort of shifting his weight leftward into nothingness. Then his right leg swung forward again. He started passing the doors. Early on, he had expected making steps to become more automatic. It had not.

In the nurses' room, Ida, Dorothy, and Jack were sitting in front of the TV. They were almost at the bottom of a blue bowl of popcorn. "Hey, Mr. Stroop," said Dorothy as he came up behind them. "You're up, eh?"

"Ball's about to drop," said Jack. "Thirty seconds." He took a swig of his Pepsi.

"Ten," said Ida.

"Nine," said Jack.

"You wanna sit down?" said Dorothy.

Loren shook his head. He could do that in a way that people understood.

"Three," said Jack.

"Two," said Ida.

"There she goes," said Jack. "It's the nineties in New York."

"Still the eighties around here," said Ida. "More's the pity."

Nevertheless, Loren felt catapulted into the future. The nineties! His dad had been a young man in the nineties—he and a pal had jumped a boxcar on the Chicago & North Western and ridden out to Seattle for a lark, stopping in North Dakota to work on a harvest gang for the spring wheat. In Seattle, they worked in a salmon canning factory for a time, and then they returned as passengers on the same train, buying food in the dining car and sleeping in white sheets. They'd arrived back home with the same amount of money they'd left with—none—but their own dads had understood—it was a lark, that was all, the prologue to a life of hard work and unremitting responsibility. And now it was the nineties all over again.

Here was another thing. If it were the nineties, it might just be too late to revolutionize American agriculture.

"You want a Coke, Mr. Stroop?" said Dorothy. "You sit down and I'll get you one."

He shook his head, and turned to the right, carefully bringing his left leg around until he could see it again. He made steps back to his room. Well, they had him. Time to stand up and admit that. What with the clutter and it being the nineties, they had him.

He pushed open the door to his room and made steps to his bed. Old Gift was still snoring. Loren sat down facing the window, hoping to look out at the half-moon and a few stars, but the light in the room reflected his own face back to him. Half of it was frowning, furrowed with anxiety. No amount of looking on the bright side, of hoping for better things, of redoubling his efforts, seemed to have affected that in the end. Half of his face, without his permission, reflected years of worry and disillusionment and sadness, and that was the living half. The other side, equally without his permission, looked smooth and serene, a bit droopy, perhaps, but mostly accepting. It was a strange thing, these two halves of his face, better than television, and he sat quietly on the bed gazing at them until the nineties had fully taken hold.

55

Death and the Maiden

DEAN HAD NOTICED that science was different from life in that in life much happened suddenly and in an unexpected way, and in Dean's opinion, life was inferior to science in this respect. If you wanted to get downright philosophical about it, the goal of his field, animal science, was to ease the oxymoronic disagreement between the two sides of the phrase. Animals, being powerful, inquisitive, and dull-witted, were particularly susceptible to sudden and unexpected events. Science intended to raise the threshold of that susceptibility. Dean had rediscovered enthusiasm for his project, for he saw that through the manipulation of bovine pregnancy, he could eliminate much of the heartbreak that had accompanied dairying since that first man had milked that first little cow. When you got right down to it, a calf embryo in the womb was just an accident waiting to happen. And he had already begun to think about future projects. Later manipulation of environment (no more pasturage, for one thing) would eliminate still more potential accidents. "No more pasturage, no more tragedy" was how he said it to himself.

It was therefore all the more surprising that Joy got so hysterical when he discoursed on this idea at the dinner table the night one of her horses had to be put down after falling on the ice in the pasture and breaking its stifle joint. It was not as though Joy were unacquainted with equine mishaps. A horse herd was, in its very essence, the mani-festation of the expression "It's always something." The useful or beautiful beasts that Joy had had to sell, put out to pasture, reserve for breeding only, or put down over the years were countless. And yes, Dean admitted, over their turkey burgers and leftover fried rice from the Chinese restaurant, each event was sobering, "but only be-cause we're in the habit of treating them as individuals. You see, Joy, their individuality is an illusion. They don't experience themselves as individuals. They are herd animals, pure and simple. Now take clon-ing. The brilliance of it, really, and I use the word 'brilliance' with the full awareness that I did not invent cloning, the BRILLIANCE of it is that it takes that very uniformity of the herd and carries it a step farther, and so the advantages of herd-ness, that synchronicity of needs and even desires that make life in a herd possible, those advantages are enhanced. I just can't help believe that the farther we travel in this direction, the better off we'll be, really, the better off the ANIMALS will be. They'll fit better into the herd, for one thing, and then once the herd is genetically programmed to live in, and be HAPPY in, controllable conditions, no pasturage no tragedy, you know, then really each—the thing is, there's an incredible opportunity for profit here, too, because you would have to charge the farmer a great deal for his clone herd, a great deal for each animal, he would have to mortgage the herd—but then, you see, he would tend to take care of each individual animal, so the life and the longevity, of course, of each beast would—Well, isn't it obvious that the individual animal as it is RELATED to the HERD, as it is IN and OF the herd, would be enhanced?''

She moaned.

Dean decided that the kindest thing was to simply ignore this. He went on. "But calf-free lactation, if I may say so, is an even simpler and, between us, an even more brilliant idea. What I envision now, in these primitive stages, is actual manipulation of the hormones. For example, the first thing we have to do is prevent the regression of the corpus luteum without there actually being an embryo in place, thereby maintaining progesterone secretion during the early stages. Now, a mechanical insertion of an inert object in utero, or perhaps a progesterone-secreting IUD—"

It was here that she actually screamed.

Dean attributed this scream to some sort of internal distress, but then she turned on him and took it out on him, saying, "Shut UP! I can't stand to hear about this anymore!"

But Dean was patient. He explained with great care. "But the early stages of any breakthrough are awkward. You could even say that, yes, there is a sacrificial generation, but the downstream benefits— Look, ultimately all of this technology will come together to produce lactating cows that are NATURALLY calf-free—the cow will reach a kind of apotheosis where all of its best, most productive selves, you know, the collective self and the individual self as sort of dissolved in, you know, I think, that's exactly the right phrase, the individual herd animal is dissolved in, or maybe not dissolved, but let's say suspended, in the herd, anyway—" He smiled to signal that he was

ON HER SIDE, but by now she was bananas, totally unavailable to reason, and she ran from the table right out the door, without her coat, too.

Dean sat there trying to decide where he had gone wrong. The gravy for the burgers was good, and after he finished his own, he reached across the table and picked up Joy's plate. She had barely touched her food.

To tell the truth, anyone he knew would agree that he had been remarkably patient over the last months with her moods, and that was probably where he had gone wrong. Sometimes you simply had to draw the line and say, no more, or they would take advantage of you. And really, it was unfair, with all the pressure from the grant, and all the work he had to do, for her to give in to these emotional displays. It was a way of sabotaging his work.

Now he remembered those early days in the fall, when he had first come up with this idea, and the fact was that Joy was against it from the start. Of course he had never attributed any ill motives to her this whole time, had he, but it added up, didn't it?

He went into the kitchen to see if there was anything more to eat, but the food had all been served, so he took out a piece of bread and began wiping up the gravy in the skillet.

He would not have thought that JOY, little JOY, would be capable of cynically subverting this project by distracting and disturbing him, but really, what else could it be? He stuck the greasy bread in his mouth. You know, women always accused him of being obtuse about emotional things, but he had figured this one out, hadn't he?

With a small thrill of triumph, he opened the refrigerator door and began to forage for something else to feed his mighty hunger.

MEANWHILE, Joy could hardly feel the cold. Listening to Dean was getting more and more like receiving muffled blows, let's say being hit over and over with a sofa pillow. It didn't hurt, it didn't raise bruises, and you could go on letting it happen for weeks, until you realized that the experience was numbing, and probably meant to be numbing. All fall, Joy had wondered why those companies were so eager to invest in Dean's harebrained scheme. Clearly, they had been numbed into it by a barrage of sentences that circled back and back, yet spiralled forward and forward. Eventually you nodded just to have it stop.

It was intolerable that he should go on and on in the usual way today. It was as if whatever she said made no difference. She had clearly told him that Brandy had died, her favorite horse, the irreplaceably and dearly worst horse in the herd. She had SAID that. How explicit did she have to be? How many times did she have to mention the horse's name in order for Dean to remember which one this was?

And the death had been a sad one, too. It had all happened right in front of her when she was forking the noon hay off the back of the pickup. It was snowing, and she was hurrying because of the cold. Some horses were gathered around the vehicle, and others were trotting in from another part of the pasture. Brandy was one of those. They were used to jostling each other, and Joy had hardly noticed, except that Brandy had been jostled and slipped and gone down and stayed down. The others pressed past her, and Joy had thrown out the last of the hay and then jumped down herself to break it up, all the time expecting Brandy to rise, but the horse simply flailed and grunted.

Then Joy had thought to help her by throwing a rope around her neck and pulling—sometimes your weight was enough to counterbalance gravity—but as soon as she got the rope around her neck, Brandy stopped flailing and lay still, and Joy saw blood on the snow. She dared not break her own rule of never tending to a down horse without a helper—those struggling, panicky back hooves could nail you without warning—so she had rushed to the truck and raced into the barn and found Harvey and called the vet. The three of them were back out to the pasture in ten minutes, with the portable X-ray machine. But there was no need to X-ray. The bone was through the skin. The vet had put the horse to sleep right there.

She was alive and then she was dead. Joy was still shaking from the suddenness of it. Somehow, it would have helped if they had gotten her into the truck and then into a stall, if Joy had fed her one last meal, or two or three. If they had contemplated the choices over a night or two. But Joy had known instantaneously and absolutely that inflicting that sort of pain on the animal was pointless, and death was the likeliest result no matter what. When the vet looked at her for the decision, she had made it at once. Now, selfishly, she regretted it, because she could not get over the suddenness of it, could not could not could not.

It didn't help that Joy agreed with much of the substance of Dean's rain of remarks. The deaths of animals were taxing precisely because you gave them names and then they began to accrete personalities every time you said "Don't put Frenchman in the paddock with Rudy, they always fight," or "Brandy doesn't mind having her teeth floated," or "King really took to jumping, didn't he?" With preference came point of view; with point of view, personality; with personality, uniqueness; with uniqueness, grief. Of course Brandy didn't experience her own death the way Joy imagined it, but Joy couldn't stop imagining how she would have felt, anyway, just trotting in, focused on the hay, looking forward to something good, then the sensation of the nudge, the going down, the pain, more pain, then oblivion. Joy couldn't stop thinking about those moments before the nudge, when everything would have seemed normal and pleasant to the horse, when the animal's only thought was anticipation of the sweet, summery hay.

Joy shook her head and started to run. Down the street, she saw the Red Stick County Bank time display: 6:47, twenty-three degrees. Sometime later she ran past her old apartment without realizing it. The world was dark and cold. She neither saw the dark nor felt the cold.

DEAN WAS full. He sat back in his chair and it came to him—he couldn't eat another bite. He could bite another bite, yes. His mouth still hungered. But he couldn't contain another morsel. He pushed his chair away from the table, got up, and staggered into the living room, where he fell into his recliner. He was well aware that by the hall clock it was after seven and Joy had been gone for over an hour. He reached for the TV remote, but he didn't press any buttons. He couldn't, so taken was he by a gastric pain. Now this was unusual. He had never eaten too much to work the remote before. The pain travelled upward, then diagonally across. It was succeeded by another, then another. Then it subsided long enough for Dean to push the on button and note that "Cosby" was on, then it started again.

Appendicitis? Dean pushed himself out of the recliner and headed for the downstairs bathroom. A stool and urine check, for blood, couldn't hurt. On the way to the bathroom, he tried touching his chin to his chest. He knew for a fact that if you had a brain tumor, you would be unable to touch your chin to your chest. Given the concept of referred pain, a pain anywhere in your body could be a symptom of distress anywhere else in your body. As he sat down on the toilet, he raised his left arm, allowing any potential shooting pains (which he imagined as passengers waiting for a train) easy access. Shooting pains in your left arm meant a heart attack, as everyone knew. After he got off the toilet (no blood), he checked some moles on his shoulder in the mirror. They did not seem to have changed in any way. He wondered where he had put that pamphlet on the seven danger signs of cancer.

Just then he heard the front door open. He thought of a greeting— "I hope you're satisfied," but spoken in a gentle voice, as if he really did hope she was satisfied. He shook his shoulders and patted the front of his shirt. He bared his teeth, and flicked away a piece of something dark with his fingernail. Then and only then, fully prepared, did he come out of the bathroom. Joy was leaning against the wall. Behind her, the front door was wide open.

"Good Lord!" said Dean. "Heat is expensive!" He brushed past her and slammed the door, then he turned and said, "I hope you're—"

She was looking at him, but not as if she recognized him. Her entire body was shaking, too, in waves of shivers that ran from her head to her feet. He reached out and laid the back of his fingers against her cheek, and they seemed to burn with the cold. He said, "Joy? Are you okay? I don't see why you ran out of here without your coat! Jesus. You've just got a little shirt on." He put his arm around her to help her to the couch, and her eyes closed. Her whole body was like her cheek, burningly chilled. She fell against his arm, and he picked her up. "Fuck, Joy!" he said. "You know better than this!" He carried her to the couch and covered her with an afghan, then picked up the phone and called Helen.

Helen was there in two minutes. "Don't chafe her hands," she exclaimed. "Her hands aren't the problem! Take off your clothes!" She ran up the stairs. As if divining his reluctance, she shouted from the landing, "TAKE OFF YOUR CLOTHES!" Dean took off his clothes. Helen returned with a blanket and the comforter from the bed. Joy seemed to have lost consciousness. "Good," said Helen. She spread the comforter and blanket on the floor. "Lie down." Soon she had Joy's clothes off her, and immediately after that, she had Dean and Joy wrapped up together in a hot cocoon. "Hug her," she said. "Put your leg over her. Pull her skin up to yours." She went to the closet and got an old wool hat of Dean's, nice and loose, and pulled it down over the top of Joy's head.

Joy's small body next to his was cold and inert. Her skin seemed waxy and thick, and he felt as if he were spreading around her.

Helen said, "Think of radiators."

"What?"

"Do you know what mental imaging is? It's a way of concentrating your physical forces. Think of radiators glowing red, blowing heat, giving off warmth. Just pick some kind of radiators that you are familiar with, and focus on that thought. Close your eyes."

It was easier to think of Joy as an ice cube.

"Don't think of Joy being cold," said Helen. "Think of yourself being warm. Radiators. Steam. Hot metal lobes. Pipes. moisture coursing through, up from the boiler. Pouring coal into the firebox, building heat. More steam. Each rounded metal surface of your body pulsating with heat."

It was intoxicating in a way. His forehead began to sweat, and then his thighs and his chest, but he didn't mind. He felt Joy soften a little, warm a little. A while later, he heard Ivar's voice, then Helen's voice, but he had gone out of the state of mind that would have allowed him to understand what they were saying. Every so often, he felt Helen's hands pull the comforter tighter, or wipe his forehead. Once or twice, he felt Joy move against him. After some period of time, Helen's voice said, distinctly, right in his ear, "The ambulance is here," and then they were loosening the covers and he was wiggling out, down to his underwear, which his belly hung over just a little, in front of everyone, and they were wheeling Joy out on the gurney, all covered up as if she were dead, but Helen was smiling and Ivar was holding the door, and Dean's own feeling was indescribable, almost a dizziness, almost a chill, almost a not recognizing his own house.

"Good job," said Helen. "Put your clothes on and Ivar will drive us to the hospital."

He said, "How long did we do that?"

"Oh, well, it took the ambulance about fifteen minutes, so probably you were wrapped up with her about a half an hour."

"It seemed like forever. It seemed like we were . . ." He paused, rooted around for just what it seemed like . . . "It seemed like we were buried in a common grave. But it was all right. I brought her back from the dead."

Helen had gone to get her coat, but Ivar patted him on the back and said, "Maybe you did, Dean. Maybe you did."

56

Less Talk, More Action

THANKS TO budgetary constraints and new controls over university "publishing" ("The university defines 'publishing' as the production of hard copy materials by means of any computer printer, photoduplicating machine, or fax machine owned by the university and coming under departmental budgeting lines.—*University Operation Manual*, p. B-15") that had taken effect over the New Year ("Memo: In an effort to restrict uncontrolled publishing [see *UOM*, 1989–1990, p. B-15], and the costs accruing therefrom, this office now requires the filing of Form B-2/54 one week before the publication of any literature designed to use more than two hundred sheets of paper. Departments and faculty members are urged to communicate through the computer network, by use of E-mail or voice mail. Our university investment in the VAX@ computer system will thus be made even more fruitful and efficient, while unnecessary usage of paper products will be minimized. Strict paper usage restrictions will be enforced by this office"), Chairman X was forced to pull from an old cupboard a ditto machine which was indeed still owned by the university (university equipment inventory number 254-0009) but which did not fall under "publishing" guidelines. He then bought from the secretary ten Thermo-Faxes and two reams of ditto paper. With his own money.

It was like riding a bicycle. Once you had dittoed a flyer, you could always ditto a flyer.

He printed out the two-sided piece of "literature" on his Mac, using the secondhand laser printer he had purchased the previous spring. A large headline, to which he had given a moist, jungly feel with his graphics program, read, "Do You Know Where the Last Virgin Cloud Forest in the Western Hemisphere Is?" Then, in smaller letters, he wrote, "Do You Know That Our University Is Working to Destroy That Very Same Cloud Forest?"

In some ways, it was a relief to be living in an apartment on his own and not having to answer to the Lady X, because she would surely have made him alter that one, since it was only the fact that the university was paying a salary to Gift the pompous craven toad that implicated the university as a whole. She would have said that the fact that the university was also paying him de-implicated them, as it were. But the line had to serve its inflammatory purpose, and so he left it.

One of his Mac utilities, which he had heretofore used only for writing marginal notes on rough drafts of scientific papers, came in handy for repeating "Stop the Destruction!" three or four times in the margins around the text.

It was a pretty good leaflet. On the front side, he had made himself stick to the point—the threatened gold mine under the cloud forest, the link between Seven Stones Mining and Arlen Martin's other companies, the crawling, greedy, execrable role of Gift. His Mac had formatted the front in the traditional two columns, and it looked good. On the back, he had allowed himself to expound a little on the historical role of agricultural universities in damaging Third World ecosystems by imposing an inappropriate model of industrial agriculture on tropical areas. Front side—call to action; flip side—education. That, too, was a time-honored arrangement. He did not plan to depart from it in future leaflets, either.

They were all printed, waiting for the first day of the second semester. Chairman X and his inner circle of horticulture students (who had needed no encouragement to shift the focus of their fervor from the ag school to the cloud forest) had agreed that the steps in front of Lafayette Hall, the front door of the economics department building, and the cafeteria entrance of the student commons were the best spots for leafletting. Hopes were high. It was possible that many of the students on campus had never been leafletted before in their entire lives, and had developed no immunities at all against leafletting.

Chairman X got up from his rented couch in his rented apartment under the rather stark overhead light fixture (the only light in the room), and went over to the shelves by the door, where he stood with a small smile on his face and admired the stack of leaflets for the fifth or sixth time. Tomorrow was the day. Some students had suggested that the leafleteers each take a stack home with them, but Chairman X had been unable to part with them. Normally, he did not find beauty in human artifacts, but he found beauty in these—the columns on the front side were not too long, not too short. The headlines were just the right size. The marginal exhortations to stop the destruction were readable even in purple ink. He liked the prose style, too. He liked the way they had been hand-cranked, counted in that old way by the cranker mumbling to herself because the counter was broken.

They were young, and he was young, too. Instead of the guerrilla war of attrition they had been fighting against the College of Agriculture for all these years, they had a frontal assault to win. Tomorrow the attack would begin. Chairman X planned to hand-deliver to Gift himself this, the first work of the Coalition to Stop the Destruction.

Chairman X reached out and straightened a corner of the stack and went back to sitting on the couch. It was just after eight. He had nothing to do except be ready. He had, in fact, forgotten that there would be this time to fill between the departure of the students and the dawn of the new tomorrow. He had no TV, not even any books. He had moved out of the Lady X's house with only the wallet in his pocket and a change of clothes in a brown paper bag. She had told him he was posturing. He had told her that nothing suited him better that shucking all of that bullshit. "Including your toothbrush?" she had challenged.

"Including every single thing that reminds me of this life," he had shot back.

Then he had, dramatically, he thought, mounted the steps of a city bus and disappeared from their life forever.

The worth of these gestures, he had made clear when he saw her the next day, was spiritual and symbolic. He in fact could not broadly modify his material existence, mostly because of the children but also because his computer and all his books and tools were at the house. Spiritually, though, he was definitely removed to a new plane.

He realized that Cecelia must have returned, since classes were to start the next day. Cecelia had been so constantly in his mind since he had begun putting together this action that he had forgotten she was out of town. Well, okay, he had forgotten everything, including eating, sleeping, changing his clothes, calling the Lady X before he came over to the house (some new rule she had made that he simply couldn't keep track of), taking the eldest to her orthodontist's appointment, a lot of things. But he hadn't forgotten that he HAD children, as the Lady X accused. He had tried to get them to agree to skip school the next day and help with the leafletting, but they had refused.

Well, but Cecelia! He found his coat.

The lights of her duplex were blazing. As soon as he got off the bus he saw them, and they pulled him into a jog, though the sidewalks were plenty icy. He clambered up the steps, which had not been cleared, and rang the bell. He did not notice the large, booted footprints that had paced the snow on the porch before his.

She was wearing the red sweater, the black leggings, the bulky socks, all the things he loved. Her hair was twisted up in a large barrette. When she opened the door, he stepped into the aura of her fragrance, and though the desire to grab her and embrace her tightly only came to him right then, it felt like a longing he had been harboring the whole month, so he said, "Oh, God, Cecelia! I've missed you like crazy." Over her shoulder and through wisps of her hair, he saw a tall, good-looking guy appear in the doorway of the kitchen. Even though he was surprised at this, Chairman X had the presence of mind to hang on to Cecelia, to hug her more tightly. That was the way, in such circumstances, that you staked your claim.

SO THIS WAS the guy, thought Tim. He could tell, because though this guy was little and wiry, not more than an inch or two taller than Cecelia, who was five-five *maybe*, Cecelia seemed to disappear into the guy's coat, like a doll he was putting into his pocket.

The guy wasn't someone Tim knew, even by sight, and he didn't really look like a university type, unless maybe someone from the physical plant, but when Cecelia introduced him, Tim recognized the name—a famous eccentric, the author of countless letters to the student newspaper, a former faculty senator who could still be relied upon for colorful quotes about the university in the *State Journal*. So this was that guy, thought Tim, who stepped forward with a grin. He was not grinning AT the guy, he was grinning WITH him, since in fact he had agreed with many of the guy's polemicals over the years—starting the school year on September 10, for example, would open up Labor Day weekend for a last fling on the East Coast and still give him time to get back for a leisurely beginning of fall classes. "I'm Tim," he said, "Tim Monahan. I'm familiar with your work."

Chairman X pulled his knitted hat off his head by the tassel and jammed it in his pocket. "You've read the leaflet?" he said.

"The leaflet?"

"The Coalition leaflet? We aren't leafletting until tomorrow."

"Oh. No, I meant, you know, letters to the editor, quotes in the *Journal*."

"Oh, yeah?" The guy seemed pleased. Everyone did. Tim had found "I'm familiar with your work" to be a surefire opening line.

Cecelia didn't seem to notice that the word "work" had the magical effect of shifting the Chairman's attention from her to Tim, but Tim did. Another thing he noticed was that Cecelia couldn't take her eyes off this guy. When he slipped out of his coat, she patted it as she hung it up. She even took a surreptitious whiff of the collar and smiled. He knew he was watching her indulge in a secret and passionate weakness. Her feelings were so naked that anyone else besides him would have looked away. Partly to escape his gaze, he thought, she ducked into the kitchen, carolling, "Go ahead and sit down, I'll make some tea!"

The Chairman strode into the living room as if it were his, without even glancing around, as Tim had done, to check out new decorative gestures (and there were some—Cecelia had brought lots of things back from L.A., and the place, in Tim's opinion, was beginning to take shape). He threw himself down in the first seat he came to and picked up the *New York Times Magazine* Tim had brought over that evening. He didn't look at it, however. Instead, he said, "So, do you work here, too?"

"At the university?"

"Well, yeah."

"Sure. I teach creative writing. I'm a novelist."

"Huh."

"I guess you're not familiar with my work."

"I don't read novels, sorry."

In that case, Tim thought, he would be perfectly safe in appropriating every detail about this guy, from his grizzly thin hair, which stood up in every direction, to his sharp, edgy blue gaze to his inside-out sweater to his baggy, multi-pocketed pants, to his much-scuffed Red Wing boots, which were so old and well oiled that they looked like they conformed to every little slope and plane of each of his feet. Tim admired the hands, too, which were enormous, with long, muscular fingers and big curved thumbs. The Chairman seemed oblivious to observation. Tim said, "So, you're putting out some sort of leaflet?"

"This is an action. A real action. We aren't stopping with a leaflet."

"What's the objective?"

"Do you know where the last virgin cloud forest in the western hemisphere is?"

"Yes, actually—"

"Do you know that this university is working to destroy it?"

"I didn't realize anyone here was involved besides—"

"I personally intend to wreck the career and, with luck, the life of that piece of shit Gift if it's the last thing I do."

"Oh, really?" said Tim.

Chairman X didn't like tea, as Tim did, so Cecelia ended up making coffee, and then there wasn't any instant, so she had to drip some, and wash a couple of cups, since she hadn't done the dishes yet that weekend. Even so, she estimated she had only been in the kitchen five or ten minutes. That was how long it took Chairman X and Tim to, as it were, find each other, get together on the couch, bend over the coffee table, come up with a piece of paper and a pen, and start working on strategy and tactics. When she set the coffee down at Chairman X's elbow, the very man who had clutched her to himself not fifteen minutes before in an ecstasy of reunion, he said, "Thanks, honey."

She said, "What?"

He looked up with a happy smile. "Thanks. Thanks for the coffee."

Cecelia turned to Tim. "Tim, weren't you just leaving?"

Tim, who in Cecelia's opinion was often insensitive but never unobservant, said, "Actually, I was."

"Where to?" challenged the Chairman.

"Well, I was going to the gym."

"For what?" The Chairman seemed astounded.

"To work out."

"To work out?" It was as if he didn't understand the words. Cecelia said, "Tim likes to stay in shape. You know, swim, lift weights?"

The Chairman's focus was so completely on Tim that she seemed not to be there. He said, to Tim, "You take time out for that?"

"I make regular aerobic and weight-resistance exercise a part of my routine, yes."

"Well, now, you see," said the Chairman, "here's a perfect example of what I'm talking about. You drive over there alone in your car, then you attach yourself to some machine that runs on electricity, and you do that by yourself, then you take a shower, which uses heated water as well as depleting the aquifer, then you drive yourself home. Why don't you just take a walk or dig in the garden?"

Cecelia said, "It's three degrees out there and there's seventeen inches of snow cover."

"Yes, but in the spring?"

"Well," said Tim, "I don't want to."

The thing was, thought Cecelia, that it was the very fire of the Chairman's innocence that attracted her. In the month since she'd last seen him, Cecelia thought she'd made steady progress toward a rational understanding of their relationship: going nowhere, offering her no social, emotional, or spiritual benefits. Even so (this was the rational part), it was compelling, the way he attached himself to things as easily and as wholeheartedly as a child—sometimes you needed a change from the cautious norm adhered to by every other man you knew. Watching him with Tim gave her a (perfectly reasonable) occasion to thrill at the energy he gave off, full of plans and charged with both hope and resolve, as well as time to incubate her (thoroughly considered) response. For now, she was content to play a role that normally she couldn't stand, the sweet-helpful-coffee-toting-girl role. It was a shell that would burst to powder with the first passionate touch of his hand.

Tim said, "I could go later, I guess."

"Good," said the Chairman, picking up the pen again. "You wouldn't believe how fired up some of my students are about this. They've been waiting twenty years for it."

"Your students have been waiting twenty years?" said Cecelia. "How old are they?"

"Did I say twenty?"

"Yes, but, you know," said Tim, "some people do wait their whole lives for something, and it's only when that thing arrives that they find out that they've been waiting rather than living."

Mmmmmmmm, thought Cecelia, shuddering and moistening her lips. Then she said, "You know, when I told my mother, she got right on the phone with her second cousin's son's wife, who's a representative in the senate there, and it turned out that she went to school with the daughter of the minister of the environment."

Both men lifted their heads and looked right at her.

57

Mass Media

I T W A S amazing, thought Dr. Lionel Gift, how they had orchestrated the whole thing during his winter recess. He would not have given them credit for the foresight or the connections if he hadn't seen it himself. Nevertheless, it happened just the way they probably had planned it—at the very moment when he took the flyer from an unknown student, thinking it must be about a bargain airfare package for spring vacation or something, just then that little nobody from the horticulture department stepped up to him, and handed him another copy, and his grimy finger pointed to Gift's own name in the first line, and Gift saw that the flyer was about himself and his report for Arlen Martin. As if the humiliation of having his name bandied about the campus like that weren't enough, when he had at last escaped to his office, set his cup of coffee on his desk, and opened the paper, there he was again, on the front page of *The New York Times*. Admittedly, he was below the fold, and his name was mentioned only once on that page, in connection with "New Pressures on Central American Countries to Exploit Resources in Protected Regions." But the fact that his name appeared at all would tip Martin off about the source of the leak. Gift set his coffee cup down with trembling hand. And then the phone rang. It was HER voice. She was saying, "Professor Gee-eft? Mr. Martin on the line for you, honey."

"Thank you," he whispered.

"Ly-nle?" brayed the little Texas billionaire. "Let me read you something."

"I've read it," whispered Dr. Gift.

" 'According to a recent report for Horizontal Technologies and Seven Stones Mining, prepared by economist Dr. Lionel Gift of Moo University, gold mining in the Tierra del Madre cloud forest would be not only feasible but desirable. Dr. Gift's report indicated that negotiations between Horizontal and the Costa Rican government were proceeding, and that "certain highly placed members of the government have a distinctly favorable view of the operation. Discreet and precisely targeted payments to these and other officials could well have the desired effect." The report also indicated that the allegations of environmental groups, that a single American corporation had been buying up land around the forest for cattle ranches, were well founded. Under various names, Horizontal Technologies and the TransNational-America Corporation appear to have been buying and deforesting the land, then running cattle over the resulting pasturage. While the information in Dr. Gift's report has not been confirmed or denied by the Costa Rican government, sources in San José did say that Dr. Gift, a well-known figure in Costa Rica, and others from Horizontal had visited the country recently, "as far as I know, just to vacation," said the unnamed official.' "

"I hadn't gotten that far," whispered Dr. Gift.

"What DO you have to say about this, Professor?" said Martin.

"I was meaning to call you before Christmas—" whispered Gift.

"Goddamnit, I can't hear you," shouted Martin.

Dr. Lionel Gift set the receiver down in its cradle and left his office, removing his beeper from his belt and setting it on his desk as he did so.

DR. CATES, who read the *Wall Street Journal*, did not see the piece.

DR. JELLINEK, who flipped the "Auto Return" button on his television remote between "Good Morning America" and the "Today" show, hadn't seen a daily *Times* in two years or more.

DR. LEVY, who read the *State Journal*, clipped out and posted on her refrigerator a long article entitled "Easy Cleaning Solutions Substitute for Potential Hazards."

DR. BELL, who got her mail first thing in the morning, was reading a review of *Writing a Woman's Life* by Carolyn Heilbrun in *The Hungry Mind Review*.

PROVOST IVAR HARSTAD WAS halfway through a 7:30 a.m. root canal appointment with his oral surgeon.

. . .

Ms. Elaine Dobbs-Jellinek had asked her new secretary, Bill Bartle, to find her a copy of the *Times*, which she tried to read at least twice a week (though preferably on Tuesdays for the Science section and on Wednesdays for the Living section), but he seemed inexplicably unwilling to do so.

Dr. Bo Jones had decided years before that nothing was so repetitive as news. When his wife, who was sitting across from him at the breakfast table, said, "Hey, Moo U. made it into the *Times*," and then read an excerpt of the article, he tuned her out, as he did every morning, in favor of an article in *Successful Farming* called "Hog Personality: Will Tailoring Your Operation to Known Breed Characteristics Prove Economical in the Long Run?"

Dr. Cecelia Sanchez was asleep.

Professor Timothy Monahan was standing in front of the honors freshman English class he had been coerced into teaching by his chairman in accordance with new university guidelines on putting higher-ranking faculty into the undergraduate classroom. He was telling the students that they would be required to purchase a subscription to the daily *New York Times* at campus rates (twelve dollars per semester), and that they would discuss articles in the newspaper at least once a week. A tall student seated toward the back of the room raised his hand.

"Yes?" said Tim. "Let's see, you're Frank Carson, right?"

"Yes. Sir."

Tim pricked up his ears at the measured, serious tone of voice. Always a sign of trouble. Tim nodded for the kid to go on.

"Mr. Monahan, some of us consider *The New York Times* to be purveyors of militantly anti-Christian bias, and would prefer not to support it with our patronage."

Tim smiled congenially. "Look at it as just another required text, okay? We can talk about those issues as they come up."

"I'm not saying this because it is run by Jews, sir. I am not an anti-

Semite. The problem is that most reporters and editors are well-known atheists and agnostics. Believing Jews are just a step away from Christians, really, like believing Moslems on the other side. But these atheists and agnostics are in another category, and some of us can't support them. It's repugnant to us."

"How many?" said Tim, whose original plan had been to discuss the Gift article as an example of "objective" rhetoric, only slipping in incidentally his own role in its conception. Four students raised their hands—Carson, another boy, and two girls, one of them the prettiest in the class, who looked around as she did so in an agony of embarrassment. Tim picked on her. "Let's see, your name is Joellen, right?"

She nodded.

"Joellen, why don't you want to subscribe to an entirely mainstream and universally respected newspaper like *The New York Times*?"

She turned red. When she opened her mouth to speak, nothing came out.

"Go ahead. Take your time."

She stared at her desk. Finally, she mumbled, "It's the mouthpiece of Satan."

"Pardon me?" said Tim.

She spoke up, just a degree. She said, "When people read *The New York Times*, they are led to doubt the goodness of the Lord and are drawn away from their faith."

Tim said, "This is an honors class, right?"

Frank Carson smoothly interjected, "How about this idea, sir? We can subscribe to a Christian paper, too. Then, every time we talk about an article from the *Times*, we can also talk about an article from that paper."

Most of the other students smiled, relieved that a compromise they considered fair had been tentatively reached. Tim made a point of unclenching his fists under his desk, not without reflecting that one of them could have made satisfying contact with Frank Carson's jaw. He looked at his watch. Twenty minutes gone to the most ridiculous discussion Tim had ever been a party to. Another hand went up. Tim nodded, looked briefly at the attendance sheet. "You're Samir?" he said.

The young man nodded. Then he said, "I will be reading no Christian newspapers. Only if we read Islamic newspapers as well. In your country, people are sadly misinformed about the true nature of Islam.

It is the responsibility of your institutions of higher learning to correct this flaw."

In the back of the room, Tim could see two or three of the more sophisticated-looking students begin to grin. He knew that they were grinning at his expense.

The New York Times was not sold in the town near Loren Stroop's farm, so even if he had been able to drive his truck, he would not have had easy access to an article that he certainly would have read, as it mentioned his university and one of his faculty members, whom, had he read the article, he would have felt free to call on the phone, had he been able to talk, in order to discuss the economic ramifications of his invention, which, when all was said and done, was still safe in the barn, untouched and unsabotaged by the FBI, the CIA, and the big ag companies.

DR. GARCIA PREFERRED to read the Chicago *Tribune*, because it carried more human interest articles of the sort that he liked, for example the one about the Polish Catholic firefighter, father of five, who had undergone a successful sex-change operation, but who still lived at home with his wife. The two women and their grown children were shown in numerous color photographs. It looked to Garcia like the two wore just about the same dress size. Dr. Garcia also enjoyed the frequent *Tribune* articles about nuns and priests, which was not a regular feature of the *Times*, either.

DEAN NILS HARSTAD THOUGHT it was interesting the way your eyes picked out the two words (Moo University) in a sea of print that had something to do with you. Then he stored this observation for communication to Marly later on, as he did many observations that, he thought, combined a notable fact with a subtle expansion of her horizons. On the whole, he felt, it was all for the best that she had put off the wedding again. It gave him more time to educate and mold her. Wives often took amiss as criticism what fiancées appreciated as attention.

He skimmed the article once to see if it presented any potential trouble to him personally, but it did not. Then he read it carefully.

He did not, on balance, disagree with the concept of developing the Tierra del Madre cloud forest or the land around it. Had he not devoted the best years of his life to Third World development, and if the effort had gone wrong here and there, did they not have themselves to blame? The fact was, though of course you didn't say this to their faces, those peoples didn't have the capacity for real development because they didn't possess a higher moral nature, which, Nils thought, was instilled somehow through the effects of cold weather. While on the face of it, this appeared to be a racist concept, which was why Nils never mentioned it to anyone, in fact he had the greatest respect for the moral nature of both the Lapps and the Eskimo peoples, and was willing to admit that even the Scandinavians, even the Norwegians, fell a degree or so below both of these peoples in the rigor of their moral lives.

Gift and his friends could do a lot worse than to come to Dean Nils Harstad for a little advice.

The article, of course, would present a problem for Dr. Gift. While Nils and Dr. Gift were on perfectly friendly terms, Nils was not really very sorry to see Dr. Gift, who made, as a distinguished professor, five thousand dollars a year more than Nils did as a dean (very unorthodox), have to cope with a few problems. Nor, upon reflection, was Nils all that sorry to realize that his brother, Ivar, would have some coping to do. It would remind him that in spite of all appearances, the world was a stony and unforgiving desert, and it was better to fix his attention on the eternal future. Lately, perhaps because things with Marly were getting a bit tricky, Nils had been brooding more and more on Ivar's future. It was all very well for Ivar and Helen to stroll through this earthly paradise of food and sex and friendship that they made for themselves, oblivious to him and to everything else, but a year is as a blink of the eye in the context of eternity, and there would be regrets, there would certainly be regrets.

Dean Harstad folded up the paper and threw it with some vehemence at the recycling bin.

DR. SANCHEZ WOKE UP with a start and the terrifying conviction that she had fallen and was still falling. Usually when she woke up, she turned her mind first to memories and anticipations of the Chairman touching and caressing her, but this morning that seemed like a box that she dared not unwrap, so instead of lingering in bed, she ran to the bathroom and threw water on her face.

MRS. LORAINE WALKER WASN'T a bit surprised by the article. How could she be, when the reporter had called her Friday and thanked her for being such a terrific help in linking Gift, Horizontal, Seven Stones, and Arlen Martin? She wasn't going to be surprised the following Monday, either, when another article appeared delving into Seven Stones' environmental record (shocking) and recycling that story about the timely bankruptcy of Appalachic Coal just before it was ordered to relocate or compensate the victims of that underground mine fire (appalling). Just then, as she was folding her paper and putting it in her bag to take home to Martha, the door opened and there was Gift himself. He walked right past the receptionist. Mrs. Walker put her hands on the keys of her computer and started typing. Only after he had spoken to her twice did she look up.

"Where is Ivar?"

"The provost is taking some personal time this morning."

"Have you seen this?" He set the flyer on her desk in front of her. "I'm sure there are university regulations against this sort of abomination?"

"University publishing restrictions do not cover ditto machines, as a rule. I could find out if the author used more than two hundred sheets of university-supplied ditto paper, but probably the provost would not act even if he or she did, since ditto paper costs only about a dollar twenty-five a ream." Mrs. Walker smiled cooperatively.

"I'm talking about the disrespect! I'm talking about the damage to my reputation! I'm talking about the public disclosure of confidential information!"

"I hardly think this information is confidential. Have you seen this morning's *New York Times*? I have it here somewhere. Let me see." She thought her helpful manner was practically authentic.

"WHERE IS IVAR?"

Mrs. Walker gave Dr. Gift one of her dark looks. She did not care to have anyone yell at her, and she made a mental note to do a careful audit of all of Dr. Gift's university accounts. More than one arrogant or disagreeable faculty member had sat in that hard wooden chair by her desk, kicking his heels while she asked, "Now, what exactly were these 'incidentals' you charged to your university account while you were in Phoenix at that conference? Let's itemize them, shall we, and then you can explain to me how each one relates to your research." She said to Dr. Gift, "The provost is unavailable. I will have him call you when he gets in, shall I?"

"As SOON as he gets in, got that?"

"Oh, yes, sir, I certainly have got that. Thank you, sir." Dr. Lionel Gift turned with what he considered to be emphatic dignity and departed. When he had closed the door behind himself, Mrs. Loraine Walker said to the other secretaries, "Do not mention this to the provost. Leave that to me."

They nodded.

58

You Can't Always Get
What You Want

THEIR ROOM in Dubuque House had not turned out to be the golden, lamplit haven that over Christmas vacation Keri had remembered it as being. Only a few days into the semester and everything about it was already getting on her nerves. Her mother, who had assigned her plenty of housework every day of vacation, and then followed after her, redoing everything "properly," would have been astonished at the sight of Keri scrubbing the tops of moldings and spraying Tilex in the corners of the shower stalls and buying her own Windex to clean the windows. Sometimes her mother's voice, rising to a whining pitch just below that of a silent dog whistle, came out of her own mouth as she said to Sherri, "Well, why don't you pick that stuff up? Who do you expect to pick it up, me?"

The answer, of course, was no, Sherri didn't expect anyone to pick it up. She expected it to remain on the floor. This was a dorm room, after all.

And therefore, Keri could have replied, abounding in fun and good-fellowship, four girls against the world, the way it had been in the fall. But NO! This semester the four girls were always in each other's way and their friends were always around smoking cigarettes, casting suspicious glances, keeping their mouths shut, suggesting other places to go. Keri's own friends did the same thing, except for the smoking cigarettes part.

The worst thing was that from time to time in the fall, she had longed to be back home on the farm, especially after harvest, when the pace of work would have slowed and her father would have been around and maybe her mother would have made something he liked for dinner, and they would have eaten at the kitchen table, then done the dishes together in water so hot that her father, who washed, would wear rubber gloves, and she and her sister would have pretended to drop the plates and then maybe they all would have watched something on TV, but when she got home it never happened quite that way, and the farm seemed incredibly quiet and her days incredibly endless, so she longed to be back at school, with Sherri reeling out some story about how drunk she had gotten the night before, and Diane laughing, and Mary shaking her head in benign disbelief, but in two weeks back, that hadn't happened, either. Mary always had friends with her, black friends, who gave off the distinct impression that they did not like Keri; Sherri had gained some weight and was spending what Keri viewed as a dangerous amount of time at the gym; and Diane had a new boyfriend, a Theta Chi with a Mustang. He and Diane were actively pursuing a merger of their corporate assets at the frat house.

Everyone had reverted to type, including Keri, who had spent her Christmas money on three crewneck sweaters in foamy pink, lemon yellow, and navy blue, colors none of the others could or would wear, as if she didn't plan to loan out her clothes ever again.

The worst thing was that the more she stayed around the room, waiting for something between the four of them to gel, the more it came to seem, even to her, that the room was her domain, a sign that she (1) had nothing better to do, (2) was too much like a mom and not enough like a kid, (3) had illusions about the others that would not be borne out by events, (4) had stalled in some stage of adjustment to university life that the others had passed through, (5) all, some, or none of the above.

But she stayed around anyway, studying on her bed with the radio on low, looking up and saying, "Hi!" if any of the others came in, "How's it going?" getting, she saw in the mirror, the way she always got in the winter, pink and rabbity-looking around the eyes and nose.

"WHAT'S THE MATTER with you?" said Sherri. "Are you sick or something?"

As usual, Keri just shrugged.

Sherri crossed to the refrigerator and took out her afternoon's ration of cigarettes, three. What you did (this was all her own idea) was, you got something out of the vending machine whether you wanted it or not, but before you unwrapped it, you lit a cigarette and smoked it as fast as you could, then, while you were stubbing out the butt, and the taste of the cigarette was still in your mouth, you started eating whatever it was that you had bought, and you ate it quickly, more or less stuffing it right down your throat. Then after that, you really didn't want anything else, nothing to eat, and no more cigarettes, either. Sherri thought it was a brilliant dieting method. The psychological part was that you didn't do the same thing when you ate something low-fat or good for you—you let yourself enjoy that. She hadn't told anybody about it, though, and didn't plan to until the effects were visible. A week or so? Well, who could tell, the whole method could turn out to be so great that she could patent it or something. She put the rest of the cigarettes back in the refrigerator and said, "You want to come to the gym?"

"Haven't you been to the gym already today?"

"Not really."

"What does that mean?"

"I just rode the bike a little. It doesn't count if I don't go at least forty minutes on the stair climber."

"That girl down on the third floor—"

"I know, that girl down on the third floor spent all her time at the gym and turned out to be bulemic and now she's at Red Stick Hospital in an eating disorders program."

"Well?"

"Well, we all saw her. She was thin already. She was crazy. I'm not crazy."

"You—"

"I gained seventeen pounds in the fall. When I got home over Christmas, it just hit me that I was the same old Sherri as I used to be. I'm lucky to be here for the spring semester. I could be back there, taking night courses at the junior college. When I go home in May, I'm just not going to be the same old Sherri, I'm just not. So if I go to the gym and pay attention to that, all the other stuff seems to follow. If I don't go to the gym and let all that slide, than all the other stuff slides, too."

Keri sighed.

"So what's the problem with you, anyway?"

"Nothing. It's just that everybody seems to be going their separate ways all of a sudden."

"What's wrong with that?"

"I liked it the way it was the first semester."

"You mean everyone hanging around the room?"

"Well, yeah, I guess."

"It's a big campus. It's like a town, but all the facilities are a hell of a lot newer and nicer than the ones in my town. You're from a city"—(Keri blushed to think that Sherri still believed this lie)—"so maybe you don't realize what a change it is, but when I got back to Fishburn over break and saw that the only thing to do was STILL hanging out at the A and W, I said to myself that I wasn't going to waste my chances ever again. Come on, we'll get suits and go swimming, too. You get to see all the old faculty members nearly naked. The women you can see really naked. It's kind of scary what they've let happen to their tits."

"I was going to study."

Sherri pulled on her sweatpants. "Well, it's up to you." She shrugged, grabbed her bag, and slammed the door on her way out.

MARY HAD TO admit that she was a little irritated to find Keri still there when she got back from her two o'clock English class. She had counted on having the room to herself. "How's it going?" Keri said, just the way she always did, so Mary said, "I thought you had your lab Thursday afternoon."

"It was changed to Tuesday."

"I have art all afternoon Tuesday!"

"So?"

Mary recollected herself before she revealed the size of her disappointment. The fact was that it had gotten so that she only felt comfortable in the room when she was alone. She left right after breakfast and came back right before bed, but that schedule was beginning to make her feel homeless and she didn't like that, either, hauling all her books with her all day, spending too much time in the library, hanging out with Hassan until he got a little bored with her.

She pursed her lips in annoyance and hung up her coat, then climbed onto her bunk with her statistics book. Keri had apparently gone back to reading, and maybe it would be okay if she really had, but she kept sighing and fidgeting and bouncing on the bed. She was eating something, too. She rustled the paper very softly, clearly trying not to disturb Mary, but the very softness of the rustle made Mary feel crazy. And then she coughed a tiny, martyred cough into her hand or her pillow or something. Mary said, "You can cough in a normal tone of voice if you have to."

"That's all right."

Whining again, thought Mary.

More silence, silence that distracted Mary until she couldn't even focus on her statistics textbook enough to recognize the words.

But she didn't want to talk. That's what Keri wanted her to do, to talk about something, and that's exactly what she herself did not want to do, what she had made up her mind that she wasn't going to do anymore. It was just the way her friend Divonne said it was: First of all, none of them knew any other black people, so you had to explain every little thing ("And even after you do that, they get half of it wrong," said Divonne), then they assumed that you were talking not just for yourself but for all black people, so they got nervous or offended or something, so then you had to explain more. It was too time-consuming and wasn't getting her anywhere. Her plan for the next fall was to live with Divonne and some other black women in an apartment they knew they could get about three blocks from campus. "The whole idea of that dorm is typical of them," said Divonne. "They *pay* you to be like them." At this apartment where they would move, the women celebrated Kwanzaa and other African holidays, and two of the women had actually been to West Africa on a tour last summer.

It was a good plan, but not one that she intended to divulge to Carol. For one thing, it would cost her about a hundred dollars a month more to live away from Dubuque House—that was twelve hundred dollars a year that Carol would resent, and her resentment earned interest depending on the prime rate. Twelve hundred dollars now amounted to a certain larger amount later that they would need to move to that terrific kitchen-bath combination, or else a certain longer time that it would take them to get there. One or the other— that was how the numbers worked. Or maybe she expected Malcolm or Cyrus to make up for her? Oh, Mary could hear everything Carol would have to say on the subject, but Carol wasn't here, and she didn't understand living in Dubuque House the way Divonne did.

Mary's main problem this semester was that she was irritable. It was like being premenstrual all the time. No, her main problem was that she felt guilty about being irritable. For that reason, she had come to especially admire Divonne, whom she had found hard to take in the fall. Divonne claimed irritability as her birthright, and made an art of it, rather the way Carol did, but with this difference, that Divonne supported her and agreed with her rather than criticizing and prodding her.

Keri sighed. It was a long, vulnerable, unhappy sigh that seemed to re-echo off the walls and resonate with all the self-pity that white girls had for themselves. Mary slammed her book shut.

"What's the matter?" Keri's voice rose, anxious and sheepish. That's what white girls were always asking their boyfriends. Every time you eavesdropped on a conversation between a white couple, she would be saying, "What's the matter?" or "What are you thinking?" or "Are you upset about something?" and he would be saying, "Nothing, no problem, don't worry about it."

Mary said, "Nothing."

"You sounded like you were mad about something."

"Don't worry about it."

"Then you are mad about something?"

"Why do you say that?"

"Because if you weren't mad about something, then you would have said so, but you said, 'Don't worry about IT,' so I know there's an 'it.' "

"There's no 'it.' "

"Okay." Another whine, then another sigh. Mary sat immobile, paralyzed by tension, pressing her back against the wall. She found herself counting. Maybe she was counting seconds? At any rate, just as she reached thirty, Keri's voice pierced her again. "Really, what's the matter?"

Mary flopped down on her chest and hung her head over the edge of the bunk. Keri was propped on her elbow, looking up at her, a textbook open on her pillow. Her look was anxious and supplicating, asking for something, whatever it was, that Mary didn't have to give, so she said, "Stop whining all the time! WHAT do you have to whine about? Your parents are paying for you to go here, they give you an allowance and all these clothes! You look like a Barbie doll, so all the guys are slobbering over you. Good Lord, girl, isn't that enough for you?"

Mary had never actually watched a white person flush before, at least this close up. The other girl really did turn bright red all at once. It couldn't be blood rushing anywhere, it was too quick for that. It had to be all those constricted veins opening up at the same time. It was probably good for her. Then her jaw dropped. Mary sat up and opened her statistics book again.

"I'm sorry," came the voice.

"You didn't DO anything," said Mary.

"But you said—"

"Are you sorry for who you are, then? I don't believe that. Nobody's actually sorry to be white and beautiful and from a rich family. I read about a study they did once where they asked some white kids how much money they would take just to be themselves, but black. They each wanted fifty million dollars."

"We aren't rich."

It was an odd conversation, Mary thought. Neither of them could see the other, and Keri's replies seemed to come from the walls, from hidden speakers, maybe, with a quality of disembodied truth. Her own remarks took on that quality, too, because she wasn't addressing them to anyone, she was announcing them. She said, "Didn't you hear what I said?"

"Yes. We aren't rich. Having a lot of farmland isn't like being—"

Now Divonne, Mary thought, would love this. And at that moment, the door slammed open and Diane shot into the room. "There's a riot!" she cried. "Come on! You should see it! There's a riot over at Lafayette Hall!"

Race! thought Mary.

Alcohol! thought Keri.

They hopped off their bunks and put on their coats.

"Maybe it's tuition hikes," said Diane.

59

Conspiracy Theory

Reuters, January 20, 1990: Sources in San José today confirmed that the Costa Rican government, long one of the most stable in Central America, has been rocked recently by allegations of corruption. The unnamed source asserted, "The payoffs we are investigating have been made to very low-level local officials. No one in the central government is implicated. We do not understand where these stories and rumors originated, but they are false." President Molina yesterday named Horacio Dominguin, a San José court justice, to investigate allegations that high-level officials of the liberal Social Democracy party had received more than $25 million worth of bribes.

The bribery allegations surfaced suddenly last week during a parliamentary speech delivered by Hector Salazar, a member of the ultraconservative Victory party. Representative Salazar showed videotapes of bags of money being delivered to Oscar Montez, the secretary of state, and to Juan Molina, the brother of President Roberto Molina. The showing of the tape caused an uproar in San José, with many stating that those seen receiving the money were not recognizable as Mr. Montez or Mr. Molina. Mr. Molina and Mr. Montez denied having taken the bribes.

The Washington *Post*, January 20, 1990: Mr. Richard Winston, spokesman for the Central American monitoring group Guerrilla Watch, announced today in a special press conference that members of Guerrilla Watch had recently noticed "suspicious activity" along the border between Costa Rica and its northern neighbor, Nicaragua. "We have evidence," said Mr. Winston, "that shipments of arms are crossing the border from Costa Rica to Nicaragua. These arms are being supplied to insurgent Sandinista forces."

Mr. Winston asserted that the Sandinistas, who are waging a hotly contested election with Violetta Chamorro, are about to resume fighting. Spokesmen for the Sandinistas denied Mr. Winston's allegations. "There is no movement of arms that we know of," said General José Ortega, brother of Nicaraguan President Daniel Ortega.

At his press conference, Mr. Winston played videotapes showing, he alleged, trucks belonging to the Costa Rican government "filled with weapons and ammunition" crossing the border into Nicaragua and being unloaded at warehouses allegedly under the control of the Sandinistas. That Costa Rica has no standing army was seen to cast doubt upon Mr. Winston's allegations.

A spokesman for the Bush administration declared that these allegations, should they prove correct, "could seriously damage relations between the U.S. and Costa Rica. They are playing a dangerous game."

The *Wall Street Journal*, January 22, 1990: While company officials refuse to either confirm or deny it, knowledgeable sources insist that Seven Stones Mining, one of the Northwest's oldest and largest mining corporations, is near collapse, and may file for Chapter XI protection from creditors within days. The price of the company's stock fell 3 points today on the New York Stock Exchange. Forty-five percent of Seven Stones has been owned by the TransNationalAmerica Corporation for over a year, but the parent company has been unable to raise profits or stem hemorrhaging costs. The price of TransNational stock fell 5 points as the rumors about Seven Stones hit the market, but by close of trading had rallied 2¼ points. Billionaire Arlen Martin, who made his first fortune in chicken processing, told reporters, "Sometimes you can crow, sometimes you gotta squawk, but that's business." Mr. Martin did not seem unduly perturbed by the bankruptcy rumors.

The Washington *Post*, January 23, 1990: Representative John H. Gonner (R–Alaska) and Representative George D. Comer (D–Texas) today introduced a bill that would provide $150 million in interest-free loans and tax rebates to western mining corporations based in Alaska, Montana, and Texas. "These states are in trouble because of this recession, and these industries are most deeply affected. If we give them a little help now, then when the recession eases, every American will reap the benefits," said Representative Gonner. Representative Comer remarked, "The American people don't want to see these companies go under. Jobs are lost, towns die, people's lives are destroyed. The American people are tired of that."

When questioned about which companies might benefit from the program, Representative Comer remarked, "Well, you can't hide the fact that Seven Stones Mining is in trouble. That's a legendary company, in all the history books. Companies like that were what made America great. The American people don't like to see those kinds of companies in trouble. It shakes their faith in the economy."

While passage of the bill is uncertain, the White House has signalled that it looks favorably upon "preserving essential American industries."

The New York Times, January 24, 1990: Officials in the Bush administration are surprised by the quick escalation of the new crisis in Central America. With rising threats of violence against one fragile new democracy and another, historically more stable government in turmoil, the State Department is looking worriedly southward.

"Nicaragua and Costa Rica are key," said one State Department official. "You can see that just by looking at a map. If these two fall, then all the gains of the last few years are threatened."

The suddenness of the crisis only highlights the volatility of politics in a region that has seen more than its share of unrest. Though officials don't like to say so, the unraveling of the Nicaraguan government would challenge the success of Reagan-era policies in Central America. "To be frank," said one official, "we thought we were done with that." The almost certain election of the Chamorro government next month has been widely seen by the Bush administration as a significant foreign policy victory. At the same time, Costa Rica was considered so stable that no State Department staff are assigned to monitor events there. "Mostly, people go there on vacation and come back saying they had a great time," said one unnamed official. "That's the sort of reports we've been filing."

The moderate Costa Rican government has been reeling from rumors, largely unsubstantiated, of corruption in high places, weapons sales to Sandinistas across the border, and faltering economic growth. Inflation here, which now stands at a moderate (for Central America) 15 percent per year, could go as high as 30 or 40 percent. Investors, heretofore enthusiastic, have recently become more skittish. "Money likes to be safe," said economist Lionel Gift, a widely respected expert on the Costa Rican economy.

Many suspect that if the present government falls, the commitment of the Costa Rican government to environmental preservation, a commitment which some say is the strongest in the western hemisphere, could falter.

State Journal, January 26, 1990: "Profile: Local Professor Also Acts on the World Stage," by Dahl Kroger, features writer.

When *The New York Times* wants a quote from an expert on Central American countries like Costa Rica, they don't call anyone at Harvard or Yale, they call local professor Lionel Gift, who lives at 4250 Agana Street, downtown. "I'm on some Rolodex there," observes the professor, with casual modesty. "They've got to call someone, and I have had a lot of experience down in Central America, though not only there."

Professor Gift is a trim, well-dressed man, his hair a little thin on the top—the perfect image of a midwestern college professor. He even stores his glasses on the top of his head, then searches his desk for them, but appearances are deceiving. The professor is widely known for his steel-trap mind. Fellow economist and departmental chairman Edward Cozy remarks, "Lionel hasn't been afraid to wade into the mire of the real world. Most economists feel more at home with numbers than they do with money. Lionel feels just as at home with money."

Dr. Gift's home, where he lives alone, is decorated with quiet elegance. The dining room, and Dr. Gift's office, are panelled in golden oak. The kitchen features every convenience. Dr. Gift is modestly proud of what he has done to the house. "You can bring a little eastern elegance to the Midwest if you really want to," he says with a self-deprecating smile. "The basic materials you have to work with after you've bought the house are solid and of good quality. I've enjoyed bringing my own taste and style to bear on this place. I feel as though it's something of a jewel box. Modest and unassuming on the outside, but quite nice within." He shows people around almost eagerly, saying, "I'm too busy with consulting and teaching to be very social, so I don't often have a party. It's nice to have someone see what's been done."

Professor Gift was born in South Dakota, in the small town of Hoary. "There isn't even a post office there, now," he says. "But I'm grateful for that sort of modest boyhood. I think it gives me insight into what people who find themselves on the periphery of things want and need. My father was a local banker who worked all the time trying to keep his business going through the Depression. I've inherited that habit. To me, that way of working is a real midwestern characteristic, too. Sometimes I'm glad I've inherited it, and sometimes I'm not."

How does it feel to be a local VIP? "There's a certain responsibility that goes with it," Gift remarks thoughtfully, "but most of the time I'm too busy to think about it. Fame is, I think, the oddest side of success. It's there and not there at the same time. You have to be aware that little things that you do have a larger-than-life quality about them. I try to remember that."

The departing visitor can't help likening the man to the home—a modest appearance concealing a treasure of style and intelligence.

State Journal, January 29, 1990: To the Editor, I cannot remember the time when I have read a piece of fawning, shoe-licking journalism of the repellent magnitude of your recent "profile" of Lionel Gift. Did the subject write it himself? Why did the author take no note of the large number of students and faculty on campus who, at this present moment, are protesting recent actions by Dr. Gift that endanger the largest and best remaining cloud forest in the western hemisphere? I know why. The writer was much more interested in the "quiet elegance" of Gift's house! What kind of journalism is that? Has the *State Journal* sunk so much lower than its customary level that it simply issues press releases now? Where is the investigative reporting on important issues? A thousand species are disappearing every day. Our natural world is teetering on the brink of disaster, and writers in the *State Journal* tiddle on about oak panelling and kitchen conveniences. This sort of journalism is not only maddening, it is dangerous. Please cancel my subscription."

State Journal, January 30, 1990: "Faculty, Administrators Injured in Campus Melee."

Two administrators and one faculty member suffered minor injuries today as a state university campus rally erupted into violence. Most of the windows of Lafayette Hall, a state university administration building, were broken by rock throwing as the peaceful rally sponsored by a campus political group called "Stop the Destruction" turned ugly. Officials were taken by surprise. In an exclusive interview, Provost Ivar Harstad told the *Journal*, "We would never have expected anything like this in the depths of winter."

Although there was some racial taunting as police moved in to quell the disturbance, the unrest does not seem to have been racially motivated.

One injured administrator, Elaine Dobbs-Jellinek, a vice-president for development, was taken to County Hospital with a minor head wound. "Elaine was terrific," said Provost Harstad. "As soon as she heard the yelling outside, she went straight out there and told them to quiet down." Ms. Dobbs-Jellinek was listed in good condition this evening.

More seriously injured was the chairman of the horticulture department, who remains unconscious and is listed in fair condition. The circumstances of this faculty member's injury are clouded, but he is reputed to be the leader of the group that called the rally, "Stop the Destruction."

In a related story, Governor Orville T. Early this afternoon announced a ban on political organizations at the campuses of the state university system. "The people of this state don't like these deconstructionists," said Governor Early. When informed that no English professors had taken part in the violence, the governor said, "So what? They're all closet deconstructionists out there. We're going to get rid of them one and all."

Today's rally began as a sunrise vigil in front of Lafayette Hall. The silent participants, holding candles and warming their hands with their breath, carried signs reading "Don't rape the virgin" and "People aren't rare, macaws are." Out of the thirty-seven thousand students, the group numbered under fifty, most of them graduate students in horticulture.

"The organization did have a permit to gather," said Provost Harstad, who has come under fire for allowing the protest to get out of hand. "All sorts of groups, from fundamentalist sects to rock bands, hold rallies on the campus. We had no reason to expect that this group would be any different from the rest."

An investigation by reporters of the *State Journal* has revealed an irregularity in the permit, however. Rather than having been signed by Provost Harstad, this particular permit was signed by Mrs. Loraine Walker, Provost Harstad's secretary. While Mrs. Walker has assured reporters that such a procedure was routine, university Associate Vice-President Robert W. Brown said this evening that "inquiries are being made."

In a late-breaking development, the *Journal* has learned that the protest group "Stop the Destruction," which allegedly catalyzed around university sponsorship of a study approving gold mining in the last virgin cloud forest in the western hemisphere, located in Peru, will move their protest to the state capital, where the state board of regents is meeting this week. City police say, "Let them come. We're ready for them."

Transcript—lead news story, KSAT-TV News, January 30, 1990.

"Violent protest today at the state university campus. More after this.

"It seemed like a return to the late nineteen-sixties today, when a violent protest broke out in front of the main administration building up at the state university. Three people were hurt and many windows were broken in a fracas that lasted more than two hours. Reporter Sarah Hobby has more. Sarah? What's going on up there?"

"Well, Steve, things are quiet now, but it was quite a scene here a few hours ago. It seems that one group, called "Stop the Destruction," has been holding a vigil in front of Lafayette Hall here for each of the last three days. I have one of their flyers here, and the problem seems to be university sponsorship of ecologically destructive mining in Central America, though the flyer also talks about biodiversity, destruction of the ozone layer, the greenhouse effect, and overpopulation."

"How did the vigil escalate, Sarah?"

"Well, Steve, it seems that after three days, the vigil had drawn quite a crowd, and somehow a fight began between two faculty members."

"Two faculty members?"

"Yes, Steve, in fact the chairman of the horticulture department seems to have tried to throttle the dean of extension, who was passing on his way to lunch. It seems that they were longtime adversaries. We understand that the horticulture chairman is in the hospital as we speak, but that the dean suffered only very minor injuries."

"What's the reaction up there, Sarah?"

"Well, Steve, most people are shocked, of course, though one student did voice the feelings of many when he said, 'Wow, you should have seen these old dudes rolling around in the snow and fighting. It blew me away, man!' "

"Thank you, Sarah. We'll have more on this story as it comes into our newsroom."

State Journal, January 31, 1990: "Provost Denies Allegations."

Provost Ivar Harstad denied today that the university was sponsoring a gold mine under a rain forest in Peru. Recent allegations by a campus protest group have alerted environmental organizations both inside and outside of the state, who promised to mobilize lobbying efforts to prevent the mining. In a prepared statement, Provost Harstad declared, "This university is not in the mining business. We are in the business of education." The statement denied the allegation that a university-sponsored report had promoted such mining. "While individual faculty members may be hired as consultants by certain corporations, the university itself does not act in such a capacity. We have no interests in Peru, India, China, or anywhere else in the Third World."

Noticias Mercurios de San José, 1 de febrero, 1990.

Hoy, en una acción no esperada, el senador Hector Salazar retractó las acusaciónes de soborno que hizo hace diez dias en la Asemblea Nacional. En un comentario preparado, el senador Salazar dijo que había estado mal informado por sus fuentes sobre el origen de las fotos que el había enseñado y de las figuras que identificó en el 19 de enero como el secretario del estado Oscar Montez y Juan Molina, un abogado de San José y hermano del presidente Roberto Molina. El senador Salazar se negó a responder a preguntas después de su corto comentario, pero un miembro de su gabinete, Ana Guzman, luego dijo a periodistas que las fotografías aparecen ser fotos fijas de una película de Hollywood filmada en Costa Rica el otoño pasado. "Cualquier persona puede estar mal informado," dijo ella.

Miembros del partido de la Democracia Social se levantaron en sus pies demandando que el senador Salazar y los oficiales del partido de la Victoria se desculparan, pero el senador Salazar dejó la cámara inmediatamente después de que leyó su comentario.

El presidente Molina después expresó satisfacción que la crisis reciente parecía haber pasado. "Nuestra dedicación a la paz y al gobierno honesto nunca ha fallado," dijo. Cuando los periodistas le preguntaron sobre qué piensa del hecho que los habían confundido a su hermano y al secretario del estado por los actores norteamericanos Mel Gibson y Dennis Quaid, el presidente Molina dijo, "¡El fotógrafo tenía que estar usando unos lentes muy, muy largos!"

State Journal, February 5, 1990: "Governor Proposes Cuts."

In a memorandum to the state board of regents today, Governor Orville T. Early proposed another round of cuts in state support of education. The governor said that he would press for a reversion of $5 million from the budget of the state university. In order to fund the reversion, he suggested that the university administration "fire all those bozos up there who are getting the sons and daughters of the people of this state stirred up. That's what the people of this state want and that's what they are going to get." When asked whether the budget reversion was designed to be a punitive one, in light of recent protests on the campus, Governor Early said, "You bet."

60

Ob-La-Di, Ob-La-Da

MARLY, who had finished her shift after lunch and gone home without passing Lafayette Hall, was just waking up from a long nap when Nils called her from the emergency room at the hospital. She looked at her watch as she answered. It was nearly seven and she had slept through Father's suppertime. Where was Father, anyway? She picked up the phone on the fourth ring after calling out, "Father? Father? You here?" and receiving no answer. Rooms were dark.

". . . pick me up because Ivar is all involved with the police," said Nils.

"What are you talking about?"

"Well, my dear, you'll be happy to know that my injuries seem to be very slight, although I am sure that there will be neck problems later on. And I am going to press charges against that little man—"

"Nils, I've been asleep, so I really don't know what you are talking about."

"This sort of thing is at the root of our social ills, in my opinion. I don't think anyone could accuse me of being a vindictive man, and I can truly say that I don't feel any anger at the *person*, only at the *act*—"

"What act?"

Shortly thereafter, Marly Hellmich realized that she had missed the only exciting thing to happen in this town in her lifetime.

Nils was waiting, his coat buttoned, his hat on, and his leather gloves in his hand, in the chair closest to the door of the emergency entrance, so that as soon as Marly walked in, she saw him. That is, before she had prepared herself to see him. He stood up with a courtly smile, saying, "There you are, my dear."

Two of his fingers were taped together and he had a circular white bandage attached to his forehead. He put his hand on her shoulder. He looked, even more than usual, as if he had had his throat slit, been turned upside down, and drained of blood. "Not too fast," he said as she led him to her car.

"Nils, are you really all right? You look terrible."

"It has been a trial, my dear. Did you see me on the local news? I know I was on KCOM, but only for a split second, as they were carrying me off the field. Would you mind opening the door, my dear? I am just so very stiff."

As he got into the car, his muffler slipped down, and she saw the bruises around his neck, standing out violet against the deathly pale flesh. She looked away.

As she pushed the key into the ignition, she said, "Who in the world attacked you, Nils?"

He drew himself up with a groan. "A very unimportant little man, my dear, that chairman of the horticulture department. He is a madman, in my opinion, a regular Luddite. I've been patient with him for years, turning my cheek week after week to one insult after another. Well." Nils' voice went very soft, and Marly strained to hear it. "He. Is. In. Deep. Shit. This. Time." Marly gave out a bark of laughter, but Nils pretended not to hear her.

She drove carefully, slowing for yellow lights, looking for oncoming cars at stop signs as if they might pop into sight without warning from another dimension and crash right into her. Perhaps she was still disoriented from her nap, Marly thought.

Nils said, "The accusations he made against me were highly unwarranted. The coca plant isn't even grown in Ceylon, as far as I know! It is not criminal to plant corn in Asia . . ." His voice trailed off.

Marly didn't answer, a victim of her own guilty conscience. Hadn't this man, her husband-to-be, treated her from the first moment with kindness and generosity? Hadn't he taken her as he found her, accepted Father and all the rest of her crazy family, spent money on her, promised to spend more? In some way, that hurt her the most, that he had bought her clothes and pieces of jewelry, that he had bought her father a Lane recliner, deprecating the gift with the remark that it would fit nicely with the furniture in the big brick house. Father used that recliner all the time now, sat right down in it, swinging his rear from side to side and screwing his shoulders into the luxuriously padded chair back, finding all the comfort there was to find. Nils' fiscal surplus and her lifelong deprivation had seemed to her from the first like tab A and slot B—a perfect fit—but now as she drove carefully along, his gifts struck her as poignant.

Her sympathies lay with his attacker, not with him. Without even knowing the other man's motive, Marly could supply one of her own.

There he had been (she imagined), standing on the sidewalk, and here came Nils Harstad, pale and bustling and self-important, and he had just wanted to. That was all. He had felt his hands clench into fists and his body tense. Nils could provoke that. He could make you just want to punch him or strangle him or trip him. As Nils came along the sidewalk, his feet turned out, his face wide and bland, the wanting had grown unbearable, the hands had risen of themselves, a throttling had commenced.

It was reassuring in a way, because it made her same desires not so much her fault after all.

They pulled up at his big brick house. He opened his door, but she did not touch hers. He said, "Do come in, my dear. Ivar isn't home, and it would be sweet to feel your gentle touch on my fevered brow."

Marly sat still.

"I will tell you all about it."

"Really, Nils. Really. I haven't made Father his supper yet. You know how he is. Maybe I'll come back later. You'll be all right, I bet."

After a long quiet moment, Nils pushed the squeaky door on his side all the way open (not like the door of the Lincoln, which practically opened itself, heavy as it was) and hoisted himself out with a little groan. Marly sat curled over the steering wheel. When, almost to the door, he turned, she gave him a big wave and a bright smile.

IVAR LAY on Helen's couch, listening to Mozart's Sinfonia Concertante on the CD player. He couldn't see anything, though, because Helen had placed an extremely fragrant warm cloth over his face. Now she was in the kitchen, making some little delicious thing to eat, something to revive him before he had to get back to his office for a meeting with the president.

Ivar understood his position perfectly, and more than that, he accepted it as his office. The university had become a broad, bare field in the center of which he stood alone, while everyone else covered their heads and fled. His job was to stand there, smiling, pretending that everything was fine, while sniper fire from the press, the regents, the legislature, the governor's office, the faculty senate, and the parents of students ricocheted all around him. He had to keep smiling and use certain words, "concerned," "situation," "of course," over and over again. Other, truer words and phrases ran through his head. "Fall guy" was one.

He heard steps, then Helen said, "Why don't we just eat right here at the coffee table?"

Ivar removed the cloth from his face. There she was above him, smiling, a plate in each hand. When he sat up, he saw that there was a triangle of pizza on his plate, no banal wedge of pepperoni and cheese, but a collage of sun-dried tomatoes, artichoke hearts, feta, walnuts, roasted garlic cloves, and fresh basil giving off the most delicate column of fragrant steam.

She sat down and set his plate in front of him. She said, "Did you reach the doctor?"

"Oh, yes, and Nils, too. The doctor says there's nothing to worry about, and Nils is spending the evening with Marly, so I think we're fine on that front."

"What about, you know, the Chairman?"

"Nils is not going to be arrested. At least four witnesses say that Nils was already ten feet away from him when X slipped on the ice and fell, and that it was cracking the back of his head on the wall of the fountain there that knocked him unconscious. And he was the attacker. Everyone is agreed on that."

"Elaine is at home. She's got a lump over her eye, but they didn't think she needed to be kept under observation since she never lost consciousness. I said I would go over there later."

In fact, Ivar was angry at all three of them, not especially for anything they had done, just for who they were: a man easily provoked, a man often provoking, and a woman who enjoyed it when all eyes were upon her. He bit off the tip of his piece of pizza. Anchovies, too. He chewed appreciatively. He said, "No students hurt, thank God. What a nightmare that would be." He ate another bite, watching Helen lift her glass of Lambrusco (given the meeting and who the president was, a Friend of Bill who considered AA the crossroads of America and the greatest fund-raising network in the world, he had decided to have mineral water himself), and said, "What if I have to go back to the physics department?"

"What goes up must come down, Ivar."

"I'd have to study up just to teach introductory physics now. I'm that far behind."

"I'm sure it won't come to that."

"You know, I was very romantic about physics when I first started. I came in through astronomy and the big bang theory, but actually, I was more drawn to the steady state theory. Studying physics was my method of contemplation. All through college and grad school, I put myself to sleep every night by imagining that the universe was inside my head, so vast and silent. I could lie there with my eyes closed and contemplate the universal darkness or, if I was in a different mood, I could contemplate the random scatterings of light. Darkness or light. Darkness THEN light. It worked. Every night I eased off into perfect rest, and slept eight productive hours. That was the point. I wasn't like some of the others, who really got excited devising experiments or arguing about strong force and weak force. Apart from getting to sleep, my only real interest was how Oppenheimer got all those warring personalities to live together in the desert. I didn't know a single other physicist who wasn't bored by just the idea of personality. I think that I've loved being an administrator after all." He sighed.

"Would you like another piece?" said Helen. "It's nearly eight."

"Let's get married," he said. He saw that she could not help looking shocked at this, so he pressed on. "Let's get married in spite of the fact that we aren't the marrying kind, even though I'm asking you at the wrong time and for all the wrong reasons. I want to marry out of fear and for security, and because Nils is getting married! I want to live here because Marly and Father are invading my space, so I want to invade yours! I'm getting old and I feel alone and I want to feel less alone!"

Helen got up and went to the closet. She returned with his coat. She seemed to have retreated light-years.

He looked up at her and said, "Our getting married can't be justified by reason or convention. We're happy the way we are. Our relationship is satisfying to both of us just the way it is. There's no reason it can't go on like this for the rest of our lives. We would like it if it did. But, Helen—"

He finished the last bite of pizza and stood up, wiping his mouth on his napkin. She helped him into his coat as if, he thought, she was hardly in the room.

"—Helen, I want to. I want to get married. To you, that is. I want to get married to you!"

"Ivar—" She walked him to the door.

"Say yes just for now, for all the wrong reasons and at exactly the wrong time. Just for now. Let the word 'yes' cross your lips."

She said, "Yes."

He opened the door and walked out onto the stoop, not daring to look at her. He went down the steps to the sidewalk. His car, he thought, would be cold and unwelcoming. He wanted her to call him back one time, just once.

Then, behind him, she shouted, "Careful on the ice and don't let them fire Mrs. Walker!"

BETH HADN'T BEEN sure of the exact hospital protocol for ex-wives who weren't really married to their husbands even though everyone they knew thought they were, who had four children with said non-husbands, but whose children were not speaking to their father because he-had-taken-up-with-a-younger-woman even though according to the terms of their nonmarital compact that no one knew about, outside sexual liaisons were encouraged, at least in theory, in order to subvert the capitalist tradition of marriage as a property relationship and the consequent intrusion of the corporation into private life. On a simpler level, Beth did not know whether X would want her there when he regained consciousness. On the other hand, he would not know whether he wanted her there, either, because he was so in the habit of mistrusting his desires that he never consulted them if he could possibly avoid it. The children, who had been there for about an hour and were now at home with a baby-sitter, were no help. Their notions of protocol did not, to begin with, include having a father who instigated political actions in front of university administration buildings. Beth had been in the room for a while. He was still unconscious, though the doctors said that he seemed to be mostly fine. His CAT scan showed a little swelling at the site of the injury, but no underlying damage. They implied, without saying so, that he chose to be unconscious. Her comment, also implied, was "Well, I wouldn't put that past him." Now she was in the vestibule of the front entrance, having a cigarette, her first in eight years. The smoke was simultaneously horrible and delicious. Across the parking lot in the darkness, picking her way around the ice, came a woman Beth knew for certain was The Woman.

Here was a protocol challenge that Beth knew well.

As the woman approached, Beth gave her the obligatory once-over. Nice boots, nice hat, but it was only twenty degrees out, and this woman was bundled up for twenty below. A hothouse flower. When she opened the door and came into the vestibule, she stopped to stamp her feet, and took off her hat and mittens. Dark hair cascaded over her shoulders. Her hands were pale and graceful and long-fingered. She slipped one of them under her hair and lifted it out of her collar.

Protocol demanded that Beth give her a meaningful glance, communicating their, well, not relationship, exactly, but their emotional juxtaposition. Beth did not. Instead, she stubbed out her cigarette and followed the woman back into the hospital as if there were no link at all.

The woman held the elevator for her and, when Beth got on, said pleasantly, "What floor?"

"Four," said Beth.

"Oh," said the woman. "Me, too. I have a friend who was beaten unconscious in the riot today."

"Really?" said Beth.

The woman teared up. The area around her eyes was so delicate that it reddened at once, as if the skin she had there was the very best, most translucent available skin. She said, "It's been hard to find out what happened. I was here earlier."

Missed you, thought Beth.

"But he was still unconscious then. People who were there say it was shocking."

"Oh, really," said Beth.

The woman fell silent. If they really had been strangers visiting different patients, Beth would have offered her story, but she didn't. The elevator stopped, the door opened, and Beth followed the woman out. Of course, in her deception, she hadn't reckoned with the nurses' station. One of the nurses looked up as the elevator dinged and said, "Oh! Mrs. X! We think he's waking up!" The woman spun around and stared at her.

Beth smiled and held out her hand. "Oh!" she said. "You must be Cecelia! How lovely to meet you! I'm Beth." Cecelia shook her hand.

In the end, they went in together, Beth holding the door for Cecelia, but then Cecelia remained at the end of the bed while Beth stationed herself where he would see her when his eyes opened.

And she was sure his eyes opened. She was watching. They opened and she could swear that he saw her, but then they closed and stayed closed. No fluttering, no struggling toward consciousness. He had seen her and was now playing possum, she thought. After another ten minutes, during which she held his hand and pretended, for Cecelia's benefit, to be tenderly concerned, she turned to Cecelia and said, "There's nothing we can do here. Let's go out into the waiting room for a bit." Cecelia, teary-eyed again at the sight of the large bandage on the back of his head, nodded.

When the door closed behind them, Chairman X opened his eyes and looked around, then shook himself a little. Mimicking a light coma was hard work, especially if she had a hold of your hand. Signs of life were like electricity that could not help passing across that connection, no matter how industriously you visualized your hand as a boiled noodle, etc. He took a deep breath. His head was throbbing, the room twisted a little to the left, and he was glad the light was dim. One display on the monitor he was attached to said, "69." That would be heartbeat. Another said, "97.9." That would be temperature. He was fine, then.

There had been someone in the room with her, probably the eldest. While he had not wanted to talk to his daughter any more than he had wanted to talk to the Lady X, it was nice to think that she cared enough to be there, watching from the foot of the bed. Chairman X smiled.

All in all, it had been a good day's work. He did not quite understand why he was in the hospital or what day it was—the last thing he remembered was hearing the crowd shout, "Stop the Destruction! Stop the Destruction!" Clearly something had happened after that—perhaps one of the cops had hit him over the head with the butt of his pistol?—but he savored the memories he had. Even more students—almost thirty of them—had shown up for the third dawn vigil as had shown up for the first two. Around breakfast time and then around ten a.m. he had worked the crowd, now numbering a hundred or more—firing them up, first about the virgin cloud forest in Costa Rica, then about the ozone layer, global warming, habitat destruction, declining biodiversity, overpopulation. He'd talked and talked, and they'd shouted right back at him. Years of teaching had given him the lung capacity and the improvisational skill to go on and on, spinning out information in great eloquent nets that he threw over the heads of the listeners. He drew them in. They were his.

Without thinking, he reached for the telephone and dialed an outside line. He needed to ask Joe, his graduate assistant, if the vigil was on for the next day.

OUT IN THE WAITING ROOM, Cecelia was saying, "No! They always say that, that the prisoner hung himself in despair or something like that. He was beaten!"

Beth made her voice soothing. "I know, Cecilia, they do always say that, and most of the time it *is* a lie, but in this case, he really did slip on the ice and hit his head on the fountain! I believe it. Joe saw it. Joe is on his side. That's what happened."

JOE WAS SAYING to Chairman X, "Goddamn! You mean you don't remember jumping Dean Harstad? Shit, man! You were trying to throttle his eyeballs right out of their sockets! You kept shouting, 'Admit it! Admit it! Admit the Green Revolution was evil! Admit cocaine is the ultimate cash crop! Admit your life is a bankrupt evil waste!' "

"I don't remember anything about that," said Chairman X.

"You don't remember rolling around in the snow? Fuck, man, I think you even bit him! You were ticked off, man!" Joe sounded full of admiration, and Chairman X found it tempting to give in to that.

"And then I fell on the ice and hit my head and was knocked out? He didn't do this to me?"

"No, man, we pulled you off him, and some old guy was helping him over to student health, and you were just standing there, and then you were down, man!"

"Where was Gift? Did I attack him, too?"

"Shit, I don't know. I mean, no, you didn't attack him, and I don't have any idea where he is."

AT THE NURSES' STATION, one of the nurses said to another one, "Look at that. His phone's lit up. I thought he was supposed to be unconscious."

CECELIA WAS SAYING, "You know, to tell the truth, I don't always get the feeling that he does think about me too much. For a while there, he was calling me up ten times a day, but it was always to tell me the name of another species that would be threatened by the gold mine. Over Christmas, I made up my mind that too much of the energy of this whole thing came from me—"

"I know what you mean, though over the years, I've gotten used to that. But just by the way he told me about you, I could tell you were something special. It wasn't just looks, either—"

"The thing is, he thinks I'm from Costa Rica, but I'm from L.A. My father is Mexican. The link to Costa Rica is fairly tenuous, actually, but he can't seem to get over it. One thing I would do"—Cecelia eyed Beth, amazed that she was about to make this confidence, but really Beth had a certain way about her, and Cecelia had bottled all of this up for so long—"when he would press me for stories about Costa Rica, I would just make them up. They were, well, lies, really." Cecelia looked down at her hands, overcome by an actual feeling of shame. "I wanted him to keep coming over."

"It sounds like you were very lonely."

AFTER THE NURSE finally left, Chairman X relaxed, opened his eyes, and let himself think about what Joe had told him. He had done it! He had actually thrown himself upon that turd Harstad, wrestled him to the ground, tried to strangle the truth out of him, and he couldn't even remember it! If he fought to get beneath his headache to his memories, as he had twice since hanging up the phone, there was nothing new there at all, only the old image of what it might, would, could, feel like with his hands around Harstad's throat and Harstad's water-colored eyes popping and his blue lips croaking, "I'm sorry I destroyed indigenous agricultural systems! I'm sorry I imposed monocultures on delicate and diverse ecosystems! I'm sorry I was so arrogant and so stupid at the same time! I'm sorry I treated people who were well adapted to their ecological niches like fools and knaves!" He found no image, alas, of what it DID feel like. Chairman X looked at his hands. He had heard of kinesthetic memory, but that was something you couldn't actually revisit. If he recalled correctly, that was simply the promise that if he ever got hold of Harstad again, his muscles and ligaments would already know what to do with him.

Of course, and this unwelcome thought was entirely unredeemed, he hadn't laid a finger on Gift. Gift, as usual, floated above what you might call the slaughter on a cloud of money. When his fists clenched themselves at this thought, Chairman X's head hurt so much that he wished he was still unconscious.

AT THE NURSES' STATION, one nurse said to the other, "His vitals are entirely normal, but I couldn't get a rise out of him."

"Maybe he just wants to be left alone. He's awake, though. What we'll do is, if the telephone light goes on again, one of us will just go in and surprise him while he's talking."

"What about them?" She gestured toward Beth and Cecelia, who were deep in conversation.

"Wife. Mistress. I've seen it a thousand times. I say it'll be a lot better all around if we just let the two of them work it out between them."

IT WAS late, almost two. The riot, Gary thought, had been terrific, a real experience for his literary alter ego, Larry. He didn't want to write about it too quickly, though, because Mr. Monahan had always advised letting things settle, steep, ferment, lie dormant, lie fallow, germinate, etc. Still, he'd had his notebook out the whole time, writing down notes. He was especially proud of one section: "Some woman comes out in a red coat. The guy I'm standing next to says to this other guy, 'Bet you a six-pack of Molson's that I can get this through that little window in the door there,' the other guy says, 'You're on,' and then he beaned her right on the forehead, and the two guys were just standing there saying, 'Fuck, man! Fuck, man! Did anybody see us? Fuck, you hit her, man! Shhh! Fuck, did you mean to hit her? Nah! I meant to get it in that broken window, man, and she stepped right in the fucking way! What if she's fuckin' dead, man? She's not dead! Fuck! I can't believe it! Let's get the fuck out of here!' " He had taken down the dialogue just the way Mr. Monahan had had them do it the first semester, only by now he was faster, and got it down more accurately. It was good dialogue, too, dramatic, though not, he realized, especially revealing of the idiosyncratic personalities of his characters. He would have to add that on his own.

And it wasn't long after getting down that great piece of dialogue that he ran into Bob's old girlfriend, Diane. Mmmm. Diane. She had on a new leather jacket, dark green, and a woolly hat that matched perfectly and these terrific black boots, and she'd been veeerrrrry friendly, possibly because of the dangerous situation they were in with the riot and all. So he kind of hung out with her, and then they went out to eat and to the movies, and then out for something else to eat, and the long and the short of it was that Gary was in love. He hadn't gotten her back to Dubuque House until after one.

He had this terrific feeling, all jazzed up and happy. The rest of the semester to come looked entirely different now. Mmmm mmm mmmm. Of course, it wasn't going to be all that easy with Bob around, but where there was a will there was a way. Mmmmm. Gary pulled out his chair and sat down at his computer. He pressed "Enter," and the screensaver disappeared. Oh, he thought, ahhhhhhh. "Name of Document to Open?" read the screen. Gary poised his hands above the keys for a moment, then typed in, "DONNA.Doc."

"Donna"

a story by Gary Olson

High above the Manhattan skyline, Donna Halvorson, chairperson of the board, Megavestments Corporation of the World, turned from her computer screen and stared out the window. It was 2:18 in the morning, and Donna could see no one else in any other office working so late. "Where did I go wrong?" said Donna to herself, her perfectly manicured hand straying over her five-thousand-dollar wool pinstripe suit jacket. "I have everything I've ever dreamed of, but

Part Five

61

Downsizing

WHEN PEOPLE at the conference saw Margaret's university affiliation on her identification badge, they all said, "Oh! I saw that on the news! Didn't you have a—"

"Wasn't that amazing?" purred Margaret. "Campus unrest at this time of the year?" That was all she felt like saying about it. Back home, the program-cutting scissors that had been snipping and trimming here and there had suddenly turned into a circular saw and all departments, from the grandest spruces over in the Biotechnology buildings to the narrowest willows in Speech and Theater Arts were at that very moment being fed to it like so many logs. Margaret found herself waiting for someone, maybe anyone at the conference in a higher-level administrative capacity to remark, "You must be looking for another position. As a matter of fact, at our university—" (Yale, Berkeley, Margaret fantasized, or, in another mood, the University of Hawaii, or of the Virgin Islands). Surely she could jump, maybe she could jump, couldn't she of all people jump—Ah, but here, halfway between Sea World and the Magic Kingdom, every detail of home and job slipped farther away by the minute.

As a precaution in case her plane went down, Margaret had graded and turned back all tests and exams and brought up to date all attendance sheets and records of in-class work, as well as rereading her will. She had made a special trip to the benefits office to include her new nephew, aged nine months, on the list of beneficiaries of her university life insurance policy. That was the old her, the Margaret she had thought of as her authentic self.

Since coming here, though, she had deconstructed, and gladly. The Margaret who would have looked around the lobby, her room, the rest of the grounds, and said, "So this is what they've been keeping from us," had vanished and the new Margaret looked around and said, "I want this." No, that was wrong, too. She didn't *say* anything at all. The desire was in her flesh. Her mind was in the backseat and the car was driving itself.

It started when she opened her eyes on the peachy pink and succulent green color scheme of her room that said to her, "Lie back, roll over, slip more deeply between the smooth sheets, your breakfast will be here soon!" Did she turn on "Morning Edition"? The radio was at her fingertips. Or even the "Today" show? The TV remote was already in her hand. No! She turned on the hotel's very own weather channel, which featured panoramic shots of the grounds and a soothing voice predicting light breezes, "temps" between seventy-five and eighty, and plenty of sunshine, interspersed with clips of blizzards elsewhere and a gravelly, despairing male voice saying, "Another large storm is tracking through the midsection of the country, dropping freezing rain and snow over a wide area." After watching the weather channel as if spellbound for the hour that it took her to spoon half a perfect melon into her mouth with a few bites of croissant, chased by a tall glass of orange juice, she got up and put on her swimsuit, feeling just enough ambition to go to the pool. Her room had a view of the pool. Fourteen stories below her private balcony, it drew her dreamy gaze, a hex-cut aquamarine, a jewel that you could enter. When she looked down at the other swimmers, she saw the surface of the stone close magically over them, smooth, mysterious, and inviting.

After all these years (her little bitty passenger intellect laughed nervously at this), she felt at last like the princess, a role her "authentic self" would have disdained, but here she was, possessed of the magic power, partaking of the magic food. That there were many other princes and princesses at the conference made no difference, in fact soothed her. Twenty laps in the jewel the first day, thirty laps the second, then she stopped counting. The conference didn't start till two in the afternoon, then it lasted only two hours before they broke for cocktails and dinner. The evening presentation went on for only an hour.

She had been taken by surprise; it seemed that she couldn't resist this inexorable and exquisitely pleasurable extraction of her "authentic self." On the third day, she went into the hotel dress shop and bought a silk cocktail dress for five hundred dollars. It featured the same colors as her room, and it slid over her body like the water in the pool, only catching deliciously at her shoulders and clinging there. The skirt seemed to float on its own gentle breeze. She put it on her MasterCard, the one she kept only for emergencies and almost never actually used. At the cocktail party that night, she saw Cates looking at her across the twilit patio as if he didn't realize who she was and hadn't seen her at hundreds of committee meetings over the years.

That evening she sat up late, no makeup and no stockings and no shoes, but unable just yet to take off her new dress, and she read the paper she was to present the next afternoon. She was sitting on the bed, and she could see herself in the mirror beside the TV, the dress glowing, her skin burnished in the single circle of golden light shed by her reading lamp. Looks-wise, she was ordinarily a girl who did her best and settled for that, but tonight she ravished herself. And the paper wasn't bad, either.

It was therefore all the more surprising when, the next morning, she was informed by the manager that due to a sudden notification by the corporate sponsor of the conference, something called Horizontal Technologies, the rest of the conference was being cancelled and, unfortunately, the management of the resort would have to ask the guests to guarantee room and restaurant charges that they had already incurred. With a coercive and challenging smile, the young woman (ten years younger than Margaret at least) ripped her bill out of the computer printer and flourished it in her direction. At the bottom of the page, right by the words "total charges," her glance picked out the number 3,198.24 the way a frog picks a mosquito from the air. Then Margaret saw her own hand lifting to meet the page and felt her own mouth smiling. A good, good, good girl, she said, "Oh. Thank you."

"Will there be any problem with that, Professor?"

"Oh," said Margaret, grinning madly. "Of course not."

THE KNOCK at the door of Dr. Dean Jellinek's lab was almost inaudible. If he hadn't been alone in there, working at his computer (which, because of its state-of-the-art engineering, was almost silent), he might not have answered the door, might not have been surprised at the sight of three men, one of them small and owlishly bespectacled, in the sort of outmoded brown suit and cowboy boots that executives of agricultural companies favored, the other two brawny, in slacks and big jackets. One of these was pushing a dolly. "Yes?" he said, carefully measuring into his tone his busyness, his general importance around the university as the recipient of a large grant, and his kindly willingness to be helpful.

The little man, whose voice he instantly recognized as that of his phone buddy and teammate Samuels, of Western Egg and Milk, said to the two others, "There's the computer. That must be a box of backup disks beside it. Take those, too. And the printer." He stepped past Dean and looked around the lab. "The rest of it seems to be university property. Okay." And the two larger men bore down upon the treasure-house of Dean's intellectual life, plucked its cord out of the wall, and in two minutes were out the door with the equipment on the dolly, heading toward the elevator.

"Wait a—" said Dean. Could it be that Samuels, of all people, a guy who loved Magic Johnson as much as he himself did, would do him harm? He looked around the doorframe again, to see if two other big guys were bringing him an even better computer.

Samuels, meanwhile, had drawn forth a piece of paper and his glasses, which he put on. He read, " 'In seizing the aforesaid equipment, the company recognizes that some of Dr. Jellinek's own intellectual property, that is, work not pertaining to the calf-free lactation project, may be stored in the computer's memory bank. This work will be copied from that memory bank onto floppy disks and returned to Dr. Jellinek by our very best computer technicians, and then deleted from the computer. Dr. Jellinek will not be charged for computer disks so employed, but they will be provided, gratis, by Western Egg and Milk.' " Here, Samuels gave him a beneficent smile, then continued, " 'All work pertaining to the calf-free lactation project is the property of Western Egg and Milk, its parent companies, and its subsidiaries, and may be utilized by any or all of these companies, may be sold, patented, published, or utilized in any other way that the company sees fit, in accordance with contracts between Western Egg and Milk and Dr. Jellinek. The seizure of the above equipment hereby terminates any and all agreements made between Dr. Dean Jellinek and Western Egg and Milk and any of its representatives.' "

"Samuels!" said Dean.

"That's me," replied the little man.

"What's going on?"

"Restructuring, is all. It might not be that bad. Getting rid of the fat, you see. Personally, I'm pretty safe. For one thing, I don't believe all that stuff about the pension plan. You can't be panicked by wild rumors, that's what I told my wife. And I've got feelers out to some other companies. Personally, I'm in pretty good shape. I could get sent down to the minors, but only to, say, Omaha, not to, say, Chillicothe. And my wife has a good job with—"

"You can't take my computer!"

"I have to."

"Why?"

"Now, Dean, you're being a little naive." He handed Dean the sheet of paper.

"You can't take my computer!"

"We took it."

"Bring it back!"

"Dean." Samuels stepped up close to Dean and looked him right in the eye. His voice was soft and friendly. "Sue me." He said. "I mean that."

EVEN THOUGH Dr. John Cates had discovered the cancellation of the conference long after everyone else (they had gotten out to break-fast and the Magic Kingdom by eight and hadn't returned until almost nine), he was able to reflect with some complacence that he had already delivered his paper. In addition to this, he happened to have the letter with him, the one that stated that all his conference charges (and they were itemized, as per his request) were guaranteed by conference officials (whose names were also on the letter) and corporate sponsors (ditto). When the little girl at the desk demanded his credit card, Dr. Cates had drawn himself up to his full height and shaken his head. He had, however, allowed them to Xerox his letter before giving it back to him. All this business had been conducted behind bright shielding smiles, and was now concluded, like most of his business, to Dr. Cates' advantage.

But the conference was over, no two ways about that, and so they were packing to move to another hotel—only three days to go and no reason to change their first-class airline reservations (Dr. Cates had checked to be sure that nothing could or would happen to those). His wife had found them a pleasant hotel even closer to Sea World (he had those tickets right in his wallet), and they were almost ready to load the rental car and leave (in the end, the resort had been happy to accommodate his wish to leave after normal checkout time and not be charged for that day, in exchange for his agreement not to enter into protracted negotiations right there in the lobby—he could tell they thought that a tall black man with a wife in African garb was capable of anything).

All things considered, Cates had handled the whole thing superbly, and if his son, Daniel, would stop screaming that he didn't WANT to go to another hotel, he liked THIS hotel, Dr. Cates thought that the boy would agree. In general, Dr. Cates tried to show Daniel by example how it was possible to maintain dignity, keep your voice down, and still get what you wanted. This lesson he expected to seep into Daniel's consciousness eventually, according to the principle of tedious repetition. Until that time, however, Daniel seemed to persist in a nasty habit of angry tantrums that tried even Dr. Cates' patience and were probably the reason that he and his wife had never had another child.

His wife came in from the bedroom of the suite, carrying her makeup case, and set it beside the door. That was it for the luggage, so he said to her, "You looked under the bed?"

"What?"

He raised his voice so she could hear him over the screaming. "I SAID, 'DID YOU LOOK UNDER THE BED?' "

She nodded.

"I CHECKED UNDER THE COUCHES AND IN ALL THE DRAWERS. THAT SHOULD BE IT, THEN. READY?"

She nodded again.

He picked up the phone to call for the rental car, but then put it down again. He knew that the bellman would hear the shouting in the background, "Listen to me! I want to stay here! I like it here! Listen to me!" He sat quietly for a moment, waiting, but nothing happened, so he went into the bedroom of the suite and closed the door. The diminution of noise was a welcome relief. He called for the car, and went into the bathroom, closed that door, and unzipped his pants. He didn't really have to urinate, but he didn't want to take advantage of his wife by purely and simply hiding out. After expelling the last possible drop, then taking enormous care over washing his hands, he sighed and went out.

Over the years, Daniel had trained himself to sustain a tantrum beyond any normal human limits, thus he was still going full steam when the bellman, exactly the one bellman, an older black man, that Dr. Cates had hoped was off duty, appeared with the luggage cart, and to the accompaniment of Daniel's shouting, the luggage was loaded on the cart. The three adults moved off, and Dr. Cates knew that the man was actively restraining himself from knocking the kid's head against the wall or, at the very least, making some remark, giving some advice on the order of "Say no and mean it." Daniel followed them, shrieking. At the car, Dr. John Cates did do what he had sworn he would not do and known, in the end, he would do: He gave the bellman a very large tip and a single, uncontrollably sheepish, desperate smile.

ONCE UPON a time, Elaine Dobbs-Jellinek had lit a cigarette whenever she picked up the phone. Now, instead, she ran her fingers meditatively over the lump above her left eye. She pressed. It hurt and felt good at the same time. Her interest in touching it did not flag as the days went by.

"This is Dr. Bo Jones."

"Dr. Bo! How are you? Well, I'm sorry to say that I have some bad news for you, Dr. Bo. It looks like the museum is out of the picture. Yes. No chickens. No nothing. The chicken expert's report was very favorable, oh yes. No problem with that, but the granting institution seems to have run into some fiscal difficulties. I'm so sorry."

Elaine knew that she had this habit, when delivering bad news, of sounding like she was having a conversation—replying to questions and remarks—even though her interlocutor hadn't actually spoken. It was just that they were always so silent; they were no help at all if you wanted to get all the information across as quickly as possible.

"It's not as though the chicken museum was undeserving of support. That's not it at all. It is entirely a failure on the other side, and so"—Dr. Bo had been silent for a very long time, and Elaine found herself making a promise that she hadn't by any means intended to make—"this office has decided to find another granting organization that might take over the chicken idea, because it is still an excellent idea. Dr. Bo?"—wasn't he just the type—big and florid—for a heart attack?—"Dr. Bo?"

"Yes, ma'am?"

"Are you all right?"

"Why, yes, I am. I never wanted a chicken museum and I couldn't abide that so-called chicken expert. Now, if you'll excuse me, I have some packing to do, because I am leaving on a very long trip to central Asia."

"Then you don't support continued efforts to find a funding organization—"

"Do what you want, young lady."

After she hung up, Elaine found that she was pressing so hard on her lump that it was giving her a throbbing headache. When she took her fingers away, the headache subsided with an almost liquid, flowing feeling. It was a wonderful sensation, and she decided to try it just once more before beginning on the rest of the afternoon's work.

"MARTIN'S FLAVORBUST?"

"BY TEXAS BILLIONAIRE STANDARDS, the ranch near Spur where Arlen Martin has retreated isn't much, a hundred thousand acres more or less. Unlike some other west Texas ranches, it isn't depicted in any atlas. Under state law, whatever happens to Martin and his tangle of corporations, the ranch, his homestead, will continue to be inalienably his, along with his Lear jet. 'My mule,' says Martin. 'That Lear jet is just like a mule, and in Texas you can't ever be so poor that they can take your mule.'

"There are a few cattle roaming the landscape, but Martin considers them of little more interest than the scrub cactus and the mesquite. 'Look over there!' he exclaims, slamming the Land Rover to a halt. 'Ah, you missed it.'

" 'What?'

" 'One of the boars! The place is teeming with wild boars we brought in from Asia. Best hunting there is. If I retire, and I'm not saying I will and I'm not saying I won't, I could do worse than hunt boar everyday. I bet you didn't know that wild chickens are pretty vicious, too. When most folks think of the chicken, they think hen, they think egg. Not me. I think about that beady rooster gaze, that focus—' "

Dr. Lionel Gift set down the *Texas Monthly* article he was reading, noting the author (Lawrence Wright), and allowed himself a little smile at Arlen Martin's expense. It was clear that Martin had learned little from the collapse of Seven Stones Mining and the subsequent, probably fatal, weakening of the whole TransNational empire. He showed none of the philosophical perspicacity that he, Lionel Gift, showed. But Dr. Gift was certain that Arlen Martin, who, according to the *Wall Street Journal*, was undergoing "reorganization," too, would eventually feel the same thrill of appreciation Dr. Gift felt at the operation of hidden truths in the lives of men. The market, after all, had acted to correct TransNational's overextension—that was one thing—and Dr. Gift had long ago cashed all checks and invested all monies accruing to him through his contract with the company—that was another. He had invested the money in high-tech ceramics, a wave of the future.

But it did not matter, really, who he was or who Martin was, where, in particular, the money came from or where it went. Individuals and individual companies were but flickering pauses in the eternal exchange of fiscal energy. Restlessly it flowed here and it flowed there. No one man could stop it or direct it; all were equally doomed to watch the golden streams flow through their clutching fingers. Finally, you had to take solace and even inspiration from that very evanescence. As he told his packed house of fifteen hundred customers, we spend our whole lives thinking that value is an object, and collecting gold, or diamonds, or stocks and bonds, but even while you are piling it up, even while you are watching it, value is flowing ceaselessly into and out of it.

The customers left the auditorium hushed and chastened, and back in his office, Dr. Gift jotted down a bon mot about teaching, "As old as I am, and I've seen two generations of 'students,' as it were, by now, even I am still evolving. Experiences teach teachers, too, you know." After jotting it down, he admired it a little, then filed it under "Interviews: Teaching."

Memo
From: Provost
To: Faculty Senate
Subject: Projected further cutbacks

It now appears that certain programs that we thought we had saved from the budgetary axe must be cut. As you know, the governor has ordered another $2 million in reversions from the university budget, over and above the $10 million ordered in the fall. This reversion, which must be completed by June 30, is to be made permanent, and may be followed by others. The board of governors has denied rumors that the reversion is intended to punish the university for last month's unfortunate episode of campus unrest. The faculty should be aware that other grant monies that we thought we could count on to compensate for earlier cutbacks have also dried up, so the picture is bleak. I now feel that it is in the best interests of the whole university community that these cutback decisions take place as soon as possible, so that affected parties have a number of months to make alternative career plans.

62

Stormy Weather

LOREN STROOP WASN'T fooled by this little inner blossom of energy and well-being. Nor was he surprised that it coincided with the snowstorm he had been listening to them talk about on the weather radio. It was full day when he finally sat up and put his feet on the floor, but the old house was creaking in the gale and the fireplace damper was rattling, too—he could hear it two rooms away. That damper didn't start to rattle until the wind speed hit about forty-five from the northwest, so, Loren reflected, it was blowing pretty good out there.

Loren reached for his cane and pushed himself up out of the bed, then turned his head carefully, all the way to the left, to see with his right eye if he'd left anything lying in his path. It turned out that if he watched himself, he could get around the house well enough, because, unlike in that rehab place, long familiarity supplied information that his senses did not. Even outside, where he'd been only a few times since his return, he felt much less disoriented than he did up at that place.

Lots of days, Loren waited to rise until the visiting nurse or one of the Millers came over, but one look out the window was enough to tell him that no one was going to get here today. On the kitchen calendar, he ran his finger over the laboriously x-ed-out days until he came to the first blank one—March 2. That would be today. Well, people would be saying that this was a late storm, but it wasn't. Just ask him. With his right eye, he gave the clock a gander, too. It was after nine. After nine, March 2, 1990. He pushed the button of the weather radio with his right forefinger and a soothing voice filled the room: ". . . has blanketed the region. At eight o'clock at Red Stick International Airport, snow accumulations measured four inches, with three to five more inches expected. High winds, gusting to fifty-five miles per hour—" The thing was, he no longer looked at the TV at all, not even CNN. Every day, all day, he listened to the round of voices from the weather bureau giving nature's news. Highs, lows, precipitation, weather advisories, road conditions, sunshine, wind, temperature ranges. If he wanted something visual, then he looked out the window. It was the exact combination of the ephemeral and the eternal that a dying man needed to know about.

The Millers and the visiting nurse had prepared him for the possibility of no one being able to get through to him for a day or two. Joe Miller had bought him one of those phones that you could keep with you, and if you wanted to dial, you just had to push one number, not seven or eleven. "Mem 1" was the Millers, "Mem 2" was the cops, and "Mem 3" was the visiting nurse. Plus, there was food in the freezer that he just had to defrost in the microwave, instant coffee, you name it. They had even paid up his heat through the end of April, so that couldn't go out. The electric, too. And Joe Miller had rigged up a deal that turned all the lights on, in the house and in the yard, at sundown, then turned them off about midnight, all except the pole lights by the barn, which stayed on all night as a deterrent to the FBI, the CIA, and the big ag companies. Oh, he was well taken care of.

Loren opened the kitchen closet and found what he was looking for, his bulletproof vest. He put it on over his pajama shirt and zipped it up. It fit kind of loose, which told him how much weight he had lost—it had fit kind of snug before. Then he pulled his chair over to the closet and sat down on it and put on his boots. They were plenty stiff, and he didn't have any socks on, but that was okay. Everything was okay.

After the boots and the vest, he was kind of winded, so he rested by looking at the clock (almost ten-thirty) and the calendar (still March 2) again. Then he stood up and took his insulated coat off the hanger. He hadn't had to button for himself since the brain attack, but he managed by watching his left hand rest right by the button, and then pushing the buttonhole against it with his right. Three. That was enough.

What this blossom of energy was for was getting out to the barn and having a look at the machine. Then, he knew, nature would take its course.

The boots were surprisingly heavy—that was the measure of how weak he was now, weak as a cat, and it wasn't so easy to open the door, either, until the wind took it and slammed it back against the house. You didn't want to leave it like that, letting all the heat out, but he didn't have much choice. He stood with his cane in the doorway. Behind him, the one girl who worked for the weather bureau was saying, "There was heavy snowfall reported south-southeast of a line extending from St. Paul, Minnesota, to Tulsa, Oklahoma, and this storm system was moving east at approximately thirty-five miles per hour."

He stepped into the wind, his eyes on the barn. That was how you got there—not by looking at your feet, but by looking at your goal— wasn't that what his father had told him long ago at the beginning of the century, and wasn't that how he had lived his life? Keep your eyes up and your feet moving.

The wind pressed him hard from the left, so that he had to put both hands on his cane. And he had forgotten his gloves, hadn't he. He stepped farther into the yard. It was plenty hard to see the barn in this wind, too. His eyes were all tearing up. Still, he made some steps, three or four, then two more. When the cane went out from under him and he fell forward into the snow, it was almost a relief. Yes, really, he thought with a touch of surprise, almost a relief that he didn't have to keep his eyes up and his feet moving anymore. He could give up and relax and just listen to the voice on the weather radio threading through the howl of the storm, "Interstate 100 is one hundred percent snow- and ice-covered. Interstate 99 North is seventy-five percent snow- and ice-covered, while Interstate 99 South is one hundred percent snow- and ice-covered. Due to high winds and drifting conditions, the state highway patrol has closed Interstate 92 west of—" The voice faded, then, as Loren concentrated every last iota of his attention upon it, it surged again—"If you must travel, a severe weather travel kit should include extra blankets, a powerful flashlight with extra batteries, a twenty-five-pound bag of sand, a small shovel, and roadside flares. Be sure to leave plenty of time to reach your destination."

63

Golden Arches

THE CHOICE WAS pretty stark: after McDonald's put a franchise in the commons, everybody who worked there could either quit or go to work for McDonald's. Lilian, who was the kitchen shop steward, didn't have to point out that McDonald's was not a signatory to any contract negotiated by AFSCME. McDonald's was McDonald's, and there would be no more bar-b-qued beef on bun w/ slaw cup or, for alternative eaters, noodle-cheese bake w/ pumpernickel slice.

Marly knew what they all were thinking—she was the anointed one, Cinderella, who would be moving into the big brick house when the jobs ran out, living the leisure life while the rest of them rustled up Big Macs or else looked on enviously at the Big Mac rustlers from the perspective of long-term unemployment. And on top of that, there was talk about giving work-study students the McDonald's jobs—that way there wouldn't be any possibility of an inconvenient benefits snarl. It was a progressive plan that everyone loved from the governor on down. O.T. had in fact been quoted in the *State Journal* as wondering aloud whether McDonald's would like to franchise every state-run eating establishment. Longtime capitol-watchers were well aware that "wondering aloud" about ludicrous ideas was Governor Early's method of trying out new policies—he was a strong adherent of the theory that a well-prepared public could gag down anything, and would, in fact, clamor for it if you suggested it often enough and kept everyone waiting long enough.

McDonald's, it was said, would be in by the end of March, so Marly went to Lilian and remarked that she had three weeks of paid vacation coming, and she wanted to take it now, while it still existed. "So when are you leaving?" said Lilian, and Marly said, "Tomorrow."

When five a.m. rolled around, Marly got up as usual and made Father's breakfast, which she set on the bottom shelf of the refrigerator under a cloth napkin, just the way he liked it, cup of coffee and all. Father was a great promoter of the microwave oven, because of the health benefits of double-cooking your food. Marly had not told him about leaving her job. The sun came up on the aftereffects of the previous day's storm just as she was folding and stacking her underwear.

She was surprised to note that she didn't have a suitcase, but then, she had never actually left town, had she? Out of a nation of restless movers, travellers, seekers, she alone, perhaps, had never gone anywhere that she couldn't return from in time to sleep in her own bed. Even Father, in his wilder days, had been to Chicago, Denver, and Fort Wayne. Even her brother had been to Houston for a Billy Graham crusade. She put her clothes in a plastic bag from the market, tied the handles together, and put that bag inside another. Into her purse, she put her Bible, the three hundred dollars she had gotten out of her account the evening before, the hat she was knitting for her niece, and a Snickers bar. She did not have a credit card or any photographs of Father or the other members of the family.

Twenty minutes later, she was carrying her plastic bag of clothes down Red Stick Avenue. She passed the university easily enough. Years of proximity had mingled her essence with that of the university even less than she had thought. With the coming of McDonald's, the institution had popped her out, intact and undigested, unaffected by critical thinking, the scientific method, empirical inquiry, or reasoned disputation. With reciprocal relief, she trudged past the scene of fifteen years of working life without a single pang or lingering thought.

When she passed her church ten minutes later, though, things were entirely different. She knew the cars in the parking lot—Mary and Eileen and Rita were there cleaning for the Wednesday service. She could easily turn her steps into the plowed driveway and join them. They would be laughing—the three of them were great laughers— but after all, when they saw her, their laughter would turn into smiles—more polite and more respectful. As Nils Harstad's wife-to-be, she had long ago become a degree untrustworthy. This whole winter, the more she tried to insert herself back into the slot she had once so easily fit—just Marly—the more the behavior of the other women had pushed her out of that slot and into another one—big shot, lucky duck, first among equals. She had tried to accept and not resent their changed attitude, to give that resentment to Jesus to deal with, but now, as she walked slowly past, craning her neck to see into the windows (stained glass was coming next year, promised their pastor), she knew for a fact that the mix was different inside her, too—resentment did color her feelings toward them. Were she to walk in and pick up a broom, things would be awkward, and that would annoy her, and her annoyance would prove to them that she had changed, and later they would compare notes and when and how and how much she had changed would become a piece of knowledge about her that everyone shared.

Well, she had changed. Ten minutes later, on the outskirts of town, she felt a still greater rush of sadness as she surveyed the snow-covered fields and the wide, enamelled sky than she had at any moment before. She had changed because she was tired of Jesus, the way He came to you and sat with you, the way He had to be a man in order to be human. Everybody in her church was always talking about how happy it made them that Jesus was right there, at your elbow, helping you along and keeping you on the right path. What could be better than a personal savior? But Marly resented the way Jesus counted on you needing Him like that. He never stepped back. He always wanted something from you. You always had to do something to please Him.

She came to the top of the hill. The road beside her continued up, over the bridge. The snowy drift at her feet spread away like a giant apron past the highway below and into the dark filigree of the woods beyond. The pattern of it was rather grand—the rounded shapes of the hills and the horizon carved by the precise parallels of the highway, the quiet blazing azure, white, and black of the natural world animated by the hurtling bright colors of cars and trucks, and Marly herself the only visible human. The grandeur of it was peaceful and soothing. She felt invited into the picture, perhaps noticed, but not focused on. Jesus, she thought, was back in town, nosing into everybody's concerns but God was here, large and beautiful and satisfyingly impersonal.

Marly turned her head at the sound of big gears downshifting. A green tractor-trailer had pulled off the highway and was rolling up the access ramp. As she looked at it, the driver sounded his air horn. Marly pushed the strap of her handbag higher on her shoulder, and ran to meet him as the big diesel idled to a stop at the sign.

The door was already open when she got there. She threw her plastic bag upward onto the seat, and clamored into the cab.

"Hey," he said.

"Hey," she said.

"Been waiting long?"

"Just got here. What time is it?"

" 'Bout eight. I left Ann Arbor about four."

He eased the truck across the road and down the on-ramp. As they picked up speed, Marly's heart began to lift and expand like a balloon. She said, "I forgot to ask you where we were going."

"How about San Francisco, that sound good?"

"Travis," she said, "that sounds like heaven."

64

A Little Deconstruction

CHAIRMAN X PREFERRED to think that as a young man he would have pressed on no matter what. That Nils Harstad was filing charges, that the board of governors had reprimanded him, that his own department had censured him and stripped him of his chairmanship as of June 30 ("Professor X" didn't have much of a ring, he thought), that he had been vilified in the press ("well-known campus hothead," "called by some, a 'space cadet' " were only two of the quotes)—all of this would have only spurred him on in the old days, a little resistance he could use like weights to build greater strength, greater effort.

As a middle-aged man, though, he was distracted by his students (the cloud forest being saved, they thought their work was over), his children (divorce—a lot they knew—was bad enough, but would he lose his job? Would they have to move out of their house? They couldn't stop asking him about it), Cecelia (wanting sex), Beth (wanting meaningful conversations). With lawyers, there were meetings, depositions, late-night phone conversations. With administrators and faculty and students, there were more meetings. With the children, there was an overabundance of quality time at Burger King, Wendy's, and McDonald's, where they ordered cheeseburgers ("Hold the meat"), and no Beth to help him through it. With Cecelia, there were arguments. With Beth, there were knowing looks and nods, as if she had been predicting something like this all along. With everyone, there were endless explanations which each of these people tried to steer toward the personal, when clearly the issues were social and environmental. He couldn't help it if in order to understand why he had attacked Nils Harstad (and everyone agreed that he had, even though he couldn't remember a single delicious moment) he had to explain the whole history of Third World agricultural development.

And so it was pleasant to think of how resolute and uncompromising he would have been as a young man if he hadn't been the way he really had been, which was hopeful and well-meaning, always expecting people to come to their senses and devote their means and their lives selflessly to the common good.

At any rate, the result of it all was that when the crane with its clam bucket came and bit down Old Meats, he didn't have the heart to order his troops to lie down in front of it, or, indeed, to lie down in front of it himself. About all the heart he had was to stand in the middle of Ames Road and watch.

The dump trucks with their loads of brick and mortar rolled over the frozen beds, no doubt compacting the hitherto friable and springy soil into a species of rock. Their wheels spun through the snow and found purchase in the most valuable thing Chairman X had ever produced—a whole world of fertility, a delicate structure of clay, sand, humus, air spaces, water molecules, phosphorous, potash, and nitrogen. Loamy, black, and mounded carefully up. Chairman X liked to think of it as a many-chambered mansion sheltering an unknowable variety of life-forms that worked away in the darkness outside all attempts of the human mind to classify, simplify, objectify. Now he watched as knobby tire treads rumbled over countless spots that he and his helpers had never dared to step on; diesel exhaust settled over raised beds that had never seen a pesticide or a petrofertilizer. Bulbs and roots and corms and rhizomes that he had left to winter over, carefully protected with a layer of compost and another of leaves, whose shoots and stalks and leaves and flowers he had looked forward to seeing in the spring, found themselves uncovered, pulverized, and thrown into the air by the heavy grinding wheels.

The clam bucket bit through brick, mortar, and living peach and apricot wood indiscriminately. There was no saving the trees, much less the flavor of the fruit, which depended as much on the circumstances of the trees as their genetic endowment. That warm red southfacing expanse of weathered brick wall, that particular type of soil, and that perfect microclimate for growing peaches and apricots this far north was gone forever.

The cloud forest he had never seen was saved (the Costa Rican government had even decided to buy up the cattle ranches around the forest, and, strapped for cash, TransNational had decided to sell them), but the garden he had spent most of his adult life tending was destroyed.

The demolition went fast. Just about the only feeling he experienced besides numbness was surprise at that.

. . .

WITH DR. BO JONES in Frunze, Kirghizia, negotiating in English for horses to ride into the mountains after wild hogs with people who only spoke Turkic and a little Russian, no one had bothered to mention to Bob Carlson that Old Meats was slated for demolition or that the outlook for both his hog and his job was clouded at best. Having stayed up late completing a three-page English paper entitled "Yukio Mishima and Ernest Hemingway: A Comparative Study," Bob had visited Earl Butz around six, when all was quiet and apparently eternal around Old Meats. The first thing he noticed at ten, when he came in sight of the building again, was that two of the walls were already gone and that in addition to the clam bucket, they had brought in a wrecking ball and begun on the concrete floor.

The change was so enormous that it was stunning, and Bob stood there, stunned, for a good five minutes. After that, he ran toward the first dump truck, and then toward the clam bucket crane, then toward another dump truck, shouting and waving his arms, but there was so much noise that he couldn't attract any attention. The snowy ground was slippery, and he fell and scraped his gloveless hands, but he scrambled up again, only to be confronted by a large man in coveralls and a hard hat shouting, "Didn't you see the sign, kid? Get out of here! This is a restricted area!"

"Wait!" cried Bob. "Wait! Where's Earl? Where's the hog!"

The man turned away. "Don't know, kid, but you gotta get outta here. If you got a problem, go over to the physical plant or something."

Bob ran toward the building, or he ran two steps toward the building, but big hard hands grabbed his shoulders and turned him around. The man's face, which he stuck right in Bob's, was red and angry. It shouted, "Get the fuck out of here, kid!"

"Listen to me! There's a hog in there!"

"He'll be bacon soon enough, kid. If you get in the way again, I'll call the cops!"

Bob backed away.

MRS. LORAINE WALKER COULD HEAR the demolition from her office, even with the windows closed. Old Meats was, after all, right in the center of the campus. When she glanced out the window, which was newly reglazed since the riot, she could see a puff of dust in the otherwise clear air above the demolition site. Mrs. Loraine Walker knew that the horticulture garden was falling victim to the budget cuts that had required the destruction of Old Meats, but that particular horticulture garden, pleasant as it was, was unauthorized. The authorized site had remained, through the years, flat, untended, arid, ignored despite any number of directives addressed to that little man, sent by Mrs. Loraine Walker over Ivar Harstad's signature.

She spoke aloud to herself. "He was warned," she said. Which did not mean that she felt no regret about the garden. One thing she had learned lately, something she had mentioned to Martha only the night before, was that sometimes it was necessary to suspend two or more contradictory thoughts in your mind at the same time. What it led to was a degree of softening, didn't it? Someone who acted on principle all the time, as Mrs. Loraine Walker was in the habit of doing, inevitably felt uncomfortable with this blurring, this softening. Mrs. Walker squirmed in her chair.

To tell the truth, everywhere she turned lately she was confronted by something that made her uncomfortable. Safe herself because of her investments and her job tenure, she saw clearly that Ivar was not safe. A fugitive fondness for him prevented her from retreating wholeheartedly into the argument that those were the wages of the job he'd taken on willingly. And there was Nils, too, a bland, complacent, provoking man, the sort whose self-satisfaction always seemed to be asking for it, but now that he had gotten it, Mrs. Walker couldn't uphold her moral standard. Every time he shambled into the office, looking despondently for his twin, she softened yet again. She got him coffee, she listened for the umpteenth time to the news that the Hellmich woman had sent him a letter from Bolinas, California, she gentled her voice instead of sharply setting him straight when she said, "Well, Dean Harstad, perhaps the relationship was doomed from the beginning—" and patted his shoulder when he said, "All my dreams—" in that pathetic way. And then there was Elaine Dobbs-Jellinek. Given Mrs. Walker's carefully thought through and extremely well founded antipathy to the woman, you would have thought that the sight of her felled by a rioter's stone, which Mrs. Walker had seen through this very window, the sight of the woman lying still and white on the steps, splayed out in her red coat, her hands spread in surprise so that her red fingernails throbbed against the snow like so many drops of blood, well, you would have thought such a sight would have carried an element of satisfaction, but Mrs. Walker had felt only horror. Mrs. Walker glanced at the window as if, like a movie, the scene might suddenly flash across it again.

Then she stood up and reached for her coat. Perhaps there was a reason she wanted to go have a look at the demolition of Old Meats, but for once in her life she didn't know what it was; for once in her life she acted on simple desire.

ALL KERI WAS THINKING about was getting to her 11:30 statistics class. She hadn't even bothered to button her coat or put on her mittens, and her neck and fingers were tingling in the cold. She dodged right, then dodged left, avoiding the seething streams of students rushing to classes on the side of the campus that she was just leaving. Then, of course, there were other clots of students, talking, kissing, teasing each other, and flirting. There were professors with briefcases striding right down the center of the walks and people on bicycles shouting, "On your left!" as if, were you to step into their path, your injuries would be your fault. Even though the walks were partly covered with ice, there were also Rollerbladers—one swept around Keri from behind and zoomed ahead—he was in her class, in fact, and always wore his skates right onto the elevator and into the room. Ahead, in the distance, she could hear the rumbling collapse of bricks and mortar, but she didn't register the noise, much less wonder what it was.

WHEN THE CLAM BUCKET took its first bite out of the wall of Earl Butz' suite, Earl had been awake for quite some time. The first thing he'd done upon hearing the distant thunder of Old Meats coming down was to kick his straw into a comfy mound and curl up in it as best he could. As the noise got louder, he shook his head at it, did his best to bury his ears in the straw, but then it didn't cease, it only amplified. Earl stood up and paced his quarters restively, hardly aware of the shooting pains in his legs and trotters. As the din grew overpowering, he consulted his limited memory for a precedent, but none occurred to him. In the end, he was reduced to cowering, without a shred of dignity, in the corner of his pen most distant from the racket. While he would have preferred even then to at least give the appearance of ignoring it all, he could not do so. Then the clam bucket broke the wall, let in the dusty bright light of day and a vision of the blue sky upon two alarmed and staring black eyes. Earl pressed himself against the solid and reassuring back wall.

The air was cold. Earl gasped as the clam bucket took another bite and widened the hole. A new sensation rolled over his pale and bristly hide, the refreshing sensation of chill. It woke him right up, right out of the frightened stupor he had been declining into. He raised his snout and momentarily closed his eyes, then he staggered back to his feet.

While Earl would never have claimed that anyone was neglecting him lately—Bob still came five times a day, still kept his pen clean, still turned the radio on for him, still fed him his special mix, still scratched his back with a stick and chatted with him while he worked—it was clear that some je ne sais quoi had gone out of their whole common endeavor. Just as Bob was hardly ever weighing him anymore, or conducting other measurements, Earl himself was only going through the motions, chow-wise. True, he was going through ALL the motions—chewing, swallowing, digesting, and eliminating—his intake had not fallen off. But he didn't pay much attention to it anymore. Had Dr. Bo Jones been stateside to reflect upon the matter, he might have concluded that Earl had been bred to eat himself to death before he was a year, or at most two years, old, and as a result of death being delayed, Earl had run past the possibilities of his genetic endowment, and was now only marking time.

What was clear to Earl as the clam bucket took yet another bite and let in yet more light, air, and chill was that the change he had been waiting for was upon him, and that he had better seize his opportunity while he had the chance.

Even so, the clam bucket itself was a powerfully daunting sight, and Earl had to summon all of his inner resources to withstand the fear it aroused in him, the way it swung and crashed against the remaining walls, the deafening grinding noise as it clamped down upon and ripped away what had constituted the immutable limits of Earl Butz' world. Most hogs couldn't have stood it. Helplessly distant and frantic, Bob Carlson assumed that Earl himself couldn't stand it. But as frightened as he was by the unusual movement and noise of the object, Earl's Christmas vision had prepared him for what it disclosed—the outdoors. As soon as he saw it, he wanted to get to it, and he fully expected to find what he had found there before—a welter of fragrances, of green grass and happy hog farm sights and sounds. The bucket swung and bit, arcing closer and closer to where Earl cowered against the wall. Finally, it swung against the bars of his pen and slammed them to the floor. A few moments later, all the rumbling, roaring, and crashing subsided into silence, and all Earl could hear was the outer breeze and some distant shouts. His mound of straw lifted and blew around the room, and Earl stepped forward two or three tentative paces.

BOB, who had been running back and forth with his hands over his ears, saw the crane operator open the door of the cab and climb down, his lunch in his hand. The other men, too, came out of their trucks and headed for the trailer the company had brought in. Bob waited until they were all inside with the door closed before edging toward the building. He knew it was stupid—any of the unsupported standing walls could topple at any minute—but all he could think of was Earl. At the barricade the men had thrown up, he paused to look right and left, then he clambered over.

MRS. LORAINE WALKER SAILED into view of the big old abattoir. All was silent. She checked her watch. 11:45. She made a mental note to call the demolition company and find out if the university was being charged for time and costs or by the bid. Across the site, standing in the middle of Ames Road, she noticed that little man from the horticulture department with his head down and his hands in his pockets.

KERI WAS walking slowly, all alone, back toward Dubuque House. She had not made her class, and the statistics professor had locked the door, the way he always did, just at the tick of 11:30. She was looking at her feet, but as she went behind Berkeley Hall, just on the side where they were tearing something down, she noticed the dust in the air and glanced up.

CHAIRMAN X KEPT telling himself that he couldn't waste his day watching this, and in addition to that couldn't stand any more of the twisting pain in his chest that accompanied the sight, but even when the men were eating lunch and the machines were silent and still, he couldn't seem to tear himself away. In a life based on the principle of passionate resistance, it did not seem to him as though he had even once staved off a single evil. Quite the contrary. The forces of greed, carnivorousness, exploitation, technology, and monoculture were everywhere more firmly in control than ever before.

EARL BUTZ CAME OUT running. It was his only hope, his deepest instinct. Head down, trotters blazing, squealing like a wild razorback on the remotest Asian steppes, he blew past the giant machines, hustled over the slurry of snow, mud, and perennial roots they had made, and shot like a bobsled through a hole in their fence. Then he was on open ground, the whole campus before him. No, it was not green and fragrant, it was white and sterile. Had he expected what he knew—the farmer and his wife and dogs, other pigs, cats—he was disappointed. Here was nothing he even dimly recognized. But there was no turning back. His little home, safe and warm, was destroyed. Earl instinctively understood that he had to throw himself upon the frozen bosom of the world as he found it and hope for the best.

BOB SAW him. He had wanted to see Earl so much, to know whether he was still alive, that he couldn't quite take in the actual sight of him, as big as a Volkswagen Beetle but much faster, rocketing past. He raised his voice, as if Earl were a dog, and shouted, "Earl! Earl! Come here! Come here!" But coming on command was something he had never foreseen that Earl would need. He turned and clambered back over the fence, but Earl carried a lot of speed for such a large hog— over seven hundred pounds. As fast as Bob could go, Earl far outstripped him.

MRS. LORAINE WALKER SAW him, and saw him for what he was, the secret hog at the center of the university, about whom she had been dismissing rumors for a year. He lumbered past, his high squealing underpinned by labored breathing, his white hide streaked with red where he had scraped himself. Something about the enormous, barrelling, frightening animal struck her as poignant. Even as she jumped back, she held out her hand as if to pat him on the head.

CHAIRMAN X SAW HIM, but only from a distance, and from behind. Still preoccupied with the garden around the building, Chairman X barely glanced at the swiftly receding paleness of Earl's haunches against the paler snow. He did hear the agonized squealing, which seemed to set the chill dry air to reverberating, and seemed, to Chairman X, to be the sound of his own grief, singing all around him.

THE CAMPUS WAS not empty. Even though many students were in class, there were plenty abroad, present to stop and gawk at the flying hog and the kid running after him, but Earl had no interest in them. He looked neither right nor left as momentum carried him through space and time into a future that wasn't prepared to receive him. As if understanding that, as if admitting the resulting perplexity, Earl slowed down. And when he slowed down, he was forced to reckon with the damage that his wild run had wreaked upon his bones and sinews. The fact was that he who was bred to eat and lie around was not bred to gallop. The new and excruciating variations on his old shooting pains nearly brought him to a gasping halt.

But they did not. If he couldn't run, he would walk. He lifted his head and staggered forward. It was then that he saw Keri, standing transfixed on the sidewalk beside Berkeley Hall. Was he drawn by her green coat? By something about her odor? By an instinctive animal recognition that she had served a year as Warren County Pork Queen? He made his way toward her even though his trotters were burning and freezing with a pain that seemed to rise up from the very earth itself.

Keri stood her ground. The giant hog, a Landrace, probably, but bigger than any she had ever seen, more like a dining-room buffet than a hog, seemed to roll toward her somehow, and then stop just in front of her. He looked her in the eye, then leaned forward, as if to smell her, then fell forward onto his knees. His shooting pains focused and concentrated themselves in his left foreleg, and then exploded deep in his chest. He took a labored, heaving breath, and suddenly jerked over onto his side. His whole body trembled.

Keri knelt down and looked into his still shining black eyes, then ran her hands over his enormous feverish head. Hesitantly, she began to scratch his ears.

He gave another great shuddering breath that froze and hovered in the cold air, and then he closed his eyes.

65

The Ripple Effect

DEAN THOUGHT the picture of the hog was funny. Of course he wouldn't admit that since entering therapy, but Joy saw him smile as it passed his gaze. Now he was deep in the Sports section, and there it was across the table from her, unavoidable. Another dead animal. She was in therapy, too, and thinking *Another dead animal* in that way was very bad for her, so she looked down at her grapefruit. Arrayed around her grapefruit were five bites of Dean's "Country Sunshine Big Breakfast" that she would have to eat before they would be able to leave the restaurant: hard scrambled eggs, a piece of biscuit, a spoonful of hash brown potatoes, a half-strip of bacon, and an elderly strawberry from far far away. Dean, under the influence of his therapist, had gone from haranguing and lecturing her to nurturing and supporting her. Long breakfasts at Denny's were part of his program.

Joy's program involved choosing not to dwell on negative thoughts. That, and waiting for the medication to take hold. Her therapist had advised her to think of herself as an earthquake victim, trapped under a fallen roof beam (her mood). She didn't have to take responsibility for the earthquake or the structural damage to the building. She only had to make choices that would lead to eventual rescue—calling for aid, maintaining hope, taking care of herself, guarding her strength, sustaining her faith in the drugs, which she was to imagine as eager, highly-trained German shepherds, barking excitedly as they closed in on the little dark room where she lay captive.

Of course it didn't help that the university had notified her that the equine management program was being cut, and she was to sell the university horse herd. She personally was being transferred to the Large Animal Hospital, where she would be taking care of patients, mostly equine, but some bovine. She would suffer no cut in pay. That was what she was supposed to focus on, no cut in pay. That was the sunny side of her street.

The sunny side of Dean's street was that he was finished with competitive, destructive, soul-destroying careerism, and intended to develop his long-buried and much-atrophied female side. As a shortcut to this end, he was teaching himself to write, throw a ball, use a knife or a scissors, and press the buttons on the TV remote with his left hand. His efforts were extremely helpful to his therapy, he reported. Just the previous night, his therapist had divulged in spite of herself that she had rarely seen a patient, maybe never seen a patient—and she had been doing therapy for fifteen years (that could be seven or eight thousand patients, which would put him in the 99.97th percentile for her patients alone)—break through to his vulnerabilities as fast as Dean had. He was sure it was the right-brain training, and there would easily be an academic paper, or even a best-selling book, a program, a video in that.

And of course, Joy, as a born left-hander, had an inherent understanding of a whole realm of thought and feeling that Dean was only beginning to discover. Together, with Dean guiding Joy toward wisdom that she already possessed—!

Well, the possibilities were endless.

But the first thing he had learned in his new life was easy does it, one step at a time, slow and steady wins the race.

Joy downed the bite of hash browns and suppressed a sigh. Sighs, Joy had discovered, made Dean crazy with worry.

She put the bite of eggs onto the bite of biscuit and made herself chew it up, then swallow it. The truth was that between Dean and the two therapists, all she had to do was follow instructions and wait for her chemical rescue. Depression, which was what she had, would gradually lift. Her ruminations of the last six months, which had at least seemed true, if not reassuring, would turn out to have been contentless. The vessels of thought would fill, of their own accord, with a rosier, bubblier liquid as soon as the drugs kicked in. Even this feeling she had to contend with lately, that she had been at last cheated of everything, would drain away and be forgotten.

She picked up the strawberry by its limp stem, flipped it back and forth with her finger, then put it in her mouth. She could barely taste it. She chose not to think a negative thought, that the strawberry was tasteless, but to think rather that her taste buds, now strangely inert, would sooner or later perk up.

Dean put down the newspaper, smiled at her supportively, and after that, she couldn't actually see the hog, she could only choose whether or not to imagine him.

. . .

HELEN HAD two yearly rituals that worked as her spring tonic. She always planted early potatoes, usually a yellow boiling variety, on St. Patrick's Day, and she always threw spinach seed out the back door onto the remaining snow around the fringes of the patio. The spinach that resulted from the icy, gradually warming conditions of the snow-melt would be especially moist and dark green, sweet, succulent, and filled with vitamins, perhaps as early as the first week in May.

Of course there was pruning to do, and raking back the mulch to expose the black innards of her vegetable and flower beds to the warming rays of the sun. And there was the postequinoctial sun it-self—Helen liked to feel the prickle of it on her scalp, and the re-sponding inner surge of vitamin D going into production. All of these activities had, in the past, been guaranteed to act upon the waiting self, like smiling in the mirror acted on sadness—mere performance raised your expectation of imminent delight.

But this year, the fact was she was merely doing it. She could not bring to her progress around the yard the stateliness or significance or focus of years gone by. She didn't take the time to cut the potatoes into two or three eye-sections, but planted whole ones. She let the spinach seed fly in bunches that would have to be thinned later. She forgot to look for snowdrops, crocuses, pungent moist onion shoots. She shivered in the cool wind and hurried so that she could get back inside.

Inside, however, there was no fire in the grate, no book half-read, waiting to enthrall her again, no stockpot simmering, not even the simplest loaf of bread rising on the radiator. Inside, outside, nothing to look forward to, and, to tell the truth, no forward-looking spirit. Was this an omen of the marriage she had agreed to? In the weeks since Ivar's proposal, she had come up with no reason to get married—that is, no reason except the one—that their orbit had brought them so close to marriage that were they to rocket away from it now at her insistence, the delicious, many-layered comfort of the life they had made for the last five years might vanish altogether.

After tossing the seed, she paused for a moment, waiting for some burgeoning, springlike thing to happen to her spirit, but the flat, bleached sky held as little promise as the frozen ground and the imper-sonally cold and steady wind, which was the sort of wind you imag-ined might blow on Mars.

. . .

MARGARET WAS on the phone with the chairman of the English department at the University of Wisconsin. She kept trying to speak in a normal tone of voice, but it was impossible. The knowledge that her colleagues were passing in the corridor outside her closed door was too disconcerting. The chairman said again, "I'm sorry, Professor Bell, but could you speak up? I'm having a very hard time understanding you."

"I said, 'I might actually consider a junior position.' "

"Oh, goodness me," said the chairman. "I am sorry. We made that hire. The, uh, deans felt that we just simply couldn't afford you."

"Oh," said Margaret brightly, hiding how deeply she felt the painful pop of the stimulating, diverse, and desirable bubble that had been her imagined future in Madison, Wisconsin.

ASSOCIATE PROFESSOR TIMOTHY MONAHAN looked up from the memo on his desk (". . . regret that all promotions are frozen for FY 90–91 and into the foreseeable future") and shouted, "Come in!" and the door opened, and an extremely odd-looking woman stepped inside and started removing her coat. Only after she said, "Hola," did he realize that he was looking at Cecelia. He gasped.

She said, "Why does it seem colder today than it has all winter? I feel like I can't possibly get warm!" She let the door slam behind her.

Tim set aside his lingering distraction over the memo he had been reading and made himself look past her. Her hair was gone. The thick, curly mass that always seemed to be about to spring free of its pins and combs had disappeared, only to be replaced by a much diminished head that reminded him of an eggplant or pumpkin covered with AstroTurf. He said, trying to make his voice sound helpful, "You know, you lose sixty percent of your body heat through your scalp."

"I knew you would notice!" she exclaimed.

"I noticed." He sounded glummer than he had intended, since he didn't care about his promotion anyway, and he hadn't actually been singled out—

Cecelia sighed. "Believe me," she said, "this started as a trim."

"It'll grow back. I mean, won't it?"

"She just didn't know how to cut it, and she kept trying to even it off, and then she got panicky, and I got panicky, so we looked in some magazines and this is what happened. When she was finished, she cried, so I couldn't."

"Won't it?"

"What do you think?"

"I THINK it will grow back." He made himself sound more confident. "Of course it will grow back."

"But this is a sign. The first thing she said was that she had never seen hair like mine before. I think this is a sign that I should go back to L.A."

"Oh, Cecelia—"

"No. I mean it. It's not working out for me here. And I just got a notice that my class size is going up again in the fall, to forty students. How do you teach a foreign language to forty students at a time? That's an educational forced march! And then, a year after that I come up for review. How do I teach a hundred and twenty students per semester with any sort of care and still rework my dissertation so that I can get all the articles and the book accepted that I need to have to show I deserve tenure?" She ran her hand over her bristly head and jumped up. "But why should I want tenure? I can't even get my hair cut! I can't even get warm or make friends or feel like this will ever in a million years be my home! Why make the effort? Why bother?"

The first thought that leapt into Tim's head was, Because I wish you would. On the other hand, self-improvement-wise, he was trying to get away from the first-person point of view, move toward something more detached and omniscient-like. So he said, benign, judicious rather than pushy, selfish, "What are the possibilities out in L.A.?"

She sat down again, leaned back, lifted her heels onto his desk. "You know, Tim, that's the question of the century. I'm serious. When I was in L.A. for Christmas, I was looking at that album my mom gave us all, with pictures of my grandparents and my aunts and my mother, and the first car and the little trees, and to tell you the truth, I couldn't figure out how in the world we ever got to L.A., how it came to be that my parents CHOSE our life there. Well, of course they didn't! They ended up there. I come from a family who could have LIVED somewhere, but instead just ended up. HE used to say—"

Tim made a disapproving noise, and his eye strayed to the memo again. He turned it over so he wouldn't be tempted to read it.

"I know I promised to stop talking about him all the time, and I have improved, haven't I? But this is important!"

"Okay, okay."

"United Fruit DID drive the farmers out of business! Cash crops DID kill the town they grew up in! There WAS nothing for them to do after four generations except move on! And moving on is what L.A. IS for, but that doesn't mean you want to be there!"

Tim shrugged, demonstrating knowing skepticism at this analysis. But he couldn't sustain his habitual manner through the sadness of her next remark: "Now it's my turn to end up."

He sighed.

She crossed her ankles. She ran her hand over the top of her head. She winced. "To tell you the truth—"

They exchanged a look and Tim could see that they were thinking the same thought. Here. Ending up here was not to be desired, preferred, wished for. Then, just then, with that look, her mood passed to him, and he saw his own future: stuck at associate professor, living in a rental, his students getting younger, his writing getting repetitive, his trips to New York getting more desperate, his circle of former lovers widening until it covered the whole campus like a pond, shallow and rank.

"It's that hog," he said. "The picture of that dead hog on the front page of the paper. Maybe"—but he heard his own voice, and his own voice sounded suddenly thin and hopeless—"maybe something will turn up."

MRS. LORAINE WALKER WAS NOT accustomed to the position she now found herself in, regarding Just Plain Brown from the business side of his large mahogany desk. A person who preferred to sit, she was standing. A person who preferred to ask questions, she had just answered some. Now he beamed upon her, unchangeably good-natured.

He said, "My dear Mrs. Walker. An organization is a delicate thing. I like to think of it as a field of balanced dynamics, energy shooting in all directions, but yet energy constrained and utilized. This, this is a field sensitive to the slightest distortion, where the least little wrong thing—a backwash of energy from an unauthorized source, for example—sets up a profound trembling in the whole." His hand rested, relaxed and comfortable, on a printout of the library budget. Underneath that, Mrs. Walker knew, lay a printout of the athletic budget.

"You might say"—he continued joyfully, clearly elaborating on the theme closest to his heart—"that an organization is a sleek, predatory animal, a panther, its eyes shining, its muscles rippling beneath the thick, glossy fur, all its attention focused on the LEAP, the SINKING of the TEETH into the NECK of the PREY—! But our panther has an illness. Certain cells have grown out of their assigned place. You would call that a cancer, would you not, Mrs. Walker? For isn't cancer really an insubordination, and isn't insubordination really a cancer? Are you with me, Mrs. Walker?" He leaned across the desk, openly trying to lock her gaze onto his.

She was too smart for that, at least. She stared mildly, with respect-ful semiboredom at a spot on the wall just past his ear. She said, "I am with you, Associate Vice-President Brown."

The smile never left the rounded surfaces of his face. "Ah, Mrs. Walker. Mrs. Walker, Mrs. Walker, Mrs. Walker. Here is the point. We've attracted the attention of the governor, the legislature, and the board of governors. The president can't do without Ivar, at least right now. So Ivar is going to have to do without you."

Mrs. Walker shifted her gaze to Just Plain Brown's face. He said, "I want to assure you, Mrs. Walker, that I am fully aware of your civil service status." His voice grew even kinder and warmer. "And I know the procedures. You, Mrs. Walker, are in big trouble."

THAT WAS IT, then. The very night of the day that that big hog fell at Keri's feet, they had their discussion and it was all settled. Their minds were made up, and it was fine, really. Diane was pledging a sorority, just the one she'd had her eye on all along, the little-sister sorority to the fraternity her boyfriend belonged to, and maybe if she joined, the two of them would stop bickering all the time. Besides, it was also the blondest and the most prestigious. Keri had gotten the newspaper out that very afternoon, after the pig, and found an apartment—a studio over the drugstore across from campus. She was over there now, looking at it. It looked like Sherri would be moving in with some girls she'd known in high school who lived in a regular dorm, and so what if it wasn't her first choice (smaller room, same number of girls, of whom that Doreen, whose boyfriend Sherri had slept with in the fall, was one), financially, it was her only choice. Mary was going back to Chicago. Things hadn't worked out with Divonne, who would lose her work-study job when the cutbacks went into effect, and the only job she had been able to line up was at the McDonald's in the commons, at half the current pay, ten times the current tedium. The idea of the apartment where they were all going to celebrate Kwanzaa and explore their African heritage had popped like a bubble.

Mary preferred going back to Chicago, actually. It wasn't worth the hassle here, and she was tired of going around and around about it with Sherri, who wanted her to stay in Dubuque House and just find two more roommates. Sherri was nothing if not persistent. A hundred times a day, she said, "I just don't understand, what IS the problem? Your teachers love you, you've got a great boyfriend, AND we can store our stuff here all summer instead of sending it all back home!" The last thing Sherri wanted to do was expose her duffels to maternal scrutiny. "I mean, she thinks wearing BLACK is one of the main signs that you've had sex!"

At this, the other three girls would exclaim in unison, "Isn't it?"

Carol, who had not quite yet been told of Mary's imminent arrival in Chicago and who did think that Mary would be staying in Dubuque House over the summer, going to summer school and working on the cleaning and maintenance crew, would certainly have at least as much trouble understanding the problem, even though Mary herself knew just what it was. It was that she could not imagine herself here. She could watch herself walk across the campus, enter classrooms, study in the library, eat in the commons or in the Dubuque House dining room, dance with Hassan at a party, but still not grasp where she was going or why she was doing anything. When she thought of the campus or her classes or even her room, she was absent. There wasn't even a space where a black person should be. Embarrassed as she would have been to admit it, this seemed to be the ultimate effect of THAT TIME in the commons, and probably of the way it had been glossed over or forgotten since. No amount of friendliness on the part of her roommates (white) or approval on the part of her professors (white) or partisanship on the part of her friends (black) or affection on the part of Hassan (neither) got at the root of her problem—the longer she stayed here, and here was the whitest place she had ever been, as white as any world she would have to succeed in in order to satisfy Carol, the less she seemed to exist.

You could delve into the causes of this feeling all you liked, and if she divulged it, there would undoubtedly be more delving by everyone than she could bear, but delving into causes wouldn't erase the feeling, it would only make her feel guiltier that she had given in to it.

Her plan was to take a strong line with Carol, stronger than she had ever taken—she just wasn't as ambitious as Carol wanted her to be, success on her terms was too destructive, and furthermore she didn't have to do what she didn't want to do, and Carol couldn't make her. Adamant refusal was her trump card. It was just thinking about the fight ahead of time that was the problem.

In general, however, everything was fine. More than fine. Everything was *good*, and if people would just leave her alone, things would be even better.

KERI SAT on the edge of the bed and looked around the tiny room. If you leaned far enough in each direction, you could reach all the amenities from the bed—the closet, the hot plate, the sink, the window, the shower stall. It was the smallest room Keri had ever seen, and she almost regretted having rented it already, having impulsively paid over her deposit before the landlord even opened the door to let her in. "Really," she had said, "as long as it's clean, anything is fine with me." But now that she was here, by herself (there wasn't really enough space for the landlord to be in here with her), she was willing to narrow her definition of that term "fine" a bit. It wasn't exactly that she couldn't imagine herself living here, it was that imagining herself living here was all too easy—ensconced in the bed; no space between herself and her things for anyone else to occupy; obsessed, as she knew she would become, with keeping everything in its tiny little place. And it wasn't even so much that she feared the prospective isolation. Her fear was more or less abstract. It was rather that she welcomed it, welcomed what a relief it was going to be. She could sit on this bare bed and look around this tiny, empty room and recognize it perfectly as the mold of the person she was going to become.

WHEN BOB CALLED his parents in search of some solace and told them about Earl, his mom said, "Oh, honey! I'm so sorry, I know there's nothing I can do to help, but I'll send some cookies, how would that be? I just made gingersnaps today, I can get them in the mail tomorrow morning! And I was going to write you a note anyway, because Aunt Edna had a heart attack over the weekend, and if you think you've got problems, you should see *her*! A quadruple bypass is the least of it! You really ought to send her a card in the hospital.

While your father gets on, I'll find the address. Just a minute, honey."
Then his dad got on, and said, "Now, son, remember when those
puppies died, the German shorthairs we had such hope for, the whole
litter of four, and we'd spent a hundred bucks on the stud fee? The
problem was that we were already counting the money we were going
to sell those pups for. And then the bitch, all on her own, went out
and got pregnant again right away, and when those pups were born,
even though they weren't purebred and we couldn't sell them, those
were the best dogs we ever had, and everyone we gave a pup to said
the same thing—smart as a whip and not bad-looking, either. You
know, I always say, when something bad happens, that it might all
turn out for the best. Here's your mother, she's got something to tell
you, just a minute," and then his mother said, "Well, I must have
thrown out that slip. Bart, did you see that slip I had? It was the corner
of that envelope, that subscription envelope from that magazine, you
know which one I mean, it had some red writing on it, we talked
about signing up the other night. Now where did I put that—"

Bob, who had been tapping the open closet door with his booted
toe, suddenly kicked it shut as hard as he could.

"Oh, here it is, no, that isn't it, that's that other letter I was looking
for. I'd better put that away right now because otherwise—Oh, yes.
Edna Carlson, Hope Hospital, Hope Junction, now I can't read the
zip code, but you know they have those books at the post office, and
you can just look in there—"

Bob could hear her side of the conversation spiralling inward. Her
voice was getting softer and he could just see her gaze dropping
downward and inward.

He said, "Forget it!"

"Pardon me, dear?"

"I said, 'Forget it!' Forget Aunt Edna! I can't stand her anyway!
Who the fuck cares about Aunt Edna? You don't!"

The silence on the other end of the line told him he had caught her
attention. He made the fatal error of marshalling evidence to prove
his point. "Just last summer you said she was the most self-centered
woman you'd ever seen, that time she made Grandma wait in the rain
while she—"

"Son?" intoned his father.

And then he threw Gary's portable phone right at the window,
which broke with a glittering smash, and then the phone shot away
into the night.

66

The Provost Reflects

IVAR HAD TO admit that while the headlines were as bad as could be, the picture of Mrs. Loraine Walker, captioned "The secretary to the provost, who happened to be on the scene when the animal escaped, directs disposal of secret hog," was reassuring. A bulldozer could be seen pulling up in the background. As always, an ambience of perfect control seemed to have settled around Mrs. Walker—she had had the kid who was apparently in charge of the animal escort the weeping girl back to her room; she had breathed no word of the ultimate end of the animal's remains (what could you possibly do with such an enormous hog besides eat it, *pace* the local chapter of People for the Ethical Treatment of Animals?); she had, in short, acted as if a hurtling hog, while surprising, was hardly a matter of concern, more a joke than anything else, and the panic of those who ran, jumped, fell, or dove to get out of its way was understandable but almost, well, silly. No one, after all, was hurt.

Dr. Bo Jones, though, had come under more serious scrutiny. Ivar and Mrs. Walker were both surprised to learn from the paper that he was in central Asia, and had been for some weeks. They were also surprised to learn from the university accounting office that recent charges for food, drugs, and a work-study student (this Bob person), all unauthorized, came on top of five semesters of similar charges and, indeed, on top of a still earlier, and somewhat startling, sum that went to the refurbishing of the hog's quarters in Old Meats. All told, the amount the university had paid out for Dr. Jones' hog-fattening experiment came to $233,876.42. Nor had any grants come in to defray even a portion of these expenses. And the university accounting office had been remarkably free in communicating this information to the news media. Governor O. T. Early had been quoted as saying, "Who's in charge up there? Do I have to go in myself and kick some butt?"

What is a university? Ivar couldn't help but pause and wonder. When he'd first come to this particular university, at eighteen, he had easily found what he was looking for. It was 1953, and angular men in glasses, crewcuts, and bow ties were everywhere, a benign army of uncles, who liked to point things out with the stems of their pipes. He and Nils had themselves worn crewcuts and bow ties and answered to "Mr. Harstad" whenever they were called upon in class. Across the campus, in their own compound, protected by parietal rules and housemothers, the girls in their circle skirts and sweater sets were clearly a species apart, and were clearly being groomed for a mating ritual that Ivar and Nils eventually elected not to participate in, choosing instead to join the uncles. The place was merely a college then, a group of colleagues. It made no claims to universality.

Over the years he had learned that the uncles tended to squabble a lot, that, in fact, the more any two uncles seemed to look alike superficially, the more bitter and profound was their antagonism toward one another. Another thing he had learned was that while from the outside it did appear that the greatest change in university life had been the grand infusion of money from all federal, state, and private sources, this infusion had had no effect upon intramural hatreds—they burned no hotter, and no less hot, simply because there was lucre at stake.

He and Nils had easily understood the single promise of "a college experience" that would last as long as they made the grade. This college experience would cost their parents a rather modest sum and the return on their investment would be equally modest—a small measure of extra respect, a bit of added insurance that Nils and Ivar would live their lives in the middle class. In the fifties, colleges had to sell themselves a little. It hadn't been obvious to everyone that spending money on higher education was worth postponing a good job or an apprenticeship to a well-paying trade. One of the brochures the college had put out began, "A college education opens doors." A graphic of a hallway, two or three doors opening onto inviting groups of smiling men. A limited promise extended to a limited group.

Money was one aspect of present universality. The uncles in their crewcuts had been succeeded by other uncles in Afros, ponytails, razor cuts as up-to-the-minute as any on Wall Street, as well as by aunts in bobs or curls or chignons, aunts in blue jeans whose locks flowed to their waists, even, on one memorable occasion, by an aunt who clipped her hair very close—one quarter of an inch—and put a note on her office door advising students who desired to meet with her that she could be found on the university rifle range. Uncles and aunts all over the university taught in a universal diversity of accents. The students responded in kind.

And the university shamelessly promised everything to everyone, and charged so much that prospective students tended to believe the promises. While a state university, unlike an Ivy League institution, did not promise membership in the ruling class (Wasn't that the only real reason, Ivar thought, that four years at Harvard could cost $100,000?), Ivar's university, over the years, had made serious noises to all sorts of constituencies: Students would find good jobs, the state would see a return on its educational investment, businesses could harvest enthusiastic and well-trained workers by the hundreds, theory and technology would break through limits as old as the human race (and some lucky person would get to patent the breakthroughs). At the very least, the students could expect to think true, beautiful, and profound thoughts, and thereafter live better lives. At the very very least, students could expect to slip the parental traces, get drunk, get high, have sex, seek passion, taste freedom and irresponsibility surrounded by the best facilities that money could buy. Its limits expanding at the speed of light, the university could teach a kid, male or female, to do anything from reading a poem to turning protein molecules into digital memory, from brewing beer to reinterpreting his or her entire past.

Over the years, Ivar thought, everyone around the university had given free rein to his or her desires, and the institution had, with a fine, trembling responsiveness, answered, "Why not?" It had become, more than anything, a vast network of interlocking wishes, some of them modest, some of them impossible, many of them conflicting, many of them complementary. Ivar himself resisted neither the wishes nor those who offered funds to pay for them. The most that he could say for himself was that, from time to time, he had felt obscurely uneasy.

Dr. Bo Jones was a well-meaning old coot, no more or less benign than anyone else, inquisitive and eccentric, not unusually greedy or calculating. He had found a way to ask the questions he wanted to ask at university expense. No one had stopped him. Ivar dialed Mrs. Walker, out in the office. He said, "Mrs. Walker, try and find out who is paying for Dr. Jones' trip to, where is it?"

"Kirghizia, Ivar. I've looked into it. He seems to have gotten a grant from Mid-America Pork By-Products, which is a subsidiary of Western Egg and Milk, which is a subsidiary of—"

"The TransNationalAmerica Corporation."

Simultaneously, Ivar and Mrs. Walker sighed two large, knowing sighs. Ivar said, "Where do you think he is?"

"Well, I did speak to Mrs. Jones, and she did get a cable last night which read, 'Have found horses and guides. Setting out early in the a.m. for the mountain districts. Have received assurances that rumors of warring clans are much exaggerated.' "

"Thank you," said Ivar.

67

Deus ex Machina

IT HAD NOT escaped his secretary that Dean Nils Harstad was but a wreck of the complacent, self-important know-it-all that he had once been. The schedule that he had formerly maintained, which suited her right down to the ground because it left her plenty of time to pursue her own calling, which was selling Amway products over the telephone, had been shot to hell, and her sales had fallen off by a third. At this rate, her vacation in Cancún was in serious jeopardy. The Hellmich woman had been gone for weeks, but it looked like Dean Harstad was going to be sitting in her office with her working through every little detail of his abandonment until she quit or he retired, whichever came sooner.

It was for this reason that she felt no qualms about ushering a guy in overalls named Joe Miller into the dean's office and letting him sit there until the dean finally came in. At that point, just as the dean was hanging up his coat and readying himself to colonize his usual chair beside her desk and begin his lamentation, she said, "Oh, sir, someone is waiting for you in your office. He's been waiting since—"

The dean glanced wanly through the open doorway, and looked as though he might sit down anyway, but she stopped him. "Really, sir. He's got important papers."

The dean sighed a martyred sigh, but he did go in. Moments later, she heard him intone, "Sir, I don't know you, but let me ask you if your most cherished dreams have ever been blasted—"

"I don't know about that—" began Joe Miller, and Dean Harstad's secretary got up to close the door before pulling her client list out of her purse and dialing an outside line.

An hour later, Dean Nils Harstad, transformed into a dynamo, shot out of his office with a roar of purposefulness, pushing Joe Miller ahead of him and saying to his secretary, "Call Ivar. Tell him I'm on the way over. Tell him to stay right where he is and not move a muscle. Tell him to call the president of the university and the university lawyer and get them there."

. . .

"WELL," said Joe Miller to the phalanx of Ph.D.'s and such sitting across from him at the university's big walnut meeting table, "We've been picking up Mr. Stroop's mail at the post office all along, ever since he had that stroke he had, and went up to the rehab center. And I would take it over there, and sometimes open it for him, and he would nod if I was to keep it for him, and shake his head if I was to throw it away. And the other thing was that he took me to a place in his house where all his important papers were kept not long before he died. He didn't have a lawyer, because, as you may know"—here he nodded to Dean Harstad, the palest man Joe had ever seen next to Provost Harstad; he made a mental note to tell his wife about them, they were a sight—"he did believe that lawyers were always being paid off to show their clients' files to the FBI, the CIA, and the big ag companies."

Nils smiled warmly, as if this particular trait in Loren Stroop were especially endearing to him.

"So he had all his papers in his house, and, you know, farmers of my father's generation and Loren's generation were pretty mistrustful after their experiences in the Depression—" He coughed, reminding himself to get to the point. "Anyway, here's the will, assigning all rights in the machine to the university, with Dean Harstad here as the agent. He was a real believer in the land grant idea. He talked about it all the time. And here's the description of the machine."

The president said, "I guess I don't really understand what this machine does. I'm a mathematician, you know." He smiled his brightest fund-raising smile.

"Here's what it does," said Nils. "It plants three-foot-wide rows of corn, soybeans, and rye grass or some other groundcover, and this tail here?"—he pointed to a paragraph in the description Loren had painstakingly written out—"That covers the wheel tracks with a short, thick-growing grass. Later on, when the harvester comes in, it rides on this mat of grass."

"Lovely," muttered the president, in a tone Ivar knew was meant to suggest comprehension, but really revealed that the man was not only at a loss, but bored, too. Ivar decided to get his attention. He said, "If we can patent this machine, it could earn the university millions."

"Oh, really?" said the president, casually but unmistakably bringing his full attention to bear upon the papers on the table in front of Nils. He held out his hand. "Why is that?"

"Well," said Nils, "if it works, this machine is going to revolutionize American agriculture."

"Oh," said Joe Miller, "it works. Loren used it to plant every year for the last four years. I never saw him planting, though, because he planted in the middle of the night."

"But no one farms like this," said Just Plain Brown. "Who's going to manufacture this machine? Who's going to buy it?"

Nils smiled. He said, "As a matter of fact, the extension arm of the university performs a powerful educational function."

Joe said, "I noticed over the years that on his more sloping fields, he got a kind of terracing effect after a while. And his yields were pretty good, too, considering how chintzy Loren was with inputs."

Nils said, "If we could get hold of the man's machine, we could try it on some test plots this planting season. Bill Darling, over in Agronomy—"

The president put down the papers and gazed off into the middle distance, a smile playing over his lips.

The university lawyer said, "Maybe we should take a little ride out to Mr. Stroop's farm and have a look at the machine?"

Really, Ivar thought, millions. He tried to feel doubtful, uneasy, skeptical. There was no patent, there were no plans among the papers Joe had brought. And he tried to focus on the truths he had just been groping toward that morning, but it was like trying to look into a blazing light and see a small dark object. It was so hard that the effort came to seem futile, and the object started to vaporize and disappear. It was easier to catalogue the programs that would, or could, be saved—women's studies, art and graphic design history, Italian and Portuguese, volleyball, tennis, theater performance, nuclear engineering, medical engineering, wildlife biology, the swim team. After all, could you really resist the money, the expansion, the heavy, rumbling momentum of the whole enormous machine? All he could do realistically, he thought, was to honor his uneasiness by pausing a moment before he said, "Maybe we should get Elaine in here."

Bob Brown said, "No, no. This is big time. This baby is big enough for Jack Parker to really sink his teeth into."

"The thing is—" said Joe Miller, "and this is why I thought I should come over here today—the thing is, some people came this morning and took away the machine. Some outfit from Minnesota.

When I tried to stop them, the guy showed me a paper that he called a confiscation order."

A dead silence fell over the table.

"Who would do that?" moaned the president, his face in his shoes.

"Well," said Joe, "if you'd of asked Loren, he would of said, the FBI, the CIA, and the big ag companies."

"Where are the plans? There must be blueprints somewhere, or building plans," said Ivar.

"My wife and I have looked high and low for any sort of drawing. You know, he did all his fieldwork in a bulletproof vest. Drawings like that are just the sort of thing the old guy would have hidden, but we can't find anything, even though my wife and I have turned his place upside down. You're welcome to help us look."

BY A COINCIDENCE that was truly no less than astonishing, Dr. John Cates was, just at that moment, staring at the plans of Loren Stroop's machine. Dr. Cates hadn't thought about the plans again after taking them from the student—wasn't that around Christmastime?—and laying them on his desk. What with conferences and meetings and directing the work in his lab, he had hardly been in his office.

But just today he was in a funny mood, a newly awakened sort of mood. He'd thrown off the aftereffects of the unpleasantness in Orlando fairly quickly—it had been reassuring to be home, after all, where he could focus on his work and where Daniel spent most of his day in school (a Jekyll-and-Hyde sort of kid, he did pretty well there and had a reputation for good behavior). Surrounded by all the emblems of his success—his Volvo, his lab, his spacious house, his respectful students, grad assistants, postdoc researchers—he'd found his focus again and sensed a bonus in the offing, as well—a hypothesis was coming on, complete with ideas for experiments, thoughts about funding, all the accoutrements. What if silicon—? he thought. What if there was a temperature range within which small clusters of, say, six, twelve, and eighteen atoms of silicon exhibited the properties of both liquids and solids? And you could use benzene as a probe molecule, the way Hahn and Whetton did in California. Other ideas would come. All he had to do was wait for them. The waiting sometimes drove him crazy, but over the years he had learned that this was how he worked.

He had no anxieties about cutbacks. The right man in the right place, from the day he started the first desegregated kindergarten in St. Louis right up to today, Dr. John Cates was history's darling, and if, like all explosions, the civil rights explosion had fallout, then through the daily exercise of disciplined focus, Dr. John Cates had minimized the intrusion of that fallout into his life. The results were there for everyone to see—he was at the top of his field. He did real science. He was a credit, and not only to his race.

The hog, though, the hog in the paper was something he had not been able to get out of his thoughts. The hog in the paper was interfering with the incoming hypothesis, distracting him when he needed to be concentrating, focusing. He had even snapped at Daniel this morning when Daniel asked him about it. He had said, "Well, how should I know where the hog came from?" And Daniel had said, "Why don't you ever know anything, Dad? You just never know anything!"

Dr. John Cates had begged to differ, but then he couldn't actually think of a specific thing he did know that Daniel might be interested in, so he made the mistake of saying, "What don't I know?" and Daniel had said, "You don't know who the Fine Young Cannibals are," and it was true, he didn't.

He picked up the drawing on the desk and stared at it. He had no idea what it was, either. His hand jerked in an aborted urge to throw it down, but he didn't.

Looking at it was almost a physical sensation, his gaze moving over lines like feet walking along paths, drawn ineluctably toward the center of the drawing, which was also the center of something else, something even more interesting than the familiar objects he began to pick out here and there—a bicycle wheel, an upside-down carburetor. Cates gazed and gazed.

After a while, he realized that he was gazing into another human mind, as odd and unique as his own, a mind for which some things were clear and some things were murky (even with no knowledge of the object depicted, Dr. Cates could see a couple of connections that could be shortened and simplified), a mind that had crept over one idea in all its parts month after month, year after year, as his mind had crept over the chemistry of atomic structure year after year, and so a mind that knew the habit of perseverance. All around the mind's object were smudges, wrinkles, stains, the relics of a life, and those drew Dr. Cates, also. The object bulking large in the center, the life scattered around the periphery. Cates' gaze shifted, hypnotized, from one to the other. After he had looked long enough at the plan, it came to seem to Dr. Cates a remarkably beautiful drawing, as beautiful as any he had ever seen.

His first thought was to keep it and frame it.

His second thought was to find the artist and see if there was another one he could buy.

He sat back and looked out the window, feeling the morning's unpleasantness with Daniel slip away, and trying to think who might know, or know someone who might know. His gaze travelled along the roof lines of the buildings across the quad and settled on the cupola of Lafayette Hall.

He picked up the phone, got an operator, and said, "Hi. Would you please give me Mrs. Loraine Walker in the provost's office?"

MRS. WALKER PICKED UP the phone on the first ring. The Gang of Five (Ivar, Nils, the president in his mint green short-sleeved shirt, the university lawyer, and Just Plain Brown) were emerging from the meeting room talking about some machine. The lawyer was saying, "The patent and ownership problems could be solved, even without the machine, if we just had some sort of plans."

". . . looks like some sort of plans," said Dr. Cates, on the other end of the line. "I would love to find the artist, and—"

"Just a minute," said Mrs. Walker. She could hear an almost audible click as her fabled intuition locked into place. "Ivar?" She nearly whispered, but the five suits froze, like dogs hearing a distant whistle. "If I'm not mistaken, this is the very person you want to speak to."

"Who is it?" said Ivar, eagerly.

Mrs. Walker shrugged and moved her finger so that it touched the hang-up button on the telephone like a trigger. After a significant nanosecond, she looked into the eyes of Just Plain Brown. His smile disappeared as if it had never been there, and the knowledge that he was the hostage shot around the group of men like an electrical signal. Ivar suppressed a smile, Nils' face relaxed, the university lawyer adopted a mask of neutrality, and the president looked from Just Plain Brown to Mrs. Walker, then back, understanding at once the very high price someone was about to pay. He sucked his teeth for a second, then smiled. That someone, after all, didn't have to be him. He said, "Mrs. Walker, I don't think your value to this university can be overestimated, really. Wouldn't you agree, Fred?"

The university lawyer gave a deliberate nod.

Mrs. Walker took that as a promise.

But then, just for a second, she wondered if she really did want to save them. She could see the certainty that they would be saved return to their faces as fast as their neurons could carry it, so quickly that maybe none of them would remember this pivotal, even definitive, moment. Her finger trembled on the button with the very force of her dilemma. What was best? What did they deserve?

Mrs. Loraine Walker glanced at Ivar. He, of all of them, looked as if he didn't know the answer to that question. For that, and for that alone, she moved her finger off the trigger and held out the phone to him.

68

Paperwork

State Journal, April 23, 1990: In a surprise move, Governor Orville T. Early today eased the two-month-old budget crisis at the state university by repealing a measure that would have reverted FY 89 funds already allocated to the university back to the state. The funds, amounting to some $3 million, will enable the university to avert the widespread layoffs and program cuts that were expected to take effect early next week. In addition, the governor held out the hope that he would reinstate funds reverted earlier in the fall, and also allow the university budget to grow slightly in FY 90. He suggested, however, that "The people of the state are watching those pinheads, and they had better watch their step." When asked if he meant "eggheads," a common term for university intellectuals, Governor Early said, "Pinheads, eggheads, knuckleheads, what's the difference?"

When asked whether the revelation of a recent bequest to the university of the design for a revolutionary new piece of farm machinery played a role in his decision, the governor said, "Education is a top priority in this state, and with this governor. But God helps those who help themselves, doesn't He?" Bids for the right to develop and manufacture the machine, the brainchild of an independent farmer-inventor who recently died from the complications of a stroke, have come from as far away as Japan and Korea. Said Dr. Nils Harstad, dean of extension, "After having almost daily contact with Mr. Stroop, the inventor, over the last few years, I know how thrilled he would be at the interest of these legendary companies in his homely efforts. Our state is certainly a land of opportunity, even in these restricted times."

Memo
From: Provost's Office
To: Professor Margaret Bell
    English Department

You are hereby authorized to hire a work-study student, as per your request of September 30, 1989, on a half-time basis. Funds in the amount of two thousand dollars will be allocated to the Women's Studies budget as of July 1. Please notify this office of the name and status of your hiree before June 15.

Memo
From: Helen
To: Cecelia

I am notifying all faculty members with first- and second-year language sections that class size will revert to twenty-five students as of the beginning of the summer session. Hooray! Also, Cecelia, I would like for you to serve on the university parking committee next fall. Please let me know.

Memo
From: Professor M. Bell
To: Provost's Office

I have hired Mary Jackson, SSN 453-89-1234, as my work-study for the fall.

Thanks, Mrs. Walker!

Letter
Mrs. Bo Jones
147 Red Stick Circle

Dear Mrs. Jones,

We regret to inform you that we have been unable to make contact with your husband, Dr. Bo Jones, since he was last seen in the city of Samarkand, Uzbekistan, USSR, thirty days ago. Soviet officials report that the present turmoil in the Soviet Union had become a severe hindrance in their efforts to locate Dr. Jones or his companions. Please let me know *immediately* if you receive any word from your husband.

Yours truly,

Richard Wagner
Liaison Officer
United States Department of State

Letter
Mr. Loren Stroop
RR 2
Auburn

You May Already Be a Winner!

In only a few weeks, MR. STROOP, you could receive a check for $10 million! What are your dreams, MR. STROOP? Mail in your entry today, and your dreams, LOREN, could come true!

Memo
From: Elaine
To: Ivar

Ivar, please authorize the transfer of my secretary, William Bartle, to another office. His "preference" for not doing any work is causing gridlock over here. Matters are at an impasse.

[handwritten]
Mrs. Walker, I'm begging!!!!!! Please!!!!!!

Memo
From: Chairman of the Horticulture Department
To: Hort Interns

We will have our first meeting at the new garden site beside the bus barns on Tuesday at 4:30. I urge you to accept the extremely unpromising nature of this site as a challenge. Our preliminary surveys of the spot show that the soil is mostly clay, and remarkably compacted. Part of the site was originally a wetland, which was filled in in the 1950s with some waste matter from the university. We have not yet determined the composition of the fill, but given the university's checkered past, we may be in for an ugly surprise. The good news is that the state Department of Natural Resources has agreed to help fund cleanup of the site and restoration of the original wetland area. I have also just received word that an adjoining tract of some three hundred acres has been sold to the Nature Conservancy. Our "garden" may look considerably different when we are finished from our former garden outside Old Meats, but the possibilities are exciting ones. Please bring any preliminary ideas and sketches to the Tuesday meeting.

N.B.: Although Professor Leopold will assume chairmanship of the department on July 1, I will remain in charge of the gardens, so you can rest assured that the plans we agree upon WILL go forward. I know some of you have been wondering about this.

Memo
From: Cecelia
To: Helen

Okay, I'll serve on the committee. Hey, did you really just get married?

Letter
Mr. Richard Wagner
Liaison Officer
Department of State

Dear Mr. Wagner,

Although I have had no word from my husband, I did receive a call today from Cabela's sporting goods in Kearney, Nebraska, telling me that they have received the iced carcass of an adult male boar, apparently from my husband. It was shot on April 15, according to the note. It was sent from Kabul, Afghanistan. I asked them about the text of the note, but they said it just said, "Hi from Kabul. Regards, Dr. Bo." I gave Cabela's permission to have the carcass stuffed before it deteriorates, so you will have to contact them if you think you can find clues to his whereabouts.

Thanks for your help.

Mrs. Carla Jones

Note
Keri,

Divonne got that fellowship to West Africa after all, so even though our apartment was back on, now it's off again, and my sister won't let me move out of Dubuque House anyway, so is your apartment thing, you know, FINAL? I talked to the R.A. and he said we can have the room again next year but at least two of the present roommates have to commit to staying here. Plus all that, you know, really, I do like you, even though I know you don't think I do. I'm sure we can work things out (this is awkward), but let me know, because I have to get back to the R.A. tomorrow—

M.

Memo
From: Provost's Office
To: Dean, Clemson School of Art and Design

Please remove from the cemetery at once the artwork entitled *Balloon Pig*. This office is fully aware that the artistic apotheosis of this work, namely the projected exploding of the "pig" on May 1 that has been advertised in the *Daily*, is intended to be a revolutionary "statement" on a number of issues that have affected the campus this year. However, it is the opinion of this office that the litter resulting from the fact that the "pig" is stuffed with play money, and from the thirty-foot-in-diameter membrane itself, would prove onerous to the maintenance staff as well as destructive to the wildlife on and around the campus. And, Jan, it is my personal opinion that this thing is an eyesore. It has to go.

Mrs. Loraine Walker

Letter
Mr. Asa Barker
Collegiate Properties
4567 Red Stick Boulevard

Dear Mr. Barker,

This is to inform you that even though you won't return my deposit, I feel that I must break the lease, and so I will not be living in your apartment in the fall. I'm sorry. I'd like to say that I don't think you have been very understanding in this matter.

Very sincerely yours,

Keri Donaldson

Memo
From: Mrs. Loraine Walker
To: Dr. Lionel Gift

Sorry, Dr. Gift, I cannot reschedule the audit of your university accounts. Please bring your papers to my office at 10 a.m. Friday morning as originally scheduled.

69

Off-off-off Campus

"I'LL HAVE," said Dr. Lionel Gift with the sort of self-confidence that always gave Elaine Dobbs-Jellinek a prickling feeling on the soles of her feet, "the warm salad of field greens, with just a little balsamic vinegar on the side, no oil, and the seared medallions of salmon with the tomato–dill coulis. And bring a bottle of, let's see, the Cakebread '87 Chardonnay. Elaine?"

As much as Elaine wanted to appear as though lunches like this one were routine for her, she also wanted to eat something that she would never eat again, fatty, caloric, expensive, and trendy, something like the ballotine of rabbit in a Madeira-truffle-tomato essence. She liked all of those words, from "ballotine" (which she imagined to be a golden box of puff pastry) to "essence," except for the word "rabbit." The waiter issued a small breathy noise, the sort of noise inaudible to Dr. Lionel Gift, who was greeting people right and left, but intended to remind Elaine in clarion terms that he, the waiter, was urgently needed at many other tables. "How are the crabcakes?" said Elaine.

"Excellent, of course," purred the waiter.

And there it was. She said, "Oh, yes. I'll have the lobster claw meat in a ragout of champagne, morel mushrooms, and cream."

"Excellent choice, madame." At last he went away.

"And how are your meetings going, my dear?" remarked Dr. Lionel Gift, spreading his napkin in his lap. "Yes, hello, Howard. The Hay-Adams. Call me there."

"Oh, wonderfully well," said Elaine, all the time ignoring the fact that while Dr. Lionel Gift was staying at the Hay-Adams, she was out at the Hilton in Alexandria with what appeared to be defense contractors, and low-level ones at that. She happened to know that Jack Parker was in New York, at the Regency. She gave herself a mental shake. "Wonderfully well. Especially with the people from—"

"Yes, Fred. I did leave a message with your secretary. Will you be in after two? Ah, here we are. I think you'll like this chardonnay, Elaine. It has a nice spice. Very good, thank you."

"Embryos R Us. Oh, this is good. I like chardon—"

"Marvin! Nice to see you. Yes, the conference in Miami was quite productive. You'll be sorry you missed it!" Dr. Gift gave one of his sudden fearsome chuckles, and Elaine's toes curled in pleasure.

For his part, Dr. Gift was not at all immune to Ms. Dobbs-Jellinek's charms. It only took 10 percent of his brainpower to stroke the passing lobbyists and consultants and with the other 90 percent he was surreptitiously admiring the woman. He didn't often squire such a nicely wrapped package. From the Fendi bag to the Donna Karan suit right down to the two-inch Cole-Haan heels (which made her a respectable four inches taller than Dr. Gift), and including the Burberry raincoat he had checked for her at the door, she looked fresh and expensive and he hadn't failed to note the admiring glances of men of his acquaintance who, he also suspected, gossiped about whether he, Dr. Lionel Gift, was gay or sexless. Well, he was neither, and he knew perfectly well how to touch a woman's waist as you were steering her to her seat and how to put your hand delicately on her elbow when other men were pushing past.

And when the waiter brought her dish, her face lit up in a way that was both girlish and attractive. All in all, it was a good decision to bring her here, the most expensive restaurant in Washington, and he would deal with Mrs. Loraine Walker later—she didn't scare him, not for a moment. He had charged more than one two-hundred-dollar lunch to his research account and he didn't intend to stop now. The fact was, and he could make this clear to Ivar himself, he was a walking magnet for grant money and his every waking and sleeping moment benefitted the university in some way or other.

When the food came, Elaine gave up the hopeless task of making conversation and picked up her fork. The fact was that she had never really been attracted to Dr. Gift before. She took her first bite of the lobster and glanced over at him. The food was so good, so savory and rich and full of flavor, that he practically shone with sudden sexiness, short, round, and bald though he was. She chewed the tender meat and sucked out the juices and felt the sauce coat her tongue and roll down her throat. After that, he looked still better.

Another thing you could say in her favor, observed Dr. Gift, was that she paid her own way. What was wrong with traditional marriage, in Dr. Gift's view, and according to his principles, was that the return on one's investment was so uncertain. Look at the men he knew, almost every one of them, if you wanted the unvarnished truth, whose expectations of comfort, companionship, sexual release, and worthy inheritors had been blighted by spousal irritability, independence, coldness, or infertility. On the whole, Dr. Gift did not share the traditional faith in domesticity that had marked even the most rigorous economic thinkers.

Nor had he ever been inclined by nature or philosophy to make romantic distinctions among females, other than enjoying rather abstractly the niceties of packaging. Elaine, though, did eat her food with every indication of a full measure of insatiability, the way you should eat everything: more hungrily at the last bite than the first. At bottom, Dr. Gift admired that in anyone. He found that his own salmon sated him all too easily, and wondered if he should have ordered something else.

This, Elaine thought, this food, this life, this onslaught of power and money and decor, was what she deserved. The endless and thankless task of prying money out of state, local, nonprofit, and corporate institutions was a labor most people underestimated in every way. Her job wasn't like, say, Jack Parker's job, which was mostly a matter of holding your hat under the open spigot and saying thank you. You had to be a very special person, as she was, to do her job successfully year after year, and for her inherent specialness no one, from her father through Dean right down to the guy she was seeing currently in the plant pathology department (she had found him a grant for $100,000 the spring before), had ever TRULY appreciated her. She had to do do do when other women only had to be be be. It was unfair, but a life of one lobster lunch after another might make it more fair.

And so, as he took a piece of baguette out of the breadbasket, Dr. Lionel Gift entertained a thought, well, a notion, really, of bringing Elaine Dobbs-Jellinek, who he knew made eighty-three thousand dollars a year, under his personal umbrella. He even entertained another notion—she was not too old to produce one carefully raised son (the highest returns were always to be made on only male children), and neither, on balance, was he. He had won two university teaching awards, hadn't he?

And Elaine Dobbs-Jellinek, smiling as if amused and adjusting the rather tight waist of her jacket, entertained a notion, too. A consulting partnership might be just the ticket. She had no objections to doing the legwork, if Dr. Gift had no objections to introducing her to his connections, and if such a partnership led to more personal intercourse, well, how bad could it be?

And so, as Elaine lifted her last bite and set it on her tongue and as Dr. Gift folded the last leaf of chicory from his salad into his mouth, they thought the same thought (surely a sign that the hidden hand of the marketplace was working in their favor), Why not?

Excited, Dr. Gift poured Elaine another glass of wine. Excited, Elaine wrapped her manicure around the stem of the glass. Excited, they smiled and clinked their glasses, and then—

And then—

And then Elaine thought about how much she hated housework, and how every man she had ever known really did think that that was the woman's responsibility, and you always ended up fighting about things like socks and dust bunnies and hair in the drains, for God's sake, no matter how well-intentioned you started out.

And then Dr. Gift recalled that Elaine was said to have a son already, a cuckoo in the nest, and anyway, it was better to live by principle than by desire, and the most important principle he tried to teach his students was never to jeopardize your own return by indulging in an unproven, never to be proven, faith in the common good. The wisest course for homo economicus was the cultivation of indifference.

"Dessert?" said Dr. Gift.

"It's tempting," said Elaine, "but I suppose not. And I do have to make some calls before my next meeting." She laid her napkin on the table, and stood up. The waiter stepped forward with the check. "Thank you so much for this lovely lunch!"

"Oh, my dear," rejoined Dr. Gift, warmly, "don't thank me. Thank the citizens of our fair state."

As they made their way out, stopping, of course, to retrieve Elaine's Burberry coat from the hatcheck girl, Dr. Gift found himself being attentive, and even tender, as if something had gone another way rather than the way it, of course, had to go. On the street in front of the restaurant, he squeezed her elbow a little too lingeringly, as if he couldn't quite release her, and then, when she did depart, he felt an unaccustomed pang of loneliness.

She disappeared into the noontime crowd. Startled was how he felt, startled and disoriented. Instead of striding off, Dr. Lionel Gift looked around at the—the—yes, the indifferent Georgetown row houses, the indifferent shops and the shining indifferent cars, the indifferent sidewalks and the indifferent intersections, all seething under the indifferent sky with homines economici, who were all themselves indifferent, at least toward Dr. Lionel Gift.

As she hurried away, her high heels clapping the pavement like a smattering of applause, Elaine, too, felt disappointed, lowered somehow, as if she would never find entrance, not only to the great white buildings in the distance, or to the Hay-Adams, but to something else that she couldn't even identify. Perhaps it was the realm of self-assurance, she thought. Whatever it was, wherever it was, there, she was sure, she would not look at herself as she did now, passing the ripply glass windows of the Georgetown shops, awkward and broken into strangely vivid parts—a fat white calf, a long shoe, glaring big hands clinging to her Fendi bag, a face appalled and naked. She paused and summoned the remnants of her dignity from the farthest reaches of her inner geography, then smiled at no one in particular, and took her sunglasses from her bag.

70

Some Weddings

AFTER ALL, the children were excited about it. Even the eldest, who had given up Benetton in favor of thrift shop items and had also dyed her hair black in the girls' bathroom at the middle school, decided that her parents' long-standing failure to marry enhanced her own personal mystique. In the end it was Beth who was not so sure.

The separation (which you could hardly call a separation when he was around every day, making excuses why he couldn't take his computer to his new apartment) had lasted, if you counted up all the actual time apart, 135 nights, 8 weekends, and 12 days scattered here and there) and had confirmed what Beth knew from watching her friends divorce—you ended up with too little money, too much space, and all your free time in the middle of the night, when as a married person you would have been sleeping. Her principled intention to make up her mind about what she wanted to do with her life had come to seem more and more abstract in the face of the chaos her life was made up of. Then one night, she had found herself making plans for her sixties, when Amy would be out of the house. But the only plan she was attracted to was being one of those wiry, wizened old women, whose backyard is a colorful riot of perennials and vegetables, who put on their gardening kneepads with their jeans in the morning, and who walk to the post office at the same time every day, who volunteer and watch the polls at election time. With Him around, she already was one of those women. Her backyard boasted barely an uncultivated square inch, and her after-breakfast walk to the post office was full of the leisurely delights of chatting with neighbors, giving and receiving cuttings, bulbs, and seeds, and spying on what was sprouting, blooming, or fruiting all along the way. With Him around, she could leave the children and take the dog, have a Coke, leaf through the mail, read a magazine article or two, sit on the boards of the co-op market and the co-op bookstore, run the HIV and STD information hotline, and spend one morning a week at the women's center.

Without Him around, she could only go to the post office on her way to other tasks, there was no time even to pull the mulch off the perennial beds, much less start seedlings, and she kept saying to the neighbors and her fellow volunteers, "I'll call you."

Without Him around, it was pretty clear that she was going to have to get a regular job, probably in some department at the university, and then she would have to put Amy in day care, buy some high heels, and actually wear them.

And without her around, He was a mess, and the children could see it, clear as day, and even though her friends advised her not to fall for the temptation of taking care of him, or at least worrying about him—it was only marriage-momentum, they said—she hated to see the furtively shocked and concerned looks on the children's faces when they returned from his place, or from their outings to McDonald's. She hated to see them compose masks for her, so that they could feel they weren't worrying her. THAT job, she had always felt, was a job for mothers and fathers, not for children.

Of course, there was the unfaithfulness, the lying, the betrayal.

But once her feelings stopped being quite so hurt, she had to admit that the lying was a technical matter, the betrayal was to her self-esteem, and the unfaithfulness boiled down to a health issue more than anything else.

The question that perplexed her was the question of love. One night when she actually did get to sleep, she dreamed she was standing on white sand, to her waist in clear blue water, trying to catch darting, sparkling, platinum fish in her hands. When she woke up, she knew that the water was her inner life and the fish were love, and the difficulty was knowing whether after all these years, she loved him, even knowing, after all these years, what love was.

On the one hand, she thought he had aged well, she preferred him to the husbands of her friends, she thought their children were lucky, especially in ways they were too young to understand, to have him as their father, she knew he was a truly kind man, his passion for improving the world still sometimes turned her on, and she always felt a shock of pleasure when she nestled against the warmth of his body. Was that enough to count as love?

On the other hand, given the choice of laying down her life to save his life or the children's lives, she would without hesitation choose the children, from time to time she felt a sharp sexual desire for some

movie actor or another that she no longer felt for him, and she preferred anticipating a really delicious meal to anticipating a night of
sex. Was that enough to count as indifference?

It was much harder to get married after twenty years, three children,
five cars, and two houses than it would have been after four dates and
a weekend in Montauk.

At any rate, she had lost seventeen pounds. That was what a separation was good for.

As for Chairman (until the end of the fiscal year) X, he was willing
to concede that Marriage predated the rise of Capitalism, and while
the whole institution was tainted with exploitation and consumerism,
perhaps it was not FATALLY tainted. The women's movement, about
which he had some reservations when female aspirations were based
on individual gain, had, on the whole, shown that an alternative model
of companionate marriage was at least possible if not inevitable, and
that such a model could coexist with capitalism and afford the participants some measure of emotional and moral security. This model of
nonhierarchical coexistence, he had come to think, formed an alternative to older models wherein the triumphant force, be it man or
woman, humankind or nature, individual or community, succeeded
in overwhelming and incorporating the defeated force. And it was a
good thing he had come to think so, because he was the defeated
force, and he preferred not to face obliteration.

He had proposed the wedding through the children. How about a
cake? he had suggested. How about new clothes? How about a party
that you can each invite three friends to? How about throwing rice
and everybody getting to walk down the aisle? How about, exclaimed
the children, getting immediately into the spirit, the boys giving away
Mommy and the girls giving away Dad? How about champagne?
How about as many strawberries as anybody wants to eat, and how
about dipping them in chocolate sauce? How about, said the third,
mixing the wedding up in his mind with a birthday party, keeping
the whole thing a secret from Mommy, and then jumping out and
yelling, "Surprise, surprise!"

"No," he had said, "but why don't you be the one to ask her?"

Later, when she took him to task for that, he said, "I realized right
away that that wasn't a good idea, but I didn't have the heart to say
no. He was so excited." She scowled, but she knew she wouldn't
have either.

And so here they were. May 20, his favorite day of the year, the average last frost date. For a week, he and the children had been raking and mulching the flower beds, tying old daffodil stems out of sight, heading the tulips so that only the last perfect ones were on display. They had uncovered the roses and pruned them, fertilized the fruit trees, planted broccoli, cauliflower, peas, lettuce, chard, onions, and leeks, thinned the daylily bed, pruned the privet hedge, tied together the peonies, planted marigolds and nasturtiums and gladioli and baby's breath. For the wedding, the wedding, the wedding, the children had done more work with more enthusiasm than during any spring he could remember. Even the eldest capered from bed to bed, dressed entirely in black but wreathed entirely in smiles.

Now, while the Lady X was inside getting dressed, he was ambling here and there, choosing blooms for her bouquet. Emperor tulips, white and red, Dutch irises, yellow with purple stamens. Branches of lilacs, white and lavender, apple blossoms, plum blossoms, cherry blossoms. The mingling fragrances lifted from the basket he was carrying and made him dizzy with delight. A wedding! How was it that he had never done this before? He set down the basket in the green grass and knelt beside it, then took the flowers in his two hands and pressed them against his face. He could feel their soft petals and rough stems, smell their sweetness. He closed his eyes.

Then she was near. He sensed that before he looked and saw the hem of her new yellow dress. "Hey," she said. "People are starting to arrive!"

Still embracing the flowers, he stood up. She was right there, her fragrance mingling with theirs, and him close enough to smell the heady combination.

She said, "We'd better—"

He pressed the bouquet into her arms.

Beth felt the scratch of branches and the whisper of petals and stems against the skin of her arms, and also the force that carried them to her. She could not say that she was marrying out of principle, if the principle was love. She still did not know what love was, unless, perhaps, it was that very force, a force that called a response right out of her, right out from under her ambivalence and doubt.

She took the bouquet. Clutched it, even.

He said, "Beth. Beth. Do you take this man? Do you really? I am so sorry—"

And she said, "I do, Jake. Look at me. I am taking him and I do."

"Okay, then," said Chairman X, and here came the eldest, shouting and laughing.

ALTHOUGH IT WAS 3:37 p.m. by the hall clock when Nils Harstad came downstairs for the first time that day, he was still wearing his robe, his pajamas, and his slippers. He made an immediate right and went into the kitchen, avoiding as if by instinct all the windows in the hall, dining room, living room, and sunporch that spilled the glorious day outside into the huge, old, empty, and neglected brick house.

True enough, Ivar was taking none of the furniture to Helen's except an antique Chinese highboy that was their father's gift to him upon his graduation from college, and the mate to Nils' similar chest.

True enough, Ivar hadn't even packed any clothes for the honeymoon in Provence that was to commence in two days, after graduation.

True enough, their intercourse over the last few years, since Nils had joined his church, actually, had dwindled steadily, and what they did have to say to one another always left Nils feeling irritated and isolated.

True enough, marriage to Helen seemed, at least so far, to be making Ivar "happy."

True enough, Nils had his own life.

True enough, he was more relieved than he had let on to anyone that the young wife and the six toddlers and the transfer to Poland were not to be a part of it.

Nils sighed, shuffling like an old man from the door end of the kitchen to the coffee end. The coffee, steaming hot since early morning, had cooked down to pure caffeine, bitter as wormwood.

Once he drank it, he could think of nothing else to do except go back upstairs and get back into bed.

The phone rang. Since it was right there and he didn't have to move even a step, he picked it up.

The voice said, "I know for a fact that she brought another box over there, because I can't find the vise grips that I bought here last winter, or that roll of telephone wire, either one. I can't find a damned thing! Where did you say she went to again?"

"Bolinas, California," said Nils.

"What's her phone number again?"

"She doesn't have one. I told you that."

"Then, what am I going to do?" Father's voice modulated suddenly from angry to querulous.

Nils let the question rise out of the phone and suspend itself in his brain, in the air of the kitchen. He didn't answer, but let Father wait at the other end for a long time, long enough for them both to actually contemplate their prospects for the next twenty years. He said, "Is that buyer still interested in your house?"

"Could be. I don't know. That was forty-three thousand dollars—"

"You can—" said Nils, and stopped.

"Down the drain! What was the matter with that girl?"

It wasn't too late. Father hadn't heard him, and he could turn back right now.

"Their hands are as bands—" said Father.

"You can go ahead and sell the house and move in here," said Nils.

"What?"

"You can—"

"I HEARD you fine. You mean it?"

"It's not going to go all your way. You have to adjust to me as much as I adjust to you."

"Do I have to pay rent?"

"You can keep the forty-three thousand in a money market account."

"What's that?"

"I'll show you."

"Can I have a little dog? Marly couldn't stand a dog."

"I don't mind a little dog," said Nils. "Maybe a little dog would be nice."

"All right, then," said Father. "You've got yourself a deal."

NEXT DOOR to the wedding, Helen opened the sliding glass door of the Martins' deck and carried her drink into the afternoon air. Ivar was right behind her. Behind him, Howard Martin, Sociology, said, "Go on out. I hear the phone, and Roberta's getting the dip out of the oven."

Helen settled herself on the glider and took a sip of her gin and tonic. Ivar sat down, and she smiled at him. He smiled back. They had done a lot of gazing at each other lately, more than Helen would have thought possible after all these years. Ivar cleared his throat. He said, "What's that over there, do you think?"

Helen turned her head, and put her hand up to shade her eyes. She said, "Doesn't it look like a wedding?"

"Huh," said Ivar. They exchanged a glance and a smile. Graduation was scheduled for the following day. The day after that, they would be leaving at last for their honeymoon in Provence. Two weeks.

Helen said, "Isn't that that little man from Horticulture? What's his name?"

"Who's he marrying? I thought he was married." Ivar craned his neck.

"Maybe they're renewing their vows," said Helen.

"Do Maoists do that?"

Helen shrugged. Their gazes caught, tangled again. Martin, the sociologist, pushed the sliding glass door open with his foot and carried out the dip. He said, "Stop that, you two. The last time two people of a certain age got married in my department, two other couples got divorced and a third one went into sex therapy."

"Ugh," said Roberta, as she brought out her drink. "It took the whole department a year to recover and three years to analyze the group dynamic! I've never been to such boring parties."

"Your neighbors are getting married," said Helen.

"Well, it's about time," said Roberta. "You know, everyone always said that they were married, but I knew they weren't."

"How did you know THAT?" Howard challenged her.

"She had an air—" Roberta began, staring across the fence. Helen looked at her, interested. She shrugged. "She always seemed like she had some leeway."

"Oh, right," said Howard, scowling a bit. "Well, I wonder why they're all of a sudden getting married now."

"Because," said Helen. Her gaze returned to Ivar's as if on tracks, and Helen, who knew as well as anyone that this compulsion to look at her husband would diminish and then disappear, took the time to relish it. "Because," she said, "not only do you have to act once in a while, it's also so exhilarating to choose!"

.   .   .

TWO MILES AWAY, at the McDonald's in the commons, Bob Carlson, customer, saw Keri Donaldson, customer, the moment she walked through the door and up to the counter. He heard her distinctly when she ordered a McChicken sandwich, a small fries, and a water. Among the many footsteps of all the other customers, he made hers out as clearly as if they had been alone in the room, and he let his gaze follow her as she paused and looked around for a table. All this attention he was paying her didn't mean, though, that he failed to turn his chair and hide his head so that they wouldn't make eye contact. Not making eye contact was a reflex with him, probably rooted in his DNA. And, of course, Keri reminded him of both Earl Butz and Diane, two strong feelings that had recently, whatever their original identities, transmogrified into shame. Bob bit into his Quarter Pounder.

But then she was right there, her tray was right on his table, and she said, "Hi! Are you staying around this summer, too?"

He looked up. She had that beautiful kind smile, the smile he had seen on her face as she knelt beside Earl Butz and stroked his snowy head, the smile that was possibly the last sight Earl had seen in this world. So Bob smiled back at her, and moved his chair aside. He said, "Yeah. Yeah, I am. Want to sit down?"

She sat down.

CECELIA SAID, "Turn here."

"Why?" said Tim. "The tennis courts are right down this way. You can see—"

"Please? Just turn, just a little out of the way."

"Where are we going?"

"Nowhere."

"Don't you want to play tennis?"

"Five minutes."

He had to thread the Saab between the two rows of cars parked in front of the house, but he noticed anyway how hungrily Cecelia took it all in, how suddenly, when they had passed the house, she settled into her seat with a thump and crossed her arms over her chest. He felt in himself a little ping of jealousy, but also a larger and more precious throb of sympathy with her. He got one glance of the house. Apart from some nice flower beds, it was very modest, especially for this neighborhood. He said, "What?"

"You know. They're getting married."

"Who's getting married?" As if he didn't know.

"They are."

"Oh," said Tim.

"It's really the best thing. He doesn't even know how much the best thing it is."

"But?"

"But."

"But?"

"But I wish—"

At the end of the block, Tim turned left instead of right. Cecelia said, "Where are you going?"

"Down the alley."

"No! You're kidding!"

He turned down the alley. "Curiosity," he said, "was made to be satisfied."

"What if he sees me? What if SHE sees me? She knows who I am."

Tim slowed the car. The voice of the justice of the peace rose on the air. The corner of the backyard came into view. Tim said, "If they see you, then wave and smile and wish them well."

PROFESSOR GARCIA, best man, handed Chairman X the ring. It was a real ring, one that Garcia had persuaded the Chairman, known tightwad, to spring for. The Chairman took the ring, and Garcia saw all of the children's gazes lock onto it and watch it slip from his grasp onto her finger. Garcia's own gaze fell on them, the four youthful protagonists, thirteen, ten, six, and almost two, for whom this climactic ceremony would henceforward be the merest backdrop to the infinitely larger dramas of their own lives. That's what he loved about weddings, the way each one was the beginning of it all.

Garcia licked his lips. Even with the children, the assumption of all their friends that they were married, and the rest of the accoutrements of married life, Beth and the Chairman had never been quite so exquisitely mismatched as they were today and would be from now on, all their disjunctions magnified by the mere fact that they had chosen each other at last and over every other candidate.

The breeze lifted Beth's hair, the eldest picked up Amy without any prompting, the two boys stopped fidgeting, fragrance from the blossoming apple trees rolled over him, and a very well cared for old Saab eased down the alley and past the couple, whose eyes were closed, and who, Garcia thought, seemed to be lost in an astonishing, and even legendary, kiss.

A Note About the Author

Jane Smiley was born in Los Angeles, grew up in St. Louis, and studied at Vassar and the University of Iowa, where she received her Ph.D. She is the author of seven previous works of fiction, including *The Age of Grief*, *The Greenlanders*, *Ordinary Love & Good Will*, and *A Thousand Acres* (which was awarded both the Pulitzer Prize and the National Book Critics Circle Award). She teaches at Iowa State University and lives in Ames, Iowa.

A Note on the Type

The text of this book was set in a digitized version of Bembo,
a well-known Monotype face. Named for Pietro Bembo, the
celebrated Renaissance writer and humanist scholar who was
made a cardinal and served as secretary to Pope Leo X, the original
cutting of Bembo was made by Francesco Griffo of Bologna only
a few years after Columbus discovered America.

Sturdy, well balanced, and finely proportioned, Bembo is a
face of rare beauty, extremely legible in all of its sizes.

Composed by Crane Typesetting Service, Inc.
West Barnstable, Massachusetts

Printed and bound by Berryville Graphics
Berryville, Virginia

Designed by Cassandra J. Pappas